Mage Bond

EDEN WINTERS

ROCKY RIDGE BOOKS

ROCKY RIDGE BOOKS

Warning

This book contains adult language and themes, including graphic descriptions of sexual acts which some may find offensive. It is intended for mature readers only, of legal age to possess such material in their area.

This is a work of fiction. Any resemblance to actual people, places, or events is purely coincidental.

Editing by Carole Cummings

Cover by Jacqueline Sweet

Rocky Ridge Books

www.RockyRidgeBooks.com

Contents

Prologue

Arkenn lay on a rug by the fire, staring in rapt attention at his mother. Outside, the winds howled, and snow piled high by the door. Inside, a fire roared in the hearth, and the scent of drying herbs pervaded the air where they hung from the rafters. The perfect backdrop for his mother's tale.

"No matter how hard they fought, the two heroes couldn't defeat the evil Thomoth." Mum flipped a lock of straw-blonde hair over her shoulder, bared her teeth, and made claws with her fingers from her place on a low stool by the rug. "It was too cunning."

"What happened?" Arkenn removed his thumb from his mouth to ask. A lifted-brow glare from his grandmother kept him from returning the digit.

"The people fled."

"And came here?"

Mum nodded. "And came here." Her voice grew scary again. "But the monster followed them."

Arkenn gasped. "He's here?"

"It is in this realm. Rumors say Thomoth is neither man nor woman," Mum whispered, as though telling a secret.

Matching his mother's low voice, Arkenn asked, "Where is it?" He glanced around their cottage. Were glowing red eyes hiding in the coals?

"Don't worry." Mum mussed his hair, giving him a fond smile. "It's far away from the Quarshi mountains. You've nothing to fear here. Besides, your da, gran, and I will keep you safe."

"What about the heroes. Did they come too?"

"Of that, I'm not certain, but they vowed to fight the monster again one day—and win."

"I want to fight To-moff!" Arkenn declared, brandishing the wooden sword carved for him by his father.

"Ah, I believe you would." Mum swept him into her embrace, nuzzling noses. "Now, off to bed with you."

"Do the trick!"

"Arkenn, bed."

"The trick! I want the trick."

"Okay, just once." Mum opened her hand. A tiny pink flame danced upon her palm.

Arkenn giggled. "You make fire."

She fixed him with a stern expression. "It's to be our secret."

"Yes, Mum." Arkenn toddled over to his cot in the far corner of the room. His mother tucked him in, kissed his cheek, then joined Da and Gran in sipping tea by the fire.

The house consisted of two rooms: a common living area, where the family sat together, prepared and took meals, and Arkenn slept. His gran slept in a tiny room off the kitchen area.

Rocks and dried clay made the walls of the thatched house, its pointed roof allowing his parents a private loft for sleeping. His father being the village healer and hunter meant they didn't have to share their home with livestock at night when cold winds blew down from the mountains. The wolves' mournful cries echoed on still nights.

"You shouldn't be filling his head with such stories," Gran said, in tones Arkenn struggled to hear. "They'll keep the child up at night from bad dreams."

"Arkenn's made of stern stuff." That was Da. Always jumping to Arkenn and Mum's defense against his own mother.

"He has a right to know his heritage." Mum's soft voice lulled. As Arkenn slipped off to sleep, she added, "Because someday the battle might be his.

"But if so, he won't be alone. There are always two."

Chapter One

C orn stalks whipped at Arkenn's face. Faster! He must run faster! Surely the braying grew closer each moment. Damnation for the villagers releasing the dogs.

A stone caught his foot, sending him crashing to his knees. *Must keep going, can't stop.* Sucking in a deep breath, he pushed to his feet. *Run. Must run.*

On and on, charging through the twilight, leaving the fields for the forest. Branches whipped from all directions, lashing his face, his arms. He chanced a backward glance.

Flickering torches lit the night, carried by an angry mob whose shrill shouts rent the air. Some voices he recognized; others weren't clear.

His former neighbors... friends.

Now his enemies. He'd done nothing wrong.

But be born.

Pressing one hand against the pain in his side, he grasped tree limbs with his other to haul himself higher. The incline wouldn't slow the dogs.

Much.

The mountain. Arkenn must reach the mountain. The superstitious villagers would never follow him there. The full moon lit his path, a well-used animal trail. A bit of white caught his attention. Bones.

Those weren't animal bones. One of his kind not fast enough?

He didn't want to turn and fight. Without complete focus, his will might go awry. *Never use your powers for evil*, he heard in his mother's voice.

His steps slowed. Tired, so tired. One more hill. And another. He fell to his hands and knees, unable to summon the strength to rise. The braying deafened him.

The Lady his neighbors prayed to wouldn't heed his calls for help. His mere existence offended her.

Now he must die.

Alone.

Something hard slammed into his chest. Breath! He couldn't draw breath!

Another hit. Then another. Ow! He put a hand to his face. Blood trickled between his fingers. Stoning. They planned to stone him to death. Taunts and cackles surrounded him as dark shapes bearing torches wended through the trees.

The flames flickered, sending sparks and smoke into the night.

"Time to die, mage," one man spat, hefting a sizable rock.

What to do? What to do? Arkenn promised his parents never to use magic to harm another. He must run, use his power to seal a cave mouth if he reached the mountain.

Peering between the circle of villagers showed no escape routes.

Heart hammering out a frantic beat, he screamed, "What have I done? I've lived in the village since I was a child. I hunt. I helped my gran. I'm no mage. You know I'm not!" Where were his friends? Neighbors who cared? Anyone to help him.

Gran. They'd killed Gran. The truth wrenched his insides, pain released on a moan. Gran. Dear sweet Gran, who'd never hurt anyone. Arkenn didn't need to see a bloodied corpse to know they'd killed her.

What had she done? What had they seen? She kept her powers so well hidden, though with age, maybe she'd become less cautious.

Someone snarled, "Of course you're a mage. From a family of mages. We should never have allowed your like into our village. We should've had you killed alongside your parents." How had they found out? Arkenn and Gran were always so careful. The villagers had only suspected his parents—enough to have them dragged to E'Skaara for execution.

Mage. The worst accusation imaginable. No meeting of the village council. No presenting of evidence.

Just death.

Think, Arkenn, think! There had to be spells to save him, but his parents hadn't invoked magic to protect themselves. Nor had Gran, or she'd still be alive.

"My father was a healer!" Arkenn pointed to a farmer. "He saved your mate when she would have died in childbirth." He aimed his gaze at another. "And you would have lost your son if my father hadn't cared for him after he fell from a horse." One by one, he fixed his righteous anger on his accusers. Everyone here had benefitted from his father's healing touch, though at the time, they never realized he used more than herblore to help them. "All of you owe my family something."

"We owe nothing. You've likely been influencing us all along," said a widowed mother who'd received many a meal from Gran's generosity.

"'The Lady does not permit mages to live,'" a former neighbor quoted.

"Since when have you been religious? I'll bet that's the only saying you know." There wasn't even a church in the village. Never had been.

One of the village elders approached. "Which is why our village suffers from poor crops. All except for your fields."

"And you burned them to the ground. They could have fed the entire village this winter." Two plots of corn, beans, and squash, all nearly ripe for the picking. Wasted. For their arrogance.

"We will not eat tainted food."

Because of their pride, they and their children would starve this winter. Magic didn't make Gran's crops flourish, but time and attention. The fools.

High in the hills, the chill breeze brought a shiver to Arkenn's overheated flesh. Or had more than the cold caused the shiver?

The elder raised his voice, the flickering torchlight lending his face a sinister air. Around the circle, dogs whined, restrained by their owners. "Archers, come forth."

The slither and click of at least six bows nocking sounded thunderous in the sudden silence. Four men and two women stepped forward, little older than Arkenn, with grim determination on their faces and no recognition in their eyes. He'd played with them as children. One young woman's parents had approached Gran about a match with Arkenn.

Now they could so easily kill him.

He peered left and right, but none spoke in his defense. They were all in accord.

Because of mage blood, he must die.

Heart lodged in his throat, Arkenn raised his hands in supplication.

Fire engulfed the trees.

Pain. Throbbing agony. The horrible scent of burned flesh. Coughing wracked his body, but thick smoke made breathing nearly impossible. Arkenn raised his head, blinking open gritty eyes.

Carnage. Twisted, blackened tree trunks, grass nothing but a sooty mass on the ground. All around...

The horror hit suddenly. Charred bodies. Those were charred bodies of people he'd known! The elder, the miller, the archers he'd once known well. One still held the remnants of a bow. He'd killed them. Killed them all.

Lost control. What had he done?

With great effort, he hoisted himself upright. Singed fabric hung from his aching body. Grasping a scorched sapling, he climbed to his feet. His shoulder shrieked in protest.

Death all around. Was this why mages were despised? But if they were so destructive, why hadn't his parents brought down fire on their killers?

The village. Arkenn had to get back to the village. Slowly, slowly, he hobbled downhill, pausing to catch his breath whenever the wind blew untainted air in his direction.

He'd killed. Many people. Neighbors. Friends. Hot tears burned his eyes. Murderer. Worse than mage. Was he less of a murderer because he'd acted in self-defense? The sun's first rays peeked over the mountains.

At last, his energy waned. Arkenn collapsed onto a rise he'd often used as an overlook, staring down on the villagers unnoticed. Then, he'd usually been with those he called friends. Friends who'd been fully prepared to fill him with arrows.

Friends now lying dead because of Arkenn.

He touched his shoulder and winced. If not properly treated, the burn would fester, but he'd not yet learned how to heal his own injuries. Dozens of bruises and scrapes added to his pain.

Doors opened down below, children racing from their homes. At least he hadn't harmed the innocent young ones. Directly. But what would they do without their parents? For a moment, old anger flared brightly. Why not deprive them of their parents? Their parents had certainly deprived him of his own.

No. He wouldn't wish the agony of such loss on anyone. What would happen to the children now? Could he go down there, pretend nothing happened?

Unwise. Better to get away. Leave this very morn without so much as a change of clothes—clothes he no longer owned. Smoldering rubble remained of the only home he'd ever known and all his and Gran's possessions. Somewhere among those smoking timbers lay the remains of his grandmother. He'd not been here at the time, but he knew. Could he have saved her if he'd come home sooner from his hunt?

Or would he have joined her in the ash?

He couldn't stay here. Had nothing to stay for.

Goodbye, Gran. Goodbye, Mum. Goodbye, Da.

An older lady followed some of the children outside. And another, leading two goats. They were joined by an elderly man and two girls a few seasons younger than Arkenn.

Someone remained to take care of the children.

Out in the fields, only black stalks remained of Arkenn's and Gran's crops. His grandmother hadn't allowed meddling where any might see, only with the kitchen garden, hidden from prying eyes by a fence.

In the end, precaution hadn't mattered. Jealous neighbors saw success as magery instead of careful cultivation, timing, and good soil.

Arkenn focused all his energy on the villagers' unproductive plots of withered beans and barren cornstalks. Under his will, twisted brown vines rose from the ground, green and strong. In a few sevendays, the village would enjoy its best harvest ever.

May his efforts be enough.

Chapter Two

While the *Seabird's* crew went about their business, Petran fished in the river shallows, several stones' throws from the harbor. Out of sight of the ships. Yes, their "business" involved actions unsanctioned by the local constable, and no, his father wouldn't allow him to tag along.

Gold, jewels, brandy, trade goods they sold in back alleys. Booming cannons, the clash of steel... Adventure.

Seen through a porthole from his safe little cabin.

He brandished his fishing pole like a sword. *Take that!* Eighteen summers had passed since his birth. Many of the crew came on board younger still.

Yet his father's *You won't be a pirate. Yer mum would come back from the dead and take me with her* rang in his ears every time he asked.

"I'm tired of hiding below decks like a child!" he shouted at the trees. He'd finally grown reasonable, if sparse, whiskers on his chin. Even the trees weren't listening.

All manner of folk sailed upon the *Seabird*, from every point of the world, from palest blonds to those with jet black hair, some fair, some dark. The kind of adventurer or outcast who never settled in one place.

Now, with a price on their heads, they couldn't.

Petran's father wanted more for his only son than a life spent running from the law, or so he'd promised Petran's dying mum.

Petran ran one hand through his hair, or tried to. His hair long ago formed the thick, matted locks worn by many a pirate, hanging down past his shoulders, the light brown highlighted by golden sun streaks. While not allowed to earn the name "pirate," he certainly looked the part, his muscles lean, skin darkened from working on the deck of the *Seabird*.

Pirate. A title he'd never hold. No, while his father and the rest of the crew raided, whored, or took on supplies, he'd harvest freshwater fish or stay aboard the ship to avoid notice. The freshwater fish did make a nice change to a steady diet of sea creatures. Could he hope they'd bring chickens aboard today? How he'd love fresh eggs. Or meat. Actual meat. With gravy. And thick bread slathered in butter.

He'd caught enough fish for a meal already, but the sun felt so good on his shoulders, with a slight breeze coming over the river, keeping the day from being too hot.

Walk down the riverbank. Why? He was perfectly content standing here. No, *you want to explore.* A feeling, not actual words, enticed him to set down his fishing gear, putting his feet to wandering down the bank.

He tried walking in the opposite direction yet found himself turned around. What the... Well, no harm going for a stroll on such a fine day.

The occasional fluffy cloud drifted across an otherwise clear blue sky. The trees along the bank provided gentle shade. Fragrant breezes laden with the scent of pine and flowers played with the branches overhead. Of course, the crew would laugh at such fanciful nonsense. Still, Petran enjoyed time alone in the woods, away from the cramped ship, which afforded very little privacy or space.

Standing on unmoving ground made a nice change of pace.

On and on, he rambled. He should be getting back to the ship. His father wanted to set sail before sunset.

Just a little more.

Every time Petran turned back, his feet took the path away from the ship. Finally, when he could no longer see the tall masts in the harbor, he found himself on a wide strip of sand, where the river hooked to the left.

He stopped. No birdsong, no wind; even the river fell quiet.

No more sense of urgency.

Heartrending sobs made his blood run cold.

Petran picked up his pace. Someone must be in trouble. There! A figure knelt on the sand near the trees, arms wrapped around itself, swaying back and forth, wracked by uncontrollable sobs.

Petran stopped a few feet away from the miserable creature.

Anguished eyes looked up at him, as blue as the skies overhead. Pain such as Petran had never seen before stared out at him from those haunted eyes.

A man. No, a boy, really, possibly Petran's age. Dressed in tattered, blackened rags. Soot marred his cheek, and his hair bore the marks of fire.

Petran drew closer, the scent of scorch hitting his nose.

The boy winced... and fell over.

"Hey!" Petran crashed to his knees on the wet sand. "Hey, boy." He shook the boy and yanked back his hand, ripping a piece of frayed shirt in the process. Angry reddened flesh, like half-healed wounds, covered the boy's neck and shoulder. Burns. Bad ones. Here and there purple bruises mottled the exposed skin.

Petran had seen similar burns after a battle, heard moans of pain, seen horrible scars later—if the victim survived the ordeal.

Without treatment, these wounds could prove lethal.

He struggled to lift the injured boy, half carrying, half dragging him over the sand, stopping by his fishing spot to retrieve his catch and provide a reason for being gone. With any luck, the crew would still be in the local village, disposing of illicit cargo.

He could allow no witnesses to the stowaway he'd bring on board. The pirates didn't welcome strangers and weren't too kind to those with no defense or value. The boy needed help. And to get away from this place.

Two things Petran could provide.

Now to get the poor unfortunate aboard.

A splash hit his nose. He wiped the drop away. Rain. Dark, low-hanging clouds. What? The sky had been nearly cloudless. Now rain?

Rain would drive the crew below decks or to seek refuge in a tavern if still on shore.

The skies opened. Torrential rain washed the scent of fire away but soaked the stranger's rags, making him even heavier. Yet, Petran preferred carrying extra weight to finding his path barred.

Step by step, he labored. At last, they reached the *Seabird*. He hid his burden behind a cask on the dock and peered upward. No one was visible on deck. Footsteps sounded down the gangway.

A raw-boned woman ambled past, not even looking his way.

"Rymon," Petran called, stepping out to meet the quartermaster. "Where is everyone?"

"Your father decided to wait until dawn to leave due to the storm. The crew are enjoying a night in an inn. Hurry, or they'll save you no ale." The *Seabird's* most dangerous fighter winked, then dashed down the docks toward the village.

Strange, indeed. Petran's father never left the ship unattended, so there must be crew about, but out of sight.

All the better for Petran. When luck graced him with its presence, he'd be a fool to refuse the offer. He retraced his steps and helped the boy to his feet. This time, the burned youth managed to help, taking a few faltering steps. He didn't hesitate or ask where they went. His only sounds were a few grunts when Petran jostled him.

"I'm sorry," Petran repeated every few moments. Given his injuries, the boy must be in excruciating agony. A small eternity later, Petran gently laid the boy down on his own bunk, away from the crew in the far back of the cargo hold. No raiders would find the hidden cabin, allowing Petran to escape battles.

At least, that was the captain's plan.

"You're in my cabin," Petran said. "You're safe now."

Those pain-filled blue eyes stared upward. "Thank you," came out on a whisper.

The storm gave Petran time enough to drop his catch off in the galley and stock his cabin with the supplies necessary for their journey to the next port. He'd helped the ship's cook, Smutje, often enough to treat the men after a skirmish to have learned basic healing skills. Smutje liked when Petran helped. Claimed the men healed faster.

Nonsense. He just wanted to keep Petran away from the fighting. Probably at Da's urging.

The boy winced but remained quiet as Petran cleaned and smoothed salve over healing burns, bruises, and a few minor cuts. How had the boy been injured? Life among pirates taught not to ask too many questions.

Petran hummed as he worked, a tune he couldn't remember learning. At last, wounds treated, and with a few sips of broth in his belly, Petran's foundling slept.

That night, to gentle snores, Petran spread a blanket on the deck beside his bunk and curled onto his side, using his arm for a pillow. A groan sounded overhead. Petran lifted a hand, patting the boy's unburned arm. Immediately the groaning quieted.

The moment Petran dropped his hand, the whimpers began anew.

He slept with one hand on the bunk.

⚓

The boy didn't speak, didn't smile, didn't seem to hear anything Petran said, but merely nodded and accepted water and broth. Petran kept the burns clean. Though inexperienced with major injuries— Smutje saw to the more severe wounds—burns should take longer to heal, even if Petran, as Smutje said, "had a magic touch."

On their fourth day at sea, the boy sat up, wrapping his arms around his legs like he'd done the day Petran found him. "Who are you?"

It took a moment to make out the words, thick with a Northern accent. The pirates spoke many languages and dialects at sea, and the *Seabird's* native tongue included parts of them all. "I'm Petran. We're in my cabin aboard the *Seabird*." No one used surnames aboard the ship, most giving them up when they signed on as crew.

"Why did you help me?" the boy asked, voice a hoarse whisper.

"I couldn't leave you." Petran couldn't explain why. Nor could he account for the mysterious force that led him to the turn in the river.

The suspicion in those blue eyes slowly eased. The boy leaned back against the pillow. "Thank you." He patted his chest, then grimaced. Yes, he'd had a particularly nasty bruise there, now nearly healed, but still painful apparently. "I'm Arkenn."

Petran nodded at the greeting. Arkenn. If he'd been alone, he'd have rolled the name over his tongue to sample the taste. "I didn't know what else to do, so I brought you aboard." Until then, there'd been no question as to bringing him. Now, Petran doubted his actions. Most pirates were suspicious of outsiders and wouldn't have taken him in. "Is there a family looking for you?"

"No!" the boy snapped. He winced. "No. My... family is dead."

Petran envied those with the gift of saying the right things at the right time, a trait he sorely lacked. All he managed was, "I'm sorry."

The boy lifted his head, peering out Petran's small porthole to the vast expanse of sea. "Where are we going?"

"We're bound for E'Skaara, the capital city of Othor. Do you know anyone there?"

"No." Arkenn turned away. "It doesn't matter. Nothing matters."

"You matter." Petran sat on the edge of the bunk he'd surrendered to sleep on the deck.

With no warning, the boy lunged, wrapping his arms around Petran.

He cried, great, heaving sobs. Petran held him, muffling the cries against his shoulder. A world of pain flowed out with the tears, prompting many questions. No. Arkenn would share what he wanted to. So Petran held the boy in his arms for what seemed like hours, whispering nonsense words while rubbing a hand in a soothing motion up and down Arkenn's back.

The wracking sobs subsided to the occasional sniffle. Arkenn finally released one last hiccuping sob. Petran's father had constructed this cabin well. Few ever ventured here, and none who didn't know its exact location would ever find the door. They were safe.

Time for a distraction. "Where are you from, Arkenn?"

"The... the Quarshi mountains." *Sniff.* He wiped his eyes with the back of his hand.

Petran handed Arkenn a fancy handkerchief acquired during a raid. He'd kept the linen square because he liked the ruffled edges. Now it would serve a use.

The Quarshi mountains. A long way from the river where they'd met. Petran lightly mussed Arkenn's hair. "This gave it away." He'd heard of a mountain kingdom many leagues away, where the people had white hair and yellow eyes, but those weren't the Quarshi people with their blond hair and blue eyes.

Arkenn's eyes widened. "You don't think... you don't think they'll find me?"

"Who? Who'll find you? Are you running from someone?" Had someone inflicted those grievous burns?

Arkenn looked away again. "No... no one. They're all gone now."

"Good. If they're after you, then they should be gone." Petran stood, fighting off the protective instincts that made his heart pound.

"No!" Arkenn grabbed at Petran's hand. "Stay."

Petran shifted his gaze from Arkenn to the door. Shirking duty would surely bring Da down here to check on him. "I can't right now. I have watch. Lock the door, and don't let anyone in but me."

All night Petran kept watch, avoiding contact with the crew. A clear night. Lots of stars. Would Arkenn like to come above deck? No, he couldn't. Still, Petran's mind too often strayed to the mystery lying in his bunk.

As soon as dawn broke, he fled to the galley, grabbed bread, cheese, and water, then made his way to his cabin. He spotted his father twice, but duties kept the captain from noticing him.

Petran knocked on his cabin door, whispering, "It's me."

The door opened. Arkenn stood, sheet wrapped around his waist. Clean, and with nearly all his injuries healed, Petran finally realized Arkenn wasn't a boy, but no more than a summer older than Petran's own eighteen, though small.

And he was beautiful. So very beautiful. Pale skin, fair hair, and those blue eyes. He was a hand shorter than Petran, with the beginnings of a stocky build. Pink crept into Arkenn's cheeks.

What? Why... Oh. Petran averted his gaze. Staring. He'd been caught staring. "I brought you food and drink." He placed his offerings on a box he used as a table. "How are you feeling?" Once more, his gaze landed on Arkenn's shoulder. No burns. No scars, even. What? "How... how did you heal so fast?" Without making a conscious decision to do so, Petran ran his fingers lightly over the soft skin he'd seen badly burned a few days ago.

They both froze. Petran dropped his hand, settling on the end of the bunk, too far away to appear a threat.

Arkenn shivered, though heat permeated the cabin. "The burns weren't as bad as you thought, probably. What are you going to do when we reach the city? Will you go ashore?"

"This is my father's ship, which is why I have my own quarters instead of sleeping with the crew. I'm under his command. Don't worry, though. I'll find a way to get you ashore without anyone the wiser." At least, Petran hoped. Then again, no one paid him much attention. While the men and women aboard the ship fought, fucked, and otherwise interacted with each other, his father declared Petran off-limits, forever seeing him as a lad instead of the man he'd become.

I promised yer mum. Da's answer to everything.

Why can't I go on raids?
Because I promised yer mum.
Why can't I be a pirate like you?
Because I promised yer mum.
Why do I have to learn? You never did. Petran wore his belligerence like a badge of honor when asking.

Da didn't rise to the bait, merely giving a soft smile, barely visible through the scruff of his beard. *Because I promised yer mum.*

Only vague memories of Petran's mysterious mum remained, but she must have been a formidable woman for Da to work so hard at keeping promises long after her death.

Da and the crew also tolerated a horrible cook because the man taught Petran to read, write, and work with numbers. Even some healer's art.

Both brows climbed Arkenn's forehead. "Your father is the captain?"

"Yes. Jaed Three-fingers, they call him." Petran smiled. "I'll tell you a secret. The crew believes he lost two fingers to a rival captain—a captain who's now missing more than fingers." He made a face and drew a finger across his neck. "The truth is, Da caught his hand in the reins while plowing when a snake spooked the horse."

Arkenn winced.

"Yeah. He said it was pretty painful, but my mum fixed him right up. She couldn't save the fingers, though."

"If he's captain, does that mean you'll be captain one day?" Arkenn didn't seem in the least perturbed, merely curious.

"No." Petran shook his head, suppressing bitterness from his words. "He promised my mum I'd be more than a pirate. Not that I mind life at sea, but he won't hear of it. One day soon, we'll go ashore, and he'll leave without me." The thought made Petran's heart ache. The ship, his da, the crew, the sea... all he'd ever known.

He'd be abandoned, alone, with only himself to rely on.

Arkenn squirmed a bit closer on the bunk. Close enough to touch with minimal effort. Petran kept his hands to himself. "That's horrible."

Petran shrugged. "That's the way of things. It's also why I always take my share with me when we're in a port he'd deem acceptable for my future." It wouldn't be long. Petran was now a man and couldn't help looking at an attractive young crewman who'd come aboard a few seasons back.

When the new recruit returned Petran's affections, the captain left him ashore at the next village.

A pirate ain't good enough for you, Da had said.

Yeah, yeah. He'd promised Petran's mum.

Which didn't help his frustrations when the only possible lovers available were all pirates.

When he lifted his gaze, he fell into blue, blue eyes. Long denied feelings surfaced. He'd touched this man while bringing him aboard, though so fearful of Arkenn's injuries that he didn't fully appreciate the beauty or sinewy muscles. Arkenn had seemed so small that day. Looking at him now revealed a trim waist and...

The sheet billowed over the mast beneath it like foresails at full speed ahead. Petran turned away. A man lay in his bunk, someone no one else knew of. An attractive man. Sporting a cockstand. Reality beat every dream of encountering a group of mermen.

A splash of cold water doused any rising lust. They'd boarded the ship without Arkenn really being aware, and Petran wouldn't ruin those good intentions now when his foundling might feel obligated to accept advances.

Petran shot to his feet. "You need to eat and get some rest." He left the cabin before he did something regretful. Pressing his back against the door once safely on the other side, he let out a heavy breath. A few more days. Only a few more days and Arkenn could leave.

Why did the thought bring both relief and sorrow?

Petran didn't return to his cabin until after Arkenn fell asleep. Then, tossing and turning on a blanket on the deck, as discreetly as possible, Petran gave himself release, thoughts on those blue eyes and the man lying so close to him.

A man he'd have to give up.

Soon.

Chapter Three

T he sloped overhead allowed enough room to sit up but not stand on that side of Petran's cramped cabin. A wooden box doubled as a small table, filled with a few books and other booty no one else claimed. Among Petran's favorite treasures were a brass button etched with a bird's image and a glass bottle that threw colors on the bulkhead when held to the sunlight on a cloudless day.

A trunk held his clothes, doubling as a place to sit. He'd stored other items, like his sword, under the bunk. Three paces long, two paces wide. He'd always thought his cabin grand compared to sharing space with the crew, but never grander than with Arkenn present.

"These will be a loose fit, but they'll do until you find something better." Petran gave Arkenn his best clothes, taken from a raided ship last spring. The shirt matched the beautiful blue of Arkenn's eyes.

The former owner must have been a man of substance, for the shirt and trousers, though worn now, had once been of the finest quality. "I'm afraid

I have no shoes to fit you." Petran didn't wear shoes much on the ship. Easier to maintain balance on the rigging or on a storm-tossed deck barefooted.

"You've given me more than enough. I don't know how I can ever repay you." Arkenn wiped a lock of golden blond hair from his eyes.

Petran wanted to repeat the gesture with his own fingers.

But... Repay him? "You owe me nothing." Arkenn had become the closest thing to a friend of his own age Petran ever had. It wasn't like Petran paid for those clothes. The thought brought a niggling of guilt.

Which only proved his father right. Petran wasn't cut out for piracy. His heart ached at the thought of leaving Arkenn ashore, as Da planned for Petran one day. It was for the best. A pirate ship wasn't the safest place for an uncorrupted man like Arkenn. While Da's position protected Petran, the crew might see Arkenn as bounty.

Never.

"Now, when we reach port in a few days, the crew will go ashore except for watchmen. I'll slip you off the ship then."

Arkenn sat on the edge of the bunk, staring at his hands folded together in his lap. In the confines of the cabin, they wore only small clothes, a tiny porthole left open to catch the breeze. "I don't know what I would have done without you."

Petran lied, pushing the offered clothing to the side and taking a seat next to Arkenn on the bunk. "You would have been fine. Like you said, you weren't as badly injured as I'd thought." If he closed his eyes, Petran still saw the burns, smelled seared flesh. No, he'd not imagined those injuries. However, he wouldn't waste precious time together trying to puzzle out a mystery.

He'd been careful not to ask but now needed to know more. "What happened to you? You don't have to tell me if you don't want to, but you can if you need a listening ear. I'm off duty until we reach port, and then I might be needed to unload cargo." Stolen cargo, but the men his father dealt with weren't too particular as long as prices met their satisfaction.

Odd for Da to give Petran time off for no reason. However, the respite allowed more time with Arkenn.

Arkenn sighed, leaning his back against the bulkhead. "I don't know where my family came from originally, but I grew up in a mountain village they'd moved to when I was small. Any newcomers caused suspicion among the villagers. My father became the village healer and saved many lives. My mother's skill at gardening made others jealous." His sad tones already told the tale of an unhappy ending.

"Religious men came from E'Skaara, summoned by a villager." Arkenn paused the telling to take a deep breath. "They accused my parents of magery and took them away to kill them at the Lady's temple. I'm not sure why they spared me and Gran."

"What?" Even living with sometimes-ruthless pirates hadn't prepared Petran for such a brutal confession. "Why? Mages don't exist anymore." Did they? He'd keep quiet about his own suspicions.

Arkenn held his tongue for many moments, then quietly whispered, "Not anymore."

"So, what happened to your gran?"

"I don't truly know. I'd been away in the mountains for several days, hunting. When I returned, nothing remained of our house but a smoldering ruin. No one would tell me what happened to her, but the guilt in their eyes told its own tale."

"Is that how you got burned? Going in after your gran?"

Arkenn dropped his gaze and shook his head. "No. They accused me of being a mage and chased me. I... I'm not sure what happened. I was running, fell, and then woke like you found me. There must have been an attack or something because the villagers chasing me were dead." He pulled his feet onto the bed, wrapping his arms around his knees, a familiar pose. "So, I started walking. I walked until I couldn't walk anymore." He gave Petran a bittersweet smile. "Then you found me."

"Then I found you." Poor man. He'd been through so much. "Well, you're safe now. When we get to the city, you'll be safer still." Pressure filled Petran's chest at the thought of not seeing Arkenn again.

Something niggled in the back of Petran's mind, some half-truth in Arkenn's account. Had Arkenn had more to do with the villagers' deaths than he let on? But no, he was no killer. The deepest parts of Petran's soul said so, and the deepest part of his soul was never wrong.

He fought the urge to embrace Arkenn for a full twelve breaths before giving in. What harm could there be? No one here to see them; soon, they'd part, never to meet again.

Arkenn stiffened, searched Petran's face with wary eyes, then sighed and sagged against his shoulder.

Nothing had ever felt so good as Arkenn's body pressed to Petran's, like two halves of one whole. Petran didn't even try to hide his stiffening cock, though he wouldn't act on his desire. Having Arkenn once and saying goodbye might break his heart.

Arkenn sat up, fingering the pendant Petran wore around his neck. "What is this?"

Petran choked back a gasp at the feel of warm fingers against his skin—almost a caress. "It belonged to my mum. My da insisted I always wear it."

"Tell me about your mother."

How to talk about someone Petran knew so little about? "She died when I was very young. Before she did, she made my da promise he'd give me a better life than we knew and that he'd keep me safe."

"Was he always a pirate?"

"No. He gave up the sea when he met her. We moved a lot, lived many places." Sometimes in the middle of the night, Petran had woken to frantic parents hastily throwing belongings into a cart. "He'd always loved the sea. When she died, he returned to piracy."

"Does this mean anything?" Arkenn tapped the pendant with a fingertip.

"Not that I know of. It's just something pretty that caught my mum's eye. Why do you ask?"

"I've seen one like it somewhere, but I can't remember." Arkenn shook his head. "Maybe in a dream."

What a strange thing to say. "Would you like to play a game since I don't have to be on deck?" Petran couldn't prolong his absence too long, or the crew might grow suspicious, even though he'd been relieved of duty. They still expected him to join the crew for meals.

Usually, they laughed and made rude gestures about what he might be up to alone, with both men and women offering to go with him, until a quelling glare from his father stilled their tongues. Lately, more had been giving Petran meaningful glances. Yes, his father would definitely put Petran ashore before he had to start killing off crewmen for molesting his son.

Even the lad from eight seasons ago hadn't tempted Petran like Arkenn, with his blue eyes, fair hair, and way of staring with interest when he thought Petran wasn't watching.

Arkenn wasn't as bulky as some Northern men, but his muscles were firm, and his chest showed a light dusting of nearly invisible hair, noticeable more to touch than to the eye.

What would it be like to touch for more than washing or treating injuries?

Arkenn lifted his head. "What kind of game?"

"Cards. I have a deck from my mum." Petran reached into the box by the bed and pulled out the once-colorful, now faded cards, the box held together with a piece of ribbon.

Arkenn stared. "I know those cards. At least, I think I do."

Petran held the deck tightly in both hands, closing his eyes. When he reopened them, he handed the deck to Arkenn. "Cut these."

Arkenn did as told. "The gestures seem familiar. What do they mean?"

Petran shrugged. "I'm not sure, but that's what our cook does. He's never really explained." Still, even as a lad, he'd found the colorful images fascinating. He placed a card faceup in front of them both.

A man in a robe with a knapsack on his back gazed up from in front of Arkenn. "The traveler. I think my gran had some of these." He traced the figure with a fingertip. Petran had a sudden, overwhelming desire to be a card. "She read futures in the cards; she didn't play games. All the cards had meaning."

"Then what is this one? It looks scary." Two serpents, intertwined, one golden, one blue.

"It's not." Arkenn lifted the card for Petran to better see. "These are the twins."

"How can they be twins? They look so different."

"Not actual twins, but two lives intertwined. The first time she read the cards for my father and mother, Gran said she'd seen this card and knew they were meant to be together."

"Smutje, our cook, reads the cards. The rest of the crew usually play for coin." Petran stared down at the serpents, noticing now how they seemed to be embracing. What if there was something to reading the cards? Once Arkenn left, would their paths cross again?

For just a moment, hope bloomed in Petran's heart.

But no, if Petran was too good for a pirate, Arkenn was too good for Petran. One day soon, they'd go their separate ways.

In two days.

Chapter Four

Arkenn didn't remember Petran bringing him onboard the ship. He'd been too full of hurt to recall anything but wild hair and deep, caring eyes.

Over the past few days, gratitude turned to appreciation to trust. Stories from his youth told of bloodthirsty pirates, yet Petran didn't fit the mold. Oh, without a doubt, the *Seabird* terrorized merchant vessels, and what Arkenn heard of the crew made his heart grow cold.

But Petran tended Arkenn's burns, fed him, surrendered his own bed to sleep on the hard floor. Though arousal tented out his pants, he never made any advances. How many men in this same situation would have been so genteel? Soon they'd drop anchor off the coast of E'Skaara. Petran would slip from the ship and bring Arkenn ashore, then the two would never see each other again.

Petran furtively regarded Arkenn. Arkenn returned the favor. Unbonded villagers shared such looks before having the village magistrate perform a bonding ceremony.

Though a village boy had once caught Arkenn's eye, he dared not act on his desire. In time the boy's parents betrothed him to a farm girl from another village. He'd left and never returned.

Fate planned to repeat itself, taking away the second man Arkenn could give his heart and body to.

What would brushing his lips against Petran's feel like? Lying naked, skin to skin with each other. Were pirates as adverse to men with men as villagers?

Regardless, Petran's body showed the effects of desire.

On one of their last nights together, Petran smoothed his blanket on the floor where he'd been sleeping since Arkenn's arrival.

"Don't." The word left Arkenn's lips before he realized he'd decided. His heart throbbed a frantic beat. This was his one chance to discover if the lightning crackling between them would fizzle like a spark in the rain or rage into an inferno. If they'd only share a few more precious memories, he'd make the most of their time together. He'd take sweet remembrances with him upon his departure—if Petran indeed shared Arkenn's desires. "The bunk is big enough for us both." He lifted the covers, scooting over, leaving room.

Petran's throat bobbed with a hard gulp. "Are you sure?"

Not an outright no. A true pirate, one from the tales, would never have asked. "I'm sure."

The moon shone in from the open... what did Petran call the window? A porthole? Enough light to see Petran's face and glorious body. Thin, with whipcord lean muscles from hours spent working on a sailing ship, skin shaded deeply by the sun.

With a grateful smile, Petran discarded his blanket and slipped into the bunk beside Arkenn. For several moments they held themselves stiffly. Finally, Petran sighed. "If we're to be comfortable, we'll have to be close." He wriggled over and lifted his arm.

What? Oh. Arkenn placed his head on Petran's chest, half-turning to get more comfortable. His cockstand slowly rose to poke Petran's thigh. Petran laughed, and Arkenn jerked back.

Petran smiled, drawing Arkenn close again. "If we're to share a bunk, we have to get used to this."

Arkenn had never been with a man before, hadn't dared even hint at his interest in the village. "Have you... Have you ever?"

"Fucked?"

Heat blazed up Arkenn's face. How boldly Petran spoke. Of course, he'd learned to talk from pirates. "Yes."

"No. The crew sometimes find pleasure with each other, but my da swears he'll boot them off the ship if they touch me."

What? Disbelief threatened to choke Arkenn. "He doesn't approve of men with men?"

"It's not that he disapproves," Petran hurried to say, "but he thinks a pirate isn't good enough for me, among other reasons."

"What else?"

"If one of the crew got me under their sway, they could challenge Da, using me to legitimize the claim and seize control of the ship." The shoulder under Arkenn's head undulated with Petran's shrug. "And most of the ports we frequent have places where men can enjoy other men, but they aren't safe, and I'd have to go alone as most of the crew seek out women, except for Rymon, Da's quartermaster. She keeps a mate in every port."

"That's not fair for you."

"It's the way things are."

"So, you've never..."

"No, I've never. Thought about it a good bit." Petran grinned down at Arkenn. "Especially these last few days."

Once more, heat rushed up Arkenn's face to his ear tips. No one had ever said such things to him before.

Except in his dreams.

"We don't have to do anything," Petran blurted. "I'm happy to hold you. I've given that much thought too."

Petran's hair brushed against Arkenn's shoulder as they lay in the dark, the ship slowly rocking them. So much between them Arkenn couldn't find the words for. Yet, he felt a connection he didn't want to end. "I'm going to miss you," he finally said. "You've been good to me, and you didn't have to."

Even with only the moon's low light, Arkenn saw the want in Petran's dark eyes. Those eyes drew closer. And closer still.

The softest whisper of lips against lips, and then...

Arkenn opened his mouth, welcoming Petran's tongue inside. Warm, slick, everything a first kiss should be, shooting desire to Arkenn's groin. "Mmmph!" he exclaimed without breaking the contact. He rocked his hips, building friction against Petran's firmly muscled thigh.

Petran deepened the kiss, ran his hands into Arkenn's small clothes, and took Arkenn in hand. His strokes were tentative at first, becoming surer by the minute.

He let go and rolled Arkenn onto his back. "Is this okay?" he panted.

Words failed, Arkenn's body burning from every single touch. He gave a sharp nod, and slipped his small clothes down to expose his cock and balls. Resuming the kiss with a vengeance, Petran rocked against him, building pressure.

When had Petran removed his small clothes?

Gripping broad shoulders, Arkenn held on tight lest he lose his grip and the world spin out of control.

Together they thrust and moaned and writhed upon the bunk. The feel of Petran's flesh, the taste and touch forever imprinted on Arkenn's brain. He slid his hands over firm sides, clung to flexing shoulders.

Wrapping his arms around Petran, Arkenn bucked up, adding a bit more pressure to the slick-slide of their loving.

He whined into Petran's mouth, gripping tight. Oh, oh, oh! Every muscle stiffened. Hanging on the edge of ecstasy, Arkenn fought to prolong the pleasure, ultimately losing the battle. Fire blazed through him as he shot pulse after pulse between their bellies.

Petran shoved harder, breathing labored, then stilled, his cries of passion caught in Arkenn's mouth.

Reeking of sex and sweat, they lay in each other's arms, in silence, with just the creaking of the *Seabird* and their own heavy breathing around them.

So much more amazing even than Arkenn's dreams. Petran finished stripping him, using the small clothes to clean them up, then relaxed on the bed, pulling Arkenn to his chest again.

Petran's racing heart beat a steady rhythm in Arkenn's ear. Arkenn drifted off to sleep in comforting arms. Before he slipped out of consciousness, the press of lips caressed his forehead.

Though he'd just found the man, Petran would be hard to give up.

Give him up, Arkenn must.

Far too soon.

Chapter Five

P etran awoke with a jolt. What was that? The entire ship shook. *Crash! Splash!* He shot from the bunk, scrambling into his clothes without a candle. A flash lit the sky.

He darted to the porthole, heart sinking, then stopping. It restarted with a kick. Another ship.

"Wha...?" Arkenn asked, voice sleepy yet concerned.

"I don't know. I think we're under attack." Please, no. If the captain ordered an attack, he'd have given a warning. This? Someone coming after *them*. Though Petran wasn't allowed on raids, all hands hit the deck when under attack.

Arkenn struggled out of the bunk.

"No!" Petran pushed Arkenn back down with a firm hand to the chest. "Stay here. This is the safest place for you. I must go on deck." Even though Petran couldn't see well in the dark, he focused on where he thought Arkenn's eyes might be. "I'll be back. All will be well. You'll see." Fumbling under the bed produced the sword and pistol kept there for emergencies. Petran strapped his father's cast-off sword belt securely around his middle.

"But...?"

"But nothing. Stay here." About to head out the door, Petran spun, planting a kiss on what might have been Arkenn's forehead. "If anyone tries to break down the door, crawl under the bunk. There's a door in the back, my own hidey-hole. Get in there. Stay put. Don't come out until I get you, or the battle ends."

Another flash from outside illuminated the cabin for one brief moment. The fear on Arkenn's face ripped at Petran's heart.

He rushed from the small cabin, barely pausing long enough to secure the door, and climbed the ladder topside.

Boom!

He grabbed the gunwale to keep from pitching over the ship's side. In the brief flash from the cannon, he spied a hulking shape closing in. A sail with triple stars, for the Father, the Lady, and the law.

Oh, Father, preserve them.

A ship so much larger than the *Seabird*. Likely bounty hunters with one hundred or more troops ready to hack the crew to bits. They'd save only enough pirates to present a spectacle in port to keep the citizens entertained while sending a message to other pirates.

The *Seabird* hadn't been boarded—yet. Their one chance was to run. No ship carrying so much mass could beat the *Seabird* for speed.

Without being told, Petran took his place. As one of the least of the crew, he acted as a runner, collecting premeasured bags of gunpowder from the ship's hold and racing to his assigned cannon.

The pirates practiced for such an event, moving in an intricate dance. A burly man, beard shot through with silver, accepted a bag of powder and a wad of cloth from Petran, shoving both into the cannon with a rammer. Another crewmate added the cannonball while yet another poked a slender rod through the touch hole, opening the powder bag, all under the watchful eye of the master gunner.

They positioned the cannon, strapping down the ropes, then touched off the powder. Petran cringed at the report. The cannon shot backward, testing its restraints.

A pirate swabbed out the cannon before they started the process again. Pack, load, position, fire, swab. Pack, load, position, fire, swab.

The blasts from other cannons—the *Seabird*'s and the approaching vessel's—lit up the night sky. The acrid scent of gunpowder and smoke stung Petran's nose.

Again and again, the pirates working with Petran filled the cannon. Again and again, they fired, their cannon's blast echoed by five other cannons, firing in quick succession.

Petran's muscles ached. Screams of dying men rent his ears. A pirate fell, open eyes staring at nothing. Blood trickled from her mouth, soaked her shirt. The stench of burned flesh and blood added to the gunpowder and smoke.

Petran fought to keep his dinner down. Da was right—Petran wasn't meant to be a pirate.

"Take her sword!" Rymon shouted from a few feet away. "Take her sword! It's better than yours!"

A hard swallow didn't clear the bile from Petran's throat. Robbing the dead. But the quartermaster spoke true. The dead pirate didn't need a fine blade.

The living did.

"I'm sorry," he whispered, unwrapping the dead woman's fingers from the sword's hilt and replacing her blade with his. A pirate should go to their grave with sword in hand.

The captain shouted orders through the din. The report of cannon and gun grew deafening. Still, the hunters' ship came ever closer. Too close. Enemy sailors crowded the other ship's deck, ready to board the *Seabird*.

While most had learned to swing a sword from a young age, a fast-dwindling pirate crew would be no match for highly skilled bounty hunters.

Then what would happen to Petran? His da?

Arkenn.

The ship shuddered. Petran grabbed the gunwale, barely keeping his feet. Rymon staggered past, sword in hand. "Look alive, there, lad," she shouted, sweeping an assessing gaze over the deck, where the dead and dying lay.

Too many. Way too many.

Regaining his footing, Petran patted his newly acquired sword. Still there. May he not need it.

Boom! The ship rocked again, heeling to starboard. Petran slid down the deck— bare feet slipping in blood. He rolled and tumbled toward the bulwark. A hand on his arm stopped his fall. He stared up into the eyes of his Da. The ship righted. "You all right, there, son?"

Petran nodded, scrambling to his feet. His father released him, hurrying toward the possible boarding point.

Surely Petran hadn't saved Arkenn and brought him aboard to die in battle, or worse, be caught and hanged as a pirate. No! Petran struggled back to the cannon, wiping who knew what from his brow.

The other ship burst through a wall of smoke and fog, a wraith coming to take them all. He stood on deck, staring straight down an enemy cannon.

Some overwhelming power forced him to stillness, legs and arms outstretched. The too-calm wind formed a gust and then a gale, filling the sails. The *Seabird* gained speed, pulling away from the other vessel. He lowered his arms. The winds stopped.

He lifted them again. Glancing right and left, he saw pirates, weapons in hand, ready for close fighting. No one noticed him. Raising his arms higher increased the wind. What was this? How was he doing this? It couldn't be him.

Each time he lowered his arms, the wind died.

Raised arms, it was.

The battle continued around him, pirates shouting, mouths moving, yet he couldn't make out the words. Lights flashed around him.

A flash of lightning split the sky, the winds picking up. Yes, yes. If the winds prevailed, they just might escape.

Petran's arm muscles began to burn from the effort of reaching upward. Afraid to look astern at the approaching ship, Petran focused straight ahead, feeling the cooling wind on his skin.

The *Seabird* tossed upon the waves, a child's toy adrift on the ocean.

Cheers erupted from the pirates. He finally turned around. The other ship grew smaller and smaller behind them. Yes! They were getting away!

Another flash came from the enemy cannon. Quiet.
Then the world exploded.

Chapter Six

Arkenn huddled in the bunk, trying to still his trembling. If captured by pirate hunters, he'd be considered a pirate and hanged. What of Petran, who'd risked much to save Arkenn, and who was never allowed to be a pirate but even now defended his father's ship?

Arkenn watched the battle through the porthole, cringing at the screams of anger and pain. Every shriek brought terrible images of Petran, body lying broken on the deck.

Or, worse, dead.

No. He couldn't be.

The skies lit up. The other ship appeared huge compared to the *Seabird*, close enough to hear the shouts coming from its deck. Shouts from sailors who'd kill Arkenn, Petran, and anyone else aboard.

Petran couldn't be killed. Arkenn wouldn't let him. Sitting cross-legged on the bunk, he focused, demanding the strange energy he'd usually hidden to do his will. *Keep Petran safe.*

In the dark, tuning out the noise, the nose-burning stench, Arkenn put everything he had into protecting his friend. If only Gran had taught him what he needed to know instead of insisting he hide his heritage.

The ship rolled and shuddered. He clutched the side of the bunk. Thank goodness the bed seemed affixed into place.

The battle raged forever, the enemy cannon fire growing closer. Who was it? Other pirates? Pirate hunters? Neither boded well. Here Arkenn was, a runt of a man, helpless. Weak.

Facing almost certain death for the second time in recent memory.

If he survived, he'd do whatever he could to never feel this desperation again. He'd become someone others could depend on for salvation, like he did Petran.

Lightning flashed outside the window. Cheers sounded from the deck above. Were they winning? Getting away?

The ship shuddered, shattering his concentration. A direct hit? Screaming. Shouted orders.

Footsteps on the ladder.

More than one set. Three, at least.

Arkenn darted under the bunk, pushing assorted whatevers out of the way. Petran had dug under here before leaving. If the people approaching saw a mess, they might assume Petran made it. Where was that door in the back?

The door to Petran's room flew open. "Put him in here, lads." The captain! Arkenn never met the man, but he must be the captain with an accent like Petran's and barking orders. The owner of the commanding voice stood only a few feet away. "Once we're clear, I'll get Smutje to tend him." Two men shuffled forward, eased something on the bunk above Arkenn's head, and pounded back up the ladder.

Which left...

"Do what you can for my son," the captain murmured, hurrying after his men.

The captain knew of Arkenn? How?

Arkenn slithered from under the bed. Light. He needed light. Usually, Petran lit a candle for brief periods, but a lamp sat high on one wall. Please let Arkenn not burn down the ship. Closing his eyes, he called to the place inside he'd avoided thinking of since leaving the village. There, deep within. Images came to mind of his mother, flame dancing on her palm.

He could do this. He *must* do this!

Fire sprang from his hand, lighting the wick. The lantern smoked slightly, but he couldn't worry about extra soot now.

He stared down at the man lying on the bed, skin ghostly pale.

Petran.

As large around as Arkenn's wrist, splintered wood protruded from Petran's shoulder. Blood. Lots of blood. On the floor, on the bunk. On Petran.

Arkenn needed to work fast. He'd observed his father healing villagers before. First, Da clouded their minds to ease the pain, calm them, and conceal his actions. Next, Mum boiled water and brought cleaning cloths. Then, Mum and Da chanted and hummed, running hands over the patient's injuries.

Though he'd thought them erased by the intervening seasons, Arkenn remembered one tune in particular. Using a drying cloth as a makeshift bandage, he squeezed the material to Petran's shoulder with one hand while grasping the spike with the other.

Words spilling fast from his tongue, he took a deep breath. If he did this wrong...

He wrenched the offending splinter away. Blood gushed. Arkenn applied pressure with the cloth. The tune changed, his mind conjuring more sounds. If they were words, he didn't know them, yet they tasted familiar on his tongue.

Lifting the bandage for short intervals, he probed the wound, removing any small wood slivers remaining.

If the battle still raged overhead, he neither knew nor cared. Petran kept his full attention. The blood slowed to a trickle, then started to clot. Three times Arkenn transferred power to the lamp. At last, he settled on the bunk, Petran's head in his lap. He continued his chanting, stroking a hand over Petran's brow. His heart spoke words in another tongue—a ward against fever.

Please let Petran be okay. Please, please, please. Little by little, both Arkenn's strength and the oil dwindled. The lantern sputtered out.

Arkenn's energy followed shortly thereafter.

He awoke with a start to footsteps on the ladder again and squirmed back under the bunk.

Light filled the room.

"There he is," an unfamiliar voice said. "Put the lantern down over there."

Judging from the light pattern, the new arrival set the lantern on the box Petran kept beside the bed. Two men, judging by footsteps.

"Let's take a look at that shoulder, my boy," the man muttered.

"Look at this!" the second man exclaimed.

"He must have come to long enough to remove the spike," the first said. "Surprised he didn't bleed out." Material ripped in the area that must be Petran's chest. "Well, would you look at that?" The man let out a low whistle. "A spike that size could've killed him. I've seen men brought down by less. But this wound? It appears days old. He either heals fast or..." The man let the sentence hang. Finally, he said, "We'll get him cleaned up, then let the captain know his son will recover."

After a few moments of water splashing, grunts, and the rustle of fabric above Arkenn, both men left the room, taking the lamp.

Petran moaned. Arkenn reached out with his mind, willing Petran to rest instead of waking to terrible pain.

Gradually Arkenn crawled out from under the bunk and peeked out the porthole. No brilliant flashes. No booms. No impacts. No shouting.

The danger was past.

He placed his hand on Petran's brow. Too hot.

Maybe the danger hadn't passed completely. Weariness pulled at Arkenn. He'd given so much of himself. Like his accidental self-defense on the mountain, he'd thrown every bit of energy into his magic. However, he'd made no conscious decision to do so then.

Petran still needed him.

Arkenn curled around the still figure on the bunk, giving in to sleep.

He awoke to the sun high in the sky and a blanket tucked over them both. A quiet "A-hem" made him jump. Oh no! One of the crew!

A man sat on Petran's clothes chest. He shared Petran's square jaw, brown hair, and dark eyes. So this must be the captain! Petran's father. "I don't know who you are or how you came aboard my ship, but I know *what* you are."

Arkenn shoved back away from Petran, whipping his head right and left. No chance of escape.

"Do I look like a religious fanatic to you?" The captain sighed and stretched his long legs as far as the cramped room allowed. He wore his hair and beard neatly cut, but no denying the likeness between father and son, though the older version sported a few gray hairs. "I saw my son when we brought him here after the battle. That was no small wound. You healed him."

"I... I..."

The captain pulled the blanket down far enough to reveal a shiny pink scar on Petran's shoulder.

Oh. Arkenn stared with wide eyes. He'd done that? His father had been able to speed healing but not cure such a grievous wound overnight. Then again, doing so would have made the villagers suspicious.

The intimidating pirate captain, slightly hooked nose so like Petran's, continued, "You have my thanks. However, I'd also like to ask a favor."

A favor? Arkenn owed the man a lot for not kicking him overboard. "Sir?"

"One day soon, I'm going to have to let my son go for his own good, so he can make his place in the world. His mother was mage-born from another place. Petran inherited her power, and she would have trained him had she survived. Since her death, I've found no mages to teach him. It is my hope that he can find his purpose in life. If possible, when that time comes, will you seek him out? Help him?"

Mage-born? Petran and his mother were mage-born? "How can I find him?"

"You'll find him." The captain smiled. "I sense a bond between you. Perhaps it's friendship, perhaps it's... more. But sooner or later, fate will reunite you."

"I'll help if I can."

The captain let out a sigh, the stiff set of his body relaxing. "That's all I can ask. I'd like to keep him with me for a few more seasons, for I'm too selfish to let him go just yet. I ask that you not let him know we talked. If he thinks I put you up to something, he might not believe you like him for himself. You do, don't you?" Brown eyes skewered Arkenn clear down to his soul, daring him to lie.

"Ye... yes, sir."

"Good. Let us pretend I still don't know you're on board. He can sneak you off the *Seabird* and be the hero, for I imagine wherever he procured you, he had rescue in mind." The captain winked. "Did he not have plans to put you ashore at E'Skaara?"

"Yes, sir. That doesn't bother you? The people in my village—"

"Were fools," the captain spat. "My Rosemary told me the strongest mage couples in her homeland were two men or two women. On winter nights, she'd tell me stories of their deeds. They were revered."

Arkenn grew relaxed enough in this man's company to ask, "What happened last night?"

The captain's mood darkened. "Pirate hunters. Somehow, they crept up on us. I fear sooner or later they'll catch me. Which is another reason to let Petran go. He's no pirate. Was never meant to be."

"How did you know what I am?"

The man grinned, nodding at Petran. "I have a bit of power on my own. Nothing beyond predicting the weather, mind you, but enough to feel a kinship." His smile fell. "I must warn you. Be careful what magic you do in E'Skaara. The Lady's temple is there, along with her zealots. You've seen Petran's amulet?"

"Yes?"

"It hides what he is. If you can't learn to hide your strength, you will be in danger."

"How can I do that?"

"Seek out the Father's priests."

Petran moaned. The captain shifted his gaze to his son.

The Father's priests. Wasn't one set of worshippers as bad as another? "What will they do?"

Once more, the captain fixed his dark gaze on Arkenn's. "Keep you alive. Or they'll try to, but that's the best deal you'll get." He rose and patted Arkenn's shoulder. "Good luck, little mage. Safe journey."

He trod toward the door. Before he closed the panel behind him, the captain added, "And if you cannot stay safe... run."

Chapter Seven

Petran stood on deck, resting his elbows on the taffrail. Mist kissed his face while salt air filled his lungs. In the distance, the vague shape of E'Skaara's harbor scarcely registered—three days later than initially planned, thanks to crew members recovering from the attack.

They'd lost six of their crew of fifty-seven, buried at sea. Another eight might never be fit for duty again.

Smutje and a few others would stay with the ship while the rest of the crew went ashore in E'Skaara.

E'Skaara, one of the few ports they could safely use and be seen as small merchants, as long as they tended to business, left without lingering, and no one asked too many questions about the damaged hull. They'd filled their cargo hold with legitimate goods, like Frescian ale and Amalgari silk, which hid less-legal items they'd offer to private collectors.

The thwack of hammers and rasp of saws in the background occasionally drowned out the squawking birds reeling overhead. How amazing that Petran escaped the battle with only a scratch. Odd, the wound that his shipmates swore had been life-threatening appeared to be a deep scar, but he'd never been injured there before, and he hadn't had time to heal from more than a glancing blow...

Footsteps approached from behind him. He stiffened, relaxing again when a familiar three-fingered hand settled near his elbow. "It's a fine eve, my son."

Son. How little Petran heard the word these days. In front of the crew, the captain called Petran by name or merely barked orders. Though he sheltered Petran in some ways, he tried to be fair to all who sailed aboard the *Seabird*.

"Aye, Da." No need to look around. His father wouldn't address Petran so within hearing of the crew.

"Yer mum used to love eves like this on our farm. Cool and clear. A perfect way to end a day she called them." A note of wistfulness crept into Da's voice.

"Do you miss her still?" This time Petran did look at his father, quick to register the change in expression talk of Mum always brought.

"Aye. A woman like no other was yer mum." Da gave Petran a fond smile. "You look more like her every day."

They remained quiet for a long time, staring out into the distance. "Petran, I don't think I ever told you how proud I am of the man you've become." Da spread his hands, indicating the ship. "This is no life for you. You deserve so much better. I promised yer mum—"

"That I'd become some kind of grand gentleman. That's not me, Da. I've no regrets. I wish you'd let me join the crew in truth." What would Petran do on land when he'd spent so much time at sea? Climbing masts, setting sails. Those were things he knew. What kind of life would he make on land?

"No!" Da softened his voice. "No. You've got good things coming to you. You're too good of a man for a pirate."

"You're a good man."

Da shook his head. "I was a good man when I was with yer mum. Now?" His weathered brow furrowed. "Now, I'm a pirate, watching over my shoulder whenever in port, scanning the horizon for hunters come to put an end to my thieving ways." He grinned and dropped the lid over one dark eye in a wink. "They gotta catch me first."

"No one is fast enough to catch the *Seabird*." Petran himself witnessed many who'd tried. They'd all failed. A memory flashed in his mind: him, on deck, arms spread wide, bringing the wind to the ship's sails.

Wind the other ship didn't benefit from.

Da's smile fell. "Luck's been with us. But luck is a fickle thing. One day here, one day gone." He placed a hand on Petran's shoulder. "Make me the same promise I made to her: that you'll be an honorable man with an honorable profession."

This same argument. Why today? "I'd make a decent life for myself aboard the *Seabird*."

"No, son. This life is not for you. Wherever you go, whatever you do, I want you to remember yer da and yer mum loved you."

For the first time since he'd been a small child, Petran asked, "Tell me about my mother." Before, his father grew tight-lipped about all but the smallest memories.

A dreamy smile crossed his father's face, so at odds with the usual scowl worn by Captain Jaed

Three-fingers. "You're of age enough to know the whole tale. I came ashore near E'Skaara late one night, fetching cargo from a smuggler. Although obviously a lady of quality, I found Rosemary out alone, walking the beach beneath the cliffs unchaperoned. Her hair was like starlight and shimmered under the moon's glow. She wasn't afraid of being alone or of me, though I must have been a sight, ragged pirate that I was." He ran his gaze up and down Petran's body. "Was scarcely past your age, I reckon. She said she needed to get far from the city. I figured she'd run from an abusive mate or father. So I took her aboard the ship, claiming she was my bond mate." His smile faded. "Once we reached Q'Dara, she told me she must go." One side of his mouth lifted. "Damn near broke my coal-black heart. When she set foot on the docks, she glanced back over her shoulder and asked, 'Well?' I left the ship that very day, taking nothing but the shirt on my back."

Petran voiced the question that he'd never gotten a complete answer to and stopped asking because of the sadness in his father's eyes whenever he asked. "What happened to her?" All he knew was she died when he was young.

Da took a deep breath, stared out at the sea, and finally nodded. "One day, I went to town with the harvest, took you along with me though you was just a wee mite. Was gone for a day or two." He paused, clutching the taffrail in a white-knuckled grip. "The Lady's Chosen came, accused your mum of wickedness. Took her away to the Lady's temple." He clenched his hands into fists. "A defenseless woman. And none of our neighbors tried to help. Instead, they watched as those men took Rosemary away."

Images flashed through Petran's mind of a beautiful woman, running, screaming, falling... taken away, tears on her face.

"No one the Lady took ever returned. I went after her, tracked her back here, where she'd run from, but never found her." Da shook his head. "I promised to keep her safe. I... failed."

"Why did they take her?" After the incident with the wind, Petran thought he knew. He needed to hear the words.

Da glanced right and left, then leaned in to murmur, "Yer mum was mage-born. Fled the city when the Lady declared death to all mages. But the Chosen brought captured mages back to the temple, drained their magic first." He balled his hands into fists, blinking a few times, chin lifted. "Yer mum never hurt anyone, used her powers for good. No one believed."

Petran knew the next part. "So you took me and a few things and returned to the sea."

Da nodded. "Mind yourself when we dock in E'Skaara. It's not a safe place for the likes of you."

The likes of you?

"The day you were born, yer mum asked me to keep you safe, do my best to raise you right. I think somehow, she knew she wouldn't be here to watch you grow into a man."

"I wish I could remember more of her." A brief smile, a flash of golden hair, a quiet laugh. Snuggles. Mum had loved him for all too short a time.

"One day, maybe you'll chance upon a lass on a beach, lost her way." Da shrugged. "Yer mum says your kind call to each other. Or maybe you'll find a lad."

A lad? Petran stiffened. What did his father know?

"Ahoy, Captain!" came a call from the crow's nest.

Da glanced up at the land growing ever closer, clapped Petran on the shoulder, then strode away. "I must ready the ship."

Well, that was... odd. Petran left the taffrail to make preparations of his own. His mother was mage-born. Why had his father never told him before? Did Da know of Petran's odd bits of wild magic that only appeared when he really needed them?

Maybe now that his father had told him, he'd answer more questions.

Later. For now, Petran had plans of his own for sneaking Arkenn ashore.

But first, one more night. Morn would be soon enough to break his own heart.

He'd once complained about his cramped bunk, but the narrow width meant his front would press against Arkenn's back throughout the night.

With Arkenn asleep, Petran could drop a kiss on the back of his neck, wrap him in a firm embrace, and miss him with a breaking heart.

With Arkenn none the wiser.

Chapter Eight

After being mostly naked for so long, wearing clothes—especially someone else's— and going into the world struck Arkenn as strange. He'd rolled the overly long trouser legs to keep from tripping, and the simple shirt hung from his shoulders.

Petran tucked Arkenn's hair into a hat, pulling the brim low. For one moment, Arkenn longed for a kiss, to feel those lips on his skin once more, like he had several times during the night when Petran thought him asleep. "Most of the townsfolk have darker skin, hair and eyes. This will keep you hidden until you're far away from the port. If any ask, tell them you're from A'shkalia, a farming community to the north. They aren't too trusting of strangers here, but they depend on A'shkalia for food, so they'll be more likely to accept you."

Arkenn nodded, trying to take in every word, while his heart grew heavier with each. "I wish you could come with me. Didn't you say your father would leave you one day? Why not come now?" The captain had said he'd have to let his son go. Why not today?

But no. Loved ones in Arkenn's life had been few and far between. So he couldn't blame a father for wanting to keep his son around as long as possible.

Petran gave a sad smile. "He's all the family I have. I'll stay with him until he finds a place he believes I'll be safe. He promised my mother. For some reason, he doesn't believe E'Skaara is for me. Given their distrust of strangers, I understand."

Yes, but Petran still had a father. Arkenn had no one but Petran. Saying so would likely cause unnecessary pain while making Arkenn appear desperate.

He *was* desperate, but their remaining time together should be pleasant.

They waited until the early hours of dawn. Petran slipped from the cabin, returning a short time later with a hunk of cheese and slightly stale bread. "Here, eat. You never know when you might get the chance again."

While Arkenn ate on the edge of the bunk, Petran continued talking. "Most of the crew went ashore after unloading the hold yesterday. Two crewmen stand guard, and Smutje is sound asleep on deck, staying here to watch the wounded. I've already told the others that I intend to take the last boat ashore to be ready when the markets open."

He got down on his hands and knees, lifted the box he kept by the bed, pulled up a loose board, and removed a leather bag. Back to Arkenn, he said, "You'll need something to tide you over." Turning, he handed Arkenn several coins.

Arkenn hadn't seen many coins in his life. The villagers bartered for necessities, and Gran had kept any money safely hidden. Had someone raided their house before setting the fire? The villagers wouldn't use Arkenn's crops, but a single man or woman might slip into the house unseen. No, he'd not think of losses now.

"These are all E'Skaara deanuits. The small ones should buy a good dinner. This one"—Petran tapped a larger coin made of some bronze material— "should cover lodging for a sevenday. This one"—he offered a shiny golden coin— "will buy a small house. Use it wisely."

Arkenn stared at his palm where Petran deposited the coins, mostly smaller ones, a few large ones, and one of the golden ones. "I can't take your money. This is a fortune." Certainly, enough to buy his whole village.

"You can and you will." Petran curled Arkenn's fingers around the offering. "I have more than enough to share with you. Now, get ready to leave. Keep the money tucked inside your shirt. There's a pocket sewn in. E'Skaara is home to some of the most gifted pickpockets in the land."

Petran made one more dash abovedeck and returned. "Come, let's go." He snuffed out the candle.

Holding his breath, Arkenn climbed the ladder after Petran. The steady sway and creak he'd grown used to now abraded his nerves.

The full moon shone over the water in this time before the dawn, and for a moment, he stopped. How beautiful. He could understand why Petran's father loved the sea, with its clean winds and adventure. Petran tugged on his hand and led him to the ship's side.

Footsteps approached.

Petran shoved Arkenn so hard that he nearly fell overboard. Oh. A small boat hung from the ship's side. Arkenn crawled in, scrambling under a burlap bag.

"So, ye be leavin' us, Petran?" The pirate's speech came out slurred.

"For a while. I promise to bring back something special for the crew."

The pirate dropped his voice, his words implying so, so much. "You can be my something special."

What? Arkenn nearly jumped from the boat, ready to defend his friend.

Petran gave a practiced laugh. "And have me da cut off your body parts? Not too special, I be thinking." Funny how Petran sounded less educated talking to this man.

A chuckle sounded above Arkenn's hiding place. "That he would. Well, then, safe travels. And if ya find a comely wench with big tits, bring her back for me."

"I'll tell her you look like me. If I told her you look like the ass-end of a mule, she'd run to the temple and declare herself a novice."

Again, the pirate chuckled. "It only happened the once. Now, get on with ya."

Petran climbed into the boat. Arkenn peeked from underneath his cover as, hand over hand, Petran worked the pulley, lowering the boat into the water. Once he'd rowed halfway to shore, he hissed, "You can come out now."

Arkenn sat across from Petran. He might find the time romantic in other circumstances, with moonlight shimmering on the water, air crisp with a salty tang.

The sea could be lovely but oh so deadly. Arkenn shuddered, recalling the battle and nearly losing

Petran. Why, oh, why, couldn't his newfound friend come with him?

Once more, the queasiness shook Arkenn's insides. This couldn't be over. It really couldn't.

"Come here," Petran said, patting the spot beside him.

Stooping low and clinging to the side to avoid flipping into the water, Arkenn made his way across the rocking boat. Yes, a land lover through and through. He started to sit a bit apart to allow rowing room.

Petran wrapped an arm around Arkenn and pulled him hip to hip. "You'll be okay. I wish I could go with you, but I can't." He stared into Arkenn's eyes. "But I'll never forget you."

Arkenn rested his head on Petran's shoulder. The captain said they'd be together one day. Though deep down Arkenn had doubts, he'd cling to any measure of hope.

They remained together, Petran awkwardly rowing around Arkenn's body. The city's gaslights grew closer by the minute. Arkenn swallowed and swallowed again, but the lump in his throat remained. Without thinking, he sought more comfort in Petran's embrace.

When they finally came ashore, pink tinged the horizon, heralding a new day. Arkenn wished he could return to yesterday, relive last night over again.

No point in pretending. His life waited on land; Petran's at sea. At least for the immediate future.

Arkenn expected Petran to let him out of the boat and row back to the *Seabird*. Instead, he clutched Arkenn's hand. "Come, I'll show you around." He dropped the hand before they moved from the deserted docks to the main street of E'Skaara.

Arkenn paused, taking in the city. Clapboard buildings with signs hanging above the doors, quaint inns, and houses. The place smelled of rotting fish and seawater. Birds whirled above, calling out to each other.

Nothing extraordinary and most certainly not expected. "The villagers say the streets are made of marble, and everything is shiny and new. That houses all have terraces, and people ride in fancy carriages."

Petran gave a soft laugh. "In the high city, maybe, where the temple of the Lady is located, and the wealthy make their home. This"—he swept out a hand— "is the lower city where the common folks live. You'll be amazed at the market."

No one else strode down the main street, though a man scarcely older than Arkenn traveled from lamp to lamp, extinguishing the flames. Arkenn had never seen street lamps before. The streets were bumpy under his bare feet and slick with morn dew.

"Cobblestones," Petran explained.

Arkenn knelt, running his hands over the smooth stones.

Petran laughed and yanked him up. "Don't do that, or they'll know you're not a local."

Heat licked up Arkenn's cheeks. "Sorry. I've never been to a city before." He rose and gazed around at the buildings. So many shops.

"Wait until you see how many people live here."

Cold raced through Arkenn's insides. People. So many people when he'd been used to few. More people meant he could disappear into their ranks, though.

They turned down a side street. Cobblestones gave way to packed dirt. Voices sounded ahead of them, coming ever closer. Finally, the narrow street widened into an open area. Even though the sun hadn't yet fully risen, men and women bustled about, setting up tables.

"Fish! Get your fresh fish!" one man called, pushing a cart laden with many different kinds of fish.

"Never eat those," Petran whispered, pointing to a rather sinister-looking blue creature with what appeared to be horns above its eyes. "It's popular with couples who believe certain parts increase their chances for children, but if it's not cooked right..." He gave an impression of puking in the gutter. "I think the fishermen started the fertility rumor to sell the worthless things."

Petran bought them each a pastry from a baker's stall. The filling tasted of some strange fruit, sweet but tart. As they wandered through market booths, Petran explained what things were and local customs.

A lesson on how to fit in, then. Which only reminded Arkenn that they must soon part. "Show me the high city."

Petran paled. "Our kind aren't welcome there. We'll be run out by the city guards. However, I can show you some better parts of the low city."

"Our kind?"

Petran rolled his shoulders in a shrug, shirt clinging to his firm muscles. "Not wealthy. The rich follow the Lady. The poor pray to the Father. Da told me they were once one and the same, two aspects of the same deity until some wealthy families claimed the female aspect for their own. So they got the Lady, leaving the Father to the poor."

They strolled, Arkenn soaking in every last word and enjoying the sticky sweetness of his fruit pastry. Petran had seen a million ports, spoke a dozen languages learned from the pirates aboard the *Seabird*, and knew about so many things. Arkenn's entire existence lay in a little mountain village he'd recently left for the first time.

At last, they both seemed to run out of words.

They sat in silence on what Petran called a jetty, staring out to sea, nothing to hear but waves beating against boards and screeching seabirds. Petran broke the silence. "I hate to see you go, but you need to find lodgings before the sun goes down, someplace safe." He tilted his head to face Arkenn, studying him for a long, long time. "I will truly miss you. I wish I could come with you, but my father doesn't want to leave me here." A quick right-left perusal showed no one around. Petran leaned in, placing a quick kiss on Arkenn's cheek. "Pl... please take care of yourself."

This was to be goodbye, then. Arkenn pressed his knuckles against his eyelids. The burning continued. A heavy weight settled in his chest. They were alone here; he'd been watching to be sure. Cradling Petran's face in his hands, he leaned in for a slow, heartfelt kiss. Petran opened his mouth, sliding his tongue along Arkenn's. Sheer paradise, this connection. Reluctantly, Arkenn pulled back. "I wish you could come with me."

Petran stared down at their joined hands. "Me too. You'll never know how much."

"If your father leaves you here in the future, do you promise to come looking for me?"

Petran brightened, one side of his mouth lifting. "I promise, but don't wait. It could be seasons. I want you to be happy. Make a good life for yourself."

No need to delay the inevitable. Blinking back tears, Arkenn rose. Only by great effort did he manage to put one foot in front of the other.

Footsteps leading away from Petran, a knife twisted in his heart with each step Arkenn took.

Chapter Nine

E ach step Arkenn strolled away added more weight to Petran's heart. Finally, he took two steps forward, then stopped. His responsibilities lay elsewhere—for now.

At least the coins might make life easier until Arkenn got on his feet.

Petran should have gone with his friend, save Da the trouble of leaving him behind, but no. Pirate Da might be, but Petran wouldn't willingly part company. His father also made clear that Petran didn't belong in this city.

Somehow, this wasn't the last he'd see of Arkenn. Clear down in his soul, Petran felt a bond, a connection. One day the insistent pull would lead them back to each other.

Or so he believed, for thinking otherwise might be too much to bear. He rubbed the scar on his shoulder.

Not being on land much, especially not in a city of this size, Petran took his time returning to the ship. He wouldn't be called on for watch until nightfall.

Hopefully, Arkenn would have found a place to stay by then. Safe. He must be kept safe.

Petran wasn't typically one for prayer, but he clutched his mother's amulet. "Father, keep him under your protection," he murmured. A shadow fell across his path. He jumped. Pickpockets wouldn't take him unawares.

The figure all in brown had him backing away. A hood hid the person's face, and not an inch of skin showed, even on this warm day. Gloves showed instead of hands.

"You've nothing to fear from me." The man's voice rumbled pleasantly.

Ah. A priest of the Father. Had the Father heard Petran's prayer? "You're a priest, right?"

"I am. I'm here to tell you that the Father heard your prayer. He will take care of your friend."

Talk about fast! Petran had barely gotten the words out. "Th... thank you."

"The Father doesn't need words to know what's on your heart," the priest explained. So how had he known Petran's question? "You'll see him again, but now isn't the time."

Petran's heart soared. "I will?"

"Yes, but only when the time is right."

"When will that be?"

"You both have journeys to take first. Yours will be hard, but you won't be alone. Keep heart. Stay strong. You'll be exactly where you were meant to be."

A shout came from behind. Petran looked away for a mere moment. When he turned back around, the priest was gone. He couldn't have gotten far. Petran raced up the street and back down, but no priest.

How strange for the man to suddenly appear and disappear just as quickly. Mulling the words over in his mind didn't help Petran figure out what the priest meant. In the end, he'd cling to the promise that he'd see Arkenn again.

Petran roamed the streets, peeking in shops at their wares or watching passersby. Maybe he shouldn't have said goodbye so soon, but waiting would only have been harder after a day spent together, showing him and Arkenn a taste of what they couldn't have.

Not now.

Petran found himself wanting to show Arkenn a beautiful pottery bowl or a scabbard of carved leather and find out which pieces his friend liked best.

His friend. He had a friend.

Most of the people Petran met took one look at him and shuffled away with something akin to horror on their faces. Barefoot, in worn breeches and a simple shirt, didn't set him apart from many of the children playing games in an alley, but his matted hair and sun-bronzed skin marked him as an outsider.

Not everyone harshly judged his looks, particularly not the kind-faced woman who'd swapped a coin for a meat pie from her pushcart, throwing in a peach crumble because he "looked like he needed some meat on his bones." Climbing riggings and subsisting primarily on fish didn't exactly make one fat.

The sun sank lower on the horizon. No more putting off the inevitable. Petran turned back toward the sound of bells as the ships in the harbor gently rocked on the waves. The always present seabirds shrieked overhead, and above all, the scent of salt spray spoke of home.

Home. His heart gave a painful squeeze. Arkenn. Petran would take comfort in the priest's words. Da waited. Petran had a job to do and would perform each task to the best of his ability. He might not earn an equal share with the crew of all the spoils they acquired, but he'd be comfortable when he did stay ashore.

He climbed the wooden walkway to the docks.

"Unhand him!" an angry woman snarled.

The distinct sound of flesh hitting flesh made him wince. "Shut your thieving mouth, witch."

Ahead, a group of men stood in a huddle. What were they doing? Slinking into the shadows, Petran watched. Out in the harbor, the Seabird floated, with two of her longboats anchored at the dock.

"String them up!" someone shouted.

String who up? Petran's heart pounded as the men turned and headed back his way. There, in their midst, Da and Rymon shuffled along, hands bound before them. "Hey!" he took a step from his hiding place. A quelling glance from his father stopped him.

"Don't worry, lad," one of the better-dressed men said, "you'll get a real good look at these filthy pirates when they're swinging from the gallows."

The gallows? No! Pain in Petran's chest choked him, nearly doubling him over. His father couldn't hang. Several boys nearly his age followed along. He neatly slipped among them.

They cheered. "We gonna see a hangin'," one crowed.

Anger boiled up inside. How dare these mere children cheer for Da's possible death? Da didn't deserve to die like a cutthroat.

Petran glanced around him. None of the others surrounding him had long, matted hair or even hair the color of his. Once more, his father made eye contact and quickly looked away, turning his back on his son.

For Petran's own good.

They'd discussed what to do in this event. Swiping hot tears with the back of his hand, Petran raced through the streets back to the kindly woman. "Have you anything to cut with?"

She pulled a knife from beneath her pushcart.

"Please." Pleading with his eyes as much as with the words, he tugged on his matted locks.

Glancing right and left, she said, "Come with me." She pushed her cart down an alleyway and stopped near the far end, mostly out of sight of passersby. Then, knife in hand, she chopped and sawed through Petran's hair, dropping the pieces onto the ground.

Tears stung his eyes. On his own. He was on his own.

The woman ran her fingers through the newly shorn strands of Petran's hair, discarding the last bits. Already he felt lighter, cooler.

"Here," she said, removing the globe from a cold lamp suspended on a pole above her cart. She dipped her fingers into the soot and ran them through his hair. Stepping back, she admired her handiwork with a slight nod. "You'll do."

Something glinted from her cleavage. Following his line of sight, she patted the medallion, so similar to his, that hung from a tie around her neck.

She poured lamp oil on his discarded hair. The mass ignited in a burst of flame that quickly died. The scent of scorched hair brought to mind injured Arkenn. But, wait! How had she set it on fire?

"We can't be found here." The woman grabbed Petran by the arm with one hand and pushed her cart with the other.

Together they exited the alley. "You there," a man shouted, fast approaching. The woman released Petran's arm, reached beneath her cart, and wrapped a hand around the knife handle. "We're searching for pirates who might have escaped into the city."

"Pirates?" The woman gasped and drew back, completely believable in her horror. "Pirates, you say?" Was she being serious? Did she not know why Petran needed her help? Would she turn him in if she did find out?

The man nodded. "Yes, ma'am. The ones we got will hang at sunset in the square. But you keep your eyes open." He shot a questioning gaze to Petran, who quickly averted his eyes.

Oh, Father, no! The heartbeat pounding in Petran's ears nearly drowned out all other sounds. He braced to run.

"Don't go scaring my nephew." The woman grasped Petran's shoulder, holding him in place with a surprisingly strong grip. "He's not quite right, poor dear." To Petran, she said, "Come along. Best be getting home with the likes of pirates about."

As soon as the man left their sight, the woman hissed, "I don't know your story, but run. Keep running. Get as far as you can from the city. And for the Father's sake, don't go to the hangings!" She hurried off, lamp swinging with her pace.

What should he do? Try to free his father? Follow the woman's urging and run? Search for Arkenn, a friendly face?

In the end, Petran followed the crowd making their way to the courtyard in front of town offices. In a small patch of grass to the left sat his father, the quartermaster, and most of their crew.

Petran peered out from around a wagon piled with barrels. Not that anyone could see him in the press of bodies. Had the whole city turned out to watch the spectacle?

Curse them! Curse them all!

One of the newer crew members stood beside a tall man dressed in black. Da and the crew glared at him.

"He has a son," the traitor said. "So high"—he held out a hand to indicate Petran's height. "Light brown-colored hair like the captain's."

Oh, if Petran had the woman's knife to slit the bastard's throat. He'd never killed a man. Yet. But it wasn't a hard and fast rule.

To keep a promise to his dead bond mate, Da spoke. "He lies. My son died of cholera two fullmoons past. We buried him at sea."

Even now, facing his own death, Da sought to protect Petran. Petran glanced around the square. There had to be some way to create a diversion, let his father slip away.

Yet his father didn't even fight. *Fight, damn you, fight!*

He'd been in worst situations than this and walked away relatively unscathed.

Petran pressed onward, but the jostling crowd wouldn't let him by. The sun sank farther below the horizon. For the first time ever, he didn't look forward to the coming of night, with its abundance of stars and cool breezes. He hid behind the horse-drawn wagon.

A diversion. What could... Stepping back, he smacked the horse's broad rump. The horse started, plowing straight through the crowd, empty barrels tumbling off the cart it pulled. Spectators scrambled out of the way.

Keeping low, Petran darted behind a water trough, then into the shadow of a building. Slowly, slowly, he wended his way through the crowd. Tuning out the screaming and flailing of the man trying to calm his horse and bring the wagon under control, Petran made his way to his da.

"Father," he hissed from behind a stack of crates.

His father's eyes widened. "No. Go!" he mouthed, whipping his head back to the front.

"Da?"

No answer.

"You there!" A man bore down on Petran.

"Go!" his father mouthed again.

Petran ran, dodging people, jumping over a dog, slipping and nearly falling in a patch of something he didn't want to think about.

A hand grabbed his arm. "No! Let me go!"

Another hand covered his mouth. "Shh," the woman from earlier said. "If you want to live, keep quiet. I told you to leave. You don't listen very well."

Not the first time Petran had heard those words.

"We're here now. Leaving will draw attention." She pulled Petran to her side and removed her hand from his mouth but kept one arm around him. "If anyone asks, I'm Auntie Addie, got that?"

Petran gulped, slowly nodding. The crowd had calmed. Maybe someone caught the horse.

Three nooses hung from the gallows. A man in black led a group of three pirates to the platform, hands tied behind their backs. Another strapping man, big and hairy as a bear, dropped nooses over their heads.

The pirates didn't say a word, and the hangman didn't ask for their last thoughts. The first pirate spat on the platform, the strapping man who'd propositioned Petran a few hours ago.

The second man... Petran's heart fell. Smutje. Without the cook, the injured stood no chance. The bastards probably killed them in their bunks.

The third young man moved his lips, eyes closed and tears dripping down his face. He wasn't even Petran's age. They'd spoken a few times on deck. The boy joined the crew after his parents' deaths left him no choice. Poor thing deserved so much better.

Couldn't Da do something? Could Petran? He slowly raised his hands. "Auntie Addie" grabbed his arm, hissing, "No! Have your senses left you? The Lady's priests would descend like wolves. Have you a wish to join your pirate friends?"

Petran stared wide-eyed at Da. So slowly Petran barely caught the movement, Da, moved his head back and forth, mouthing, "No."

Damnation! What was the use of having power if Petran couldn't use it to save those he loved?

The man standing with the traitor said, "By the power vested in me as magistrate of E'Skaara, and in the witness of a priest of the Father, I sentence you to death for piracy."

The trapdoors opened beneath the pirates' feet. With a ghastly *thunk*, they fell. Smutje, Old Willie, the new cabin boy they'd acquired three fullmoons ago. These were Petran's family.

"Auntie Addie" turned Petran into her side, hiding his eyes with one hand. "You're doing well, love. I'm sorry you have to see this."

Three by three, the crew stood on the platform one moment, dangled from ropes the next. Some fell silently, merely jerking once or twice. Others flailed. Finally, only two remained: Da and Rymon. Silent workers removed the last bodies. Full dark descended, and gas lanterns fluttered to life, casting eerie shadows over Da's face.

Da mounted the platform without a word, taking his place by a noose with the same command he'd show on the Seabird's deck. Rymon did the same. Both stared straight ahead.

"Take him, too." The man in black pointed toward the traitor.

"But... But... You promised..."

"I promised nothing," the man spat. "By your own admission, you are guilty of the crime of piracy. You are hereby sentenced to death."

The blood drained from the traitor's face. Whipping his head this way and that, he charged the crowd. He screamed as three men brought him down with punches and lay on the ground until boots and kicking silenced him.

"We have only two, then." The man in black stepped up to the platform.

Throughout the entire spectacle of the execution, a priest stood his ground. Draped in a brown hooded cloak, with not a bit of skin showing, he never so much as moved his head left to right. Was this the same man Petran had spoken to earlier?

Though his face and eyes were hidden by shadow, Da seemed to meet Petran's gaze for one brief moment in time, then focused on something far away. As clearly as if he'd spoken aloud, Petran heard, "*Goodbye, son.*"

Petran's heart dropped with the platform.

He sat on a stool by an unlit fireplace, a single lantern lighting the room. "You can't be Petran anymore," the woman who'd saved him said, working a concoction into his hair. "That's not a local name." Addie. Her name was Addie.

"Why are you helping me?" Numb. Dead inside. Petran could hardly sit still, let alone contemplate life without his father or the *Seabird*. If the wounded had died aboard ship, along with the pirates hanged today, Petran alone survived of the crew.

Addie gentled her touch, massaging Petran's scalp. "Because I sense something in you. You're no pirate whether or not you came in on that ship."

Petran choked back a sob. "But I am! My father..." He whipped his head around, causing Addie to wipe brown goo on his cheek.

She dabbed a cloth at his face, holding his chin in her other hand. Addie murmured, keeping her tone soft, "No, you're not. You're Peter, I'm your Auntie Addie, and everything's going to be fine." She brushed her lips against his forehead. "We have a lot in common, you and me. One day you'll see."

By the dark of the next new moon, Petran paddled out to the *Seabird*. Holding his breath, he dove, time and again, digging a borrowed dagger into the hull. Due to the recent sea battle, any damage might be mistaken for cannon fire.

He often paused, clinging to the hull, listening for voices. Three men, maybe four, chatted on the deck, laughter punctuating the night. If they only knew what lay beneath their feet.

His hands were raw and bloodied from barnacles when the hull gave way. He ran his fingers into the opening with one final dive and removed what he sought. Twice he nearly dropped the heavy iron box on the way to his borrowed boat. His legacy.

Once he'd secured the box, he dove again, attacking the weaknesses his father built into the ship for such an occasion.

By morn, the *Seabird* would kiss the seafloor.

May she rest in peace.

Along with his father.

The *Seabird* and her captain would sail no more.

Chapter Ten

E very step away from the docks got heavier. Arkenn stopped several times to glance over his shoulder. Each time Petran waved until Arkenn turned a corner. His heart thudded in his chest. No. This was wrong. He turned and ran back.

Petran was gone.

His one friend. Possibly the one person in the world who didn't want Arkenn dead.

Then again, Petran didn't know he'd helped a mage. The coins in Arkenn's pocket meant he'd survive for a while. Maybe he could find honest work, but doing what? There were no gardens here in the city, and the Lady's temple occupied a prominent hill. Her followers could be anywhere, ready to label him a mage and drag him to his death.

A tall figure in brown robes strode down the main thoroughfare, hide boots making no sound. He stopped, turned, and faced Arkenn.

From the folds of his hood, Arkenn saw no face, and the figure wore gloves. His garments covered him completely, head to toe. "What is your name?"

Though deep and gruff, a man's voice carried a note of kindness.

"Ark... Arkenn, sir."

The brown-robed figure pulled a pendant from the inside of his robe. "Wear this. Never take it off. When the time is right, I will find you. Use a different name, one familiar to native E'Skaarans. Above all, do not call attention to yourself." He whirled and hurried off.

Arkenn stared at the pendant.

Exactly like Petran's.

And the one he'd seen before. Who was the man? A priest, perhaps? He certainly wasn't a follower of the Lady in his drab attire. Her Chosen dressed as colorfully as exotic birds.

The men who'd taken Arkenn's parents must have bought out an entire silk seller's cart.

He slipped the charm around his neck, continuing wandering the city.

"Amos? Amos!" a bear of a man yelled, looking up and down the street. Broad shoulders, leather armor, sword gleaming at his hip. He stood two hands taller than Arkenn, much broader in the chest. "Where has that good for nothing gotten to now?" His gaze fell on Arkenn. "Boy!"

Arkenn pointed to himself. No other "boy" in sight.

"Yes, you." The man gave an impatient "come here" gesture. "What's your name, lad?"

Would word of what happened in the mountains travel this far? Down the street, a woman comforted a crying child. "Shh... Hush, Martin."

Use a different name, one familiar to native E'Skaarans.

"Martin, sir. My name's Martin." In his experience, many from lesser tiers of society used no surname, especially if they weren't the heir. Arkenn offered none.

The man nodded, stroking his faded red beard. "How would you like honest work, Martin?"

Honest work? Petran's generous offering wouldn't last forever. "What do I need to do?" Just because he'd only arrived in the city didn't mean Arkenn would automatically trust strangers. Trusting friends and neighbors nearly cost him his life.

"I am Captain Gery Enys of the city guard. I'd talked my nephew into joining—or thought I had. Unfortunately, openings don't come along every day." He ran an assessing gaze over Arkenn. No way to miss the worn, too-large clothes, bare feet dusty from the road. "You're a bit on the thin side but have sturdy bones. A few good meals, and you'll be a fine figure of a man. How old are you?"

"I've seen eighteen summers."

The captain nodded. "Then you've still plenty of time to fill out. Do you have a home?"

Should Arkenn admit the truth? No way could he lie successfully, knowing nothing of the city. "No, sir. I just arrived today."

The man rolled his eyes. "Another country lad hoping for fortune in the city, are you?"

The offered explanation beat any reasoning Arkenn might come up with. "Yes, sir. I'm a younger son. No inheritance."

"Then you'll have a bed in the barracks, and you'll feel at home with the guards. Many are like yourself, from other lands. The locals don't like foreigners. You'll be welcome if you can hold a sword and do what you're told. The accommodations aren't much, but you're given food, clothes, and a place to sleep at night." A smile peeked out of the man's beard. "What more can a young man ask?" The smile turned into a grin and elbow nudge. "The young ladies like men in uniform."

Captain Enys made a convincing recruiter but needn't have said more than "food and a place to sleep." But Arkenn—no, *Martin*—could also do without the admiring ladies and their scheming mothers. Several times he'd almost found himself with a bond mate in the village before the villagers turned on him.

He'd left village life behind. He couldn't go back, couldn't change things.

"What are the duties?" No need to make himself appear too eager. What if they found out about his crime? Not crime. Self-defense. An accident. No one knew he hadn't died with the others, did they? Would they come looking?

If they did, he'd worry when the time came. But, for now, meals and a bed sounded good. He'd make Petran's coins last as long as possible.

"Our company keeps the peace in the upper city. Not much crime among the rich, except for those who wish to steal wealth. Not like the poor sods patrolling the lower city, herding whores, chasing down cutpurses and the like at the docks. Occasionally, we even guard the temple when the public is invited."

The temple? Where Ar... Martin might be found out.

"Offer doesn't hold forever," the man said. "My fool nephew could show up any minute now."

"What must I do?" Martin. From this day forward, he'd be Martin, from a farming village to the north.

Arkenn lay dead.

Like his parents.

Captain Enys failed to mention "errand boy" when he described Martin's job with the city guard. Still, Martin had eaten a good meal, the men at his table only chided him mildly, and no backbreaking work.

Knocking out the bully who thought "little" meant "pushover" won him some respect.

He could do worse. The bed he'd been assigned, while not comfortable, might allow him a good night's sleep.

He'd miss the gentle rocking of the waves, the press of Petran's lips to the back of his neck. All part of his past. Now, to make a future. A future in which he hoped to see Petran again.

But... the temple. Though he'd joined the guards, Martin hadn't been given leather like the captain. No, he'd been given gray trousers, a gray shirt, had his hair shorn, and the scant whiskers on his face shaved. At least the sturdy boots fit his feet. He dressed the part of a messenger boy. His first assignment? Deliver papers from the magistrate to the temple priestess.

In town for a few hours only, bound to come face-to-face with the enemy. The captain's directions sent him uphill to the temple, through opulent gardens, and to the back door. Apparently, even messengers were forced to endure the temple's excesses.

The temple killed mages, like Martin's parents.

Now he'd nothing to fear. He wasn't mage-born, just a country lad, now a guard member. Martin. His name was Martin. Arkenn died over a sevenday ago, trying to reach a mountain.

He couldn't afford to be afraid. If anyone saw his fear, they might wonder at the cause. Better to remain calm. *Martin, I am Martin, a new recruit of the city guard.*

Swallowing down his attack of nerves, he raced up the hill, heart pumping. With each step, houses grew more beautiful and elaborate, shaming any in the lower city. The people he passed wore clothes more elegant than he'd ever seen. Some houses stood four stories tall, with intricate scrollwork and immaculately kept yards.

"Our kind aren't welcome there," Petran had said.

Petran. Where was he? Had he left aboard the *Seabird* yet? Did he miss Martin as much as Martin missed him?

He quietly chanted, *Please don't see me, please don't see me.* Carriages passed, or the occasional man or woman on a horse. Clusters of well-dressed people strolled along the edges of the road. None paid him more than a passing glance.

Good. He blended. At the garrison, he'd seen men and women with many skin and hair colors, speaking many dialects. A man in uniform, even a non-local recruit, wasn't cause for staring.

Closer, Martin went to his doom. He passed a low, nondescript building, too in awe of the temple to notice much else. The central tower rose high into the sky, gleaming white in the sunlight. Head-high walls separated the gardens from the street, though the grounds leading to the front door were open for all to see.

A carriage slowed to a stop, brass fittings gleaming in the sunlight, pulled by a matching pair of white horses. What might have been a family crest embellished the door. The liveried driver hopped down, opened the door, and took a gloved hand in his. A woman stepped from the carriage, possibly ten summers older than Martin. Her full skirts swirled around her as the servant assisted her from the carriage. She'd dressed all in lavender: hat, dress, gloves. A double strand of pearls graced her neck. The image of dark-haired, dark-eyed perfection.

The price of her outfit could probably feed an entire village. Once more, Martin's heart squeezed, thoughts turning to his former village—a place he would never see again. Nothing waited there for him anyway.

Head high, the fashionably dressed woman traipsed down a mosaic pathway—the tiles arranged to mimic a river—to the main temple entryway, an elegant marble arch festooned with flowering vines. The carriage driver snorted, shaking his head, disgust clear on his face. At the woman? Or the temple?

Through the gate, Martin glimpsed grass and shrubs and caught the sweet scent of roses. Quietly he approached. Steeling his nerves, he pushed open the gate.

No one about. Good. Maybe he wouldn't get found out.

"Greetings."

Martin whirled, nearly tripping over a bench. Instead of a priest hurling a stone, a young man, perhaps Martin's age, finely dressed in flowing silks, gazed up at him. His tunic hugged his lean form, swathes of silk crisscrossing his chest, exposing fitted blue trousers. Embroidered flowers in multicolored hues decorated the tunic. Satin slippers covered his feet.

"I'm Cere. Are you a new novice? You're pretty enough to be one. Where are you from? I don't see many people with hair naturally the color of yours." The most beautiful being Martin had ever seen stood before him, with pale skin, blue eyes, and fiery copper hair cascading in waves over slender shoulders.

No. Not the most beautiful. But close.

"N... no. I'm not a novice. I'm here with a message for the high priestess." Martin held up the package.

"Aww... I was hoping you were here like me." Cere stuck his lower lip out in a likely practiced pout. Confident in his beauty, this one.

"No, I'm afraid not." Every second Martin remained on temple grounds gave those with a little more experience time to find him. "Um... can you direct me to the clerk?"

"Sure! This way." The perfect specimen of upper-class breeding crooked a finger, winked, and said, "Follow me." The silk of Cere's trousers clung to his shapely buttocks. In mountain villages, men didn't openly flirt with other men.

"Thank you." Arkenn—no, Martin—tried not to stare at the temptation before him. The image blurred, becoming sun-bronzed, with light brown, shoulder-length matted hair instead of shimmering copper waves.

"You know, you don't look too old. If one of the Chosen saw you, they might make you a novice. That's how I got picked. I was playing out in front of my house one day. Two men passed by and spoke to me, then went in to talk to my father and mother." Cere flashed a grin over his shoulder. "And here I am! If I'd stayed home, I'd be working in my father's shipping business, but now"—he spun in a circle, arms wide—"I'm here. Not expected to do hard work or—"

"What do you do here?" Curiosity got the better of Martin.

"Me? I study, dance, and hope to be picked for a higher position one day. I want to be a Chosen. They have all the fun. Everyone looks up to them. They have the best clothes and their own suites. Not just a room, but a suite. Can you imagine?"

Martin couldn't, having slept in the corner at Gran's, shared a bunk with Petran on the *Seabird*, and been assigned a cot at the barracks.

Cere turned, walking backward while keeping eye contact with Martin. They passed statues of scantily dressed men and women, and polished flagstone led them through flowering shrubs. The orange, red, and yellow blossoms brought to mind flames. "We get great clothes. The food is better than we ever had at home. Not that it was bad, mind you—our housekeeper was an excellent cook—but the food here is so much richer. Only the best is ever brought to the temple."

As amusing as the young man was, Martin hadn't time to waste. "Speaking of, I need to get this message delivered, or I might not make it back to dinner tonight."

Cere stopped, face scrunched in question, then brightened. "Oh, right. Well, hurry up, then." He turned back toward the path but kept talking the whole way to the rear of the temple, the door far less ornate than the front entrance. "Here you go. Hey, come see me again sometimes. Just ask for Cere. Everybody knows me. Now, I have to get to lessons. Bye!" The colorful bird of a young man trotted off.

Martin stopped him. "One moment, Cere. When I arrived, I saw a well-dressed woman enter the temple. Another novice?"

"No." Cere grinned. "A *worshipper.*" He waggled his brows.

"What?"

"You don't know, do you?"

"Know what?"

Cere laughed, a musical sound, also likely practiced. "Above all, the Lady teaches pleasure. Worship means the highborn lady will take off her fancy gown, lie down on a bed off the main sanctuary, and wait for a Chosen to fuck her."

Wait for a Chosen to fuck her? With effort, Martin clicked his mouth shut.

"If I become a Chosen, I'll help you worship anytime." Cere winked again.

Time to finish the errand and get out of here before Martin died of shame. Sex with someone back home without being bonded ranked close to magery for stoning offenses. Then again, the villagers only honored the Lady when her edicts suited their goals.

Despite saying he must go, Cere opened the door and skipped along a short hallway, forcing Martin to keep up. Cere led him to a spacious office, though far less luxurious than the grounds or outside of the temple. A woman dressed in a blue satin gown stood from behind a desk. "You have something for me, guard?" She held out her hand.

Martin handed over the package.

"Novice Fiona." Cere bowed his way out of the office and all but ran.

"I don't think he's quiet even in his sleep." The woman tutted and handed Martin a small parcel. "For your trouble."

As he turned to leave, a man and woman entered. Martin froze. They might not be the same faces, but the robes were similar. White, gauzy fabric, crisscrossed over the heart and heavily embroidered.

The Chosen. The ones who'd come to his village and taken his parents. Had Mum and Da come to this very temple to face judgment? Fucking worshippers aside, this was what sweet little Cere wanted to become? Martin held his breath. *Please, don't let them notice me.*

The Chosen brushed right past without acknowledging his presence, speaking in low tones to the woman in blue. Taking advantage of their distraction, Martin fled.

Once safely outside, he opened the package and found a coin, unlike the ones he'd received from Petran. What was its worth? Were messengers allowed to keep any coins received?

His heart gave a lurch. Was it too much to wish Petran's father would leave him behind? The thought buoyed Martin, and he paused to enjoy the beauty of the gardens. Tomorrow he'd go to the docks to look at the ships. If the *Seabird* wasn't there, he'd search for Petran.

He returned to the garrison to find several men his age chattering away and gesturing wildly with their hands.

"Martin!" one called, who he recognized from his earlier tour of the grounds. "They caught a whole bunch of pirates and are gonna hang 'em in the lower city square. Every one." He grinned. "We're off duty and heading down there. Want to go with us?"

One man shook his head. "My mate'd have my head if I missed supper to go to a hanging."

A hanging? Pirates. A hard swallow didn't clear the lump from Martin's throat. "All of them?" *Please, please let Petran be all right. Let it be different pirates, another ship.*

"Every last one, I heard." The speaker stuck out his lip at his friend who opted to go home. "You said you'd go with me this time."

"I said no such thing. No, I'm off duty. I'm going home."

"You?" the man asked Martin.

Martin shook his head, stomach churning. "No. It's my first day. I need to find the captain."

"Maybe some other time." The man finally left, two others following behind.

Some other time? How often did they hang pirates in this city? Probably nearly as often as they killed mages.

Once sure his new friend had left. Martin paced. Could Petran be among those captured? Surely not.

Worry squirming through his insides, Martin attended his check-in with the captain, eyes fixed to the mantel clock. Finally, he retraced his steps back to the docks, getting lost a few times. The sun sank beyond the horizon. Soon he'd be expected to check in at the barracks. Where was the square the guard mentioned?

He needed to find the docks. Prove to himself Petran was all right.

Lamplighters moved along the street, lighting the gaslights one by one.

Full dark quickly descended. Martin stepped back to let a trundling cart pass. The wheel hit a pothole, and something poked out of the slatted side.

A hand. He stepped closer.

Oh, gods!

A hand with three fingers. Bile rose. Martin rushed into the alley, barely clearing the street before spewing the remnants of lunch. Hot tears streamed down his face. Petran! He should have made Petran come with him. Or kept him away from the ship longer.

Every last one.

His heart squeezed. Petran. His Petran, dead. Hanged as a pirate. No! No! No! No! No! Martin threw back his head and howled. He'd lost his family, then found someone to be his friend and possibly more. The captain said Martin would be with Petran again. Had he meant in the afterlife? How cruel could the fates be?

He sank down onto filthy flagstones, burying his face in his hands. Visions filled his mind: Petran's smile, how tenderly he'd cared for Martin's injuries, his kisses on the back of Martin's neck.

The pleasure they'd given each other. They read the cards, talked, and dreamed of a possible future together. His Petran, his beautiful Petran, gone.

That night, Martin settled into his cot in a room with dozens of snoring men and dreamed of Petran's dark eyes, staring between the slats of a horse-drawn cart.

Unseeing.

Chapter Eleven – Three Summers Later

Despite Addie insisting he leave the city, Petran stayed. No, not Petran. Peter. His name was Peter. He'd once been an adventurer, looking forward to each new port, thrilled to see land on the horizon—or more water.

Sea creatures once raced the *Seabird*; he'd slept on warm sands, eaten fruit from a tree native to only one island, far to the south. Now, he couldn't bring himself to venture past the walls of a city, even with its too many unfamiliar faces and customs. Too many rules. Some unseen force kept him here.

With the money from his father, he could have gone anywhere, lived in style, even owned a grand house near the temple, or bought a ship of his own. Though he'd have to explain how someone of his station in life came by a fortune.

Another deterrent stood in his way: a single glance at the shiny white stone temple caused a shiver. He stuck to the lower city, more easily blending in with the place he'd last seen his father.

The last place he'd seen Arkenn. He'd meet Arkenn again here in E'Skaara, if anywhere.

Market days offered a bright spot in his rather dull world. No, he wasn't searching each stall for pale hair and blue eyes; he really wasn't. Yet, every time he ventured past vendor stalls, he recalled showing Arkenn the city, sharing bites of pastry. His heart hurt from the memory of Arkenn's smiles. They should have left together. Then Petr— Peter could believe his father still sailed the seas.

He wouldn't be alone.

Sometimes Peter roamed the docks, staring out at sea to where the *Seabird* went down. Fish now swam around her rigging. Bits of conversation came back each time from the last words Arkenn spoke. The kiss Arkenn gave before parting.

Peter entertained a few discreet men from time to time, but his heart ached for one man when he lay alone in his bed at night. No amount of searching turned up the lost love he missed so badly, though they'd only known each other a short time.

As a trading hub, people came from all over to E'Skaara's harbor. Hundreds of men matched Arkenn's description, speech as varied as their clothing, but no one knew the name. Maybe he'd gone north or booked passage on another ship.

The Stone's Throw tavern catered to all kinds. If Arkenn remained in the lower city, sooner or later, their paths must cross. Keeping his artificially darkened hair closely cropped allowed Petran—no, not *Petran*, but *Peter*—to blend with the locals. With time, he managed to copy their singsong accent when he spoke.

"Peter, boy. Come here. I need you." Addie stepped out from behind the bar, wiping her hands on her apron. Peter followed her to a far table where three men sat, skin golden from the sun. "What are they saying?"

Peter tried three languages before one of the men smiled. They chatted for a moment, then Peter told Addie, "Three pints of ale, three bowls of mutton stew, and one of fish chowder." He arranged payment then, in case he wasn't around when the time came to pay.

"There's a good lad," Addie said. "I knew we kept you around for a reason." She patted his cheek and wandered back to the kitchen, jingling a pocket full of coins. Apparently, barmaids made more coin than a woman pushing a cart.

"Peter? I need another cask!" the tavernkeeper shouted from behind the bar, a stout, balding man in his later seasons.

"Yes, Mitta." Peter trudged behind the building, hoisted a cask onto his shoulder, and returned inside.

Mitta clucked his tongue. "Were but I your age again." He squeezed Peter's muscular arm, relatively larger than when he'd arrived. Now he lifted, building firmer muscles than he'd earned aboard the *Seabird*.

Three summers. Three summers since he'd settled in E'Skaara. Three summers since he'd left the world of piracy.

Three summers since he'd seen Arkenn.

One day they'd meet again. The priest said so. While Peter didn't put much stock in religion, he'd cling tightly to those words.

Addie returned from the kitchen, bringing the foreigners their meals, while Peter carried the ale, spending a few moments talking to the travelers before duties called him away again.

A young girl darted into the tavern, chattering away to Addie. Addie held up her hand. "Calm, young one."

"It's Mum! It's time!" the girl cried.

Addie nodded. "Go, girl. Tell yer mum I'mma coming." She left her apron behind the bar and lifted a brow in Mitta's direction.

Mitta waved a meaty hand. "Go, go."

Passing by Peter, Addie murmured, "Come, I need you."

Once more, Mitta raised a hand in a shooing motion. "Go on."

Peter chased after Addie. "Where are we going?"

"You'll see." For a woman twice his age and two-thirds his height, Addie managed to match Peter's longer strides. She yanked his sleeve. "Down here." They cut through an alleyway, across another road, ending at a modest cottage.

A shriek came from within. Addie hurried her steps. "Poor woman lost three babes already. I'd hate for her to lose another."

A birth? Addie brought Peter along to help with healing skills? "I know nothing about delivering babes."

"I don't need you to. Just stay here. Think good thoughts." She disappeared inside the house.

Think good thoughts? The woman inside screamed again, much louder this time. Peter cringed. The poor woman must be in agony. The little girl ran back outside, swiping at her damp cheeks.

"What's wrong?" Peter asked.

"My auntie died having a baby. Is Mum gonna die?"

When the girl talked, the shimmering eyes and little hiccups nearly broke Peter's heart. "No. She'll be fine. The babe will be fine. Soon you'll have a brother or sister."

"I had three brothers. They all died," the girl wailed.

Peter hunkered down, putting himself on eye level with the girl. "What's your name?"

"Mags."

"Well, Mags." Peter forced his voice to remain confident when he felt anything but. "Addie and I won't let anything bad happen to your mum or the babe."

"What you gonna do?"

"Pray." Peter closed his eyes, opening his mind, as he'd done the night the winds filled the *Seabird*'s sails.

He stood in a small room, the heat nearly unbearable. A woman lay on the bed, features twisted into a mask of pain, covers tented over her swollen belly.

"Shh..." Addie soothed, looking under the blanket placed over the woman's waist.

Another woman sat at the head of the bed, holding the first's hand, silent tears running down her face. The scent of blood filled Peter's nose.

The woman and her child were dying. "Do something," Addie hissed under her breath.

Peter didn't know what to do, why, or how, but he raised his arms like he had during the attack on the *Seabird*. Power. Power flowed through him, around him. So much power, making him giddy like strong drink. He pulled the power to himself.

The laboring woman screamed. Peter directed the power at her, willing her to peace, willing her to live, willing the baby to live.

The moment he stopped concentrating, the screaming began anew.

"Focus," Addie snapped.

Peter did. Using his body as a conduit, he collected and poured the mysterious power into the woman.

He didn't know how long he stayed there. Time lost all meaning.

"You did good," Addie said, from vast leagues away.

He opened his eyes to find himself still crouched outside the house, the night full dark now and stars twinkling overhead.

A haggard-looking Addie trudged out of the house and patted Peter's cheek. "You did good, but we must leave now."

They scurried away, not how they'd come, but through less desirable neighborhoods of tumbledown houses. Two men approached in the darkness. Thieves? Peter braced himself for a fight, fully prepared to push Addie behind him.

Addie's snarl sent the two men scuttling away. "I'm sad to say those might be kin," she mumbled to Peter. At last, they reached familiar territory, where gaslights lit the streets. Raucous laughter sounded from a tavern, cut off when the door slammed shut. An inebriated patron wended his way down the street.

Peter and Addie quietly padded down a side street and to her dark house off of the main road.

Upon opening the front door, Peter reached for a lantern. Addie slapped his hand away.

"No. If any watch the house, they must think us asleep. Any who might have come to the tavern, Mitta would have told we came home as you were ill."

Peter dropped into his usual chair by the hearth, totally drained.

Addie puttered about in the darkness, pressing a cup into his hands. "Here. Drink this."

His hands shook. Addie helped him get the cup to his mouth. He swallowed half of the bitter brew and gave her back the cup. One of her many healing elixirs. "Thank you. What just happened?"

Addie placed the cup on a small table and sat across from him in her own chair, letting out a weary sigh. "The women I help think the power lies in my herbal concoctions or learned skills. They don't know there's more."

Chills ran up Peter's spine. "What's more?"

Even though they were in her home, alone, she whispered, "My mum was mage-born. A healer. I'll never have her talents, but I do what I can."

Having shared the woman's cottage, the news came as no surprise. "Then why did you invite me?"

"You have power. Like me, you hide behind an amulet, but it's there, bright enough for anyone to see if they know what to look for. I would have lost the mother and daughter without your strength to lean on. I'm sorry. I put you at risk. That much power? The Chosen could have come. But I thank you."

"I... I saved her?"

"Yes, you did."

Her words merely confirmed what Peter felt down to his soul. That he had some sort of power. Lifting his hands to bring the winds. Seeing himself by the laboring mother's side, feeding her strength to endure. Yet, both those times he'd not consciously known what to do.

"Can I ask you something?" Addie patted his leg.

"Yes." Was she about to ask something too personal? She'd taken him in, never asking too many questions.

She never questioned any of her foundlings overly much.

"Do you have a lover?"

A lover? "Umm... No. Why do you ask?"

Addie remained quiet for several long moments. "Have you ever heard of a mage bond?"

"No. I've hardly heard of mages."

"Mages have power. With the right training, they can learn to do many useful things. Then some mages instinctually wield their powers. Strongest of all are those who meet someone with complimentary magic. They form a mage bond, feeding from each other's powers, each becoming stronger. The last mage I met of your talents had been in a mage bond for many seasons."

Mage bond? "What are you talking about?"

Addie sipped from the herbal concoction, the cup clicking against the table when she set it down. "I'm older than you know."

"You're not that old." If Peter had learned anything in life, it was not to comment on a lady's age.

"But I am. I was born and raised here in E'Skaara. Like many other magical folks, my parents were drawn to the power radiating from the hill. We settled here before the Lady"—she spat the epithet— "built her temple and rounded up magic practitioners. Since then, her Chosen have imprisoned any with talent to speak of, stripping them of their magic. They couldn't live without their power and died. There are few of us left."

The hair on the back of Peter's neck stood. "You're a mage?" He'd often suspected her of some magical talent, but she'd never told, so he kept quiet—both about her possible magery and his own.

Yet, she'd known. And tonight's demonstration showed what both were capable of.

Addie shook her head, hair escaping from the bun at her nape to swing over her face, barely visible in the near-darkness. "Not necessarily a mage, but I have some innate abilities. Since I'm not very powerful, my amulet hides me well. My parents, a bonded pair, weren't so lucky. I only survived because our nonmagical housekeeper swore I was her child.

"Well, I met Zahn." She flashed a brief smile. "Our magics complemented each other's, and we each grew stronger. I was sought after as a healer, while he could predict storms with great accuracy, a boon to the fishermen.

"He was turned in to the Chosen by a rival who didn't know about me. They never knew we'd bonded." Addie wrung her hands together. "I knew the instant he died, felt the power leave." She ended with a choked sob. "I vowed to help any mages who needed assistance, which is why I helped you."

"You just picked me out of a crowd?"

"No. After I cut your hair and we parted ways, a priest of the Father visited me, knew I helped those like you, and said you were important."

"You only took me in for the priest." The words sounded hurt, even to Peter's ears.

Addie gave a fond smile and cupped Peter's cheek. "I would have helped even if you were nonmagical. You're not much older than the child I lost when Zahn died would now be."

A child. She'd lost a child yet dedicated herself to keeping other women from knowing her pain. They stayed silent for a time.

"Why didn't you say anything?" Peter asked.

"Because the priest directed me to stay silent, unless there was reason not to."

"You're not being silent now."

One side of Addie's mouth curved upward in a smirk, the gesture barely visible in the scant light coming in through the window from a gas lamp. "No, I'm not. That mother and child are alive because of you."

"But I'm not a healer."

"I beg to differ, but in this instance, I borrowed from you to supplement my own strength."

Peter had thought so. "Why did you ask if I had a lover?"

"I feel you growing stronger. Not strong enough to have formed a bond, but enough to make me think your bond mate is near."

Ridiculous.

"How much did your parents tell you about mages?"

"Very little. My father met my mother when she escaped the city."

Addie nodded. "Yes, those too powerful to hide fled."

"The Chosen came for her when I was a child. Da took me to sea with him."

Addie stayed quiet for a few moments, words a mere whisper when she continued. "And I held you while he died."

Too choked up for words, Peter nodded.

"Tonight, you did a good thing, but I was foolish to involve you. Your power is greater than I ever imagined. For sure, someone in the temple felt the ripples, another reason why I've never mentioned this before. The priest said he'd come back for you when the time was right. We'll keep our heads down for now, let the storm pass."

"What about the mother and child?"

"If the Chosen go there, they'll find no evidence of magic. We took all traces with us, and anyone there will tell only of the gifted herbalist who assisted the birth." Addie shrugged. "They've come to see me before, saw nothing of interest, and left. In the past, I've put foundlings with magical potential on a ship. Got them far from here. It's you we need to hide."

"Where do they go?"

"Most I send across the sea to Adulas. Evil mages there are still known to steal magic, but I have trusted friends to keep them safe."

"Why did you allow me to stay?"

"Because you, my dear boy, are something this city hasn't seen in quite some time."

"What is that?"

"A mage who may be capable of taking on the Lady herself. And winning."

Chapter Twelve

M artin stood in the garrison's stable yard, breathing in the scent of horses, leather, hay, and what the stableboys currently raked from a stall. Horses nickered greetings or stamped their hooves in impatience. While the animals here were smaller, trained for riding instead of pulling plows, they brought to mind the shaggy, sturdier mountain beasts of his former village. Da had often lifted a much younger Martin to stroke a velvety nose or offer a carrot.

In the distance, temple bells rang, marking the hour. Shouts rose from the training grounds, along with the clangs of practice weapons. The background music to Martin's life.

Commander Enys approached, a familiar glint in his eyes.

Oh no. Not good. No escaping now. Martin willed his feet to remain still when his instincts screamed *run!* "Good morn, Commander Enys."

"And good morn to you, too, Martin."

Pleasantries over, now the commander would state his true purpose.

"Do you fancy blondes, Martin?" Going from captain to commander didn't stop Gery Enys's matchmaking. "Come. Have dinner with my family tonight."

Martin rolled his eyes. "Who is she this time?" Dinner at the commander's house usually included an unattached young lady. Some were sweet-tempered, others not so much, some kind, others spoiled. None captured Martin's heart. None ever would.

"My third sister's fifth daughter. You know, the accomplished harpist."

Third sister. Martin ticked them off on his fingers. Anna, Hannah, Susanna, or Susan? He'd lost track of the twins' names long ago. "Exactly how many sisters do you have again?"

"Seven."

"Seven sisters?" That many women under one roof at one time didn't kill each other off?

"I owe my rank to them." Commander Enys slapped a hand to Martin's shoulder, a sign he didn't intend to take no for an answer. Why was he so adamant about seeing Martin bonded?

"How so?"

"Think about it. Would you have stayed home with so many sisters? I lied about my age and joined the guards the moment they let me. My father was so proud he didn't dare call me home. Now, I'm a commander." Enys's brilliant grin peeked out from his thick beard.

The hand bled warmth into Martin's shoulder. He tutted. "Feared commander of the city guard, afraid of his own sisters."

Enys exaggerated searching the area, whispering behind his hand, "Not afraid, just smart enough to avoid them when they swarm."

Martin couldn't help prodding the man whose scowl sent new recruits scurrying. "Is that why you volunteer for extra shifts during festivals?"

"No." Enys grinned again. "I want the younger officers to have time to spend with their families."

Martin cocked an accusatory eyebrow. "While you avoid your own. Don't you think that makes you a bad brother?"

Enys patted the shoulder he'd seemingly taken possession of. "That makes me a smart man. Have you ever met my brothers-by-bonding? Since their bonding day, not a single one has made their own decisions."

"You're bonded."

"Yes, to a lovely woman who helps me avoid my sisters. Now. Dinner?" Ah, Enys, forever the diplomat.

"Not tonight. Maybe some other time." While Martin missed his own family, Enys's loud, boisterous kin didn't allow him to insert a single word into the conversation. Why would Martin commit to a lifetime of remaining silent?

Enys frowned. "It's the blonde, isn't it? Well, I have plenty of nieces of bondable age. So tell me your preferences; I'm sure we'll have a match."

Martin employed the same excuse he'd offered the last time he'd avoided dinner with the commander's family. "I cannot afford a bond mate."

"Shall I put in a word for a promotion?"

Smiling, Martin shook his head. Enys just wouldn't take no for an answer. "I am perfectly happy as an unbonded man."

"One day, you'll grow tired of being alone." Enys added a touch of persuasion to his tone.

Martin was tired now. But he'd not find the one he wanted sitting at his commander's table in a new summer dress, mind full of establishing housekeeping with a guardsman.

"At least think about it." Enys gave Martin one final back pat. "If you change your mind, you know where I live. You need my mate's cooking. You didn't gain your bulk by eating regiment food."

Martin took the reins from the approaching stable lad and swung himself onto his favorite buckskin mare's back. "I will certainly give it some thought while I'm on rounds today." He rode his mount out of the stable yard, the horse's hooves clacking against the cobblestones. Points to him for not galloping away.

Riding on horseback, patrolling the city, beat running lesser errands, like delivering packages on foot. New recruits carried parcels now. Despite what he'd told Enys, Martin had risen through the ranks to a comfortable salary, allowing him to leave the barracks for a two-room lodging, complete with a small courtyard.

The better to dodge ceaseless attempts to make him a bonded man. How many nieces found themselves bonded to guards under Commander Enys's command? It seemed for every niece he saw settled with a mate, he gained two more.

At least the guards provided a steady income for the brides, although two of Enys's nieces had joined the guards themselves.

Martin's rooms were small but clean, furnished from castoffs he'd lovingly reworked. Anything he touched seemed better for the attention.

He'd even dug his plates and eating utensils from a discard heap, painstakingly restoring them to usability. Some repaired items he even sold in the market. For someone relatively new to the city, he'd made a secure life for himself.

Having more freedom to traverse the city made avoiding his fellow guards' questions about his whereabouts easier while allowing him to rescue more castoffs.

He'd never found the priest who'd gifted him the medallion—worn tucked under his uniform tunic—in his travels, and he'd become bolder with his forays to the Lady's temple.

Fear long ago turned to rage. Rage that honest people who simply wanted to raise their child in peace were put to death. He'd already avenged Gran, albeit unintentionally. No. No dwelling on the past. How dangerous was he to kill so many people accidentally? Granted, they'd been set on killing him. Still, sometimes Martin even terrified himself.

He'd learned the areas in need of watching, in the capacity of a city guard, particularly the in-betweens located between the upper and lower city. In all his travels, he'd sought out others like himself. He couldn't be the only mage-born in this city.

No one questioned him. Did the pendant somehow protect him? He'd presented himself at the Father's temple several times, only to receive a cryptic, "This isn't your time."

When would be?

If the pendant somehow hid him from discovery, could it hide others too? What of the mysterious priest? What had become of Petran's pendant? Did it lie in his grave, or had the undertakers claimed the jewelry for their own?

Petran. For a moment, the old pain flared anew. If only Martin had known that their last kiss would be Petran's last ever. No good came from brooding over the past. Petran had been no pirate yet had paid the price for his father's choices.

Like Martin paid the price for his own heritage.

A few people called out to him in passing; some scuttled away to avoid his notice, while others paid him no mind. Lowly guards were beneath upper-city dwellers.

He rode the mare past the temple. A familiar carriage sat out front, a familiar driver helping a familiar lady down the steps. Wait! No, not the same lady. This one appeared much older. The original woman's mother?

As before, the driver clucked his tongue, shaking his head when the lady made her way into the temple. She stumbled on the stairs, prompting a novice to catch her by the elbow.

"Good day, friend," Martin told the driver, reining in his curiosity.

"Good day, sir," the man replied, reclining against the carriage. Martin's mount exchanged nickered greetings with the two horses pulling the carriage.

"Is your lady unwell?" he asked.

The driver gave a jolt, narrowing his eyes at Martin. "You can see?"

"See what?"

"How they're sucking the vitality out of the lass."

How they... Martin glanced toward the door where the woman had disappeared.

"Her family cannot see it, but every time she comes here, she leaves just a little... less."

After she worshipped with a Chosen, a killer of mages.

Martin hesitated before asking, "Tell me, sir, has she any mage blood in her family?"

The man's face purpled. "What an outrage! How dare you accuse the countess of such." Regaining his composure, he added, "You do not strike me as a native-born; thus, I give you a warning. Do not speak of mages in this city. Any mention of magical blood among the nobility would bring ruin to their family."

"I see no lawbreaking. This is no concern for the city guard." Given the force of the reply, Martin took the denial as a yes.

Mage blood. Perhaps the woman had some degree of power. Not enough to put her to death for, but enough to drain from her bit by bit. Then again, maybe the Chosen dared not take the high born outright, lest the nobility rise against them.

The man gave Martin a grateful smile. Martin rode on. He peered into the gardens but saw no sign of his friend Cere. Maybe for the best, for Martin might feel compelled to voice questions best not asked.

His rounds ran long enough for Commander Enys to be safely ensconced at home with his many sisters and nieces. The sun had retired when Martin secured the horse in the stables and returned home by foot.

His lodgings lay in the in-between, close enough to his work and the high city to offer protection but close enough to the lower city for the occasional working man or woman to wander by.

He'd taken pleasure there, but not tonight, mind full of what he'd learned about the woman at the temple.

Screams ripped the quiet. Martin froze. An argument from a nearby house? Another heart-wrenching, terrified scream put his feet into motion before his mind made the decision.

He darted down an alley, chasing the sound. This far from the main road, the gaslights barely reached. A woman turned this way and that, screaming and stepping right into the claws of some hideous creature.

"Ma'am, this way!" Martin shouted.

Still, she twisted and turned, blood soaking her dress. The scent assaulted Martin's nostrils, along with the bitter tang of fear. He thrust her behind him.

"What have we here?" her attacker asked, red staining its claws.

What, by all the gods and goddesses who'd ever lived, was that? "Leave her alone."

The thing cocked its head to the side. "You can see me?"

"Of course, I can see you. You're right there." Martin stepped back, herding the woman toward the main street.

The terrified woman clutched him from behind. "What is it? What's there?"

The monster stood to Martin's chest, shoulders broad, with a sloping forehead. The thing wore no clothes. Instead of skin, scales covered its arms and legs. "Can't you see it?" How could she not see the hideous beast?

"She can't see me. I wonder how you can." The thing circled, flicking out a forked tongue.

Martin turned, pushing the woman toward the mouth of the alley. "Run!" Instead, she took two steps and fell.

No time to help her now. Not with the attacker still a threat.

Attackers. Another figure emerged from the shadows. Two. Two horrible creatures and him unarmed. Why did the guards insist he leave his sword in the arsenal?

With no weapon, he'd no way to defend himself against sharp claws. From the corner of his eye, metal glinted, a hook used for lifting barrels. Better than nothing.

He grabbed the hook and swiped at the horrible vision from nightmares. It danced back out of reach, the hook barely abrading scaled skin.

"Very interesting," the thing closest to him said. The other loomed nearer. Both stopped suddenly, staring over Martin's shoulder.

They ran. Still clutching his makeshift weapon, heart in his throat and pounding in his ears, Martin whirled, catching a brief glimpse of brown. A priest?

The woman moaned. Martin dropped beside her, releasing the hook.

"Wha... what?" Blood trickled from her mouth. Martin slid his arm beneath her shoulders, keeping her upper body off the ground. She stiffened, then relaxed in death, head lolling to the side.

Martin stared down at the unknown woman. Why hadn't she seen her assailants?

They'd toyed with her, scaring her, enjoying her pain.

They would pay.

When he looked up, both the attackers and the figure in brown were clearly gone.

Martin filed his reports, how he'd found a man assaulting the woman, leaving off the part about scales. Who would believe him? Would they think he'd killed her? The undertaker asked few questions about casualties from the lower city, taking her body into his shop.

What were those creatures? Did anyone else know of those things? Martin could only imagine the laughter if he'd given more details in his report. He stared down at a smear of green on his clothing. Blood?

Upon arriving home, Martin checked the sturdiness of the lock on his door, ensured the windows couldn't be opened from the outside, and settled into bed. He left a candle burning.

Those things haunted his dreams, chasing him. They turned into the villagers.

He killed them with fire.

The process started all over again.

He awoke the next morn, sweat soaking his bedclothes, the horror of the night still filling his mind. Visions of the woman, dealing with the undertaker and the night guards. The hook bearing no sign of red blood saved him from further questioning. No one he knew of could do such damage to the woman's flesh with bare hands.

He rolled over in his bed and jumped back in alarm.

Next to him, in a sheath of tooled leather, lay a sword.

Martin sought out his commander, waiting by the gates until Enys strode through. "Good morn, Commander Enys. You were born to this city, were you not?"

"Aye. And my da and mum before me."

"Have you ever heard of any creature covered in scales, with sharp claws and teeth, that stood on two legs and spoke like you or me?"

Enys scratched his head beneath a layer of dark auburn hair, liberally frosted with white. "No. Is that some kind of creature the farming folk tell children about to get them to behave?" He smiled in his usual jovial fashion.

Martin couldn't let himself sound too crazy. "I went to a pub the other night and heard tales." A plausible enough answer.

Enys gave a laugh. "Men filled with ale tell many tall tales. Don't you believe none of it."

If only Martin could heed the advice.

With only two constables in the lower city, the streets were patrolled mainly by volunteers. The rich of the upper city afforded much in the way of protection, leaving the poorer of the city to fend for themselves. No one Martin spoke to shed any light on the woman's attack.

In the early morns, he practiced knife and sword with the city guards, then patrolled or escorted notables of the high city to meetings with more notable citizens. What did they have to talk about? Leveraging more taxes on the poor?

Occasionally, he escorted a wealthy merchant's son, daughter, or mate to the temple to *worship*. Even the magistrate himself came several times each sevenday.

To cavort with nubile young *Chosen*.

Then they went home. Several showed the effects after a time, like the woman from the carriage. As with the monsters, no one seemed able to see but him.

And the carriage driver.

Every eve after once more telling his fellow guards he'd not join them at a tavern, Martin took up the unexplained sword and stalked the streets.

Woe be to any creatures he might find with evil intent. The sword gleamed, obviously well-cared for. The tooled leather sheath must've cost someone a fortune. Who had snuck into his rooms, taking nothing but leaving such a valuable gift?

Every so often, while hunting, he'd catch a flash of brown from the corner of his eye.

On one such night, he focused on a person in the crowd. Something wasn't right. A sense of wrongness hung about the man. Martin followed.

Dark, dank alleys, poorly lit streets, dilapidated houses. The scent of refuse and despair. Martin trudged after the man who'd caught his attention, sending tendrils of worry squirming through his belly. At last, they reached a closed storefront. It could be a milliner, an apothecary, or even a tinker's shop. One of many similar businesses in the lower city. Martin stayed back, hiding in a recessed doorway. The man glanced around. Not a soul stirred. He lobbed a rock through the front window, crawled through, and emerged with a filled sack moments later.

Although Martin's guard unit didn't patrol this section of the city, letting a criminal walk free sent bile burning the back of his throat.

He stepped into the man's path. The thief's eyes widened. He tossed the sack to the ground, the surprise changing to determination. Quicker than most eyes could follow, he snatched a knife from beneath his cloak, dropping into a fighter's stance.

Martin flipped his cloak back to reveal his sword. "City guard," he announced.

Once more, the man swept his gaze around the deserted street. Footsteps fast approached, from where Martin couldn't tell.

The man paled. He attempted to retrieve the sack twice, then gave up, disappearing into an alley as the footsteps drew closer. The footsteps stopped abruptly.

"Who's there? I'm a city guard. Identify yourself." Perhaps another guard lurked in the shadows, in which case Martin might have to explain what business brought him out of his district.

Nothing. He returned the sack to the shop. How could he keep other thieves from entering?

As with the day in the forest when he'd been forced from his home, something burst from his fingertips, but not fire this time. For a moment, the shopfront glowed. Then, the glow dimmed, leaving a faint shimmer around the door and window.

A ward? He'd constructed a ward? His gran spoke of magical barriers once but never told him how to accomplish such a feat, refusing to train him in magery lest the knowledge lead to his discovery. Easier to pretend he wasn't a mage if he didn't know how to use his skills.

Still, the unseen owner of those footsteps didn't show. Had someone seen him perform magic? Too late to dwell on consequences now.

Martin retraced his steps. Home. He needed to return home and puzzle out this mystery. Once he reached better-traveled streets, he encountered people set about their daily lives. From some, he felt nothing. Others? The woman in the green dress cheated on her mate. Another woman silently cried inside for having to sell her body on the streets to feed her family.

A well-dressed man with a smug expression inherited a fortune after killing his brother and accusing a servant. The servant hanged.

The prostitute's guilt appeared a pale green thing compared to the man's black aura. More and more, Martin felt violence, evil, and wrongdoing all around him. However, those driven by viable needs didn't weigh as heavily on his mind.

I murdered my sister.

I stole my brother's mate.

I sold my employer's necklace and told her it was lost by the jeweler.

Guilt and gloating buffeted him from all sides, screaming into his head. Finally, he broke into a run. Had to get away! Make them quiet!

Martin bustled past a maid in the house where he lived. No! He did not want to know her innermost thoughts. He charged into his rooms, slamming the door. Back against the wooden panel, he panted. What was happening? Why had his parents died too young to instruct him in the use of any mage talents?

From what little his gran had said, reading thoughts was something only powerful mages could accomplish, perhaps one of the reasons they were deemed too dangerous to live.

He sucked in air and released the breath slowly, willing his jangled nerves to calm. Plopping down on his bed, he took his head in his hands. What was he to do? If he couldn't find other mages to teach him, he'd have to learn on his own, or else the magic might consume him.

In time, Martin learned to tune the voices out, except for the louder ones, usually from someone who'd not only hurt another but reveled in their misdeeds.

"Did you hear?" Commander Enys said when Martin came to work one day. "A wealthy merchant's daughter is offering a reward to anyone who finds her missing father."

Two days later, Martin liberated the merchant from kidnappers, delivering the grateful man to his daughter's house.

The first of many successful recoveries.

Well-paying recoveries.

But what Martin wanted most, even his skills couldn't deliver.

He couldn't raise the dead.

Chapter Thirteen – Two Autumns Later

The streets of E'Skaara weren't paved with marble slabs like the villagers once claimed. In his younger days, Martin believed every word. Now he knew the truth. Cobblestones paved the streets of the upper city, while the lower city's streets mainly consisted of packed dirt and horse shit, with cobblestones as window dressing for the main thoroughfares. Couldn't have wealthy citizens seeing dirt when they traveled from a ship to their mansions in their fine carriages.

Cloak wrapped tightly around himself to dispel the autumn chill, Martin made his way down the bustling main avenue. Taverns competed for coin, with garishly painted facades and names like the Lion's Paw and the Broken Wheel.

A pickpocket bumped into him. "Sorry, sir," the man slurred, feigning drunkenness to explain his clumsiness. Nevertheless, his thoughts clearly announced his intention to divest Martin of his coin purse.

Martin caught a bony wrist in one strong hand, yanking the man around to see eye-to-eye. "You have just taken a small leather bag from my pocket. It could be full of coins or scorpions. Which do you think?"

"Let me go!" Eyes wide, the wiry little man tried to jerk away.

Martin let out a practiced laugh. He'd learned to be intimidating since he often prowled less-desirable parts of the city. Intimidation had been his most reliable weapon—until he'd filled out and his size kept robbers and bullies at bay. Not this man.

"I asked you a question." Martin gave his captive a shake. "Why don't you open your prize and see?"

"H... here. T... ta... take it back," the man spluttered.

"Ah, but you wanted my purse enough to steal from me. If you needed coin, did you not consider asking? Perhaps I am a generous man."

The thief tried again to return the pouch.

"Open it," Martin growled.

Hands trembling, the man loosened the leather thongs holding the purse closed. The mouth gaped open. The man winced while pouring the contents onto his palm. Three shiny silver coins. The man breathed a sigh of relief.

The coins shifted between one second and the next into three scorpions, tails raised to strike.

"Yah!" the man shrieked, yanking his arm free.

This time, Martin let him go, deftly catching the discarded coins before they hit the ground. Several curious gazes met his, then snapped away, the honest folks—and dishonest—not caring to draw his attention.

Onlookers merely witnessed a man dealing with a scoundrel who received his due. Scorpions? What scorpions? Those were for the thief's eyes alone. The thief would never admit seeing coins turn into potential death and risk accusations of madness, or worse yet, magery. Who would believe a thief?

Martin would love to walk away knowing the thief departed from a life of crime. But no. Three days at most before he ventured out into the only world he knew.

Martin cut off his thoughts. He didn't want to see further into the man's future. He'd made such a mistake in the past and then found himself in conversation with someone he knew to be facing death.

Death would win. Death always won.

Deliberately keeping his steps light, Martin made his way to the Stone's Throw. He kept a cautious eye on passersby, ears tuned to scuttling in alleyways.

The place had called to him when he'd first made a delivery last sevenday to the local magistrate. Were thieves present, requiring his intervention?

Early in the eve, children still roamed the streets, some on their way home to dinner, others gathering around the inns' back doors, hoping for a handout from a kindhearted cook. They were safe from the menace the city dwellers didn't see. The unholy beings didn't take children to Martin's knowledge, and crime kept most folk safely at home during the darkest hours.

He'd been scarcely older than some of those children when he'd first arrived, knowing no one and searching for others like himself. There must be others. Gran told him so. Yet, in all his time here, he'd found no evidence. But, of course, having to keep his nature secret surely didn't help.

Woodsmoke flavored the air, generously seasoned with the ever-present aroma of sea and surf that came with living in a harbor. Pausing outside the tavern, Martin breathed deeply of bitter hops and succulent pork, the scents comforting. His mouth watered.

Go inside, something told him. Sensing no immediate danger, he slipped through the door.

"Greetings, stranger," came from a few of the patrons. "Stranger" he would stay until he provided a name, for many came and went in this harbor town.

He wouldn't provide his name, nor would he lie. "Stranger" suited in many ways.

Martin nodded in answer and located an empty seat at the bar, perusing the room for a familiar face and coming up empty. Though he'd met many E'Skaarans, he kept to himself whenever possible. Keeping others at bay helped protect his secrets.

Commander Enys asked minimal questions, with so much family to talk about that he overlooked the one-sidedness of their conversations. Plus, Martin's promotion to captain guaranteed more duty-related topics.

While he neatly dodged Enys-related females, he'd entertained himself with an Enys second-cousin-once-removed for a season until the young man left for further schooling elsewhere.

Occasionally Martin enjoyed a pint with his fellow guards or even joined the commander's family for dinner—sans nieces.

Tonight, he longed for a different kind of company.

Soot stained the dull grey walls around the cheery hearth fire, and an antique wooden clock filled the mantlepiece—likely someone's prized possession. The clock showed the same time though minutes passed by, yet no one remarked on why the proprietor hadn't repaired the clock.

The tavern maid slid an ale and a pork pie—the eve's favored dish, apparently—across the timeworn oak of the bar top. The server wore her gray-flecked brown hair in a bun. Laugh lines around her eyes crinkled when she smiled.

"Well, hello there, handsome. Haven't seen you in here before." She leaned over the bar and hissed from behind her hand. "Let me tell you, you're a sight better to look at than most of these codgers. And I take it you wouldn't pinch a lady's bottom, would you?" The brassy woman dropped an eyelid over one dark eye. "Should you find one."

"Addie! Woman, I'm thirsting to death down here."

The woman, Addie apparently, rolled her eyes, dancing away to the other end of the bar. "Hold yer horses. I'm waiting on a customer." Her voice cut over the din of the crowded room.

Martin turned his attention back to the dinner he hadn't ordered. Ale and pork pie: simple fare. Back home, the villagers ate a lot of mutton before...

No. Martin would not think of before.

The ale brought back memories of his father and the villagers socializing over a pint, though he'd been too young to join in.

Before. Always *before*. When he'd been an ordinary son of ordinary parents, destined to become a farmer and raise more lambs for the slaughter. Before the villagers summoned the Chosen and allowed his parents to be taken without interfering. Did they deserve his punishment? Maybe, though it pained him to have carried out justice without conscious thought.

He'd kept a close eye on his fingers since that day. Though he'd tried many times, except for lighting a lantern in Petran's cabin aboard the *Seabird*, he'd yet to produce fire again. Perhaps the danger brought about the defense. With no one to ask, he might never know.

Fire, like wards, possessed a mind of its own.

Martin ate in silence, soaking in the laughter, chatter, scents of his meal, ale, and a hint of soot from the fireplace. His heart ached to not feel alone, as he had from the moment he'd been driven from his home.

No, for a brief time, he hadn't been alone. A very brief time.

Too brief.

Petran. If only Petran had left the ship with him.

If only.

Here Martin found himself in the land claimed by the Lady, with her fine temple on the hill in the high city. None of her followers strayed to the lower city, where the humble folks served the Father.

Father and Lady. The Father taught service to others, hard work, and simple living, like the people who served him. The Lady taught pleasures of all kinds, living in the moment, surrounding oneself with luxury.

The reason the poor didn't pray to her.

Oh, how afraid he'd been of the Lady and her Chosen.

Now Martin hid in plain sight, walked in the temple gardens nearly daily during his patrols, passed many of her servants, and even spoke with some regularly, particularly the energetic Cere.

None pointed a finger.

At least not yet.

The locals' tales caused him to wonder about the Lady. It was said that she and the Father had been one once before they split upon economic lines. Few claimed to have seen her. Few enough that Martin doubted her existence. But her followers roamed the land, putting to death any found guilty of the sin of magery, which the Lady forbade.

Of course, none claimed to have seen the Father, either, and he'd been none too clear about his stance on mages.

The Lady's magnificent temple brought pilgrims from afar, wanting a glimpse of the rumored opulence. Their money flooded the upper city, giving the city officials reason to extol her virtues.

Who wouldn't rather worship in pleasure than in self-sacrifice? The Father never stood a chance.

Though the goddess hadn't personally struck a blow, she might as well have killed Martin's family herself. Why did she hate magic? What had magic wielders ever done to her?

Martin turned on his stool to survey the tavern. A half dozen round, rough-hewn oak tables stood in neat rows, each surrounded by six chairs. Three tables boasted full capacity, while two more held parties of three. The last remained empty.

Herbs hung drying by the hearth, adding to the scent so different from anyplace he'd ever been before but still bringing thoughts of the mountains and the herbs his gran dried in the rafters for medicines.

How gloomy Martin had become tonight. He'd not experienced a bout of homesickness in several fullmoons. Perhaps he should find a suitable man for hire for the eve.

The door opened, and a waft of cooler air swept into the tavern, bringing the scent of rain. All troubling thoughts fled his mind. Martin breathed a bit easier. Tall and sturdily built, the aproned man entering the room struck Martin as familiar. Ridiculous. He'd never set foot in this tavern before. Perhaps he'd crossed paths with the handsome man in the marketplace or on some city street.

The tavernkeeper himself, though Martin couldn't say how he knew. Maybe he reached a logical conclusion, the way the barmaid acknowledged the new arrival with a smile; how the patrons calling out to him showed reverence.

Martin's slight frame had grown into a stocky build and broad shoulders that often aided him during hunts and sparring with his fellow guards. Yet those traits, along with blond hair and blue eyes, set him apart from many locals. However, some of the wealthy in the upper city boasted light hair due to cosmetics. Since his time here, his hair had darkened from gold to wheat, but not enough to let him blend with the lower city. Thus, "stranger." In a harbor town, strangers were never in short supply, though few stayed beyond a handful of days.

In the upper city, women and men alike avoided the sun, while most lower-city dwellers had darker hair, eyes, and complexion.

The tavernkeeper was no exception. He didn't fail to capture Martin's attention with a trim figure and laughing eyes. Those eyes. Something about those eyes. The moment Martin tried to puzzle out the niggling sense of familiarity, his thoughts skittered away. What had he been thinking?

Martin greeted the tavernkeeper with a brief smile. Now there was a man he'd like in his bed this night.

The tavernkeeper nodded, returning the smile, only to have his attention called away by boisterous patrons.

Martin tuned out the crowd's thoughts surrounding him with some effort, yet from the tavernkeeper—nothing. No flicker of emotion, no traces of thought. Calm, amid a whirlwind.

A touch of disappointment lodged in Martin's heart. Something within him demanded he get closer. What a ridiculous notion. Someone like himself, destined to hide in shadows, attracted to an honest, hardworking tavernkeeper. Martin's honed instincts said that much about the man.

He shook his head at the fanciful notions. His family legacy fated him to keep to himself.

Twice since arriving in the city, he'd witnessed the murder of innocents who'd been branded mages. Neither one contained any magic, but rivals coveted their businesses, paying to grease the right palms.

Still, the dark brown hair, revealing glints of copper and gold in the lantern and firelight, the eyes dark as midnight, and the bunched muscles flexing in the tavernkeeper's back, captured Martin's attention.

An image came to mind. A dream?

Dreams were often messages, but if he'd dreamed of this man, they'd surely met before, and Martin's desires conjured images during long nights alone in his room. Yet, once again, the harder he focused on the illusive thoughts, the more they evaded his grasp.

He quietly sipped his ale. One learned so much by simply listening. No one bothered him or tried to engage him in conversation. Here, a stranger could remain a stranger unless wanting otherwise.

These people had never truly been alone in their lives.

Sometimes, though, he'd love, just for a minute, to feel connected to another. Warmth washed over Martin, a fine blanket on a winter's night. He needn't turn around.

"Good eve to you, stranger," the tavernkeeper said, sidestepping Martin's stool to place a trio of mugs on the counter. He addressed the barmaid. "Addie, another round for the travelers in the corner."

Addie, tending bar, replaced the empty tankards with full. "Aye. Can't keep that lot happy," she groused. "My pockets better jingle when they leave."

Martin pitied them if they didn't reward her appropriately for the meal with extra for herself. Addie struck him as a formidable woman.

He breathed in sweat, spices, and an honest day's work. Again, a sense of familiarity played at the edges of his senses. Then, all too soon, the man who'd caught Martin's interest lifted the drinks and disappeared back into the mass of patrons.

Martin placed a coin on the bar. "Keep the remainder."

Addie smiled, smoothing her hand down her stained homespun apron. "You come back and see me. Give these tired old eyes a pleasant sight." Well, he wouldn't be facing her wrath tonight. He couldn't say the same for the men in the corner.

Martin lifted his hood and headed back outside to a light drizzle.

At such a late hour, few honest folks roamed the streets. The dishonest ones took one look at Martin and fled.

The lights still blazed in the Lady's temple when he returned to the high city, stopping by to renew his vow of vengeance. One day. Not yet. Though what he waited for eluded him. He watched the temple dwellers through the windows, selected for their beauty, bedecked in finery and jewels. Was Cere among them tonight? Martin didn't envy them. For them, he felt only pity for believing falsely.

No kind, benevolent being put his parents to death when they'd committed no crimes.

Every night he came here, stood in this spot. Felt magic dance along his skin.

And glared at the house of his enemy.

For just a moment, a split second in time, he felt his enemy glare back.

Chapter Fourteen

Peter noticed the stranger the moment he returned from his eve walk. Most people gave off some kind of energy, something tangible.

This man? Nothing.

Addie blatantly flirted. Her bosoms would fall out of her low-cut dress if she bent over any farther. All for show. Her heart and body belonged to the long-dead Zahn. Still, her act brought coins to her apron pockets—coins she'd use to buy herbs to treat those too poor to afford a physician or apothecary. Or to book passage for some mage-born in need of sanctuary.

She looked over the stranger's head, smiled, and winked. Peter's cheeks flamed. He should never drink that much again and answer Addie's personal questions. Ever since he'd foolishly disclosed his desire for men, she'd made it her life's work to find him a mate.

As though the city would accept a male couple.

"*Don't be silly,*" she'd said. "*Lots of mage bonds formed between two men or two women in the old days.*"

Yes, back before magery brought a death sentence, when elves, fairies, and other magical creatures roamed the lands. Or so Addie said. Magical creatures fled in droves when the Lady built her temple. A few sailors mentioned them from time to time, but they mostly lived across the sea in the Myrgren Mountains of Adulas.

Though Peter swore he'd seen merfolk.

Still, the stranger intrigued, with his dark clothes, sinister air, and straw blond hair.

Those eyes! Peter grabbed hold of the bar to steady himself when the stranger turned those eyes on him. Pale hair, pale skin, a slip of a boy with eyes like those.

But no, Arkenn was long gone and could never have changed so much in so little time. Even so, Peter could look at the stranger all day and not grow bored. Something about him...

No matter how he focused, his thoughts closed on nothing, like smoke through a fist.

"Tavernkeeper!"

Peter followed the summons, bringing empty tankards to the bar—normally Addie's job—for an excuse for a better look. His hands trembled. He stood closer than necessary, breathing in the man's scent, all leather, sweat, metal, and temptation.

No, he couldn't risk his business and his good name by making improper suggestions to a stranger. For all he knew, this man was a city guard in disguise, actively looking for a lawbreaker to haul into jail, though why he'd be in the lower city, Peter didn't know.

His clothes were of good quality, though worn; neat, even stitches closing a rent in the sleeve of his shirt. But, when he brought one foot onto the rung of the barstool, he exposed a patch on the sole of his boot.

Not a wealthy man then.

Only one table remained unfilled, and by the time work ebbed enough for Peter to return to the bar, the table had filled, but the bar stood empty.

No stranger.

"Who was he?" Peter asked aloud.

"A whole lot of trouble, if you ask me," Addie said, slapping Peter on the back and cackling. "Them's the best kind." She waded into the crowd, exchanging bawdy tales with the patrons.

She'd return with her pockets full of coins—she swore the patrons surrendered them freely, and she didn't resort to magery.

No, she wouldn't. Too much at stake. Peter missed Mitta on nights like this when the former tavernkeeper who'd taken Peter under his wing would have been holding court by the hearth.

Mitta, who'd lain on his deathbed, clutching Peter's hand, declaring him nephew and heir.

Leaving Peter the owner of the Stone's Throw. How Peter missed Old Mitta, another who'd taken him in without asking too many questions, basing opinions on a man's honor and work ethic, not parentage.

Addie had the main room under control. Peter headed into the kitchen.

"Good eve," the kitchen maid said, a girl of nineteen he'd hired to help Addie.

"Good eve." Peter helped himself to some pie, perching on a stool in the corner to eat. The scent of burning wood teased his nose, though not from his own hearth fires. He sniffed the pie. Nope. Smelled fine. He stepped out into the main room, stalking straight for the back door and throwing open the wooden panel.

The smell grew stronger here. He headed toward the scent, picking up his pace. On the streets, people went about their business. Did no one else smell smoke?

The smell beckoned him away from the safety of the tavern. He searched the rooftops for a telltale orange glow and found nothing.

Yet.

Plenty of derelict buildings in this part of the city, some used by pirates to house illegal wares, others used as shelter for those without a home. Deep inside, something urged Peter on. Somewhere, someone needed him.

He hurried down the wharf at a trot, pausing to consult his senses every few moments. His breath fogged before his face. There! He darted to an abandoned warehouse, throwing open the door. Flames licked at the wooden walls, leaving char in their wake. Soon they'd reach the ceiling.

Two boys beat at flames with smoldering flour sacks.

"What are you doing? Go!" Peter ordered them, snatching the bags from their hands.

"We can't, mister. Toby's in there," the larger of the two wailed.

From a room behind them came a whine. Peter's heart stuttered. A child? "Go! I'll get him."

"Promise?"

Peter tried to keep his voice confident for the children's sake. "Promise. Wait for me at the docks."

The boys ran off on bare feet. Peter faced a wall of flames and heat. Where to begin? How could he...

Resuming the boys' task, he beat at the flames with the flour sacks. Instead of quelling the fire, the fanning sent it higher. Though he couldn't see to the second floor, he heard the rush of flames as something caught. Orange glowed through the boards overhead. No, no, no, no, no!

Now! He must stop the flames now before the warehouse collapsed! Thick, black smoke obscured his vision, stinging his nostrils, and clogging his throat. Heat battered his skin. Tears leaked from his eyes. Peter doubled over in a coughing fit. The wall between him and the child burned hot, orange, red, and blue. A child! He must save the child!

"Toby? Toby!" he cried.

A whimper answered him. Was there another way into the next room? *Father, help me!*

Like the day with the woman in labor, power sizzled through him. Heat still scorched his skin, but not from the flames. Peter raised his hands.

The flames shrank back, as though in fear of his touch. The air around him grew cooler, easier to breathe. He lowered his hands. The fire raged once more. Arms lifted, he chanted in some unknown tongue, commanding the fire to obey his will. *I am stronger than you. You must do my bidding.*

The flames shot upward once more. For one brief moment, Peter imagined a raging inferno crashing down on him and the child.

Then the flames wavered, growing smaller. His arms ached, muscles trembling. Still, he held his hands aloft. Slowly, slowly, the flames calmed, going from inferno to small fire, to embers.

In the center of the dirt floor sat a ring of stones filled with charred rags. Two stacks of smoldering flour sacks sat nearby, side by side. Had the boys tried to start a fire to warm themselves, using the flour sacks as blankets to sleep?

"Toby?" Peter called, advancing on the door, now a blackened ruin hanging from one hinge. Nothing. Oh, gods, no! Peter yanked at the door, ignoring the heat and soot on his hands. Once, twice. The door came free, falling to the floor.

"Toby?"

A matted ball of white fur huddled under a splintered wooden chair, whining and too afraid to approach. A dog. Not a child. Peter snatched the grubby creature by the scruff of the neck and inspected for injury. Nothing visible. He'd get Addie to perform a more thorough examination—on the dog and the boys.

The boys hadn't heeded his instructions, waiting by the back door instead of heading for the safety of the docks, shivering in their too-thin clothes. If the fire hadn't gone out...

Peter wouldn't take the time to consider what he'd done. Had the boys seen? Had any of the Chosen been close enough to feel his use of power? Best to leave quickly. "Come with me," he told the boys, handing over the dog to the older boy.

The boys, nearly as scruffy as the dog, bore a resemblance, the oldest maybe ten and the younger possibly six. "Do you have a home?"

The older boy glanced back at the warehouse.

Oh. Despite exhaustion and trembling from earlier fear, Peter put on a friendly face. "Come with me. There's food aplenty at the tavern. I know someone who'll want to meet you."

The older boy gave off a faint whiff of power, but the younger was too young to detect. "Where are your parents?"

"They... they're... gone," the older boy replied, eyes wary. He passed the dog to his younger brother, who'd been reaching, carefully keeping himself between the smaller boy and Peter.

"How?" The twisting of his insides said Peter already knew the answer.

"They got taken to the temple and never came back."

Peter would take them to Addie, who'd likely find someone with a ship to carry them far away from here, where they'd be given a home.

E'Skaara was no place for the mage-born.

Chapter Fifteen

Martin ran his mouth over smooth skin, exploring a chest generously spattered with hair. A moan vibrated against his tongue. Farther and farther, he explored until his mouth hit roughness. What?

He pulled back, staring at a puckered scar... and a face that haunted his dreams.

Martin awoke with a start, breath coming in heavy pants. A dream. Only a dream. Of a man with a scar on his shoulder.

He lay on his bed, pulling in air while his heart calmed. Hints of light peeked through the wooden shutters. Time to start his day. In a minute. First, he closed his eyes, imagining the man from his dreams once more, slowly stroking his cock with one hand while clutching beneath his balls with the other.

Oh, to have continued the dream, buried himself inside his fantasy's body. It had been too long since he'd plunged his cock into a willing hole.

Memories came back: a rocking ship, two fumbling young men, his first kisses...

The heat, the pressure.

Oh! He came, spurting across his furred belly.
Only a dream, but a good one.

"Are you sure you won't come to dinner?" Commander
Enys asked as he and Martin took midday meal in the
commander's office.

"Who is she?" Martin asked, picking at his roast
chicken. One thing to be said for officers—they ate
better than the men in the barracks.

Enys gave a sheepish smile. "My mate's cousin, so a
brunette this time, for variety."

Exactly as Martin feared. Now to be diplomatic.
"While your mate is a wonderful woman, I'm sure her
cousin could only be a pale shadow in comparison."

"Yes, true, but how will you know if you don't meet
her?" Enys shoved a bite of bread into his mouth, the
touch of pleading in his eyes nearly comical.

Martin laughed, shaking his head. "You're never
going to believe that I don't need a bond mate, are
you?"

"As my Esmerla tells me often, men have no idea
what they want, so they need mates to tell them."

Something had been on Martin's mind. Now that
he held rank, he felt more at ease talking to Enys as
a friend. They'd also known each other long enough
that, no matter what he said, Enys wouldn't take
offense or become suspicious.

"What do you know of the Father and the Lady?"

Enys stopped, a forkful of potatoes halfway to his
mouth. "Now, that's an abrupt change of subject. Yes,
I get it. No more talking about the never-ending line
of unattached women in my family. What do you want

to know? Esmerla attends the Father's temple and spends some morns helping the poor."

"What about the Lady?"

Enys barked a laugh. "Worshipping through pleasure? Let some stranger fuck you till you're divine?"

Wow. Enys was even less reserved than Martin hoped. "You're against it?"

"Don't get me wrong, the temple brings a lot of visitors to our city, who in turn bring coin they leave behind. If they're going to the Lady's house, they bring *lots* of coin." Enys leaned in and whispered, "And also their bodies."

"So, you *do* object. I never took you as a follower of the Father."

"I'm not, but don't tell my mate. She might question why a man of my rank always seems to be working during worship services."

Now came Martin's turn to laugh. "You do use your position to full advantage."

Enys sobered. "My great-grandfather lived here when something changed."

"What changed?"

"Until then, the Father and the Lady were worshipped together, though most called her the Mother then."

"Did anyone see her? What does she look like?"

"No one has seen her. One day, the hill began to glow. Every day changes came. All the powerful mages seemed drawn there." Enys paused a long moment. "Like my great-grandfather. He went up the hill and never returned. The Lady's followers said she'd instructed them to build a great temple. The larger the temple grew, the more mages disappeared."

Prickles of unease trailed across Martin's skin. Had the Lady used the mages' power? "Are there any more mages?" He held his breath.

Enys shook his grizzled head. "None with any great power. Occasionally the Chosen will come into the city and drag some poor soul back, usually someone they were paid to make disappear." He sighed. "You have no idea how many reports we've received. The reward you collected from finding that lady's father? None were more shocked than me that he hadn't been forced into the temple."

"If they kill people there, what happens to the bodies?" Surely someone would notice. Why wouldn't the city guard intervene?

"My great-grandfather said that some high priests can conjure fire that destroys them. I think he drank too much." Enys returned his attention to his meal.

Conjuring fire.

Not so farfetched after all.

"Why is this allowed? What about laws against killing?"

Enys sighed. "They don't apply to mages."

"What happens to the mages that are brought here?" Martin asked Cere as they lounged on a bench. Butterflies rode gardenia-scented breezes, and fountains burbled in the background. In the lower city, the air grew cool, the meager plants turning brown. Here?

Eternal summer.

"Why, they're punished, of course." Cere leaned back, showing his lean muscles to full advantage. He never merely sat—he posed, artfully arranging himself on the bench.

Martin ignored the none-too-subtle advance from seasons of practice. "Why? What have they done wrong?"

Cere shifted his gaze, first right, then left, and lowered his voice. "It's blasphemy to ask these questions."

"Oh, I'm sorry. I was just... curious."

Cere stretched his long legs out in front of him, scowl giving way to his customary grin. "That's okay. You're not from here, so you can't know. Power belongs to the Lady. The mages steal it and use it for evil. They must be punished."

Interesting. Martin's parents hadn't stolen anything. He certainly hadn't. "What does the Lady do with the power?"

"Why, everything. Without her, the sun wouldn't rise or set. Crops wouldn't grow, or babes be born."

What? "But hasn't the Lady only existed without the Father for a few generations?"

"Blasphemy!" Cere shouted, then slapped a hand over his mouth. "That's what some would have you believe, but she's always been here. She merely chose to make E'Skaara her home a few generations ago. You have to admit, she picked a wonderful spot."

"What about the Father and his teachings?"

Cere huffed. "He would condemn me for taking a man to my bed."

"Doesn't the Lady forbid that too?"

"She forbids mages from forming such bonds, but if pleasure is to be had with a man"—Cere rolled his shoulders in an elegant shrug— "then why not?"

Why not indeed. "Have you ever heard of creatures who roam the night, killing innocents?"

"Could never happen. The Lady protects the innocent." Soft chiming sounded from the temple. Cere jumped from his bench. "I have lessons. Come visit me again?"

"Of course, whenever my rounds bring me this way."

Cere darted off a few paces, stopped, and returned, rising up on his toes and brushing a kiss over Martin's lips.

Martin stood in the garden, fingers against his tingling lips, long after Cere rounded the building and disappeared from sight.

What a long day. All Martin wanted to do was kick his boots off and relax in his favorite chair.

A fire blazed in the hearth of his rented rooms, and he held his hands before the heat. His home for the past three summers smelled of sweet herbs and held a bed, a desk and chair, and a trunk for his clothes in one room. Four comfortable chairs, a table, bookcases, and a refurbished settee occupied the other room. He'd built the bookcases himself with wood leftover from a renovated mansion. The wealthy threw away things of value as inconsequential.

Very few furnishings in his home had he purchased, save for his clothes and the candles. Even the books he forced himself to read had been salvaged and repaired. The more he knew of the world, the better. Many were religious tomes about the Father and the Mother. He'd found some on the Lady, all newer volumes. Know your enemy. Also, know your possible ally, though he'd never dealt much with the Father's devout. Interesting how different some of the texts were from Cere's beliefs.

At least Martin's magery allowed him to pick up reading and writing easily, with help from Cere and Esmerla Enys. After all, she wouldn't want her relative's future mate to be illiterate, would she, should she and Commander Enys finally wear down Martin's defenses?

Stone walls, stone floor. Martin's abilities afforded him lodgings in the oldest reaches of the city, rife with residual magic practiced over the centuries.

Before mages were hunted down like vermin. But the mages had their purpose, even if the general population didn't understand. Without them, the city might one day fall to ruin.

Several books he'd scrounged told of when ships traveled the seas by magic, not sails, and how mages actually owned shops based on their particular talents, like healing or divination.

Oddly, nowhere in the city thrummed with magical energy quite like the temple and surrounding hill. Why build your fortress among so much magic if you despised those who practiced?

Then again, Cere claimed all magic belonged to the Lady, making a hill filled with power ideal. Plus, it afforded an unparalleled view of the city. No matter how wealthy a person or grand a house, they'd never compare to the opulence of the Lady's abode. Approaching visitors, either by land or sea, saw the temple before anything else.

Martin returned his book to the shelf and retired to his bedchamber. His gaze fell to the bed. An image came unbidden to mind: the tavernkeeper, naked and splayed on the mattress. Martin dreamed of the image often, to the point where he'd like to ask to see the man's shoulder to ensure the scar was real and not a product of a dream.

Until recently, Martin hadn't been aware his fantasy man actually existed. The more he considered, the more likenesses he found.

He laughed at himself. Really. As if the fates would send him images of a lover.

Martin wouldn't mind being wanted by a certain tavernkeeper. What was it about the man? Another image came to mind: a smiling face, gold-streaked brown hair in the matted style of the pirates, sun-bronzed skin.

Petran. Martin's heart ached. The man he'd met last night reminded him of Petran. Only the tavernkeeper was fair and with dark brown hair.

What had the patrons called him? Peter?

Those eyes. Those intense, dark eyes. By whatever power reigned over the universe, Martin wished the pirate boy had lived. When Martin met other mages, he'd ask who their deity was and pray to them for Petran's eternal peace.

Once more, his thoughts dissipated in a thousand directions. What had he been thinking? Something about Petran?

Martin had worked hard today, training with the sentries, patrolling the streets, and he'd love to go to the Stone's Throw for dinner and ale. Perhaps he'd speak to the tavernkeeper tonight.

No, first Martin must perform the duty he'd taken upon himself, to keep the people of this city safe. People who'd never know what he did for them.

Twirling the weapon he'd acquired without knowing how, he went through the motions of the guards at morn practice. He'd been one of their ranks for long enough to be adept at the sword, his efforts aided by the night he'd seen something he couldn't unsee. Better to know how to fight.

He changed from his daily wear into all black, shoved his sword into its scabbard, and left his rooms.

Darkness. The throbbing pulse beneath the cobblestones pounded through the thick soles of Martin's boots. This close to the waterfront, the air reeked of garbage, piss, and rotting fish. Distant shouts in a dozen languages rose from the dockhands, their workplaces lit by oil lanterns.

Light offered some protection from what lurked in shadows.

Straining to tune out the everyday noises in favor of scuttling or a slate tile slipping on the roof of the building across the narrow alley, Martin held his breath, heart beating in time with the city's.

Higher. He'd see more from a better vantage point. An upturned barrel gave him a head start, and he shimmied onto the low corner of a roof. Soft rain sprinkled his upturned face, cooling skin heated while giving chase.

He paused to enjoy the night for one brief moment, the blood pulsing through his veins.

Being alive.

Wait! The distinct rasp of claws on stone reached his ears.

No one was about in the shopping district this late at night. No mere mortals, at any rate. Silent as a shadow, he leaped from a seamstress's humble structure to a healer's, tracking his prey.

Neither the seamstress nor the healer would ever know of hunter and prey who kept themselves hidden. If the city knew what lurked through its streets at night...

Wouldn't it be better if people knew? Couldn't they better protect themselves? Yet, who would Martin tell? He'd be thrown into the building outside of town if he tried, where the citizens discarded those they labeled crazy. Have a vision? Be imprisoned.

If it was safer to hold his tongue, hold his tongue, he would.

And hunt.

He'd love to tell someone, though, to have company. Maybe Gery Enys. But no, how could Martin explain something the commander couldn't see?

Poised on the edge of a rooftop, Martin crouched, muscles bunching in his thighs and calves. While he served the city with his nocturnal tasks, the excitement pulsating through his blood added more thrill than strictly required.

He served the people.

More scuttling. The putrid odor of dead things. Grasping an ornate roofbeam in one hand, Martin silently eased himself to the ground, careful to muffle his footfalls.

He waited. Flickering lanternlight from a passerby grew closer, and he fought back a frustrated scream. His quarry spotted the light, hissing as though burned. No.

Rasping claws on tile loosened a mat of lichen that fell to the ground with a noisy splat, barely missing Martin's head. Damnation! The thing had climbed and couldn't have been more than a few feet above him.

If he'd stayed aloft, they'd be face-to-face by now.

He splashed through stagnant puddles and other vile things city dwellers poured into gutters.

Chasing through the shadows, shielded lamp in one hand, sword in the other, Martin cringed when a dark shape dropped from the roof to shuffle sideways down the alley. Though vaguely man-shaped, the thing's resemblance ended there.

Its glowing amethyst eyes locked on Martin. Then, the thing turned and fled.

Martin paused, leaning back against a rain-slicked clapboard wall to catch his breath. He'd caught wind of his quarry—it wouldn't escape. The dock warehouses on this side of the street, abandoned since nightfall, offered many nooks and crannies for nesting by otherworldly beasts. The stench of a trash-filled canal assaulted Martin's nose, the tainted scent alleviated somewhat by a steady drizzle.

Hammering footfalls shattered his respite. "Down there! He went down there!" a voice shouted. What? Who was that?

But, *down there.* So, toward him. Martin went on alert, scanning the night for his enemy, and whoever else he might encounter.

He spun on his heels. Was that the faint scraping of scale over stone, the flick of a forked tongue testing the air? He flattened against the wall. How stupid to think he could hide from eyes more suited to darkness than daylight.

A slither, a hiss, a defeated sigh. The thing slunk closer. *Thump, thump, thump* went Martin's wildly pounding heart.

A high-pitched voice pleaded, "Don't hurt me. I mean no harm."

The piteous whine sent chills marching up Martin's spine. Bracing himself, he held his lantern aloft and unshielded the flame.

These beings never spoke to him as an equal. No, they ran and ran until he caught them; they challenged him with bravado or escaped, though few had escaped once he'd learned his craft.

This one stopped... and asked for mercy. He'd never witnessed such. Weren't they like animals? Killing without regard?

Stooped on the opposite side of the narrow alleyway, a creature huddled against an empty packing crate, licking its green lips with a reptilian tongue. Vertically slitted purple irises glittered in the lantern's feeble light. "I don't want to hurt you," it mewled again.

The stuff of nightmares sat hunch-shouldered before Martin. Had this shriveled, scaled being once been a man? Or was it something else entirely? Surely Gran had never spoken of such a being. Martin fought a shudder.

The creature appeared helpless—and would until the moment the claws it currently hid sank into a victim's throat.

"This isn't my first hunt." Martin's breath hovered in front of his face a moment before becoming one with the eerie nighttime mist. He barely registered the absence of rain, too busy watching the treacherous predator with wary eyes, extending his sword toward a scaled throat.

He'd seen the damage from such claws as the being possessed. Many a throat fell victim to the razor-sharp teeth of the thing's ilk. The horrors wandered the streets at night. People couldn't see the hideous creatures, didn't know they were there.

Until the creatures struck.

The dying couldn't tell Martin what killed them.

He forcibly calmed, luring the beast into false security. Soft footfalls mixed with the pattering of water falling from the warehouse's eaves.

He'd deal with whoever approached later, keeping his eyes on his adversary. Chances were, whoever it was couldn't see the evil anyway. If only he could feel emotions or intents from the creatures like he did from people. But he didn't have time to focus on whoever approached.

Slowly, slowly the pathetic longing fled a face the color of gutter slime, replaced by a visage of pure hunger. The forked tongue flicked out again, and the thing smiled. In a far more confident voice, the eternally damned being said, "You know what I want of you, then, what I am. I'm sure to receive a handsome reward for a mage. Make your move, *priest*."

Priest?

Chapter Sixteen

T he clattering of boots upon stone forced Martin to look away, just for a second. Then, a brown cassock came into view. An actual priest?

"Ah, what have we here?" Keeping a safe distance, the newcomer peered down at the scaled monster.

The creature hissed, backing away, the wall at its back preventing escape. "I mean no harm," it whimpered, bravado fleeing in the face of a holy man.

The priest squatted, coming far closer to a shadow-dweller than Martin dared. He'd once gotten close and nearly bore scars across his cheek.

A dagger glinted against the creature's throat, tilting its head upward. After a moment, the priest stood. "You mean no harm, hmm? I suppose you've stained your claws with innocent blood by accident. You know the penalty?" The hooded man kept his tone even, without malice or condemnation.

Who was this? Where had he come from? Sure, Martin had seen priests before, but hunting night creatures?

"'Tis no worse than the fate awaiting me if I fail in my hunt." Desperate now, the thing begged, "Please, please, please, let me go." Scaly arms covered a distorted face. It crooned, rocking back and forth.

"That I cannot do," replied the priest, "for once your kind kills, they'll kill again, depriving my lord of his blessed children." The brown-clad figure stepped back, securing his dagger inside his boot. "Martin? I believe this will make your ninth kill. Do not taunt, do not maim, take no pleasure in work which needs doing." He recited the words, smoothly shifting to a language Martin shouldn't be able to understand.

"Ho... How do you know my name?"

"Later. Right now, complete the task you've taken on." Gloved hands folded together in a prayerful pose, Martin's unexpected companion resumed his strange, lilting chant.

The creature inclined its head. A single purple tear slid down its nose. "Be about it then," it said.

Martin placed his lantern on the ground and raised his sword in a two-handed grip. "May whatever you believe in have pity on your soul if you possess one."

The thing sniffed the air, eyes widening. "You! It's you!" It gave an evil smile. "No, let mercy be on you. He wants *you*."

Too late to stop his momentum, Martin brought the sharp-edged steel down with all his might. A single whimper, a plop, and the thing's head rolled into a puddle. Martin stepped back, wiping his blade on the corpse's scaled hide.

Staring down at the thing, he felt a moment of grief for taking a life. But by his actions, how many had he saved?

The priest murmured low, repeating earlier words, "There is no joy in this work that needs doing. Not for an honorable man." He whistled into the sudden silence. Answering whistles replied.

"Who is with you?" Martin asked.

"More priests, hunters like yourself. Did you believe yourself the only one taking on this task?"

Martin shook his head. "I've never seen any of you before." But maybe he had. A flash of brown here or there.

"We didn't want to be seen, but we have hunted with you many times. Ever wonder what happened to the beings that got away?"

"Yes."

The priest quietly murmured, "They didn't get away."

"Yet you show yourself tonight."

"It was time to show myself." Did the priest have to be so matter-of-fact, yet make Martin pull explanations from him? The priest chanted words Martin didn't know.

What had the thing meant? *He wants you.* Who wanted him? The Father? Martin didn't hold to any religion. Religion turned its back on him ages ago by marking him an outcast and cursing him with powers he knew little about.

The robed figure's utterances grew louder. Finally, he raised his hands, sprinkling fire onto the corpse. White-hot flames licked at scale and claw, rendering the beast to ashes in the blink of an eye.

Martin jumped back. "Who..." Flames from his fingers? "Who are you?"

Like all those summers ago. Except the priest seemed to have called the flames, controlled them.

Martin stood beside the mysterious figure, who chanted serenely until the last flame withered and died, leaving only an oily residue and the memory of a murderous horror.

"What was it exactly? I've never heard them beg for their lives before." Martin kept his voice low. Breaking the eerie silence seemed wrong somehow. Bold killers who had no remorse didn't bother him nearly as much as the one tonight.

The priest remained quiet a moment, weighing his words, no doubt. "Something that no one should be able to see. No one but the mage-born."

Martin pointed toward a spot of goo with his blade and shuddered. "And what did you just do?" So many questions rattled around his brain. Was this really happening?

With a few more muttered words in a strange tongue, the priest waved his hands. Martin focused on the cadence and inflection of each word, if not their meaning. The air glistened, glowing runes forming and drifting away. Before the last gleaming strands faded, the priest pivoted on his heel and strode from the alley. Martin followed.

Magic. This man performed magic, knew Martin's name, and made the corpse disappear.

Neat trick. Martin usually tossed the bodies into the harbor and hoped sea creatures destroyed the evidence. If they could see them.

"Wait! Why won't you answer my questions?"

The nighttime world blossomed around them as they left the warehouse district, ladies and gentlemen of pleasure plying their trade on the fringes. The areas populated this late at night wouldn't attract what could only be called a demon. Those hunted where they stood the least risk of discovery.

"A blessing, Father," a woman called out, flinging a shawl over her exposed bosom to hide her pale flesh. More than rouge stained her cheeks.

She'd dressed simply, hair hanging straight down her back, clothes clean but unadorned. So many things brought women—and men—to the streets to earn their living. Mostly, desperation. Martin might have resorted to such to keep himself fed when he'd first arrived if not for Petran's gift and Commander Enys's timely offer. An air of innocence followed the woman. She plied her trade because of need, not want.

The priest traced runes in the air that she probably saw as mere gestures and not the fading glow the symbols formed. The woman smiled. "Thank you, Father."

Another woman approached, boldly displaying her body. Jewels hung from her ears, wrists, and neck. She sneered at the first woman in passing. "A blessing, Father!" On her hung the stench of superiority, how she lorded her possessions over the other women of the streets. Already though, her beauty waned, not from age but from her unattractive inner self bleeding to the outside.

The priest ignored the entreaty. "Though my lord does not revel in pleasure as the Lady does, he smiles on the undertakings of honest workers," he told Martin.

"How about the ones you fail to bless?" In Martin's eyes, no visible difference existed between those he blessed and those he didn't, except maybe for a bit of modesty and lack of vanity when faced with a holy man. Not to the eyes, rather. Did the priest sense their guilt, shame, or emotions, like Martin?

"The lord frowns on treachery. The dishonest have no need of my lord's fortunes to line their pockets. They're doing well enough on their own and shan't prosper." Though a hood hid the priest's features, Martin still felt a razor-sharp gaze.

"Wait, stop! Who are you?"

The cassocked man swept a stately bow. "Father Dmitri, at your service. Servant of the Father, and as you've probably determined, a mage."

A mage. A living, breathing mage. "I've looked for mages a long time. So why haven't I found any before?"

"We didn't want to be found before you were ready. Yes, night after night, you roamed the city streets, unwittingly taking on a task we've always performed." Martin heard the smile in Father Dmitri's voice. "You were never alone. Had you not succeeded in your mission, we would have saved you. But you're finally prepared to face your destiny." He bobbed his head toward Martin's scabbard. "I see you're making use of our little gift."

"Gift?" Martin pulled his sword free, brandishing the blade. "My door was locked, and yet I woke one morn to find this."

"A hunter deserves a hunter's blade. Imagine trying to hack through scaled skin with a kitchen knife because you wouldn't be deterred once you set your mind to something. Although I must admit, I've never seen anyone fight with a barrel hook before." The shoulders of the hassock rose and fell in what might have been a shrug. "We felt the need to intervene. At least on a small scale."

Wait. Martin wasn't ready? "You've been watching me all this time?"

"Of course. You don't think we'd leave an untrained mage to his own devices, do you? We couldn't have you bringing attention to the lot of us living under the Lady's very nose, could we?"

We? Martin had searched for mages all this time, and they'd been under his nose all along? "You keep saying 'we'. How many of you are there?"

"Twenty. We used to number many more, until the Lady sentenced our kind to death."

"You don't look dead to me." Father Dimitri didn't much look alive either, more like a pile of brown laundry.

"You might be surprised," the priest muttered under his breath. "And please, call me Dmitri. Doing so saves time." Swiveling the opening of his hood toward the few people making their way along the street—giving Martin and Dmitri a wide berth— he said, "Come, let us find a more suitable place to hold this conversation."

Martin hoped for a tavern. A tankard of ale wouldn't go amiss. Instead, Fath... Dmitri led Martin to a park, settling himself on a bench.

"We know you, Martin. Or should I say Arkenn? We've always known of you. Have marked your progress." Dmitri dropped his voice. "We also knew your parents before you."

"You... you knew my parents?" Martin sat beside the priest, though not too close.

"Yes. Good people. They thought to hide you in a rural village, yet they were found out. I do not know how. Your mother passed her only protection to you, and it was lost."

"The amulet?" He recalled the amulet Petran wore as clear as day, of having seen similar before. He clutched his new one. "You gave this to me?"

"Yes. It conceals your magic. You still have access, but no longer does enough show to call attention to those who'd seek to destroy you."

"I... I..."

Very softly, Father Dmitri said, "Yes, we know. Although unintentional, you meted righteous judgment on the villagers for standing by and doing nothing for your parents. What they did to your grandmother. What they would have done to you."

Martin sighed. This man knew, and didn't judge. A weight lifted from his shoulders. A priest of the father absolved him of his sin. "At night, I relive that moment often. I had no control..."

"The fact that you don't use your abilities for personal gain says a lot about what kind of man you are. You work hard and earned a promotion at an early age, even without prominent family connections. I don't mean the small acts that put food in your mouth, like finding lost jewels or a lost pet. A man of your abilities could have a palace, servants, gold, and yet you do not. So tell me, Martin, what do you want?"

Having a stranger address him with such familiarity should have bothered Martin more than it did. Could be shock, and he'd panic later. "To find out and understand what I am."

"Ah. Introspection. Sometimes it's best not to know the answers beforehand. Now, how did you come to hunt the evil creatures of the night?" There was a touch of amusement in Father Dmitri's voice. He spoke with lilting cadence, voice neither old nor young, with no distinct accent known to Martin.

"One night, I heard a noise, cut down an alley, and saw two creatures attacking a woman. I chased them off. She was close to death." Martin closed his eyes in a fruitless attempt to banish the image from his mind: a young woman of the streets, torn open, gasping out her last breaths. "They'd toyed with her. Made her death as horrifying as possible. She never even saw her killers, just felt their teeth and claws."

Father Dmitri's hood dipped in a curt nod. "Yes, that is their nature. But, you see, it's not the flesh they feed upon but the emotion. Her fear, her pain. Magic grows stronger when a person is afraid. As you know firsthand."

"She was a mage?"

"No, she held so little power she didn't even know. Few of their kind would risk attacking a mage who can fight back and possibly win. Apparently, she had a mage ancestor, though, giving her a hint of residual magic, for it is that magic the creatures feed upon, amplified by her terror. Not enough magic to let her see her attackers, however, when they choose to hide themselves. What did you do after her death?"

"Every night, I sought her killers. A sevenday later, I found them. I've been hunting demons ever since."

"Demons. Yes, an apt enough name, though they don't see themselves as evil. You've been quite successful for someone self-trained."

"Why are you asking? You mentioned the hook. You already know what happened, don't you?"

"Yes, but only from my perspective. I needed to hear yours."

This was the most bizarre conversation Martin ever had. But while Dmitri seemed willing to answer questions... "How... how did you come to know about magic?"

"Same as you, I suppose. My parents were mages, and my grandparents before them. On my wo... In my village, as here, mages were once valued. We brought rains when needed, healed the sick, kept wolves away from sheep." Dmitri chuckled. "And entertained the young ones with sleight of hand during long winter eves when they grew bored. We spared many a parent's sanity."

"You said 'were'. Are they valued no more?"

Dmitri paused several moments before replying, "My village is no more. Which is why we, also, have come to this city. All of us who remain."

"The Lady's temple is here. Don't you risk much by being so close?"

"The amulets shield us from her followers, and we learned to hide what we are long ago. If she sought us herself, she might grow wiser, but she has entrusted the task of ridding the world of mages to others. They no longer look so closely because they think they've nearly accomplished their goal. They simply wait until someone reports magery. Can you imagine what would happen to the people of this city if we weren't here?"

Martin shuddered. Demons everywhere, picking off people at will. "I've heard that the Lady protects her own."

Dmitri swept out a hand toward the city. "Does it look like she cares for her own?"

Good point. "The lower city belongs to the Father. Or so I'm told. So why doesn't he help?"

The priest chuckled. "He does. He sends us, his devoted servants. Those with mage blood are drawn here, to the power, without knowing why. Some need our help."

Although Dmitri's austere sect didn't require total coverage that Martin was aware of, he'd never once glimpsed any priest's skin, only gloves, a hood, a cassock. However, the tight belt around Dmitri's middle hinted at a muscular body and thin waist.

Without warning, Dmitri stood, striding toward the high city. Martin had no choice but to hurry after him.

Leaving behind the brothel district, they entered the section of the city devoted to dining and drinking. They passed the Stone's Throw, Martin averting his eyes. The opening of Dmitri's hood swiveled Martin's way, then toward the tavern, but any hint of face remained hidden in folds of brown wool.

Oh no. The priest didn't need to study the tavern too long, lest he suspect things Martin didn't want known. Then again, if Dmitri and his sect had been watching, they probably knew Martin's comings and goings. He attempted a distraction from a sudden interest in the tavern by changing the subject. "Do you ever get used to it? The killing, I mean." Martin lengthened his stride to keep abreast of the much taller priest. Dmitri's gait never faltered.

No one could ever accuse him of dawdling.

"Do you find you haven't the nerve to banish the evil ones? Your actions speak otherwise." The tone held no mockery, merely curiosity.

"It's not that." Martin wracked his brain, searching for the proper words to explain. "It's just that, beneath the scales and strange eyes, when they speak, especially the one tonight, it seemed... more like a person. Before, I saw them only as killers, a threat to overcome. Now that I know it's not just a mindless

monster, it bothers me. Can they be reasoned with?
"

Dmitri stopped in the middle of the street so suddenly that Martin nearly collided with his back. "Do you not know what happened before the Father sanctioned hunters?"

"No. I never even knew other hunters existed until tonight."

Dmitri sighed, a deep, weary sound. "The Lady teaches the here and now, the day, the moment, the second. Little else matters. The god's teachings are steeped in history, where we've been as a society, how we've evolved, and the lessons past mistakes have taught. Before organized hunts, those creatures"— he waved in the general direction of the otherworldly being they'd recently dispatched— "were pursued by howling mobs, captured, and sometimes tortured for days. Our methods are more... compassionate. Then the mages were killed, save for a scant few who went into hiding. In time, the tales became legends and myths discounted by the common folk. Either way, *demons* cannot be allowed to survive in the land of men. Before you came to this city, a creature was killed who'd butchered hundreds in a single season." Dmitri growled, "His master grew far too strong, taking a share from the magic of those killed."

Master? At times like this, Martin wished for a deity to pray to.

Dmitri's sure footsteps halted. He spun, his brown woolen cassock swirling around his ankles. "In those dark days, I would have envied the Lady's children, for she encourages strong drink. Unfortunately, my lord does not."

"Where do demons come from? Why are they here?"

"So many questions. Do you have to know everything tonight? Actually, I should be the one interrogating you. So, do you have any ideas of where they come from?"

"No." Learning the answer might not be reassuring, either.

"And why do you stop them?"

"Because it needs to be done, and I can. I've met no one else but you who seems capable of seeing them."

Dmitri tilted his head at a thoughtful angle for a few moments more, his serious tone softening. "Come, Martin. Our duty is done for the night. Surely a young man like yourself has more to do than listen to a chatty old priest."

Not nearly chatty enough.

Martin sucked in a great lungful of air, banishing the troubled images he'd conjured. He'd been dismissed as clearly as if the priest barked an order. Never had Martin been so grateful not to be a follower of the Father and be expected to abstain from alcohol. A nearby tavern full to bursting of the god's believers said not all adhered to the strict dictates of their religion.

Tonight, he needed drink.

He resumed trekking beside his unlikely mentor, shrugging off duty in favor of more pleasing nighttime pursuits. They soon reached the parting point. On one side of the street, a marvel of marble and gilt glowed with an inner fire, light and revelry spilling from each window. Fanciful statues and curlicues graced the doorways and window frames. The lively strains of a flute drifted from the façade.

Lavish. Magnificent. One glance told of the Lady's power.

Across the street stood a startling contrast, a low, unadorned wooden building. No embellishments advertised its use, and save for the lone flicker of a single lantern, it sat quiet and dark. The Father's temple matched a deity whose worship hinged on frugality, discipline, and self-sacrifice, while the Lady's teaching promoted beauty, pleasure, and joys of the flesh.

Night after night, whenever duty and weather permitted, Martin had stood here. Had the priests witnessed his silent vows of revenge?

Dmitri inclined his head ever so slightly. "Good eve to you, Martin."

"Good eve, Father Dmitri." Martin bowed low. How odd for the houses of worship to face each other.

Only after Dmitri faded from sight behind a door did Martin recall the creature's words, *"He wants you."*

Chapter Seventeen

M artin shimmied out of his gore-splattered trousers and threw them into a corner. One of the housemaids would surely wrinkle her nose in distaste, as he'd done when dealing with the aftermath of his initial kill on his own. Though most couldn't see the creatures, they saw the mess and smelled the stench left behind.

He didn't envy those assigned to privy duty or cleaning but provided the custodians with extra coins for their trouble.

Coins most sincerely earned.

The maids smiled, took the offering, and never spoke of the matter again. The green slime on Martin's clothing bore no resemblance to their own red blood anyway. Invisibility worked on the creatures, it seemed, but not on their spilled blood.

He dampened a cloth in a basin and sponged off sweat and grime with lavender-scented water. Once clean, he selected brown hide trousers. The shirt he chose, of homespun blue linen, matched his eyes. Or so the seamstress who'd altered the garment for him said. No black clothing for him tonight, not when dressing to impress. Finer clothes in the chest at the foot of his bed and official guard uniforms awaited his duties to the high city. Still, mingling with the common folk meant blending in.

Martin tied his hair back with a leather cord. Dressed this way, he'd seem pretty ordinary among laborers and dockworkers who regularly dealt with visitors from many lands, even with his blond hair and blue eyes. At least he'd lost the nasal twang of a mountain accent.

In the upper city, particularly near the temple, no amount of money or finery would make any see him as an equal, except for Cere, likely not the shrewdest of individuals but likable all the same.

The Lady denied her servants only desires bringing harm—except to mages—or actions compromising her tenets of indulgence. In the shining temple her servants ate, drank, and indulged in pleasures of the flesh.

Martin rarely met her elite, the Chosen who hunted mages or delivered her word to the lesser folk.

Everyone was lesser to the temple dwellers.

People in the lower city worked hard days for clothes on their backs and food in their mouths. But street children pretty enough to attract the attention of her followers often found their station in life vastly improved, though Martin would have hidden from anyone sent by the Lady.

Wrongness seemed to pulse from the Chosen, and Martin avoided getting close enough to feel their thoughts and emotions. Once a street child entered the Lady's service, Martin never saw them again, not even on temple grounds. Maybe they avoided the streets and had a better life. Perhaps a fate far more sinister befell them.

Time spent hunting wolves before his life went downhill had built Martin's instincts for tracking prey, finely honing his skills at determining the danger of a situation.

Most temple dwellers were city-born, from elite families, cherished and raised in luxury. Perhaps bags of gold accompanied a novice's arrival at the temple.

The streets outside Martin's rooms held little interest for the Lady's followers. However, he reveled in the life thrumming through the neighborhoods, drank in the vitality. Reminders of village life before he came here.

The good parts, not the bad.

The mud walls of his family's house grew damp in summer rains and cold in winter when his mother stuffed the house's few windows with scrap cloth to keep out the weather. She could easily have stopped the cold sneaking through the cracks with power the neighbors didn't possess. Instead, the terror of discovery meant she'd rather endure the cold.

How awful to live in constant fear, not for yourself but your family.

More awful still to have no family to fear for.

Martin's living quarters were part of a large, once-elegant house, divided now into multiple lodgings. His walls were smooth gray stone, hung with worn tapestries. Instead of frigid water from a well, maids filled his basin with warm water. Steaming baths waited at the back of the dwelling, used by the dozen tenants housed here. He rarely met another soul while bathing. Of course, he customarily bathed long after the rest of the house retired and seldom took meals in the common dining room, preferring to fend for himself.

He wasn't considered rich but supported himself quite comfortably, and his living arrangements were grand by some people's standards.

Most of Petran's coins lay hidden under a stone paver beneath Martin's bed, along with money earned from finding lost people, pets, and possessions. Enough to buy a fine house or travel to another land where others might consider him wealthy. Neither option held appeal.

No, Martin waited. For what, he didn't know.

The worn patchwork quilt of his youth paled in comparison with the brilliant starburst pattern of the much-mended satin spread out on a bed wide enough to hold him much more comfortably than his humble pallet back home.

Though he lacked for nothing, thoughts of home brought an ache to his heart. The early snows would soon fall in the mountains, though the city's weather remained milder and would do so throughout the winter.

No. Not home. A place he'd never see again.

Because it ceased to exist with the loss of his parents. No longer was snow a mysterious delight, nor the spring rains a blessing. Life took on a hard, real edge, wiping away the wide-eyed wonder of childhood.

Martin opened his shutters, gazing upward to study the stars for portents. Though not skilled enough to read signs in the flurry of a hunt, pieces of the future revealed themselves when he paused to consider.

The books he'd read left much to be desired. Would Father Dmitri contact him again? Could Martin ask for knowledge? Surely the priest wouldn't reveal himself only to disappear again. Anyone who'd watched Martin for so long before giving such truth must have plans.

To avoid another unintentional massacre, Martin needed to learn the extent of his powers, and how to use them. How to control them.

The glittering lights in the heavens whispered no secrets this night. The Guardian held watch over the city, a constellation visible as the warmer season faded. The Guardian, a figure entirely hidden by a hooded robe.

Martin applied the finishing touches to his garb: a knife strapped to his forearm, hidden under a billowy sleeve, another in his boot. The temple stood in the best part of the city, where unnecessary guards roamed the nighttime streets in pairs.

His destination lay in a less wealthy area, though still a far cry above the city at its very worst. No one stopped him on his way through nearly empty streets. Voices carried from houses he passed. A whiff brought the scents of roasting meats or perhaps an herb-laden stew.

His stomach growled, urging him to quicken his pace.

Songs. Laughter. Snippets of conversation. Nothing of importance.

The night bird's call to seek its mate brought a smile to his lips. Happy hunting, indeed.

Sputters from the gaslights overhead blended with his footsteps over cobblestones. He stepped out of the way of a horse-drawn carriage, curtained windows hiding the occupants from view.

He'd not been designed for city living. Give him plains, mountains, rivers. Yet, every time he seriously considered leaving, something held him back. He strolled up the paved hill, casting a brief glance at the silent, dark building across the street before standing in front of the Lady's temple. One day. One day soon, the Lady would pay for the murder of his parents and so many more.

Martin gazed at the squat unassuming structure housing the Father's temple. Father Dmitri likely wasn't given to social calls. How did he spend his eve, working the coiled tension of hunting from his system? Prayer? Meditation?

Still, the creature's comment weighed on Martin's mind. *He wants you.*

Tomorrow. If he had to storm the Father's temple or appear in the capacity of a city guard, Martin would track Father Dmitri down tomorrow and ask. Then again, demons were treacherous. Martin's recent kill likely only said the words to plant seeds of fear.

Never trust the word of a demon.

Residual energy from the night's hunt needed slaking. Martin whistled while traversing the street southward with a spring in his step used for hunting men, not demons.

A handful of minutes later, he sat at the bar in the Stone's Throw with a cup of ale and a bowl of chowder.

And still didn't summon the nerve to talk to the tavernkeeper.

Chapter Eighteen

Peter stood on the dock, watching a ship's lights growing smaller and smaller. His heart ached for the *Seabird*, faraway ports, the adventure of the sea, his father, his father's crew...

Arkenn.

For a few indulgent moments, he allowed the memories to return: finding Arkenn, burned and broken, nursing him to health, holding each other in bed.

Peter rubbed his shoulder. The more time passed, the more convinced he became that his injury had been as grievous as the crew claimed. Arkenn healed him. Like Peter now realized he'd helped Arkenn's healing. May Arkenn be somewhere far from here. Somewhere safe. Somewhere fanatics didn't kill mages.

Had Arkenn found a lover, making a good life for himself? Did a ragged pirate's son ever cross his mind?

The two boys Peter found in the warehouse now nestled aboard the ship he watched, on their way to their new life, with a couple who'd keep them safe—along with their little dog, all of them much cleaner after Addie's tender attentions.

From somewhere, she'd procured an amulet for each of the boys. Coin helped. What would Da say if he knew Peter spent the *Seabird's* ill-gotten gains on getting mage-born out of the city?

Nothing stopped Peter from leaving. He could sell the tavern, for he'd gotten offers, or surrender it to Addie, but where would he go? Besides, his heart said he must stay here, for what he couldn't say.

A tiny flicker on the ship's deck could have been the older boy saying goodbye. Hopefully, the ship wouldn't suffer the same fate as the warehouse.

Peter turned away, making his way back to the main street, still bustling with nighttime activity.

A handsome young man caught his eye. "Eve', sir." He tipped his hat in the way Peter knew meant he'd put himself on offer. While men with men were judged harshly, supply and demand meant a plentiful selection of male night workers.

The man was slight, with light hair, and for a moment...

Nah. The man caught Peter staring and gave a languid smile. "Looking for some company? Someone to keep you warm on this chilly night?"

Peter shook himself out of memories. "What? Oh, no. My apologies. No offense."

"None taken." The man drifted close enough for Peter to smell his bathing soap. "Some other time, perhaps?"

"We'll see." If not for a full tavern awaiting his attention, would Peter have accepted the offer? How long since he'd enjoyed the pleasures another man could bring? How much longer could he do without?

He no longer lived with Addie, not that she'd have cared who he brought home, but still, word about his desire for men in the wrong ears could hurt business, which could hurt Addie, and hurt the young mages she found and secreted out of harm's way.

The night air held the crispness of autumn, bringing to mind lands where leaves turned gold, red, and orange. Then snows came. Snow seldom fell in E'Skaara. The trees here also never lost their leaves. Maybe someday Peter would go adventuring again, enjoy such sights once more.

Travel to lands he'd heard of in stories.

He cut down an alleyway to avoid additional propositions, taking a shortcut learned long ago.

Ssssllllllssshhhh! What was that slithering noise? Peter paused, squinting into the dimness. "Hello? Is anyone there?" A flash of purple flickered at the edge of his sight, gone when he turned. Must have been a trick of the darkness or perhaps a cat's eye.

If so, why did his heart pound so wildly? He hurried, quickly making the next turn.

And stopped cold. A figure stood before him, holding a lantern.

"Don't be afraid. I'm not here to harm you." A man's voice, soft and melodic. The blinding light kept Peter from seeing clearly.

"Who are you?"

"A priest of the Father. You're not safe here. Leave."

"Why am I not safe?"

Without answering, the priest brushed past, a swirl of wool sweeping around his ankles. Shrill whistles sounded from the next alley.

Peter took the priest's advice and ran.

Peter lifted the last of the chairs onto the tables so Addie could clean the floor.

"Nice crowd tonight," she said, clinking the proof in her apron pockets. "They know how to appreciate my... talents."

Not to mention her ample breasts nearly spilling from her dress. *My little moneymakers,* she called them. Then she'd cackle and add, *"Maybe not so little."* Yes, she enticed clientele, who left disappointed. Local prostitutes should give Addie a cut of their pay for sending the frustrated men into their arms.

"It was a decent night." Peter might never grow wealthy lodging travelers and serving ale, but he made a good living, a far better living than he had any right to, without the ever-present threat of a hangman's noose. He'd hidden away his father's legacy, using only when needed. Much went to the poor Addie helped. She didn't ask where it came from, and Peter didn't volunteer the information. Addie knew his previous profession.

Peter eyed the stool where the handsome stranger sometimes sat, all dark, brooding and quiet.

Something about the man struck Peter as familiar. Arkenn had blond hair and blue eyes, but the man who came in silently and left without saying much had too much width to his shoulders and appeared taller. No lovely mountain lilt added interest to the words, whenever he did speak. No, he sounded E'Skaara born and raised.

Besides, Peter looked for Arkenn and never found him. But, of course, in a city of this size, easy to overlook someone who traveled in different circles, even if blond hair and blue eyes narrowed the choices.

In his time in this city, Peter often swore he'd found Arkenn, only to embarrass himself when the person he approached turned out to be someone else.

His heart couldn't take much more disappointment.

Both past and present, Peter's professions taught him what to look for and how to study people. Yet, there was more to the stranger than met the eye, the way he balanced on his stool as if poised to fight at a moment's notice. Hard to miss the knife up his sleeve, or the one in his boot that inhibited the movement of his right ankle, the way he constantly swept his gaze from side to side.

The way he paused when his gaze fell on Peter, though not in an unfriendly way.

Assassin, perhaps? Hardly the first to grace this city.

Soldier? Guard? Some dangerous profession, surely.

Long, sturdy fingers gripped the spoon when the stranger ate his stew. Peter shuddered, imagining those fingers on his skin. For the sake of that skin and his livelihood, he'd best not get caught staring. On a ship, no one cared how men occupied themselves with each other. However, most landed locals followed the edicts of the Father, at least to a degree. Any regard Peter harbored for the stranger wouldn't be tolerated. Still, how closely could a former pirate possibly follow the temple's teachings?

He'd felt the man's eyes upon him. If only the stranger stayed until all other patrons left... No, such thinking would do Peter no good. No good at all.

Who was the mysterious stranger who hadn't divulged his name or spoken more than a handful of words? Although he spoke like a native speaker without mixing in unfamiliar words as many travelers did, he didn't share the locals' coloring or bearing. Perhaps a younger son, driven away to protect an older sibling's claim to the family's legacy.

Most left on ships, overestimating their abilities, never to return.

The man definitely watched Peter. Too bad he always arrived during the busiest part of the night, when Peter had no time to socialize.

And left before the crowd dwindled.

"I'm taking my leave of you." Addie pulled her shawl off the back of the chair she'd placed near the fire to warm. Though the city enjoyed milder temperatures regardless of the season, nights grew cold from incoming sea breezes, enhanced by the recent unrelenting rains.

"Shall I walk with you?" Peter asked as he did every night. In the beginning, when he'd only worked at the tavern, he'd climbed the stairs at her house to his small room, but once he'd inherited the Stone's Throw from Mitta and become a business owner, he moved above the tavern.

Addie patted his cheek. "No need for that. Any cutpurses are likely to be my kin." Peter locked the door behind her. A *squeak, squeak, squeak,* unmistakable to anyone listening, sounded in the rooms above his head. He'd rented to a bonded couple and two men claiming to be cousins.

The noise wasn't coming from the couple's room. If the crowd hadn't left the tavern, Peter would never have heard the sound.

Although Addie was no stranger to the goings-on of travelers, he'd rather not have her here to grin and make suggestions of him joining the lodgers.

"Meddling woman. I cannot wait until your nephews and nieces reach bondable age so you can matchmake for them and leave me alone," he often grumbled.

Addie always snickered, unrepentant. She never reminded him of how they'd met, how she'd rescued him from the streets and treated him like one of her own.

"Oh! Oooooh!" came from the ceiling, followed by silence. If she bore witness, Peter didn't even want to imagine what the saucy-tongued Addie would say. He shifted his rising cock in his trousers and fled the room, assailed by visions of the "cousins," one buried deep in the other's body.

His mind, however, chose to add those frantic sex noises to the visage of a mysterious patron.

The lovers were probably asleep when Peter finished preparations for the next day and climbed into his loft bedroom. Thoughts went through his head: the stranger, the *Seabird*, the boys he'd sent on a journey.

His odd walk back revisited his mind. The slithering sound. The priest.

The priest's words:

You're not safe here. Leave.

Could a former pirate and mage-born be safe anywhere?

Chapter Nineteen

Martin handed the tightly wrapped parcel to the temple clerk, arching to stretch his back. Today, a small delivery conducted on foot, only because the commander asked for this special favor.

"Martin! You're back!" came an excited voice from behind.

He should have known he'd not escape the temple grounds without being spotted. Martin turned to face a delicately-built young man with high cheekbones, smooth, unblemished skin, and copper waves, dressed in clothes far finer than Martin would ever own. The perfect, typical temple dweller.

Cere had grown during their acquaintance, nearly of an age with Martin, but still retaining delicate features Martin never possessed. "Come with me to the garden?"

As much as he'd like to truly be a friend, Martin must be careful, especially after Cere kissed him. "I'm afraid I am needed. I have other duties." Somehow Cere had wriggled his way into Martin's affections with his puppyish need for attention.

But yet, how could Martin resist such a hopeful smile? "Well, maybe a moment." Please let Cere not mention the kiss. There was no room in Martin's life for kisses from a temple novice.

Cere led the way to the gardens. Even late into the season, flowers bloomed. The paths were strewn with shining white pebbles, matching the temple's walls. Vine-covered arbors offered shade; ornate benches beckoned the weary to pause a moment, rest, and enjoy the meticulously kept gardens.

Or rather, beckoned the weary elite. Martin bet the tavernkeeper of the Stone's Throw had never seen anything so fine.

No other novices roamed the pathways, just an army of gardeners. Oh, how many working people it took to keep this temple lavish.

"You know you're attractive enough to join us, don't you?"

This old argument. Martin shook his head. "I have no use for a life of leisure. I like my freedom to roam the city too much."

"If you joined the order, you could stay here with me." Cere gave Martin a smile that likely lured many to his bed.

Cere was Martin's one regret, befriending one of the Lady's own. He'd only meant to infiltrate, not engage. A city guard and occasional deliveryman, he should have been invisible. This temple-dweller alone saw him. Acknowledged him.

So different from all the others, who barely acknowledged Martin's new rank of Captain. "You know I can't."

"You won't." Cere pouted.

Martin lifted his shoulders in a shrug. "Even if I presented myself, I am far past the age to be a novice."

Cere ran an appreciative gaze over Martin's body. "If you don't try, you'll never know." After a moment, his smile fell, as did his gaze. "I must go. Will you be back soon?"

"Yes. In a few days."

"I will see you then, my friend. Look for me?" Without waiting for a reply, Cere took another path, disappearing around a tree.

Without a kiss. Good.

Martin sighed, staring after one of his few friends in this place. While he didn't enjoy the gossip of others, he had no wish to alienate anyone.

The very man he wanted to see waited across the street when he stepped from the gardens.

Brown gloves, boots, cassock, and a hood hid every inch of the priest. Martin had never caught a single glimpse of skin. Likewise, Dmitri's accent revealed nothing—he could have been from anywhere. The same held true for the other priests Martin saw.

Martin's blue, red, and green uniform stood out in stark contrast. Not as fine as the novice's clothing, but he'd passed approval for leaving the garrison.

"Good day, Father."

"Good day, Martin."

"What can I do for you?" Let the priest speak his own heart. Maybe he'd see Martin's demands as proper payment for whatever he wanted.

"Walk with me."

Martin fell into step beside Dmitri, meandering around the side of the temple, stopping before an open portico.

Ah, so that's where Cere hurried off to.

Two by two, the novices paired off, facing each other in a spirited, quick-footed dance while an instructor patted out the rhythm with his hands. Twice, Cere stumbled, regaining his footing before the instructor noticed.

Martin stood in silence beside Father Dmitri until the instructor barked an order, sending the dancers scampering. Martin could almost hear their collective sighs of relief.

Dmitri nodded toward the now-empty dancefloor. "Did you know the dance moves they practice were once used in battle?"

Martin laughed, imagining the novices, dressed in gaudy, exotic bird colors, trying to fight. "Their tenets are against violence, are they not?" He shrugged. "Well, except for killing mages."

"Yes, but peace is fleeting, and sometimes a fight is required. Plus, they have no idea where the moves came from. Here..." Dmitri gestured with a gloved hand toward his chest. "Perform that last dance, imagining a dagger in your hand."

Martin snorted. The priest hadn't steered him wrong yet, however. He assumed the stance of the first move.

"Dagger," Dmitri reminded, pulling a glinting blade from his cloak.

Martin's eyes widened. While he'd used a sword to decapitate demons and concealed daggers on his person for protection, he'd never brandished one on the street in daylight. He took the hilt, eyeing the blade. Such a tiny thing. He glanced up at his unlikely mentor.

If the guards on duty passed by now, they'd undoubtedly have questions. What was the penalty for attacking a member of the clergy? Especially since Martin's bulk dwarfed the priest's, though Dmitri towered over him.

"Just because something is small doesn't mean it's not useful."

Martin resumed his stance. Replaying the dance cadence in his head, he went through the movements. Overhand, underhand... He clearly pictured what would have happened to his arm if Cere had managed force when his wrist met his dancing partner's.

Eyes wide, Martin increased his pace. Instead of air, he visualized a man's head, neatly kicking an imaginary chin, then whirled to slide a dagger between ribs had Dmitri not spun out of the way.

"Again." This time, Dmitri assumed a defensive stance.

Martin countered, recalling movements early in the set. Once more, his body fell into a rhythm, muscles flexing as he spun, very nearly connecting.

Dmitri danced away. "Again."

Time after time, Dmitri altered his stance, driving Martin to improvise and combine moves in new ways.

Finally, Dmitri stepped back, bowing his head. "Well done for your first lesson."

Martin huffed for breath, resting his hands on his knees. He'd never exerted this much energy on a dance before.

Though his face remained hidden, a smile came across in Dmitri's words. "You catch on quickly."

Martin offered the knife.

Dmitri's hood swiveled back and forth. "Keep it. You never know when you might have need."

Need? Martin never faced much threat unless hunting, when a rigid length of steel gave protection, and his own, less fine daggers offered a threat to cutpurses in the night. He'd long ago learned to discourage thieves with a mere growl—or a fist if they proved persistent.

Illusions of scorpions when necessary.

The blade of Dmitri's gift glowed, a sheen of blue, green, and yellow dancing on the metal when its movement caught the light. Runes ran up either side of the bone hilt. Such a beautiful thing to come from a plain-living man. Martin would have to invent stories of how such a fine weapon came into his possession, or he'd be questioned endlessly by his fellow guards.

Martin slipped the knife into his belt, angling the blade to do no harm.

"Walk with me." Dmitri led them away from the temple. No one seemed bothered by a man wielding a knife during the whole exercise. Had Dmitri somehow kept them from being seen?

Martin strode beside Dmitri. "Why do you watch me? Don't your edicts teach against fraternizing with those not of your faith? None of your kind ever tried to convert me. Why not?" He'd heard tales of priests accosting people in the streets, preaching the way of the Father, attempting to lure passersby from the Lady.

They weren't often successful.

A chuckle came from under the priest's hood. "It's not that the Father would reject your service for being a nonbeliever, but you have your own path laid out before you."

"A path? Ever since my parents died, I've been merely existing. It's like I'm waiting for something, but I know not what."

Dmitri stopped, clutched his hands together, hood tipping down. "I mentioned knowing your parents. Your mother was dear to me."

"Dear to you!" Martin whirled, the pain he'd kept for so long shifting to anger. "Why didn't you protect her like you did me? Why did you let her die?"

"Because she was too far away. I thought her safe." Genuine regret sounded within the words.

Too far away? She'd been brought to E'Skaara, hadn't she? "Not good enough! You're a mage—"

Dmitri's voice remained eerily quiet. "She's not the only one who suffered. During that time, hundreds died or took missing within a few sevendays. I barely kept the few who lived in the city safe." He paused and whispered, "Some I failed."

As much as Martin would love to hate him, Dmitri lost people too. "How did you know her?"

Dmitri turned away, facing the sea in the distance. "She and I shared a homeland."

"Where is that? She never said." So much about Martin's mother remained secret, but he'd heard his parents and grandmother talking late at night when they thought he slept.

A note of wistfulness crept into Dmitri's voice. "Someplace far away that we never speak of."

"Where there were mages, and they practiced freely."

"Yes. An enemy came in the night, so to speak, and we fled in every direction. Some came to E'Skaara; some took refuge in other lands."

"What happened to them? The ones who went elsewhere."

"Most were discovered and put to death. Those of us who survived took to the cloth. Who would ever think to look beneath a priest's robes for a mage?"

"Why didn't you hide me, then, instead of giving me an amulet and letting me fend for myself?" Martin nearly barked the accusation.

This time, Dmitri's calm gave way to a bit of a growl. "We chanted many a night over your amulet's creation long before giving the gift. So you see, we knew you were coming."

"How?"

Dmitri chuckled. "We're mages."

Would hitting a priest get Martin arrested? "But why all this hiding? Why didn't you just talk to me?"

"You needed to find your own way, and we needed time to assess your abilities. Though you were mage-born, how did we really know you possessed a useable gift or that you wouldn't betray us?"

Martin scoffed. "A mage betraying another mage."

"Sadly, it has happened. Now, come along, enough talk of the past. Let us speak of the present." Dmitri resumed his long strides. "The Lady's followers will announce the Chosen next fullmoon."

"Ah, the Choosing, when the Lady picks the novices who'll serve her more closely." And the ones who'll fuck worshippers. Martin failed to keep the bitterness from his voice.

"Your friend Cere hopes to be chosen for service."

Martin whipped his head around to face Dmitri. "How do you know that? And how do you know he's my friend?"

"I'm a mage."

Martin glowered.

Dmitri sighed. "I know he hopes to be Chosen because any novice who's been here as long as he is bound to want better things. Would you want to be a novice all your life, waiting on the whims of the more powerful? And I know he is your friend because he waits by the gate on days you're on duty."

No, Martin wouldn't want to serve the more powerful. He wouldn't want to be in service at all. "All those people around him and Cere still seemed so... lonely. He's asked me to present myself to the temple elders many times. I have no desire to join with those who killed my parents. Besides, Chosen rarely venture from the confines of the temple. I'd no longer hunt demons in the night, no longer be free to wander the city after dark."

"No longer be free to visit a certain tavern," Dmitri supplied, a touch of mischief in his voice.

Martin stopped, a chill running down his spine. "You... you know about that?"

"You'd be surprised what I know. However, there's nothing wrong with drinking among the common folk. It's a credit to your skill that they haven't figured out your true nature. Most of the folk on this end of town, well, let's say they don't hold most guards in high esteem. But I've often wondered how the Lady's followers can serve a people they do not know, save for those who arrive in fine carriages. We priests walk among the people, bestowing the Father's blessing on the deserving. We do not call the joining of two bodies worship. Joining between lovers is sacred, but still, not worship." Dmitri sniffed. "There's little difference between the matron in silk and the fisherman who works the wharves when it comes to finding paid pleasure. Money crosses palms to get what they want."

Martin passed a hand through his hair. "Cere says I look the part, but I'd never be mistaken for one of the Lady's ilk." Not with his lack of adornment and modest clothing when he left the high city. No earrings graced his ears nor bangles, his wrists. They'd cause too much noise, a constant annoyance to Martin's hunter soul.

"You wouldn't. Which gives you an advantage. You can blend in among the common folk. You've never shown interest in religion. You do what you do because it's right, not because you feel it necessary to appease some higher power."

Martin resumed walking. "Are we going to the docks?" The scent of salt air carried on the breeze. He felt out of place in his visit-the-temple formal uniform, drawing questioning glances from passersby on streets where he normally evaded notice.

"We're merely going for a walk."

Martin's hackles rose, but he didn't let his inward concern show.

"Sometimes, our paths are clear and direct. Other times the way grows murky." Dmitri's words kept pace with his footfalls. "Then there are those who aren't meant to follow the path but to blaze their own trail."

Did the man ever just speak his mind and not talk in riddles? "Something troubles me, Father."

"Oh? And what might that be?"

Martin sucked in a deep breath. After so many hours mulling over a few short words, he'd nearly convinced himself he'd imagined them. "The night we met, that creat... demon told me his master wanted me. Who is his master, and why would his master want me?"

If Martin hadn't been watching so closely, he might have missed the sudden tightening of Dmitri's shoulders. "Those were his exact words?"

"Yes." Ah, so Dmitri didn't know everything.

For several blocks, Dmitri said nothing, finally breaking the silence with, "I suppose his master wants as much magic as he can claim, and you have strong magical potential. But, Martin?"

"Yes?"

"Please be cautious when you leave home at night."

Martin stopped short. What were they...? Why were they...?

The tavern.

"Enjoy your eve. Meet me outside your dwelling tomorrow after dark." Dmitri reached under his cloak and withdrew a hide-covered tome. "Read. And practice."

Martin cast his gaze across the street to the familiar place where he'd spent eves, pocketing the book.

"Why have you brought me here?" Did Dmitri know something more than Martin's longing for good ale and companionship?

No answer.

He turned and found himself alone. Dressed as a guard, he'd never dare enter the tavern. Not tonight. Still, why bring him here?

He heard Dmitri's words again. *You'd be surprised what I know.*

Chapter Twenty

P eter put his hand out to grab a dirty cup from a table. The cup flew into his hand. What? He staggered back, the cup crashing on the hearthstones. The pottery shattered.

"What's wrong, Peter?" Addie glanced up from where she counted coins on the bar top. Her night's haul gleamed under lantern light.

Peter's heart lodged in his throat. He didn't just see that! He'd not been in need, when his power normally manifested. What if someone had borne witness? "Di... did you see that?"

"See what?" Addie resumed her counting.

He held his hand out again. Nothing.

Addie came out from behind the bar and patted him on the shoulder. "Peter, love, you're tired. Go upstairs. Get some rest, or better yet, come home with me. We'll share a pint by the fire like old times."

Sure. Tired. Maybe Peter imagined the whole thing or knocked the cup to the floor accidentally. Perhaps he should talk to Addie. But not tonight, when exhaustion scrambled his thoughts. He rubbed his burning eyes with his thumb and forefinger. "That's all right. You can go on home."

Grabbing his shoulders, the stronger-than-she-looked woman spun him around and gave him a shove toward the storeroom. "Go on, now. I'll clean up."

"But—"

"You heard me, now, go!" Addie placed her hands on her hips in a gesture known to strike fear into the hearts of stronger men than Peter.

It took him three more of her threats to give up and climb to his loft. He *was* tired. Motions wooden, he bathed in cool water from the basin, washing away sweat and grime. Tomorrow he'd take the time to visit the bathhouse. If he went early, he'd get fresh water.

Or fresher than usual.

Not bothering to don a nightshirt, he settled down in bed with a sigh. Sometimes, when he grew tired, he could almost feel the sway of the *Seabird* beneath his tiny bed, not much larger than his old bunk.

The bunk had been big enough when needed, however. For a moment, he indulged memories of a warm body in his embrace, brushing his lips against Arkenn's shoulder, and wondered, as he did far too often, what became of his friend.

No, not his friend. His love. *May he have found a comfortable life.* Still, Peter's heart ached for what might have been.

He yawned, frowning at the light in his room. Right. He should have blown out the lamp *before* getting into bed. Sitting, he reached... The lantern went out.

He jumped back as far as the wall let him. Had a breeze swept through? Never happened before.

Focusing all his will, he imagined a flame dancing on the wick. Nothing.

Yes, he'd made things happen before, but usually under dire circumstances, not day-to-day tasks. Or without his even wanting.

Maybe Addie was right. Peter needed sleep.

The river stretched out before Peter, the sun warm on his skin. The place seemed familiar. He'd been in the city for so long that he couldn't recall the last time he'd been alone in the countryside. Trees. Birds. Definitely not the city.

He strode along the riverbank, nowhere to go, enjoying the day. An overwhelming urge hit. He must hurry! Quickening his pace, he followed where the feeling led him.

A body lay still on a sandy bank.

Peter slowed. The body let out a low moan, so not dead. He drew closer. A boy lay there with light-colored hair, darkened in places by blood, dirt, and debris. The bitter stench of burned flesh hit Peter's nose.

Bending low, he placed his hand on the boy's shoulder and gently rolled him to his back.

The tavern stranger stared up at him.

Peter bolted upright. He'd thought of Arkenn last night, which explained the dream. But why the stranger's face? Then he noticed the brightness.

The lantern burned in the corner.

He must be losing his mind. Peter couldn't make objects move or light a lantern without a match. His magic didn't work like that. He'd put out a fire before but never lit one. What if he lost control totally, and odd things happened in front of customers? He'd be dragged away to the Lady's priests.

And then they might turn their attention to Addie...

No. He couldn't let that happen. Maybe he'd fallen asleep with the lamp on and simply couldn't remember. Deep in his heart, though, Peter knew better. He stared out his tiny window at the waking day. With bleary eyes, he dressed and climbed down the ladder.

"You're a sight, you are," Addie mumbled, rising on her toes to kiss Peter's cheek as she came in the door with a laden basket. "Didn't sleep at all last night, did ya?" She stared at him more closely. "And you're not grinning, so you didn't lose sleep for the only worthwhile reason."

Peter snorted, taking the basket from her hands. "You stay awake plenty of nights."

"Someone has to help the wee ones into the world."

"What do you do for the easy births? Hand the mum an ale and say, 'Push.'"

Addie winked. "Something like that, I'd say."

He followed her into the kitchen, placing the basket on the counter. "Chicken? Since when do you cook chicken more than once per sevenday?"

"Thought I'd give our guests a change of taste."

"We're in a port town. Locals expect fish."

"Ah, but your stranger isn't local. A farm lad, do you think? He might like a bit of chicken."

"You're changing your normal fare for a man who rarely comes?" Though if chicken lured the stranger in, Peter might have to build a coop behind the tavern.

"He'll be here tonight." Addie smiled.

"Don't tell me you're sweet on him." Should Peter be jealous?

Addie slapped his arm. "He's too young for me, not that I wouldn't like teaching the boy a thing or two. But I done gone and picked him out for you."

"Me?" Peter's mouth dropped open. Addie had become like a mother to him, but surely, she didn't know him that well. "What makes you think—"

"He's a pretty one, ain't he? Got that mysterious outsider thing going on. And those eyes! I bet if he ever takes off those clothes—"

"Addie!" Peter did not need the image she'd planted in his head. Now he'd never get any work done. "He probably won't even be here tonight."

"He'll be here." Addie hip-bumped Peter out of the way. "Don't you have mugs to polish and barrels to... straighten or something? Get out of my kitchen and let me work."

Peter saluted like one of his father's men, a former soldier, used to.

Despite his best efforts not to, every few minutes, Peter stared at the door once the sun set.

Addie brushed past with a tray full of ale. "He'll be here," she said, whisking across the room, full skirts rustling.

Chapter Twenty-one

M artin met no one while slipping out of the house. Faint lights shone from some of the windows across the street, simple lanterns or candles. For a moment, he envied those people, safe in their snug little houses, surrounded by loved ones, with no idea of what lurked in the streets.

Nor of the ones who stayed in harm's way to keep them safe.

Martin reached out with his senses, combing the area, focusing on a dark shape slipping from the shadows.

"Good eve, Martin."

"Good eve, Father Dmitri."

Side by side, they strode down the street, Martin resting a hand on the hilt of his sword.

"Dmitri," Dmitri corrected. "And you don't need your weapon tonight. We won't be hunting physically."

"How else is there to hunt?"

A chuckle emerged from beneath Dmitri's hood. "Ah, young Martin, you have so much to learn."

"I'm not that young."

"Yet I am ancient."

The soft soles of their boots made no clatter on the cobblestones, and their simple garb earned no stares. They were invisible, no one, unseen.

Keeping the innocent safe while they slept.

The silence became too much for Martin to bear. "The creatures we kill speak like men. Were they ever men?"

"Yes, and no," Dmitri replied. "Don't limit your thinking. More beings draw breath than you or I can ever know. Who are we to decide that only our form qualifies as men? Like most species, there are also females of their race."

"Females?"

"Yes. They are highly prized and rarely seen. They do not involve themselves in hunting."

"One said he had a master." Martin rifled through his memories of all he'd read in the priest's book. Some more powerful creature controlled the pitiful excuses they dispatched. Martin barely contained a shudder. He'd never seen a master. Had no desire to.

"He did."

"Have you ever seen a master?" The book contained some chilling tales of vicious, remorseless evil. Of course, the book also spoke of different "realms" and "worlds." What did that even mean?

If Martin could unread the book, he would. He could've lived his whole life not seeing the images portrayed in those drawings or reading the accounts of unfortunate souls who'd had the bad luck to be in the wrong place at the wrong time. The evil he'd read about. Whole realms destroyed. What was a realm? Didn't much matter what they were if something destroyed it, along with millions of lives.

He'd never known such evil until the night he'd tried to save a woman. He'd wanted answers, wanted to meet someone like himself.

Martin should have been more careful about what he wished for.

Back home, hunters sometimes found an animal or even the remains of people left behind by some monstrous predator. Had demons existed in the mountains too? So many places for them to hide. Maybe they'd been there all along, and any unlucky enough to cross their paths didn't live to tell the tale.

And died, never knowing what attacked them.

Martin slept easier before discovering the true nature of such beasts. Here, the priests took care of the deaths they couldn't prevent with their hunts.

Dmitri stopped, the opening of his hood swiveling Martin's way. "Not *a* master. *The* master. Yes, I've encountered him, and barely escaped with my life. It's why I and the other mages fled my home. Or rather, one of the reasons."

Martin shuddered. "If the master is so powerful, why use minions to do their bidding? Why don't they come themselves?"

"*He* cannot. There is a barrier he cannot cross."

"Why not?"

"Because of those like us."

Dmitri ducked down an alley, leaving Martin struggling to catch the priest's longer strides. They left the road, picking their way down an embankment until they stood beneath the stone bridge separating the city from the rest of the world.

Dmitri lifted Martin's hand to the bridge support. He ran one of Martin's fingertips over the smooth indentions in the stone.

"Runes!" Those were mage marks. If mages were considered evil and destroyed, why were their marks allowed to remain?

"Yes, runes. Most cities have them. Few would last long in these dark days without proper wards. Remote villages were never worth the demons' time. This city, however, is a gateway and the easiest crossing point. The wards were designed to keep outsiders away. Unfortunately, as you can see, they're failing."

"Who created the wards? Can they repair them?"

"One thousand mages created these runes. You wouldn't find one hundred with enough power in all the lands put together. We are a dying breed. And when we do..." Dmitri shook himself. "Stop asking questions. We have many more to check on this night."

"You never really told me. Where do the demons come from?"

"Did you read the book like I asked?"

"Some of it. It's a large book." Martin read until the wee hours and only managed about a fourth of the pages.

"They come from other realms like the book says."

"What are realms?"

Dmitri huffed out a longsuffering sigh. "It's all in the book. So read. And once you're finished with the first book, I'll bring you another."

"Another?" Martin had never read a book that large from cover to cover in his life, and his haphazard education meant it probably took him much longer than one of Dmitri's sect. "How many books are there?"

"Seven hundred ninety-four."

Martin's mouth dropped open. Were there that many books in the world? Surely, Dmitri jested. "Seven hundred..."

"...ninety-four."

"Why so many?"

"Mages fleeing my homeland each brought as many books as we could to preserve the knowledge of our ancestors. Only those remain. So much knowledge lost."

"Would the missing books have told us how to repair the wards?"

"Doubtful. But the ones we have will tell you something useful."

"What's that?"

"They will teach you how to use your magic. Now, take my hand. Don't let go."

Prickles crawling along Martin's spine, he took Dmitri's hand. Dmitri gestured with his other hand, up, down, side to side. The air shimmered. He stepped into the spot, taking Martin with him.

Martin floated, gently buffeted by unseen winds. Images flitted through his mind; some scenes could be from places he'd seen before, with beings similar to himself. Other images were bizarre, filled with strange inhabitants. Hundreds of images flashed by in quick succession. Where was he?

A tug on his hand pulled Martin back through the shimmering air to the spot he'd occupied beside the bridge. His heart pounded.

"Do you understand now?" Dmitri asked.

"Understand what?" The ground suddenly seemed unsteady under Martin's feet.

"What you saw were different realms, some similar to ours, others bear no resemblance."

"So, the demons came from one of those other realms?"

"Yes."

"What about the others? Do they ever come through?" Some of those creatures would star in Martin's nightmares.

"Sometimes, but if they're not suited for our realm, they don't live long enough to be seen."

"But—"

"Read the books."

Martin plodded through the streets of the lower city. Words and phrases in an unfamiliar language dogged his heels. Once mastered, they tended to invade the brain and never leave.

Night after night he'd trudged through the darkness, seeking out the hidden runes with Father Dmitri. They no longer relied on lanterns, though Martin carried one in case someone observed him. Now, he merely opened his hand, letting a round ball of mage light guide his steps.

Similar to the flame Martin's mother used to call for his amusement.

Mage light.

Mages. The power they'd had. How would it be to conjure fire when needed and make the rains fall during a drought? Mages were good. Necessary, even. Why, then, was the Lady and her priests so against them?

Every night, after putting in a full day with the guards and more with Father Dmitri or reading,

Martin fell into bed in the wee hours, too exhausted to think of naught but sleep.

Magic was real, not merely some story handed down. And magic lived in him as surely as it had his parents. But, even if he'd been given the great gift Dmitri claimed, he was still a man with a man's needs.

Perhaps the good father had noticed Martin's longing glances becoming more frequent each time they passed the tavern. Whatever the reason for a night's respite, Dmitri had given Martin an eve free from studies. Martin had no intention of wasting a moment of his eve off.

"Greetings, stranger," resounded around the well-lit tavern as Martin opened the door and slipped inside. The light and good cheer chased away the lingering inner chill.

Martin's head swam with symbols and sounds—symbols and sounds he should have begun learning long ago.

The large stone hearth occupied much of one wall, the granite indistinguishable from the walls, save for soot stains.

The tempting scent of roasted chicken drifted from the kitchen. Chicken. How long since he'd eaten roasted chicken? The garrison served mainly fish, or stews, or fish stew, or something better eaten without dwelling too hard on the ingredients.

Exposed beams displayed similar markings to the walls, bearing witness to their age, and steps wound around the far side of the hearth, leading upstairs to rooms for hire, no doubt.

Comfortable. Homey.

Martin usually only went to the lower tavern floor and never worried what else might lie in the squat stone building. His lessons with Father Dmitri instilled the necessity of paying attention to all his surroundings.

The barmaid approached, handing Martin a full mug of ale and placing a plate of roasted chicken with potatoes before him without asking his pleasure. "Aye, love! And welcome!"

A heavy iron pendant hung from a thong around her neck, perfectly positioned to draw eyes toward her breasts. Her profession belied her outward symbol of servitude to the Father. Something else peeked from her bodice.

A medallion? She tucked the token back into her ample cleavage. Interesting. He'd have to ask Father Dmitri about the woman.

Martin accepted the ale and added silver to the coffers, thinking, as he so often did, about Petran's brief explanation of coins.

He lifted his cup in a silent toast and drank to the boy who'd saved his life. Quietly, he enjoyed his meal. Oh, heaven. Was that rosemary on the chicken? Delicious. While eating, he studied the room but found no sign of the tavernkeeper.

Sipping on the finely crafted drink, he maneuvered his way around patrons to the tables in the back. No matter what tavern he'd chosen for an eve's entertainment during his time in E'Skaara, there were always tables in the back. Tables in the back meant games of chance.

Or so the patrons thought. Time to put his newly learned skills to use.

Did they not know the dice they rolled and cards they played had once held significance in future-telling? According to Father Dmitri, many former skills were lost in time by those who believed themselves no longer in need of divining abilities.

Martin knew a little about the cards. Dmitri taught him so much more.

About everything.

He leaned against the far wall, angling for a view of the cards of the two nearer players, amusing himself with the knowledge he'd gain that they never dreamed they revealed.

A short man, facial tattoos marking him as a sailor from a distant land, with too little hair and too much bragging, drew from a deck on the table. The black swan.

The man seated to his left drew the fallen soldier.

Martin sucked in a surprised breath, quickly perusing the surrounding area to ensure no one saw his reaction. No need to tip off a soon-to-be criminal. He eased his hold on the part of him that blocked out thoughts, focusing on these two men. Others' thoughts tried to encroach, but he pushed them back. The older man bore no ill intent.

The sailor? Stealing, cheating. He'd abandoned a pregnant mate.

These men saw only a game of chance. The cards revealed the future to Martin.

Play by play increased his alarm. The elderly man seated by the sailor stood no chance of surviving the eve without intervention. Though Martin didn't know these men, he couldn't in good conscience allow the unfolding crime to take place.

He'd longed for a legitimate reason to speak to the tavernkeeper, but tonight left him little choice.

Retracing his steps, he sought out the serving woman. "Fine ale," he said. "Might I give my compliments to the tavernkeeper?"

The woman smiled. "Why, of course, sir." Beckoning with her hand, defying balance with the tray of drinks on her other, she led the way across the floor towards a partially open door. The knowing look she tossed over her shoulder gave Martin pause. "I'd wondered when you two would get around to speaking."

Whatever did she mean? "His name is Peter?"

"Aye, sir."

A ridiculous question dropped from Martin's mouth. "He reminds me of an old friend. Is he from E'Skaara?"

The woman's open manner closed. Martin swore the temperature dropped. "Born and raised here, sir."

"He doesn't strike me as a local."

The woman spun, somehow managing not to drop the drinks. Martin had once seen the same fierce protectiveness in a mother wolf defending her cubs. "I suppose I should know, him being the son of my own dear sister, may the Father bless her soul."

Martin raised his hands, taking a step backward. "I meant no harm. I'm from a village north of here myself." Oh, how easily the oft-repeated lie fell from Martin's tongue, while the small ray of hope that had somehow bloomed in his chest died a brutal death. Peter was E'Skaaran.

The woman visibly deflated. "Apologies, sir. I've been told I'm a bit overbearing at times, her dying so young and leaving him all alone in the world."

Overbearing at times? While she wasn't a tyrant by any means, he'd established early on who ruled the confines of the Stone's Throw. "Understandable. You'd get along with my gran."

For a moment, they locked gazes, some kind of understanding passing between them. "*I mean him no harm,*" Martin willed her to understand.

Her own message said, "*Hurt him and die.*" Finally, she nodded. "You'll do."

Do for what? Martin reeled, playing back the conversation to better understand what just happened. One thing for sure, she'd put to rest any fantasies about Peter somehow being Petran.

The woman pushed the door open farther. "Peter. A patron would like a word." She turned on her heel and left Martin to stare in rapt fascination at the gloriously fashioned rear in a pair of thin cotton trousers, aimed in his direction.

The man grunted and rose, tossing a cask over one brawny shoulder.

Oh, my. Martin's mouth went dry. While wiry muscles weren't anything new on dockworkers used to running, swimming, and climbing, this man's biceps were nearly as firm as the cask.

Martin had seen the tavernkeeper in action many times before, but at a distance, or in passing, not close up. Not close enough to reach out and touch without having to avoid prying eyes.

The air grew nearly too thick to breathe.

"Excuse me." The tavernkeeper strode through the door, plopped the cask on the bar, and returned. "Peter," he said, inclining his head.

"Martin."

Laughter erupted from the tavern. Martin winced. No having a conversation in this din. He opened his mouth to request another venue when Peter abruptly kicked the door closed, muffling the noise somewhat, but leaving enough of a crack to keep an eye on the room.

And the card game at the back table.

"Sorry about that." Peter leaned against the far wall, impressive muscles bulging in the arms he crossed over his chest.

Martin gave a hard swallow past the dryness in his throat. What had he been about to say? Besides ample muscles, Peter's intense brown eyes drew attention. His dark hair, which burnished red near the firelight, appeared subdued now in the light of a single lantern.

"Addie said you wished to see me." Peter lowered himself on an upended cask, pointing to another for Martin.

Rough rock walls surrounded them, cool, and a good place to keep extra stock. A lantern hung from the wall, casting shadows upon the mountain of a man.

Wrenching his fascination from the enticing view of chest hair peeking through the open V-neck of a work-rumpled shirt, Martin recalled his purpose and sat down on a cask, politely angling away to avoid revealing his attraction.

"I told her I wished to compliment your fine ale." Martin lifted his mug in salute.

A smile lit Peter's face, causing squirmy feelings in Martin's insides. Still, something about the man seemed guarded, reserved. "My uncle Mitta's recipe and his father's before him."

Martin hated chasing away the smile with unpleasant news. "I discovered something while observing a card game at the back table that I think you should know." He sucked in a deep breath. How could he impart his news without exposing himself?

He kept an eye on the table through the cracked door, ensuring both card players remained seated.

"Oh?" The smile fled Peter's face. After a moment, he relaxed his rigid stance. "Is Old Man Farley cheating again?"

"I'm afraid I do not know of whom you speak. However, cheating pales in comparison to what I've seen." And what Martin felt.

"Tell, friend." Peter appeared all earnest intent, concern wrinkling his brow.

Ah, so Martin had been promoted from "stranger" to "friend," had he? If only Peter continued the sentiment after Martin imparted his news. "First, you must promise not to tell anyone what I know or how I know it." He ran a finger along the side of his mug.

Peter's throat worked. "Will anyone be harmed if I do?"

"Only me. Many may be harmed if I don't trust you with my secrets." The intended victim had a family, lands, tenants. He was a good landlord. His people would suffer greatly with his passing.

"Then you have my oath." The tavernkeeper pulled a leather strand from beneath his shirt and kissed the bronze image. An image of the Father? While his establishment served drink, forbidden by the god, apparently, this man chose the tenets he kept.

"You are a man of faith?"

Peter laughed, a rich, throaty sound. Honest. "Not really." He shrugged, palms up before latching his gaze to Martin's.

Not that Martin believed much in Dmitri's god either.

"Tell me this news of yours." Peter appeared calm, though clenching his fists gave away his nervousness.

Martin took a deep breath. "There is a man at the back table, a sailor, I believe. He hasn't the money to pay his debts and intends to rob the elderly gentleman sitting next to him. You'll find the victim's body behind your establishment next sunrise."

Chapter Twenty-two

P eter glared, narrowing his eyes. "How do you
know this? You wouldn't be the first charlatan
who came in hoping for free drinks or more for
fortune-telling."

Martin gave him a rueful smile. "You promised not
to ask me, remember?" Trust came easier through
Martin's observations of this decent man.

Still, Peter glowered. "I am a man of my word."

Martin took a sip of the excellent ale remaining in his
mug. "I read his cards, but I promise you, I am no mere
fortune-teller."

Peter rose and cracked open the door wider, gazing
out into the tavern. "The gentleman in question is a
regular customer. The sailor isn't known to me. Many
men come with the ships; they never stay. Most never
start trouble. But I've... I've felt something from him,
something unsettling."

"Is there a way you can quietly warn the intended
victim?" The less personal involvement on Martin's
part, the better.

"I believe there is." Peter strode out into the tavern, directly toward the endangered customer. Startled into action, Martin trailed behind him. "Ah, my dear sir, I believe you have had enough ale for one eve. Allow me to offer you a room for the night. I would never forgive myself if you stumbled in the dark and didn't make your way home safely."

Martin watched the sailor's face, the surprise, the anger, and finally, the realization. The would-be murderer raised his gaze to meet Martin's. Martin donned a knowing smile.

The elderly gentleman gazed at Peter with wide eyes. "Surely, I haven't had that much to drink this eve."

Peter smiled, giving the man a friendly pat on the back. "That's what they all say. Why don't you go upstairs? I'll prepare a room."

The tavernkeeper escorted the man upstairs, returning a few minutes later alone. Martin sat at a table, keeping an eye on the sailor. Eventually, the man rose, made his apologies, and stumbled in the direction of the back door and the privy.

Martin met Peter's gaze and followed the sailor. The sailor stumbled down the alley, circled back to the front of the building, and hurried toward the docks.

Having lived in the city—with all the curiosity of the young—for the last few seasons gave Martin the advantage over a ported sailor. He cut through back alleys, emerging in front of the man. "Where are you going in such a hurry, friend?" The gas lamps lining the streets gave enough light to clearly see his quarry.

The man stuttered to a halt. "What business is it of yours?"

"Because you left owing a good bit of money for drink and food, not to mention your gambling debts."

Guarding the city against evil meant evil in all its forms, right?

The man scowled. "Get out of my way. I don't answer to you."

Martin shook out his limbs, bouncing on the balls of his feet, warming muscles for the dancing exercises Dmitri enhanced into fighting lessons. He'd not practiced yet today. Why not now? "But you see, it is my business. Maintaining order in the city is my business." The sailor didn't need to know the particulars or that Martin's position as Captain of the City Guard only meant the upper city. He had no jurisdiction here.

All toughness and sinew, the roughhewn man reached inside his tattered jacket and yanked a knife from an inner pocket. Martin smiled. Now the game got interesting. With clumsy motions, the sailor slashed. Martin expertly danced out of the way. How could the man know Martin practiced these moves daily since learning them outside of a temple?

Martin pulled Dmitri's knife from his belt. Even after only a few lessons, the runes on the knife handle felt familiar, the weapon becoming an extension of his hand. Where he willed, the knife obeyed.

Martin twirled and wove, grinning all the while.

The man slashed.

Martin spun out of the way. His assailant's actions might as well have been slogging through mud. Martin sliced a neat line down the man's sleeve, avoiding skin. "That was your warning. Next time, blade tastes flesh."

The man wheezed, growing slower by the minute. He jabbed. Martin dove, knocking the man from his feet, rolling back to standing in one smooth motion.

The sailor rose a moment later. His shipmates might think him a worthy fighter. Martin did not.

This time, when the man charged, Martin sidestepped, trailing his blade down the path on the sleeve. A thin red line appeared. The knife hummed as though tasting blood aroused its appetite.

The man screamed, slashing blindly, unwilling to admit defeat.

Without really trying, Martin avoided each clumsy lunge. He didn't need to read thoughts to know intent.

He darted around his tiring opponent and levered one arm behind the sailor's back. The man screamed again, this time dropping the knife.

Too easy, leaving Martin barely winded. He'd hoped for a good workout, at least. Sour body odor stung his nose, nearly making him loosen his hold. "On what ship do you sail?"

"That is not your business." The sailor spat on the ground.

"I've already told you that it is." Power surged through Martin's veins, the thrill of the hunt, the pursuit. The capture.

The man struggled but proved no match for a trained fighter. Martin dropped his voice to a sinister murmur. "Take me to your captain, and we'll collect the money you owe. How you pay him back is your problem."

"Like hell, I will." The man struggled anew.

Martin chuckled; a rehearsed sound aimed to raise the man's hackles. "Suppose I should tell him that you planned to kill an innocent man to cover your debts." Martin turned the sailor to catch his horrified expression, feeling a deep sense of satisfaction.

Merchant ship's captains were a suspicious lot, unlikely to risk the Father's wrath by employing a man with blood on his hands, lest foul weather beset them.

The midnight hour approached as Martin made his way back to the tavern, money bag in hand and memories of a ship's captain clouting the sailor upside the head. A kinsman, no less. Not Martin's problem. He'd succeeded in his mission to protect the innocent.

He stopped short. Protecting the innocent? A tenet of the Father. For how long had Martin taken the mission to heart, never realizing his desire to right wrongs had as much to do with Dmitri's teachings as his own da's?

Light still shone in the tavern window when he arrived, though dim, and the great door resisted his push. Had he returned too late? Martin tapped lightly. With the tavern shut down for the eve, he didn't really expect a reply. Peter opened the door in trousers and loose-fitting shirt, apron discarded at some point, holding a broom in his hand. His eyes widened.

"Martin? You came back?" The flush coloring Peter's cheeks shouldn't have brought such joy.

Martin lifted the money bag he'd gotten from the captain. Peter's eyes widened even further. "What is that?"

"It's what is owed to you and yours." Martin dropped the bag onto Peter's outstretched hand. "His ship's captain is none too pleased but is a man of honor and made good on the debt."

"By the... Would you like to come in?"

"The hour is late." Martin glanced around the room, never before having seen the cozy interior free of patrons. Alone. Alone with Peter. The man Martin despaired of ever working up the nerve to speak to. He wouldn't push if Peter wanted him to leave.

But he had questions. So many questions.

And more than a little desire.

"We're closed, but at the very least, I owe you another ale." Peter discarded the broom against the wall and pulled two tankards from a shelf behind the bar. "Though I promised not to ask, my curiosity burns how you knew what the sailor intended."

Martin shrugged, weighing his words with great care. "I learned to read people a long time ago, and my mother always said drawing the black swan meant ill intent." Not the whole truth, but enough. Although the hour was late, Martin had no real desire to leave. Not truly knowing why, he stepped more fully into the tavern and closed the door behind him.

Peter gave him another dazzling smile. "Make yourself comfortable by the fire."

During his adventure, Martin hadn't noticed the cold, having shut everything else from his mind but his mission. He placed his cloak on the back of the chair and wandered over to the hearth, holding his fingers over the embers.

Peter returned with two tankards. The amber liquid glinted in the firelight. Martin's gaze fell on a deck of cards left lying on a table. Peter followed his gaze. "Do you play?"

"I have." Martin would never confess how long it had been since he'd viewed a deck of cards as a mere game. If he stared hard enough, he'd start seeing Petran's features on Peter's face. No, Petran was dead. Every time Martin thought of the hanging on his first day in the city, his heart ached.

Every time he tried to see Petran in Peter... What had he been thinking, again?

Peter sat at the table, expertly shuffling the deck. "Care for a game while we drink our ale? I can't thank you enough for retrieving the money. I run an honest business but still cannot afford for many people to walk out on their bills. Plus, by law, the man he shortchanged may look to me for his winnings."

All the more reason for Martin to have gotten involved in something he probably shouldn't have. He sat down across from Peter. "Then, by all means, deal. But, I must tell you, I don't gamble."

Peter chuckled. In the short time Martin had known him, the man laughed a lot, as attested by the crinkles at the corners of his eyes. He'd certainly filled the room with his booming friendly cheer during Martin's visits. "Neither do I. I'd rather spend the money on my business than lining someone else's pocket. As I said before, I'm an honest man. Honest men don't last long as gamblers." He eyed Martin from beneath his lashes.

The warmth in those eyes sent squirming sensations through Martin's insides. Oh, for those eyes to be turned up at him while Peter sank to his knees... Pushing aside thoughts best reserved for later, Martin toasted with his ale. "Truer words were never spoken." Did Peter even realize he closed his eyes, enclosing the deck in his hands for a moment?

As one would before a card reading.

Peter handed the deck to Martin, who cut the cards, then Peter dealt them four each.

Martin lifted his. The dove, the opening rose, the less-traveled path... The lovers.

Peace, new beginnings, a long journey, and the card that needed no interpretation.

Martin reached for the deck, stilling the trembling from his fingers as he lifted one card. The sinking feeling in his chest named the card without his even looking. The judge.

He was to be tested and judged, but what would be the outcome?

Unknowing of the pounding of Martin's heart, Peter calmly lifted a card and smiled. Likely, by Peter's estimation, the dove carried five points, the opening rose two, the less-traveled path one, and the lovers seven. The judge counted for ten in a game.

One more card to go. Martin took a sip of his ale. Maybe cards weren't such a good idea after all. At last, he lifted the final card: the black sorcerer. Dark forces lay in his path. Perhaps, but didn't they already? Just last eve, he'd killed a demon. Or was it the eve before?

He raised his eyes to catch Peter studying him, those startling dark eyes seeing clear down to Martin's soul. Neither moved. Outside, a carriage clattered down the cobblestones, and overhead, a guest coughed in one of the rooms. Martin couldn't look away. With every passing moment, his heart beat faster. Wiping his hands on his trousers didn't make them less damp.

He laid down his cards face up. Without taking his eyes from Martin's, Peter did the same.

To him this was just a game of chance. "I win," Peter crowed.

Which meant Martin lost. Judging by the images, he was bound to do so much more. Good thing Peter didn't know the hidden meaning of the cards.

Peter pulled a card from his stack and held it suspended over Martin's. A flush suffused his face. Closing his eyes, he placed his card on Martin's with a bleak smile. Then again, maybe he did see the significance of their choices.

A pair of lovers lay on the table.

At that moment, the patron who owed Martin a life debt staggered down the stairs. "Peter, might I get a nightcap?"

Martin sighed and drifted out into the night.

Chapter Twenty-three

S o close! They'd been so close! Then the man they sought to save interrupted.

Peter pushed aside frustration to ask his patron, "How much did the sailor owe you in bets?" He hefted the purse Martin left.

The old man scratched his balding head. "Let me see, about two silvers, I think."

Probably an exaggeration, but the purse could easily spare two silvers. Peter handed the customer his coins. "Here you are."

He shared a drink with his long-time customer, then the man toddled back upstairs to bed, enjoying himself immensely at getting a free room and a handsome sum in bet winnings.

Peter deducted the amount needed for the sailor's meal and drink. A goodly amount remained. If Martin couldn't be convinced to take it back, Addie would use the windfall, providing for those in the neighborhood who'd fallen on hard times or helping mage-borns leave the city.

Sitting at the table he'd shared with the handsome Martin, Peter stared out into the night. A priest of the Father wandered by, followed by two more. No business remained open at this hour. Where were they going?

The hairs on the back of Peter's neck prickled as he recalled the priest's warning. He had no desire at all to step out into the night. Usually, he enjoyed a walk after work. Every self-preservation instinct he owned screamed at him not to go out. He rose, darting outside just long enough to secure the shutters over the windows, then returned to the safety of the tavern, locking the door behind him.

Whether mage abilities spoke to him or his imagination ran wild, something outside needed to stay out. But what of the priests, in their brown head-to-toe clothing? Were they safe?

The one he'd met in the alley hadn't been afraid.

He snuffed all the lanterns save one, banked the fire, and made his way to his room with the remaining light. Martin was out there tonight. Was he safe?

Something told Peter that Martin could take care of himself. The money in the pouch spoke of his skill.

The lantern flickered, casting sinister shadows on the walls and the one tiny window of Peter's bedchamber. Surely he didn't need shutters over a glass scarcely larger than his head, up this high.

His bed creaked when he sat down, and he stared out the window, recalling the porthole on the *Seabird*, how he'd grown up in that little cabin, his father keeping him safe. He longed for the sea breezes, the slapping of waves against the hull, the gentle swaying lulling him to sleep.

He snuffed the lantern and lay down. It had been a long day. Spinning thoughts kept him awake until the wee hours of the morn.

Peter was moving, carried between two of the crew, staring up at the frantic eyes of his father. Why was Da afraid? Nothing scared him. The crewmen placed Peter on his bunk. White-hot pain shot through his shoulder. He'd have screamed if he'd had the breath.

Blood soaked his clothes. His, or someone else's? He'd seen someone die, right? The crew left. His father stayed. The captain should be on deck. They were under attack.

Weren't they?

His father spoke low, but not to Peter. Maybe he prayed. Only, Peter had never known his father to pray. Peter gasped for breath, every inhale pure agony.

When his father finished speaking, he left and closed the door.

Someone else was there. Who? How badly was Peter injured? Just a scratch, right? Soon healed into a puckered scar.

The someone sat on the floor beside the bunk, crooning, wiping Peter's chest with a damp cloth. The pain dulled to a faint throbbing. He looked up. The wall-mounted lantern that he rarely used cast shadows and light over the face of a young man, eyes as blue as a summer sky.

"I..." Peter began.

"Shh... Rest. It's going to be all right. Everything is going to be all right."

Peter slept fitfully, swimming to the surface of consciousness, only to plunge down again. The presence never left, calming him, wrapping him in a sense of security. Nothing bad could happen, not with this man nearby.

There had been blood. Lots of it. And pain. A shaft of wood sticking from Peter's body.

He blinked his eyes open and pressed his fingers to his shoulder. A scar. Only a scar. His clothing that night had been drenched in drying blood, as were his blankets. Someone else's, maybe? How many of the crew had they lost?

A young man slept on the deck by the bunk, one arm over the side, hand clinging to Peter's.

Peter squirmed to see who was there.

Sky blue eyes stared up at him.

Peter bolted upright, flinging the covers aside and patting his shoulder. A scar. Just a scar. He searched the blankets, but couldn't see in the dark. The lantern flared to life. He wouldn't even bother to question at this point.

No blood, though sweat drenched his skin. Sitting on the side of the bed, he buried his face in his hands.

It'd been a long time since he'd had such a vivid dream of his father and the *Seabird*.

He removed his face from his hands and ran tentative fingers over his scar. He'd been impaled by a piece of splintered wood. His father pleaded with him not to die. They'd taken him to his cabin.

Where he'd been healed.

Blue eyes. Chills prickled up Peter's spine.

A mage. He'd been in the presence of another mage.

In the distance, an eerie howl shattered the quiet. He extinguished his lantern and peered outside. In the street in front of his tavern, a lone figure stood under a gas lamp, wrapped in brown wool. The figure stood still, hood turned up as though looking straight at Peter.

Peter dove back under his covers. Lately, his powers had grown stronger, providing light, moving objects. What if he did something like that in front of the wrong person? Like a Chosen.

When he peeked out the window again, the priest was gone.

He stayed awake, staring at the walls for the rest of the night.

Chapter Twenty-four

Something seemed different, something Martin couldn't name. People seemed more subdued, the city holding its breath, waiting. For what, he didn't know.

He stared across the desk at Commander Enys. "What's going on?"

"You feel it too?" Enys dropped his feet from the desk to the floor, waving a hand toward the straight-backed, uncomfortable chair he deliberately put in his office to encourage some of the more eager butt kissers not to stay.

Martin plopped down into the chair. "Something is off."

"We're receiving more missing person reports than even you can keep up with." Enys handed a sheet of parchment across the desk.

Normally, the demons' victims, if reported at all, didn't warrant the attention of the city guards. Scanning the list made Martin's blood run cold. "Children?"

"Yes. Two young boys, aged ten and six. Dock rats, no parents." At least Enys's voice wasn't full of derision. He didn't mean the term as a slight, merely used the word he'd been taught.

Unlike most citizens of the upper city. "Who reported them missing?"

"Some of the other children approached a school matron. She promised to pass on the word, even though she didn't teach the boys in question." Enys gave a weary smile, reclaiming the missive from Martin's hand. "My niece, as it turns out."

Surely the demons hadn't started claiming children. Wouldn't Dimitri have said?

"There is no reward, but my Esmerla does charity work down by the docks and knew the boys. I'd take it as a personal favor if you'd look into the matter."

The descriptions weren't very good, two young boys with brown hair and eyes. No one even knew their real names. The street kids all went by nicknames, the better to avoid the constables. It could have been half the kids on that end of the city. Martin looked up. "They had a pet dog. Did anyone find the dog?"

"No."

Wherever the boys were, they'd taken their dog. Did they possess mage blood? "They weren't taken to the Lady's temple, were they?"

Enys leaned back in his chair, folding his hands over the expanding belly he'd grown in the time Martin had known him. "No one knows, but they didn't seem the sort that would appeal as novices. Too lowborn, not pretty enough."

Who in the lower city might talk to a guard? Oh, yes, though better not reveal Martin's position to a certain tavernkeeper who might be privy to local gossip. "I might have someone I can ask."

Enys gave a curt nod. "I thought you might. Usually, I'd send someone of lesser rank, but you've seen our typical investigators. They strut around, boasting much while accomplishing little. You? You blend. And you're also not of the E'Skaara nobility, with your looks. Those in the lower city might talk to you when they wouldn't talk to others."

Too true, especially since Martin's forays into the dock district made him familiar. He picked up the next parchment sheet on the desk. "How about this one? A countess?"

This time, Enys sighed. "Strike her off the list. They found her dead this morn, two blocks from the Lady's temple. No obvious signs of injury. She'd been there to worship two nights ago and never returned home."

The countess Martin had seen withering. Maybe she'd been drained of all vitality, her body removed from the temple to avoid scandal. "What about her carriage driver?"

"Driver?" Enys cocked a brow. "What do you know?"

"You don't expect a lady of her station to walk to the temple."

"Hmm..." Enys rubbed his chin, fingers rasping on copper stubble. "I'll dispatch an inquisitor to her home. You think her death might be murder?"

"Possibly." Though not easily explainable without Martin saying too much. "I have a friend at the temple who might know more."

"Go. See your friend as the temple is closer than the docks. Then ask about the boys. Most of the other cases can wait."

Martin didn't share Enys's opinion. When someone went missing, the faster the guards investigated, the greater the chance of finding them alive. But Martin couldn't argue with his superior.

"I'll go home and change. It's time I paid a visit to the temple anyway." He stood, placing the parchment on the desk. Though he'd love to be wrong, the death of the missing countess might be easily solved. But what if demons had gotten her instead?

"Shall I have the stable boy bring around your usual mount?"

"No." Martin shook his head. Riding on horseback meant official business and notice. Better not to draw too much attention, though simple dress stood out more than a uniform in the case of the temple.

On a stone bench in the Lady's courtyard, Martin found Cere, midday sun glinting down and shimmering off the fountain's water at the center. A statue of three maidens poured urns into the basin below, the falling water tinkling like laughter. The immaculate gardens perfumed the air with jasmine, gardenia, and herb scents.

Flowers that didn't grow in any other part of the city this season. Just the temple grounds.

Doves hooted from the treetops, and a guinea fowl wandered past, seven chirping keets in her wake. Here, even the fowl remained unaffected by the cooling temperatures outside the garden wall. As much as he hated everything the temple represented, Martin loved the gardens, particularly at this time of day when most initiates were about their studies.

He could take a few moments' enjoyment before returning to his duties if not for worry over the two boys.

Martin needed to finish here and be on his way.

What would Peter think of this serene place, used to the busy city as he was? What was he doing now? Cooking for the night's dinner, tending bar for early arrivals? Without a doubt, Peter wasn't sitting idly in a courtyard contemplating life.

Would he smile at the clumsy guinea keets? Would he put a gardenia blossom to his nose and take a sniff? Would he even recognize Martin, dressed in royal blue satin trousers with an elaborately embroidered jacket? Anyone taking a quick look might mistake him for a wealthy patron. When new, Martin's well-oiled boots likely cost more than Peter saw in a sevenday. Bought secondhand and embellished with Martin's newfound skills, they looked quite nice indeed but not nice enough to draw too much attention.

Alone. For a few moments, amid a bustling city, Martin was alone—save for Cere.

As a child, he had often climbed the highest mountain peaks, allowing him to stare down on the world from a lofty vantage point. Vast open spaces unfolded beneath his feet. No people. Here, people mingled everywhere. Rare was a moment of solitude.

At the time, he'd never heard the ocean waves, never seen a ship at port.

Had Peter ever seen the mountains? Ever breathed in the early morn mists or trudged through hip-high snow in winter? What would he make of Martin's homeland?

And why did Martin want so badly to take him there?

Cere rose from his bench and grinned. "Martin! I'd hoped to see you today." He paused and studied Martin's face. "Whoa ho! It looks like someone lost sleep last night. Good hunting, I take it?"

Martin hid a wince, though he knew the temple novice meant a different type of hunting.

Cere sat and patted a spot on the bench beside him. Martin sat. He'd never admit to watching Cere dancing, then turning those dance moves into fighting skills.

It wasn't an outright lie to make creative use of the truth. "Good hunting, indeed, Cere." Let him think Martin captured a lover during the hunt.

Would he have if he hadn't been interrupted?

A bit of the light left Cere's eyes. What? Part of temple life meant pleasure with other novices. This particular novice likely never lacked partners, spending his days in luxury. In contrast, Martin spent his days practicing with other guards, patrolling the city, managing the men under his authority, and consulting with his commander. Then he spent most of his eves practicing fighting moves, using those skills while demon hunting, and reading ancient tomes, trying to learn all he could about the mysterious mages.

Dmitri had shared something without demanding Martin's confidence. Still, there had to be reasons the symbols protecting the city weren't common knowledge.

Or why they'd begun to fail, allowing demons through.

"You must tell me all about it."

Martin detected a hint of jealousy in Cere's tone.

Martin enjoyed freedom others didn't have, or rather, didn't realize they lacked. Novices likely spared no thought for what might lie outside the temple or outside the market and better areas of E'Skaara. Martin mingled with the common folk, strangers from many lands, followers of the Father, and — tavernkeepers.

He turned his face to hide a smile. Tavernkeepers. "Don't tell me you'd prefer haunting seedy dock taverns over this." Martin waved a hand to indicate the opulent temple grounds.

Cere laughed, sending his ringlets bouncing with a head shake. "Oh no, my friend. You may have the alleyways, the stinking sewers, and the bad parts of the city where the common folk roam while I, myself, am safely tucked into my bed." He waggled his brows. "And maybe not alone."

Martin snorted. "When have you ever slept alone?" In the seasons of their friendship, Cere had filled out some but still remained lithe. And very attractive.

Cere slapped a hand over his heart, releasing a put-upon sigh. "We live such austere lives here. Why would I not take all the advantages offered?"

"Austere lives?" Martin pointedly raked his gaze up and down Cere's body, from his copper curls down his green brocade jacket, purple breeches, and green velvet boots.

"Oh, yes. As I tell my family in my letters back home. Would you believe that they actually feel sorry for me?" Cere let out a musical laugh.

Martin rolled his eyes. If ever there was drama to be had, he'd find Cere in the center. "And pray tell, what lucky man or woman found themselves in your bed last night?"

Cere stretched his long legs out in front of him, leaning back on his arms. The pose appeared so casual, a young man at leisure. Martin knew the stance for what it was: intended seduction, whether a conscious effort or not. "I couldn't decide, so I took one of each."

One of each? Martin would be content with one. The same one every night, in fact. Dangerous thoughts when such desires skirted the edges of the Father's religion. "Then lucky for you to be a servant of the Lady and not the Father."

"Oh, yes, very lucky for them. What about you, my friend?"

"What about me?"

"Have you been a good follower of the Lady and found a man or a woman to fill your bed? Or do you release your prey after capture?"

A good follower of the Lady. One who worshiped by indulging in pleasure. Well, Martin might certainly meet those criteria if given half a chance. He let out an exaggerated sigh. "Sadly, I read late into the night, alone in my room." True enough, if he mentally added "after I came home in the wee hours" to his confession.

Cere shivered. "I saw you with a Father's priest a few times outside the gates. I don't understand how you can spend so much time with him. He's so... sinister."

"Father Dmitri?" Really? Martin found Father Dmitri friendly if a little contained.

"Yes! He's always covered head to toe. Have you ever even seen his face?"

No, Martin never caught sight of Dmitri's face. "No, I haven't. What's it to me if he stays covered?"

Cere grinned, whispering, though none were near enough to overhear, "They say he's horrendous under there. No nose, one eye."

Martin barked a laugh. "He's far too keen of sight to be missing an eye." He dismissed the rumor, though why he felt the need to defend one friend from another eluded him. But, wait! Martin considered Dmitri a friend?

"Still, it's funny, don't you think?" Cere continued. "Do the other priests cover themselves?"

Martin thought back over glimpses in the dark: no triumphant flash of teeth, hand signals always given with gloves. "I've only met a few. All stay covered. Just the priests, though. The acolytes dressed like common men."

"Are they ugly?"

"What?"

"The acolytes. Are they ugly?"

"Well, the Lady takes the pretty ones, so all that's left is ugly, right?" Martin snapped his mouth closed. The acolytes were far from ugly, but they seemed to strive to be plain. Would they be beautiful in the finery Cere wore for worship?

Probably.

Until recently, Martin's unkind words wouldn't have bothered him. Now he felt the need to peer over his shoulder to see who stood there.

A vision filled his head of a very non-ugly tavernkeeper who followed the Father's teachings, more or less, with the pendulum definitely swinging toward "less" as of late, with his subtle flirting. Would Cere consider Peter too coarse for beauty? "The value of a man lies not in his looks." While Martin usually enjoyed conversations with Cere, he needed to hurry past the pleasantries and get to the true purpose of his visit.

Cere made a big show of an eye roll. "You've been hanging around those priests too long. You're starting to sound like them. But looks sure don't hurt." Cere laughed, reminding Martin of the youngster he'd been when Martin first arrived.

Martin saw an opening. "Speaking of looks. Have any new novices come in lately? One ten, one six, with a dog?"

Cere wrinkled his nose. "Dogs aren't allowed on the premises, though one of the Chosen keeps a cat."

"So, no new novices?"

"None." Cere rested his hands on the bench, fingers a breath away from Martin's. "They won't seek new novices until after the Choosing." Giving Martin a coy smile, Cere gazed up from underneath his lashes. "It's a holy day. The public is allowed to attend. Please say you'll come." He yanked on Martin's tunic. "This becomes you. It would be perfect."

The Choosing, already? Time had slipped past quickly. "I haven't thought about it, really." Though Cere occasionally mentioned the event.

"What if I'm like Aramon and stay a novice forever and never advance to Chosen?" Cere scrunched his face.

"He's not been here forever. He's only twenty-seven winters, you said." Still, Aramon became the fodder of whispers and a cautionary tale of what happened if the Lady claimed you but didn't call you into her special service. Martin sat through enough litanies from Cere to know.

"Yes, and anyone else not Chosen by age thirty usually goes home. He'll have to stay here because he has nowhere to go."

What would Martin's life have been like if he'd been taken to the temple at a young age like Cere? To never hunt. Never learn about runes and magic.

Never see Peter.

"Please say you'll come," Cere implored again, eyes pleading.

Martin risked much simply by being on temple grounds; entering the building during a religious event when most of the Lady's followers would be in attendance was a whole new level of danger. Still, one look at Cere's hopeful gaze made Martin give in. "I will if I can."

The humor left Cere's face. "I have something to tell you."

"What?" Perhaps a liking for another novice.

Cere bit his lip, gripping the bench he sat on with both hands. "You must promise not the tell anyone."

Martin laughed. "Who would I tell?"

Cere nodded. "I heard there were cellars beneath the temple and went to look."

"And what did you find?"

"A woman, lying on a table. She looked... she looked dead."

"What did she look like?"

"Blonde hair, lots of jewels. It was a strange thing. One moment she seemed young, the next old."

The countess? Had Cere volunteered the information Martin sought?

"What happens to worshippers? Do they continue to come back?" Martin prodded.

Cere tipped his head to the side. "Not that I recall. They come for a time, then we see them less." He beamed. "Always more to take their place."

Martin bet. "Do you know what happened to her?"

"No. I heard someone coming so I hid. They were gone when I came back out, and so was she."

Interesting. "Were they novices?"

"Chosen, I think." Cere spoke in hushed tones. "Oh, Martin, what if I'm not picked for Chosen? I couldn't bear to go back to my father's house. My family is so proud of me. To know I'd failed..."

Though the mere thought of serving the Lady made Martin's flesh crawl, he patted Cere's hand. "You'll be picked. I'm sure of it."

Cere's full lips curved into a smile. "Yeah, you're right. I'll be looking for you. You'd better come." He rose from the bench. "I must be going. Take care, my friend."

"Same to you, Cere."

Martin strode away. The temple sat on a hill, the source of so much power—power the Lady forbade any to use.

He glanced up at the marvel of stone, the crowning jewel of E'Skaara.

A place of malevolent intent. Like a stench, the rottenness permeated Martin's senses. Could he possibly convince Cere to leave this place?

Not likely.

He strode out of the gates, hackles prickling. Like evil watched him.

And still two missing children.

Now dressed for the lower city, Martin strolled down the street, pacing to keep up with Dmitri. Men, barely more than boys, lit the gas lights, one after the other. "What happened to the countess, whose body they found?" he ventured.

"A Chosen drained her powers. She died."

"Does this happen a lot?"

"No. Power is channeled from the worshippers through the Chosen to the Lady. The Chosen who killed the countess hoped to keep some of the power for himself. He's been drained and died. The others were told he's been sent on a mission, so no one will suspect what actually happened. The Lady's priests are a hard lot."

Damnation! And Dmitri managed the whole explanation in dry tones, showing little emotion except for a touch of contempt.

Would the same happen to Cere one day? "Will her death be investigated by anyone other than the city guard?" She'd been nobility, after all.

Dmitri slowed his long strides. "The Royal Palace is two days' hard ride from E'Skaara. As long as the city pays proper tribute, the king doesn't involve himself with local matters, giving magistrates far too much power. The woman's mate has not asked for an investigation, so there will be none. I'm told he's already promoted his favorite mistress into her post." Dmitri heaved out a sigh. "More than likely, money changed hands."

So much for the glamorous life of those in the high city. Commander Enys and his bond mate had no fancy house, and she walked to do her shopping, never riding in a fine carriage, yet they were happy. If she passed, Martin doubted Enys would ever give his heart away again.

Esmerla Enys would take the commander's very soul with her to the afterlife. And if she died under suspicious circumstances, Enys would tear the city apart to avenge her.

"Two children are missing from the docks." Why not ask Dmitri since he seemed to be answering questions tonight? Martin seriously doubted much happening in this city escaped Dmitri's notice.

Maybe Martin should bring all his questions here, as the priest seemed more current on gossip than even Cere.

"They aren't missing. Someone knows where they are and chooses not to share the information."

No one did cryptic like Father Dmitri. "Who?"

"Someone who knew they were in danger in this city and arranged to send them away."

Danger? "They were mage-born."

"Yes."

"Who saved them?"

"Other mage-born."

"More live in this city? Besides priests?" Sometimes Dmitri chatted on and on. Other times, he tried Martin's patience. Then again, if Martin said so, Dmitri might reply, *"That's the point."*

Dmitri stopped suddenly, nearly sending Martin careening into him. "Did you honestly think yourself the only one?"

"I've been searching since I arrived in the city. I've found no one but priests." However, Martin had recently seen medallions similar to his own. So, not merely a coincidence.

"You weren't meant to."

"Why not?" So much wasted time! Martin could have been learning!

Dmitri kept his voice infuriatingly calm. "The time wasn't right."

"Now you're telling me about them, why?" For a moment, Martin recalled how frustrated he'd been every time he asked a question growing up, and his gran answered, "*You'll understand when you're older.*"

"Because, my little mage, now the time *is* right. Eyes kept closed will open."

Something flickered at the corner of Martin's sight. By the time he turned back, Dmitri was gone.

Chapter Twenty-five

T he sun rose, the sun set, and after midday, rains
chased customers into the tavern, where they
enjoyed pints until the downpour abated. Still, no sign
of Martin.

What could Peter expect? The man's mannerisms
and speech marked him of the high city for all his plain
clothes. Surely a lowly tavern serving working folks'
fare couldn't hold much appeal over time.

"He says he's from a village north of the city," Addie
had said.

"North of the city" wasn't a good description, with
E'Skaara being a southern port.

Peter closed his eyes, recalling the boy who'd shared
his bunk. If this man was indeed the boy he'd rescued,
with whom he'd spent time on board the *Seabird*,
Martin definitely didn't remember.

Or pretended not to. Peter would keep his
suspicions to himself—for now. See what game Martin
might be playing. And how dangerous.

After all, he'd known Arkenn less than two
sevendays, with one of them in pain and healing most

of those days. But, then again, maybe Martin had better things to think of than a skinny, sun-browned pirate lad.

Longing not to be alone in the world could also create delusions. One of Da's crew spent two seasons stranded on a small island. When rescued, he swore a beautiful woman lived there with him. The crew searched the whole island but found no sign of anyone else.

Besides, Martin was much stockier of build than Arkenn. Though they shared similar eyes and hair, Arkenn likely left the city seasons ago. And wouldn't any mountain-bred men share similar traits, like the native E'Skaarans favored each other? Arkenn also spoke with a lilting mountaineer accent.

Even if Martin wasn't Arkenn, he still wouldn't pay someone like Peter any attention.

And why would he? You're a pirate's son and tavernkeeper. Nothing.

Still, night after night, Peter watched and waited, hope dying more with each passing eve. Maybe Martin really was from a farming village north of the city. How often before had Peter sworn he'd spotted Arkenn, only to be disappointed?

"I'll close, Addie. You run along home."

Addie folded her apron, flashing Peter a smile. "Are you running me off?"

"No? Why would I do that?" Why was the meddlesome woman grinning?

"I think you're about to have company." With a giggle and a wave, she bid Peter good night and slipped out the door, which she left open.

Had Addie lost her mind? Peter crossed the room, intent on blocking the eve chill. A shadow fell over the doorway. "I'm sorry, we're clo—" The ability to speak fled Peter's mind when the shadow stepped into the light.

"If I promise to help you clean, will you share a pint and a game of cards?" Martin pulled off black gloves and pushed back the hood of his cloak.

Martin. Dressed in black from head to toe, firelight washing over his high cheekbones and uncertain smile. For a moment, they merely stared at each other.

Peter shook himself out of the spell. "I'm nearly finished, and how could I say no to the savior of my customers?" Stupid, stupid. Why couldn't he think of something better to say? Why was forming words into coherent sentences so hard?

Wait. Had this vision asked a question? Oh, yes. Right. "I can do that." Peter hurried over to the bar, returning with two pints of his best. Thank the Father the pints hadn't come of their own volition when Martin or anyone else might see. More and more, lately, Peter had to hide unexplained occurrences.

Martin sat at the table, shuffling a deck of worn cards with nimble fingers while staring at the dying fire. Without looking at the deck, he dealt their hands. Peter took the opposite chair.

Oh, nice selection. Peter added the points, spreading his cards on the table.

They both drew one final card to place on top of the others.

The lovers and the joined souls.

Peter stared at the cards, then lifted his gaze. Martin's expression remained unreadable.

Although many used cards simply as a game, those of Peter's acquaintance often used them to divine the future, settle disputes, or make crucial decisions. Even the captain of the *Seabird* had bent an ear for those who read the deck.

How many pirates owed their lives to the cards when forewarning steered them around storms or away from harbors where they'd likely find a noose around their necks?

Until that fateful day...

Now, Peter stared at the cards dealt tonight; some he knew the meaning of, some he didn't. However, there was no mistaking the image of two robed figures, bodies twined together. No matter how many decks he'd seen, he'd never been able to determine if the lovers were a man and woman, two men, or two women.

Martin remained stock still. Why had he come here tonight? Though his clothes were designed to blend in with the ordinary tavern patrons, his bearing and state of cleanliness declared him of the upper city.

Had he come to spy on the common people? Had he come to spy for some specific reason? Surely Peter didn't still have a price on his head for serving on a pirate ship long ago.

Unless Martin suspected him of magery.

Peter swallowed, then swallowed again, fighting against the knot of worry gathered in his throat. Could Martin hear the hammering of his heart? Peter glanced up, then back to the cards. His eyes rose to meet Martin's intense gaze as though of their own choosing. There would be no better chance. The next few minutes decided fate.

Martin hadn't come here for a friendly game of cards or a pint of passable ale. No, he'd timed his arrival to when he'd likely find Peter alone. The intensity in his bright blue eyes. Ale couldn't ease the dryness in Peter's mouth.

He'd stood at a crossroads several times in life: when he'd rescued a boy and taken him aboard the *Seabird*; when he'd dawdled in the city and hadn't been caught with the rest of the crew.

When he'd chosen to stay in the city after his father's passing.

It seemed he'd reached yet another turning point. He could pretend he didn't understand, gently ease Martin out the door, or...

He could reach out his hand for what he'd deprived himself of for so long.

Did he deny the future depicted on the table and risk his destiny walking out the door? Or should he throw caution into the winds and act on the fantasies he'd indulged ever since laying eyes on this man?

Martin read the sailor's cards the night he'd saved the gambling patron and must know the portents now before them.

Lovers and the entwined souls. The heat in Martin's gaze spoke of his interest. Another like Peter, who desired men.

Peter took a deep breath and stood on the precipice, ignoring the chasm at his feet.

And leaped.

Chapter Twenty-six

M artin's heart hammered harder than when he'd been quarry. He wouldn't make the first move. The Father's followers believed cards were merely playthings for games of chance. If he didn't move, he couldn't pressure Peter into something he wasn't prepared for.

Something Martin wasn't prepared for.

He'd noticed Peter at their first meeting and caught furtive glances from the corner of his eyes. This was wrong. Pleasure with others was nothing new, yet Martin never dallied with someone he might want to keep around.

Since Petran.

Would he stop if he crossed this line, or might Peter become an addiction?

Martin had no great regard for the Father or the Lady, but he truly believed in Fate.

Yes, Fate saw the cards on the table. Some would say she'd guided them herself, she who controlled the world, moving her followers across a giant game board to exactly where she desired.

This could be no mere dalliance. If Martin gave in to temptation and followed the cards, he wouldn't be satisfied with one single taste. Like a tale he'd learned in childhood, of a man who'd found a fantastic tree while wandering in the woods, heavy with the most delicious fruit he'd ever tasted.

The man took a few fruits back home, only to find an empty sack when he reached his village. He spent the rest of his days searching for the tree. Nothing he ate ever satisfied him again.

Would that be the story of Martin's life if he joined his mouth, his body, to Peter's?

As one, they stood. Peter stepped forward, raising a trembling hand to Martin's cheek. Fire flashed across Martin's skin wherever the fingers touched. Eyes as dark as a midnight sea searched Martin's face. A hard swallow didn't dislodge the lump in his throat.

At last, Peter said, "It appears the cards have named us lovers."

No card game anymore, their cards remained on the table, points untallied.

Martin froze, unable to move. He knew the next movement of the dance, should have stepped back, should have paused longer to consider the consequences of their actions, shouldn't have even come here to begin with. But no, he'd returned; he'd read his destiny in the cards. Too late now.

Peter brought his lips to Martin's ear. "A secret for a secret." The warmth of his breath drew prickles on the back of Martin's neck.

A secret for a secret. Martin read cards, but they both wanted men.

Martin lost before the battle truly began, leaning forward and brushing his lips against Peter's. The clench of his heart said the cards were right. Lacing his fingers in dark hair, Martin held Peter in place while plundering his mouth.

With the flick of a fingertip, he created a ward, something he'd recently mastered with Dmitri. Anyone coming near would feel the compulsion to look some other way. Not invisible, but hidden all the same.

Peter flinched, but only for a moment. He moaned, bringing his other hand to cup Martin's face between his palms. He remained passive, allowing Martin to explore his mouth for a moment. Had Martin misread the situation?

One gentle swipe of his tongue, then another, brought Peter into the dance. Tentative. Unsure... Innocent?

Martin stepped back. "Did I merely startle you, or are you unused to such attention?"

Peter said nothing, but the rapid pounding of the pulse point in his neck betrayed him.

Oh, he was a man of the Father, even if he didn't follow all the tenets. Martin offered him a way out. "I could leave, pretend I never was here, never come back."

"This isn't a good idea," Peter replied, voice trembling. However, he didn't release his hold.

Parts of Martin tried to tell him that this *was* a good idea. A good idea indeed.

Grabbing his cloak from the back of the chair, Martin wrested free of Peter's grasp. A surprisingly firm grip clutched his arm and spun him. Before he knew what happened, Peter connected their mouths again, invading, conquering, and kissing Martin like a drowning man clinging to a lifeline.

The kiss sealed both their fates.

Martin pulled away, downing a mouthful of ale to aid his suddenly dry mouth, and held out his hand. No going back now. He'd seen his future. To be sure, he eyed Peter's cards: the novice, the watcher, the port, the lovers, the condemned man.

The novice: If not a virgin, then a man unskilled in the art of love. The watcher: the one destined to wait, though for what remained unknown. The port: an easy card to understand. Already Peter had established himself as solid and dependable. A port in a storm. The lovers. The condemned man: the one who couldn't escape fate.

Martin closed his eyes and blew out a breath.

Peter circuited the room, snuffing lanterns one by one. Finally, the last, he lifted from the mantelpiece and offered Martin his free hand.

May whatever forces guided Martin's path forgive him. He laced his fingers with Peter's and allowed the lover the cards granted to guide him.

Peter led Martin, not upstairs to the rooms overhead, but to the storeroom where they'd first spoken. He let go of Martin's hand, a note of apology on his lips, and climbed a corner ladder with one hand, disappearing through a square hole in the ceiling with the lantern.

The storeroom darkened.

Martin should go. Run back to his own rooms. If he wanted mere release, any number of men would welcome him into their beds. Though he wasn't wealthy or well-bred, many of the upper parts of the city liked a little danger in the night.

Or he could go to the barracks and choose from among their ranks. Though men with men or women with women wasn't openly accepted, guards often chose to turn a blind eye.

Why, then, was he here? What advantage did this humble working man with callused hands have over the most beautiful young men and women in the city?

Instead of running, Martin climbed, nearly hitting his head on the sloped ceiling. They must be under the building's eaves.

The room paled in comparison to Martin's rooms, with a rough-hewn wooden bed, likely supported by ropes, and what had to be a feather mattress, possibly chicken, as goose feathers were saved for those who could afford the best.

The blankets were worn but serviceable. Clothes hung from the rafters, a spare pair of trousers and a shirt. A small keg served as a table, holding socks, a bone needle, and thread. Peter did his own darning.

Herbs drying from the rafters perfumed the space with lavender, a far cry from the dried blooms sewn inside linen squares found in the marketplace to sweeten clothes chests.

"It's not much." Peter inspected the floor, prompting Martin to follow suit. Plain brown boards smoothed by seasons of foot travel. A worn rag rug took up space by the bed, easier on the feet during cold winter morns than wood.

"I'm not here to see your room." Kissing Peter seemed both stupid and the best idea ever. No need to fight. Martin wanted this man for more reasons than he cared to name. The cards had spoken. He'd worry about tomorrow tomorrow.

Until then, he'd make the most of the hours until dawn.

He melded himself to Peter, taking in the scent of ale and smoked meat, soap, and sweat. Honest sweat from an honest day's work.

Peter's hands weren't soft, he didn't smell of perfume, and his clothes' rough fabric would chafe the sensitive skin of some of the upper city lovers Martin had taken.

For Martin, a hunter, the soft life held no appeal, nor pretty, stylish fops with practiced words and empty promises. Good enough for a tumble, but nothing he'd keep around.

Once more, Peter cupped Martin's face in rough hands, brushing a light touch of lips across Martin's.

Martin melted into the kiss, fumbling with Peter's shirt. The soft rustle of fabric sounded abnormally loud in the otherwise quiet room.

The lantern painted the ridges and muscles of Peter's body in shadows and light.

Martin ran his hand over Peter's shoulders and chest, exploring, sending feather-light touches over smooth skin, raising goose flesh, or slowing his progress to explore the long scar on Peter's shoulder. He froze, attention riveted to Peter's face.

The scar.

Like a spell breaking, Martin finally saw, truly saw the man before him. Why hadn't he known before? Something as plain as the nose on his face.

Because, my little mage, now the time is right. Eyes kept closed will now open.

The realization sent Martin reeling. He steadied himself with a hand on the wall. "Petran? I... I thought you were dead. They said... they said they'd killed the entire crew of the *Seabird.*"

Peter gave him a sad smile. "I thought maybe you didn't remember me. Or didn't want to. We didn't know each other long, and I wasn't sure it was you. My mind clouded when I thought of you." He waved a hand, indicating Martin's body. "You've changed."

"As have you. Oh, damnation, Petran. I thought you were dead!" Martin pulled Peter to him, burying his face in Peter's neck.

Peter wrapped Martin in his arms, holding him through the sobs. "Shh... I didn't go directly back to the ship that day. My da and the crew were arrested while I wandered the streets." He ran a finger over Martin's cheek. "For many moons, I stayed hidden, until taking work here. I didn't know if you'd forgotten me or didn't want to admit we'd known each other, or if it was really you... Arkenn."

Shock. Horror. All the seasons Martin dreamed of this man, of a horrible end. They held each other, loneliness dissolving like they'd never been apart.

"It really is you." Martin gave Peter one last hard embrace and pulled back. "Your hair..." He touched a dark curl.

"Dyed. Addie found me, took pity on me, cut my hair, told me to leave the city. But..." Peter cast his gaze downward. "But I couldn't leave E'Skaara, not when I stood even a small chance of meeting you again. I found work. A purpose."

"Addie said you were born here in E'Skaara. That you were her nephew."

Peter gave a sly smile. "That's what she's said since the day we met. To protect me."

Captain Jaed Three-fingers had foretold Martin being drawn to Petran—Peter. And he had been. He simply hadn't understood at the time.

The time wasn't right.

"I wasn't sure if I recognized you, but even if it was you, I didn't know if you wanted to acknowledge once being friends with a pirate."

"Not a pirate. You were never a pirate." Martin lifted the charm hanging from Peter's neck, similar to his own and the one his mother once wore.

Similar to the one the barmaid wore.

Mage-born. Peter was mage-born and wore an amulet designed to hide him from those who might otherwise sense his magic.

Which might be why Martin hadn't recognized him. Then again, Dmitri's words implied the Father blinded Martin to the truth. If he'd known about Petran before, they might have fled someplace safe.

Not fulfilled whatever destiny Dmitri hinted at.

The truth registered. Peter's father had hidden him on a pirate ship, keeping him from stressful situations like raids and fighting to avoid his accidental use of magic.

Like Martin's parents had attempted to hide him. He'd love to remove both pendants and feel their power combine.

The lovers. The card didn't mean they would become lovers, but that they were already. Two lovers. Reunited. They came together in a flurry of mouths and hands, breath mingling.

The buttons at first defied Martin's fingers, their trembling rendering them nearly useless. At last, he removed his shirt.

The coarseness of Peter's fingers should have irritated Martin's skin, but instead, they shot fire straight to parts of him long immune to the allure of others. His skin burned, craving each touch—yet every touch left him longing for more.

Though Peter's caresses were tentative, the bulge in his trousers said he desired too.

For a moment, Martin clearly imagined the card: the novice. A man likely unskilled in the joys of the flesh. A man who desired men, living in a community where such was unaccepted, likely avoided the risks of following through on his passions.

Had what little they'd done aboard the *Seabird* been Peter's only experience with another man? Or was it Martin alone who caused Peter's nervousness?

No time like the present to discover the man's secrets.

A secret for a secret.

Martin sank to the floor, employing grace acquired from hours spent learning dance and fighting moves. Peter gasped, jerking back. Martin gripped slender hips, pressing his face against the hard column of flesh straining inside the confines of Peter's trousers. Long, slender, but substantial, in perfect proportion to the rest of Peter's body. The masculine scent of him swelled Martin's cock further. What an enticing smell. He breathed deeply.

Unlacing the ties on Peter's trousers, Martin buried his face in rough curls.

Peter stiffened above him. "We mustn't!" he hissed.

Martin drew back, sorrowfully leaving the wondrous part of Peter he hoped to get better acquainted with. "Why mustn't we?"

"The... the Father forbids it."

"Yet you don't follow the faith."

"I do not." Peter deflated.

"You've not done this before?"

"Yes, but with... well..."

"Street workers?"

Peter paused a moment before nodding. "And sailors. Here for only a few hours."

"Is it perhaps that you do not want this with me?" Martin traced his lips over Peter's hip, pressing kisses to trembling thighs. Peter's hardness naysaid Martin's question, but the shy ones needed room to make up their own minds.

Peter? Shy? Where was the fearless pirate lad Martin remembered so fondly?

Hiding in plain sight. Keeping his head down. Not drawing undue attention.

If Peter changed his mind, all for the better, as Martin lacked the power of will to walk away.

"I do... I mean."

"That's all either of us needs to know." Martin opened his mouth, taking Peter deeply, ending any hope of returning to his life unchanged.

When he pulled away, Peter murmured low, "If we do this, I won't be able to let you go."

For a moment, panic threatened, then vanished. Petran. Peter. One and the same. And somehow, Martin had been blocked from seeing the truth until now. Here. All alone. No, he'd not be able to let go either.

How he'd cried for this boy. No, not a boy. Not anymore.

Peter gasped, gripping Martin's head, but didn't push away, instead burying his fingers in the strands of Martin's hair, rocking his hips ever so slightly.

Martin grinned around his mouthful.

"Yes," Peter hissed, cupping the back of Martin's head.

With a chuckle guaranteed to add vibration, Martin resumed showing Peter what a mouth could do.

Peter groaned, legs shaking.

The taste of Peter shot flames to Martin's groin, the touch of shyness threatening Martin's skilled moves. He longed to please, see his card-destined lover come undone by his touch. How had such a gentle soul come from a pirate background and remained so untainted by life? At least by Martin's worldly standards.

When they'd met, Martin had been the sheltered village lad, Peter the well-traveled, who spoke several languages, read books for fun—had been the more sophisticated of the two.

They'd somehow switched places during their time in E'Skaara.

"I'm going to..." Peter gasped.

Oh, no, he didn't. Martin pressed behind Peter's balls, yanking his mouth back.

"No!" Peter whimpered, hips bucking.

Martin did his best not to laugh. Ah, how sweet Peter was, wanting, not quite bold enough to ask for release.

Martin rose to his feet, wrapped his arm around Peter, and slowly, slowly, brought him to the bed while maintaining a sensual play of tongue against tongue. He urged Peter onto the mattress, then climbed on top, supporting his weight on his arms.

Grinding against a firm thigh, Martin's cock hardened to the point of pain. If he didn't get relief soon... He opened his trousers and pulled out his cock to rub against Peter's.

Peter brushed his hands lightly over Martin's ass, then jerked his hands away. "May I?"

Laughing, Martin clasped Peter's hand and returned it to the round globe of his ass. "You may do anything to me that you like."

The time for words ended. Peter explored Martin's body with nips, bites, licks, and kisses. Martin held back, not wanting to scare his reticent lover away with too much too soon.

His mind flashed to a cramped cabin, two young men twisted together on a tiny bunk.

How could this be Petran, here, now? When so long, Martin imagined him lost forever. But oh, how he ached for this man in his arms. Ached to bury himself to the hilt in Peter's muscular ass, do what Martin hadn't known to ask for in their youth.

Leave a lasting impression.

"I've not kissed anyone in seasons," Peter whispered. "Not since you."

Sadly, Martin couldn't say the same. "Then I'd better make this good." He claimed Peter's mouth again, skimming his hands down Peter's hard, sleekly muscled body, all plains and angles. A day's growth of whiskers tickled Martin's face.

He hadn't brought any oil, not expecting to see his fantasies realized. Likely Peter kept cooking oil in the tavern but no leaving the bed to hunt.

Gathering the drops at the tip of Peter's cock, Martin worked his hand around both their shafts, shoving into his hand.

"Wha..." Furrows appeared between Peter's brow. "Oh," he said on a sharp exhale. "I didn't..."

Martin silenced him with a kiss. Rocking down, Martin met Peter's upward thrusts, reveling in his scent, the feel of him, those fathomless brown eyes, tugging Martin down, where he might drown if not careful.

Normally, he'd practice the art of coupling, engage every lesson he'd been taught, to have those lessons returned, seeking release devoid of passion.

What Peter lacked in skill, he more than made up in enthusiasm, moaning out garbled words—some in what sounded like other languages—urging Martin on. No one ever responded so sincerely, shooting flames of lust straight through Martin.

Peter cried out, bucking in reckless abandon. Martin's grip slid more easily. Oh, damnation! "Ah, ah, ah!" Lightning wracked his body, filling his mind with stars and light. Ecstasy coursed over him like a storm tide, leaving him winded, sated, and wrung out.

Static crackled along his skin, energy dancing between Martin and his lover. Yes, his lover. Then. Now. No time to think of the future at the moment.

That was... That was...

Martin collapsed onto the narrow bed. Stars danced behind his closed eyelids. Aftershocks shook his body. What had just happened? He'd never lost control before. Lovemaking, like everything else, required precision and skillful motions.

Yet this man, this simple man, bypassed all Martin's experience. He lay on his back, panting, trying to reassert control over his body.

Petra... No. Peter. Peter didn't move. Oh. Poor fellow likely didn't know what to do now. On a whim, Martin rolled over, nestling against Peter's firm side.

Peter relaxed and exhaled. "That was good."

Martin chuckled. Not the usual sweet praise, but any word in Peter's voice made Martin's heart soar. The words were spoken on a surprised laugh, not by rote, and with just the two of them, sated after sex, Peter's tension eased, making him sound more like his old self.

The boy Martin now realized he'd fallen in love with seasons upon seasons ago.

And loved still.

He really should redress and get back to his own rooms. Yet the modest bed offered comfort his much larger bed in his much larger bedroom did not.

Here on Peter's small cot, Martin could freely recall the rocking ship, the two of them tangled together, treasuring every moment, knowing they had so few remaining before they'd part for good.

Rain pattered against the roof. He had no desire to be soaked through out on the streets nor draw undue attention by hiring a carriage if he managed to find one this late.

Shifting into a more comfortable position allowed him to capture more of Peter's warmth. Martin might as well admit the truth: it wasn't the rain or fear of discovery keeping him in this bed.

Peter tightened an arm around him. "It's pouring outside. Stay the night?"

Martin shouldn't. He really shouldn't.

Peter kissed him again. Umm... Why did he need to leave again?

They wriggled free from the rest of their clothing and cleaned themselves at the basin in the corner of the room. A moment after Peter doused the lantern, what Martin saw registered in his mind.

The scar on Peter's shoulder.

From a wound healed by magic. A wound Martin healed by magic. Had their healing each other tied them together in some way?

With Peter in his arms, Martin slipped into sleep.

He woke early, drinking his fill of the man sleeping peacefully on the bed, imagining the tangled blond strands and deeply tanned skin of Petran's—no, Peter's—youth.

The name change might take some getting used to.

Here comfort reigned. Martin could gladly give up all responsibility and stay in this tiny room forever, now that he'd found his heart again. Outside the door lurked horrors few knew of, magic, and sinister beings.

Martin's world, which waited for him outside this safe haven. Leaving now might be the hardest thing he'd ever done since parting from the pirate's son seasons ago.

Chapter Twenty-seven

The Father's great hall paled in comparison to the Lady's. Instead of huge, airy windows, only gas lamps and candles illuminated the severe interior, devoid of ornate furnishings, music, or laughter. Yet, the cool stone walls offered a refuge, a sense of peace lacking at the opulent temple across the way.

The outward façade showed a simple wooden building. In reality, the temple stretched far underground.

Sweet herbs smoldered in lanterns around the room, chasing back the expected mustiness from a chamber cut off from fresh air.

The chairs Martin and Dmitri sat upon amounted to little more than cushionless boxes, functional, if not necessarily comfortable. No rugs covered the floor. Still, sitting allowed for greater concentration on the matter at hand. Moreover, no one stood a chance of sneaking into this place, as every footfall echoed off stone.

"Mage fire has no effect on their living flesh, yet can completely consume a dead demon." Green-tinged flames licked at Father Dmitri's gloved fingers, dying when he closed his fist.

Martin focused all his attention on his spread palm. A tiny blue flame sprang to life, withered, and died. Although Dmitri backed him in several demon fights, Martin best not to lay all cards on the table at once by showing his full strength. However, his efforts failed to pay off. For a moment, he remembered his mother entertaining him with her own flames.

"Concentrate, Martin. You seem distracted today."

So like Dmitri to notice. Martin closed his hand. There'd be no conjuring with so much on his mind. "Father, have you ever done anything you regretted?" Not that Martin regretted his time with Peter. Far from it. But to now know the man's taste, the feel of him...

The dark hood swiveled Martin's way. "We all have regrets, have done things we're not proud of. Learning from our mistakes is how we grow."

"Have you... have you ever wanted someone? I mean, for more than one night? The Father's priests are allowed lovers, right? Like the Lady's are?"

Dmitri stayed silent a long moment before answering. "My sect doesn't encourage taking others casually into our beds or hearts. Any we bring there must be... special."

Oh, really? "Was there someone special to you?" Martin saw priests as truly spiritual beings and hadn't expected one to confess to such baser emotions as love.

Dmitri let out a sigh. "There was."

"She's not with you now?" Yes, Martin asked rude questions but needed to know.

"Why do you say 'she'?" Again, no humor, no condemnation, simply a question.

"Your religion frowns on two men or two women, or so I'm told." Though the gossip from Esmerla Enys and her sister-by-bonding didn't count as reliable information.

Good women, both, but far too prone to chin-wagging. Of course, they probably got their information from Enys himself.

"Yes, it does. But while the Father's servants do their best to follow his teachings, we're still mortal. The heart travels of its own accord."

"So, *he's* not with you now?"

"No." Dmitri's brown hood swept back and forth.

"Do you regret it?"

"I regret how I lost him." Dmitri rose abruptly and strode away.

What? A holy man? Martin hurried to catch up. He passed other priests and their novices, working in appointed places throughout the room. A silencing spell hid their murmurings from Martin's ears.

He caught Dmitri at the door, barely remembering to swipe his hand over the lintel runes before slamming into an invisible wall. It only took twice for him to learn.

Martin followed his mentor into a courtyard far less lavish than the Lady's. Dmitri sat on a plain wooden bench, patting the spot beside him.

Martin sat.

For several long moments, the silence lingered. Then, finally, Dmitri said, "We all must choose our own path. The Choosing is days away when your friend Cere hopes to be called more deeply into the Lady's service. Once one gives themselves to her care, there is no going back."

Martin winced. "Should I try to discourage him?"

"He, like you, has the right to determine his own path. He would not listen." Dmitri shrugged. "What can we offer him? He also has a destiny to fulfill. You turned down any chance to serve her, and while you're welcome to join the priests here, I see you traveling a different road."

"Is it the same way with the Father? The permanence."

"No. His servants are free to come and go as they please. Were I to suddenly take a notion to try my hand at farming, I'm free to do so with the Father's blessing. However, like you, I have a destiny."

Destiny? Now Dmitri sounded like the card deck from the Stone's Throw.

"Have you ever thought of leaving?"

Dmitri hung his head. "After I lost my first love, I met someone I might have had a second chance with. After I'd sworn myself to service many seasons ago, I rescued a man attacked by demons. Because he'd seen them, I couldn't simply return him to his home. He'd been injured, so I found a cottage and nursed him back to health."

Martin had never heard of anyone besides a hunter surviving a demon attack. "What happened then?"

"As is often the case, when two people share time together, they bond. I hadn't intended to grow attached, and yet I did." A smile showed in Dmitri's voice. "Those were some of the simplest days of my life, talking to him and taking walks in the forest as he regained strength. He'd traveled the world over and seen many things. Told stories of his adventures." Dmitri placed a splayed hand over his chest. "My heart didn't stand a chance."

"You... you loved him?"

"With all of my heart that my old love and the Father didn't possess."

"But you couldn't be with him."

Dmitri shook his head. "I wanted to. The Father knew I wanted to. In fact, I'd considered breaking my vows to be with him." He faced away.

"What happened?"

"Demons hate hunters, for good reason. If they can't destroy us, they hurt us how they can. The demons returned for him. I... I wasn't there."

Visions appeared in Martin's head. If he didn't let his tavernkeeper go, would that be Peter's fate?

"Every day, I ask myself if he'd still be alive and happy if I'd just let him go, hadn't acted on my feelings. Another part of me says I'd be a poorer man if I'd never known his love."

Dmitri had acknowledged Martin's nighttime forays to the tavern, and likely told this story as a cautionary tale. *"You'd be surprised what I know."*

If Martin continued visiting the tavern, would he know Peter's love one day? Would demons target Peter to hurt Martin?

He must stay away. Though his heart hurt at the thought, he must stuff his feelings down deep, distance himself, and focus on being a hunter for Peter's sake.

Though the longing and sorrow might kill him.

When he opened his hand, a golden flame danced across his palm. Time to focus on magic, setting aside thoughts of the man with lighter hair hiding beneath a coating of dye, and intensely dark eyes.

If only Peter stopped haunting Martin's dreams. And if only Martin could walk away, now that he'd found the man he'd despaired of ever seeing again. Even now, as he prepared to roam the streets in search of demons, he knew where his night would end.

Dmitri continued, "My lover was not a mage, so we couldn't form a mage bond. Other mages would never have involved themselves so."

"What's a mage bond?" Martin never saw a reference to such in his books.

"In the land I'm from, mages formed pairs with complementary magic. Strong practitioners burn bright. Without an opposite to keep them grounded, their power grows wild. Unpredictable."

"But I don't have another mage to pair with."

"Don't you?"

Because, my little mage, now the time is right. Eyes kept closed will now open.

"Peter. You know of Peter."

"My sect knew of Petran the moment he set foot in E'Skaara, just as we knew about you, Arkenn."

"Wait. What? You knew about him? About us?"

"Yes, we did."

Anger caught Martin in an iron grip. "For many seasons, I mourned the death of my friend. You knew he was alive and didn't tell me?" He grasped the bottom of Dmitri's hood and yanked him to his feet—and stood with an empty robe in his grasp.

He dropped the robe. Immediately, the robe rose from the ground, forming into Dmitri's familiar shape.

Martin jumped backward, falling and scrambling away. "What did you do? How did you..."

"You have much to learn, Martin." Dmitri held out his gloved hand.

Martin stared at the hand for a long moment, heart racing. Dmitri hadn't simply disappeared, then reappeared somewhere else. Had he?

Dmitri wriggled his fingers. "I'm the same priest who's protected you all along. Why should seeing another aspect of my powers alarm you so? Don't you know I'd never use any power against you?"

Slowly, Martin clutched the offered hand and allowed Dmitri to help him up. Would Martin one day manage such a feat as disappearing?

Dmitri continued the conversation as though nothing unusual had happened. "Why do you think the Father prohibits two men or two women together?"

"Mine is not to question your god." Martin would like to ask a few questions with his fists about why he and Peter were kept apart and how Dmitri knew of them. Although, much more demonstration of holy power might turn Martin into a true believer.

"Mage bond pairs are extremely powerful, especially when they bond young. But, if not guided, they go rogue, use their powers for evil, not good. Which is why mages as a whole were considered dangerous."

"I don't understand. It's the Lady's people who took my parents."

"Who do you fear most in this world?"

A few sevendays ago, he'd say he feared nothing or no one. Now... "Someone who could take away all I hold dear."

Dmitri turned his head in the direction of the Lady's temple, where a tall spire shot toward the sky. "So does she. And the only thing she holds dear is power."

"That still doesn't explain why you kept Petran and me... Peter...apart."

"Doesn't it? Could you have held off a novice guard when you were young?"

"Well, no, but..."

"Congratulations, you have found your mage bond. Do you have any idea how rare that is? But if you'd received no training, what would happen if you held a sword on an experienced fighter?"

"He'd likely take my weapon and kill me."

"Precisely."

Though Martin couldn't see Dmitri's eyes, he felt a hot stare boring into him.

"You needed to mature, for us to see what you would become, how strong you were before we trained you. Why make a man give up the life he knows if he'll be of no service?"

"And you've been watching me all along." Hadn't Dmitri said something similar before?

"We gave you the amulet to hide you and keep you safe."

"What about Peter?"

"One of our trusted servants, a minor practitioner, kept an eye on him until the time came for you to reunite. He was in no danger, and wards prevented any from seeing him as the pirate lad. Even you, until now."

"Why now?"

"Because you'll need your bond for the next level of your training."

"I need to ask one more thing." A hard thing to ask, but something Martin very much wanted to know. "Is the Father real?"

Dmitri slowly shook his head, tutting. "Do you believe he is real?"

Did he? "I don't know. I've prayed to him in times of trouble." And hoped the Father protected him from the Lady.

"And did you feel comforted?" Dmitri folded his arms inside the sleeves of his robe.

"Somewhat."

"At that moment, you believed in him."

"Yes, I guess I did. But is he really there?"

"Whenever you believe in him, at that moment, he is real to you."

"Is the Lady real?"

Dmitri remained silent for a few moments, then quietly answered, "Very much so. But she's not what you think she is. Which is why you must train."

Chapter Twenty-eight

M artin.

Peter closed his eyes and leaned on the tavern's hearth, recalling arms around him, lips against lips, the deep thrum of *something* underneath. A rightness. Tiny sparks igniting when skin touched skin. A missing piece of himself, restored.

From the moment he'd been drawn to a badly injured Arkenn on the riverbank, there'd been something about him. So much time apart should have dampened the pull.

Yet time and distance only increased Peter's want for his foundling.

Only, he'd woken to an empty bed. Would Arkenn... Martin come back? Fate couldn't have brought them together, only to separate them again.

All those seasons ago, nestled together on Peter's bunk. First, he'd nursed Martin back to health, then Martin returned the favor. Peter never told a soul his suspicions about Martin's magery. How had he managed to hide his powers, living in a city where one wrong move meant a death sentence?

He should have run, gotten as far from E'Skaara as possible. Yet, he'd stayed. Why?

Peter would have to ask him, if Martin graced the Stone's Throw's door again. The late eve crowd departed, his three lodgers trudging upstairs to their rooms long before closing. Tonight, no squeaking bed ropes chased back the quiet. Not a sound, not even the ticking of the mantel clock. No surprise. He'd liked the workmanship when he'd inherited the place but never got around to having the faulty mechanisms repaired.

He dawdled, sent Addie home, took his time sweeping.

Tick, tick, tick...

Peter spun, facing the hearth. The clock's pendulum swung back and forth, ticking off the moments. What? How? An accidental fall to the floor broke parts inside, Old Mitta had told him.

Suddenly prickles rose on Peter's neck, warmth flowing into his belly. He wasn't alone. Slowly, slowly, he turned to face the street.

There, under a lantern, stood a familiar figure, dressed in black.

They stared at each other for long moments, frozen. The figure crossed the street in a few long strides.

Peter jerked his shoulders back, reanimating and hurrying toward the door. One minute Martin stood outside, looking in on a world where he felt so out of place at times; the next moment, warmth surrounded him when he stepped out of the cold, both physical and proverbial, and into the light.

Peter greeted him with a bashful smile. "What brings you down here to my humble establishment at this hour?"

He didn't bar the way, ushering Martin farther inside. Martin winked, tightness unfurling inside of him at the welcome. "We're sharers of secrets, are we not?" Shyness had never been a problem, yet Martin hefted the weight of each word before allowing it to leave his mouth. "Would you believe I have business with the tavernkeeper?" Too much filled his mind, had kept him awake at night. Things Peter might not be ready to hear if the priests had kept him so isolated from the knowledge of who, or what, Peter and Martin were.

Peter whipped his gaze to the floor, the bloom of color on his pale cheeks answering louder than words.

Footsteps overhead had Peter gazing ceilingward. He bustled over to the front door, grasping the cloak and hat hanging from a hook and wrapping himself inside worn wool. "Walk with me?"

"Aren't you afraid of cutpurses or other evils roaming the streets at night?" Martin asked, even though they'd be as safe outside as in—he'd see to it.

"Not with you." A gentle smile lifted the corner of Peter's mouth, etching a dimple into his cheek. "Why do you think no one approaches you? You're... dangerous." He shrugged one shoulder. "Besides, anyone who can run down a murderous sailor and return with nary a scratch must be someone to be reckoned with."

Peter didn't know half of the matter. Martin raised a brow.

Peter chuckled. "As Aggie says, anyone out on a night like tonight is bound to be a relative of hers. I'll simply threaten to tell her. No wise man risks her wrath."

Martin supposed not. He strolled outside, then waited as Peter locked the door and pocketed the key. "Where to?"

Peter nodded toward the end of the road. "There's a pier that the locals use for fishing. When I can't sleep, I go there, watch the ships' lanterns bobbing in the bay."

Did he miss the sea? The *Seabird*? His father?

Martin paced beside Peter, breath fogging. Chill fingers of the coming winter caressed Martin's face and stung his nose, or chill for E'Skaara. The scent of smoke mingled with seawater and the ever-present fishy odor of the harbor district. They left cobblestones for packed earth.

"You said Aggie's family," Martin ventured. "What about your own? You didn't tell me a lot during our brief time together."

Peter pulled his hat down more firmly over his ears. "Da was the only member of my family I knew of after my mum died. With him gone, it's just me. I've never felt the need to take a mate, though many have tried to persuade me." He gave a wry chuckle. "Da told stories of my grandmother. Tough when she had to be, with a kind heart. She never let circumstances get in her way and raised my father alone."

"She sounds like a good woman." Those words held a lot of meaning to Martin, who'd met good women who sold their bodies to feed their families and others who'd been called good without the slightest bit of love in their hearts.

Peter barked out a rueful laugh. "It depends on who you ask. The townsfolk saw her as a woman of ill repute, spat on the ground when she passed. Da saw her as a woman who did what she had to in order to raise the son she refused to sell no matter the sum offered her."

Shock halted Martin's steps. "Sell?"

Peter continued on, bootheels clicking over the packed dirt. Martin hurried to catch up. "People here think there's a huge divide between the rich and the poor." He shook his head. "Where she was from, the rich *owned* the poor."

Now came Martin's turn to gasp. "Surely not. For what purpose?"

Voice even, carrying none of the contempt the subject deserved, Peter replied, "For servants mostly, but many found other uses for a comely young lad." He spoke so casually.

Breath wouldn't come. People would have used Peter's Da? "But don't your people follow the ways of the Father? Isn't that forbidden?"

"People have a way of twisting doctrines to suit their own whims. Two men together are forbidden, but if you take an indentured servant, and... Well, they don't have the same rights in that world and aren't considered equals. One of Grandmother's... friends owned a merchant vessel and promised to take care of my da. She kissed Da, saw him safely on the ship, and he never saw her again. When he returned home a few seasons later, someone else lived in the house, and all her things were gone. Sold, most likely. He didn't realize at the time that, with no one to protect her, she'd fall prey to dishonest neighbors."

"That's horrible." Demons didn't only live in shadows, apparently.

Peter shrugged. "It's the way of the world. I've seen atrocities committed by pirates. Nothing came close to what's been done by so-called *decent* people, in the name of their deity, no less. She was kinder than any of them."

While Martin grew up working hard for his supper, he'd slept safely in his bed at night. Never would he have dreamed another, especially a mere child, faced such horrors. Yet, he'd seen street children here. Were they at such risk? "Your... your mother died when you were a small child."

Peter removed his hat, running fingers through dark, cropped hair so different from the gold highlighted brown mass Martin remembered. "My father took me to sea, not trusting our neighbors not to take advantage."

"They worshipped the Father?"

Peter nodded, lips pulled tight.

Dmitri's religion allowed such? Wait until Martin saw the priest again. "But you got away."

"I got away. Some tried to say I'd be better off with a local farming family with too many daughters and no sons. They actually came in the night and demanded Da hand me over." Peter gave a toothy grin. "My father was a persuasive man, particularly when he held a blade at your neck."

Martin's father? Holding a blade at someone's neck? A scythe, maybe. "So, you lived the life of a pirate." Envy sank hooks into Martin's heart. He missed his parents, but Peter had his da for a time. Oh. The envy twisted into guilt. The captain died horribly, leaving Peter as alone as Martin. "You've lived on the sea. Saw other lands."

"Yes." Peter stepped onto the pier, placing his hands on the railing. He stared out over the dark water. Lanterns hung from ships in the harbor twinkled, tiny stars reflecting off the bay.

"Why settle here, then, if you had the world to choose from? Do you have any connections in E'Skaara? Your mother's people, perhaps? Didn't your father meet her here?" Martin regretted his words the moment Peter's shoulders slumped. He couldn't recall everything that Peter had said about family.

"I have no one, anywhere. But I also had no desire to dance on the end of a rope, never having known life." More quietly, he added, "Known love. Da protected me from the crew's advances. Though I'd have loved to stay at sea, as far as anyone knows, my ill uncle called for me here, I worked for him, and I took over his business when he died. The man in question had no kin and willingly went along with Addie's plan in exchange for not allowing the magistrate to benefit from his death. Mitta was a good man. I greatly respected him." Muscles twitched in Peter's jaw. "What about you? I've searched for you for so many seasons, you know. I gave up, figuring you must have left the city."

Once again, guilt sank in its icy blade. Martin drew fingers through his hair, admitting only part of the truth. "I've never fit in with the others here, so keep mostly to myself. I'm a city guard." How much, if anything, should he say of Dmitri? He cocked his head to the side, facing Peter, and turned the topic away from himself. "And you, who've seen not only the city but the world. Don't you long to see what's beyond the next voyage?"

"Sometimes. But sometimes you have to sacrifice what you want for survival." The longing in Peter's gaze said he'd sacrificed more than just the sea.

Never had Martin seen such hunger turned his way, not from anyone, the women who thought he'd make a fine bond mate, not even the demons starving for his power. He sent his senses out, seeking, seeking. No waking minds were close enough to him or Peter to make out faces or voices.

With slowness bordering on pain, Martin leaned in, inch by inch, until Peter's ale-scented breath warmed his face.

Peter's eyes widened, and he sucked in a startled breath before resignation filled his shadowy features. Keeping his eyes open, he held his ground, neither meeting Martin's mouth nor retreating.

Did he not want this?

Martin pressed his lips to Peter's, who held rock still. After a moment, he relaxed, his mouth pliant, opening to accept Martin's tongue. Gently stroking, Martin began a slow dance, not the passionate play of tongue-on-tongue he wanted. If he proceeded too quickly, Peter might run.

If he ran, Martin wouldn't chase him.

The pull in Martin's heart couldn't be denied, and his own loneliness clouded his mind before deserting him to the comfort of Peter's arms.

"Let's go home," Peter said, arm around Martin's waist.

Martin awoke in Peter's bed early the following day and dressed quickly, giving Peter a quick kiss on the forehead before hurrying off for his morn meeting with the guards under his command.

Chapter Twenty-nine

W hat had Peter done? He wiped down the bar for something to do, his nerves jangling on edge. One thing to dream of another man in the privacy of his loft room, another entirely to take one there.

More than once.

He'd escaped others' advances on the *Seabird* due to his father's intervention. But, even after leaving the *Seabird,* he rarely gave in to the impulse to have another man in an alley or other out-of-the-way place. Get each other off and go their own way, no talking. Definitely no kissing.

Except for a young man he'd once found near death, whose life seemed irrevocably entwined with Peter's.

Looking back on all the times he'd said no to a potential lover, he'd compared them to a memory and found them lacking. Even the most accomplished lovers couldn't compete with the fumbling of the right virgin in his cabin.

The mere thought of the man now known as Martin caused Peter's cock to swell, though he'd not seen

Martin in a sevenday. No. Not here. Not now. Not in his tavern, surrounded by customers.

He swiped a hand over the back of his neck. Good crowd tonight, come for plentiful ale and Addie's fish stew and crusty bread. "Have some more, love!" she encouraged a customer in her loud, booming voice while trading an empty bowl for a full one.

The rooms overhead were all rented for the sevenday, a rare occurrence. All should have been fine.

Still, unease prickled Peter's spine, the sense of being watched. He turned. Only a group of laughing men by the fireplace, swapping tall tales. A few women kept a polite distance in the corner.

Nothing. All in his head.

He swiped a cloth over a vacated table. An adjacent card player bumped an elbow against Peter, dropping a card on the floor. "Sorry, mate," the man said in a foreign accent.

"No harm done." Peter bent to retrieve the card. The black cloud. Even he, with his limited experience, recognized a bad omen. Which certainly didn't help his already rising disquiet.

Stop being ridiculous, he chided himself. *Just a bunch of superstitious nonsense.*

The door opened, a gust of wind sweeping into the room. Peter looked up, as he had for every customer since he and Martin had last shared a bed. No one. Someone must've failed to secure the latch. He crossed the floor in three long strides, glancing right and left at the street. A few sailors strolled together, too far away to have opened the door.

Black as pitch tonight, save for the flickering gaslights feebly illuminating shopfronts. For some reason, their light didn't travel as far as expected, individual spots of brightness quickly fading to dark. A fine fog drifted in the air, creating halos around the lamp globes.

A shout from near the hearth yanked him from his reverie. "Yo! Tavernkeeper! Another round."

Peter shut the door with a sigh and returned to work. Keep busy. Yeah. He'd keep busy until the unnerving feeling in the pit of his stomach passed. Hours flowed by in quick succession, allowing little time to dwell on Martin or the eve's eeriness.

The eve wound down, guests retreated upstairs, and the tavern regulars drifted in ones and twos out into the night. Peter focused on cleaning.

"Addie, I'm stepping out back."

"Alone? Why that's no fun at all. Please tell me you 'ave a handsome fella waiting back there for you." Addie gave him a saucy wink.

Peter ducked away to hide his heated cheeks. Did the woman have to blurt out every single thought to pop into her head? He rolled an empty barrel out the back door. Pale gas lamps across the street gave him little light by which to see. He froze, the hairs on his arms rising. What was that scuttling sound? "Who's there? Show yourself."

Nothing. Maybe his imagination ran away with him. Addie hadn't sent someone back here to play a prank, had she? Or perhaps she'd escalated her matchmaking game. But no, she'd met Martin. Based on her innuendo, she'd figured out the mutual attraction there, though Peter hadn't confessed to knowing the man seasons ago.

Peter rolled the barrel across the alleyway to join four others. He'd need to replenish his supply of ale soon. Lots of ships this season meant plenty of thirsty customers. He'd long since stopped brewing his own ale and gave his benefactor's recipe to another, who kept him well supplied.

A flash of movement from the corner of his eye caught his attention. More scuttling, slithering like scale over stone. His heart beat wildly in his chest. Had the sailor Martin accosted returned for a bit of payback? "I'm warning you. I'm armed," Peter lied.

Nothing. "Peter, stop scaring yourself. You're jumping at shadows," he mumbled. He stacked the barrel with the others.

Slither.

He whirled. Gaslight reflected in a pair of eyes—a pair of eyes set between him and the door. Slitted eyes.

A cat? A dog? Not with eyes like that. Peter gulped. He'd heard tales of evil creatures roaming the streets. Stories told to keep young ones in line. There were no such things as demons. Couldn't be. He'd have seen one in all his time spent in the city if there were. Addie had lived her whole life here, and she'd never mentioned such a thing.

The eyes drew closer. Peter stepped back—careening with a wall. No escape. "What do you want?"

More slithering, like claws on stone. The thing broke from the shadows, all long teeth and claws, with scales for skin. "Not much," the thing hissed, flicking out a forked tongue. "Just the pitiful thing your puny race calls a soul."

His soul?

Peter gathered his courage to run. The thing cut off his access to the tavern, but surely he could sprint down the alley and find another place to hide.

"Run," the horrifying vision said with an evil chuckle. "So much more fun to give chase. No one wants easy prey. But my master wants you. He thinks you'll make perfect bait."

Bait?

The creature lifted its head, giving an audible sniff. "Perhaps there's more to you than meets the eye. You can see me."

Backed against the wall, Peter glanced right and left. If he... He slipped down the side of the wall. He'd left an ax near the woodpile.

The creature shifted sideways, tracking Peter's movement. Keeping his eye on the stuff of nightmares, Peter groped in the dark.

One step, two steps. Peter's foot hit something. The woodpile! Slowly, slowly, he slid his hand downward. The ax handle seemed to jump into his hand. He wrapped his fingers around his one chance. This horrifying... thing planned to harvest his soul?

Never.

Peter swung.

The axe head bounced off the thing's skin, the handle ripping free of his grasp. For the mercy of the Father! For one brief moment, Peter froze.

Then he ran. With no idea where his path led, he sped between buildings, boot soles slipping on the rain-slicked cobblestones.

Claws on stones followed on his heels.

Where could he go? The thing stayed between him and the tavern. The waterfront? Where was a constable when he needed one?

In the much safer high city. No more sailors on the street. Even the night workers were absent. Mist kissed Peter's skin as he tore down the abandoned street.

If only he possessed a sharp length of steel. Even though he'd not used those skills in quite some time, poor swordsmanship would still be better than going unarmed.

His heartbeat pounded in his ears, matching his footfalls up one street, down another. Lights shone from the windows of a hatmaker's shop. Heart in his throat, he paused long enough to beat on the door. "Help! Help me!" Nothing.

Tiring now, he grew desperate, throwing himself at doors again and again.

Those slitted eyes appeared at the end of the street. No time to waste. He ran again.

In the darkness, he barely stopped in time to avoid hitting a wall. He groped blindly for a door, a weapon, anything.

Turning, he pressed his back to rough bricks and watched in horror as his doom approached. Peter caught his breath, readying himself for the agony of claws and teeth. Why couldn't he conjure a sword as readily as he conjured flame these days?

Peter tried to recall prayers to the Father, or any handy deity, for surely, he'd soon breathe his last.

Oh, Father. His heart pounded in his chest, pulse racing in his ears. This was it. He'd only found Martin. Now he'd never see the boy he'd loved again.

Loved. He'd loved Arkenn. Might soon love Martin if he didn't already.

Too late. He'd die tonight.

Two shrill whistles came from above. A dark shape dropped from the building's roof, a hint of metal glinting unnaturally in the gloom.

The thing hissed, drawing back. "Go away, hunter. I have no quarrel with you."

"Ah, but you do." A hood hid the man's face, and his low voice rumbled with menace. "This man is mine."

The fighter rolled, rising in front of the horror in the blink of an eye, putting himself between Peter and the thing he'd narrowly avoided. The man growled in Peter's direction, "Leave here. As fast as you can. Don't look back."

He'd like nothing better, but... "What of you?"

"He's met his match," the stranger said, in tones nearly too low to hear.

Did Peter recognize the voice?

"Go!" the man commanded.

Keeping his eyes on the two dangerous shapes in the dark, Peter slipped past the thing, retracing his steps down the darkened street. "I cannot leave you." No way would he abandon someone to that... that... thing.

"Go!" the man shouted.

Peter went. Calls, like sea birds, echoed through the streets. Halfway back to the tavern, he passed a man in a priest's cassock, strolling purposely the other way.

"Blessings, Father," Peter said in automatic response, from hearing Da's pleas many times when fleeing a storm or the magistrate's men.

"Blessings given." The priest's steps never faltered.

"Do not go that way," Peter said, clutching a loose sleeve. "You know not what awaits."

"I know." The priest gently placed a gloved hand on Peter's. "All will be fine."

One moment they stood together; the next, the priest was gone.

Still shaken, Peter stared into the darkness for one long moment. An unholy shriek sent him hurrying back to safety.

But was anywhere safe from what he'd just seen?

Chapter Thirty

Martin's heart nearly leaped from his body. The demon closed in, its putrid green skin glowing. That same heart almost stopped when, even in the darkness, he recognized the demon's prey.

He halted himself from charging in. A blind attack wouldn't help anyone. *Picture him as anyone else, not Peter. Don't make this hunt personal.*

But weren't they all?

Always before, Martin remained hunter-calm. Now, he'd strike with a vengeance. First, to get his bearings. Determine the demon's location, size, and fighting ability. Then, check for escape routes for the victim.

He gave two piercing whistles, announcing his find to Dmitri and other hunters.

Angling toward the roof ledge, Martin bunched his muscles, searching the ground for the best place to land, ever mindful of slippery tiles. Foolish mistakes made in haste would not help Peter.

Closer. Closer.

Martin leaped, dropping to one knee, brandishing his Father-blessed dagger.

The thing hissed, retreating in the face of a predator. "Go away, hunter. I have no quarrel with you."

"Ah, but you do." Martin threw back his hood so as not to obstruct his peripheral vision. Fear crept into anger. How dare this demon attack Martin's own? Through the dim light, he clearly saw runes metaphysically etched on Peter's aura.

Had the demon marked him?

No! Two twined figures. The crackle of static between Peter and Martin. Had Martin somehow marked this man as his? He spoke the truth. The thing could clearly see the glowing runes, devise its meaning, as Peter could clearly see the demon. "This man is mine."

Martin rolled and came up in front of the horror. Monster at his front, Peter at his back. Without turning, Martin snapped, "Leave here. As fast as you can. Don't look back."

"What of you?"

Calm settled over Martin. "He's met his match." Once Peter left, Martin could deal with the problem at hand. Did Peter recognize Martin's voice? "Go!" The sooner Peter left, the better.

Soon Martin would seek his lover, explain. Swear him to secrecy.

If Peter even let Martin inside the tavern again after discovering the truth.

Peter sidled around the creature, pausing at the mouth of the alley. Martin couldn't make out the words for the roaring in his ears.

"Go!" Martin breathed a sigh of relief when Peter rounded the corner, footsteps pounding away.

Good. Now to focus on the task at hand.

The demon was no weak mewling creature like some of Martin's lesser kills. This being tracked his steps. An older one.

Harder to kill.

Glowing eyes approached. Two demons?

One shifted to Martin's right, the other to the left.

"Ah, hunter, our master will be pleased when we bring you back."

Bring you back?

Martin tossed the knife from one hand to the other and back again. Weight balanced on the balls of his feet, he watched, searching for bunched muscles or other signs of attack.

Two? He'd dealt with two before, but only with Dmitri's help. Where were the priests?

Even footfalls sounded behind him. A wave of relief swept over Martin. Dmitri.

"Good eve to you, Martin." Dmitri's voice remained calm, as though merely exchanging a pleasant greeting on the street.

Martin inclined his head without taking his eyes from the predators of the night. "Father."

Voice unnervingly serene, Dmitri asked, "Shall we dance?"

"Love to." Martin turned, putting himself back-to-back with his mentor.

"This is none of your affair, Dmitri," the first demon hissed. "You don't want to anger the master."

The demon knew the priest's name?

"Your master can do to himself things followers of the Father won't speak of," Dmitri replied.

"You mean he can go fuck himself?" Martin asked.

"That *is* what I said," Dmitri shot back.

The second demon lunged. Martin danced away. He returned his knife to his belt and yanked his sword from the scabbard between his shoulder blades.

"Fond of your head?" he asked his adversary.

The thing swiped with long claws. Martin ducked. A second later, he felt the sting. The claws brushed his skin, not enough to cut deeply but enough to draw blood.

Unlike many of the single demons he fought, these two were bold, fearless.

Toying with him.

"Dmitri, why aren't they retreating?" he asked.

"The demons before were testing our strength. Scouts. These are warriors."

Warrior demons?

The two scaly things fought as a team, circling, seeking an opening. Martin held his sword aloft, as did Dmitri. A few softly spoken words and green flames engulfed the priest's blade, lighting the alleyway. Illuminating a scene Martin couldn't unsee. One moment's concentration and golden flames enveloped Martin's blade. Which didn't make the scene less terrifying.

Two macabre grins on faces bearing little resemblance to people or even other demons he'd met. He'd never seen their like before.

"You can fight, but you'll not win," one taunted. "Kill us. More will come. They won't stop coming until the master ends the hunt." It grinned wide. "And he'll never end the hunt. Not until he has what he wants."

The thing leaped. Martin cried out, blocking talons with his sword. He brought the hilt down hard enough to concuss a man. This opponent was no man.

The demon snarled, kicking out at Martin's feet. Martin jumped, barely missing the blow. Behind him, a blade clanged. Against stone? Or against rocklike skin?

With no time to spare for Father Dmitri, Martin parried. The demon moved lightning-fast, its motions a blur. Martin dared not take his eyes away or swipe at the sweat on his brow. All his attention focused on the matter at hand.

Nothing in his demon hunting lessons had prepared him for this. He brought his sword down with all his might on the thing's head. Shockwaves traveled up his arms. Impervious skin? None of the demons he'd beheaded possessed such skin.

"Aim for the throat!" Dmitri shouted.

Martin shifted away, using the priest's instruction to turn dance moves into battle tactics. Whirling kept him a moving target, and a quick sidestep put him out of claws' reach. A monstrous mouth gaped, revealing rows of razor-sharp teeth.

Then the fight was upon him again. *Hack. Slash. Whirl. Thrust. Parry. Roll.* Everything came down to this moment, this fight.

Martin's limbs grew heavy, and his steps slowed. The fire on his blade sputtered out of existence. A misstep in the sudden darkness nearly sent him tumbling. "Father!" he shouted. No more. He could handle no more.

From the corner of his eye, he glimpsed a flaming sword.

Fire.

But he couldn't spare the concentration. Even with all his might, he only managed a weak flame.

Closer and closer, the demon came. Martin's back hit a wall. Trapped. The thing showed its teeth. "My master will be so pleased." It stepped forward, taloned hands outstretched.

An image flashed through Martin's mind: Peter, pressed against the wall.

Peter. He must fight for Peter.

Fiery rage swept Martin into a typhoon. This creature would not rob him of his lover. No! Rolling his anger into a ball, he summoned energy to his fingers.

Flames erupted from his fingertips, engulfing the demon in golden light.

Martin collapsed.

Chapter Thirty-one

"Are you injured?" Dmitri sidestepped his own kill in his rush to Martin's side.

Was he? The long scratches on Martin's arm hurt, exhaustion dragged him down, but he hadn't lost enough blood to be lightheaded. "Not really. Are you?"

Dmitri shook his head. Ichor smeared his cassock—blood from the demon.

Good. "I have to check—"

"The man you saved is fine, safely ensconced within his tavern. The demons planned to use him as bait, to capture you."

"What? Bait!" No, Martin couldn't put Peter in danger.

"Martin. He is well. Stay with me a while."

Instinct pulled at Martin to go see Peter for himself.

"Please," Dmitri pleaded.

Martin deflated. Dmitri had never asked him for much before. Martin stared down at the remains of two demons, then raised his gaze to the vicinity of the cloaked priest's face. "Two tonight, warriors. Why?"

"I do not know." While Dmitri's voice held his normal controlled tones, time as hunting partners clued Martin into traces of concern. "Warriors." Dmitri inched closer to the remains of Martin's opponent. "You shouldn't have been able to do that. Not on living demon flesh."

"What did I do? I just shot a fireball." Fire, like Martin once used to kill the villagers. But Dmitri said mage fire didn't harm living demon flesh. "Has it always been this way, demons in the city?" How long ago had some unknown priests created the runes to ward off evil?

A wash of flame blazed up from the bodies, momentarily turning night to day, gone in an instant. Still, the bright flash hadn't penetrated Dmitri's hood.

After the first sevenday or so, spending the eve with a faceless man and the other hunter priests grew more comfortable. Martin had not yet given in to the temptation of card reading with Dmitri in mind, too afraid of what he might discover.

And like the demons, Martin sensed no thoughts or emotions when he fixed on the priests.

Prepared to receive no answer, Martin strained to hear the next words. "Not always. In seasons past, when we numbered in the thousands, guardians patrolled the city and countryside, seeking out night wanderers. What you call demons, though they have their own name for their kind." Dmitri shrugged one shoulder. "When necessary, evil men and women."

He turned his face away, staring out into the blackness. No stars, no moon to light their night, and in this oldest part of town, few street lanterns chased back the shadows. What could he possibly be looking for? "The danger seems to have passed for a moment. We can talk."

"What do you mean, guardians?"

Dmitri let out a wistful sigh, lapsing into teaching mode. "As you may have guessed, my fellow priests and I are not from here."

"Not from E'Skaara."

Dmitri let out another sigh, this one longsuffering. "The time has come to tell you everything." They stood in the firelight, the darkness of Dmitri's clothes nearly dispelling the light. "I come from Eallarial, a world far older than yours, where we freely practiced magic. Imagine ships riding the waves from magic, never needing sails. Even ships that rode the winds." Was that a trace of wistfulness?

But ships that rode the winds? Was Dmitri toying with him? "That's ridiculous!" Though, if memory served, Martin had heard tales...

"No, it's not. Remember the many realms you witnessed the night I taught you about runes? I came from one of those other realms. Magic on my world was plentiful, as it was here, until... it... came."

"What is it?"

"The entity you call the Lady. It came here and took advantage of local religious custom, fashioning itself on the aspect of the Mother but calling itself the Lady. It arrived on my world and consumed the source of a mage's power. It lives on magic. Like here, mages were collected, with the creature draining their vitality. They were its competition for what you call magic. Great carnage ensued."

"Thomoth! My mother told me stories of Thomoth."

Dmitri's hood dipped. "That is one name the creature has used. As on your world, it posed as a deity on mine. How else to secure the goodwill of the people?"

Two silent priests slipped out of the darkness, taking up stations near the burning corpses. "Come, Martin," Dmitri said, "I need to return to the temple, and you won't rest until you see for yourself that their latest victim returned home safely." Hand on Martin's back, Dmitri led Martin away, continuing his tale. "Soon, the monster consumed nearly all of the magic on my world. The mages remaining, myself included, worked tirelessly to defeat our foe, to no avail. Even nonmages, you see, needed magic. It kept us alive until all the magic was gone and our lands lay in ruins."

The stories Mum told of Thomoth didn't even compare to what Martin learned now. "It started by killing the mages."

Dmitri's hood lifted and lowered. "The remaining mages and their families from my own realm combined resources, created a portal, and fled, except one, who had grown as evil as the creature in his own way. The creature followed. We created shields, wore amulets to conceal our nature, and hid among the people of your world. We watch for magic, other mages, protect and nurture them if we can. The strongest of us stayed here in E'Skaara, where the greatest concentration of magic is, continuing our fight to keep this creature from destroying yet another world."

"And the demons?"

Dmitri sighed. "They weren't from my realm but another drained by the Lady. They were nonmagic users who still needed magic to survive, though unaware of the fact. They are weaker, and many slip past our wards."

"Why do they kill?"

"Their victims all have a percentage of magic blood. Though demons cannot feed directly on the magic supply and alert the creature hiding beneath the Lady's temple to their presence, they consume the magic they can, generated out of fear, and return home to their master, who allows them a portion and saves the rest for himself. We call them evil. From their standpoint, they're merely doing what they must to survive."

"But they kill our kind!"

"Do our kind not kill cows and sheep to feed?"

"So, we're sheep to them."

"No, we're survival. Food in the bellies of their young."

Martin might never eat beef again. "Their master?"

"The mage we left behind. With each offering, he grows stronger. One day he'll find a way to cross over. He plans to face the creature himself. He will fail."

"He wants what you want, right? Wouldn't he be a powerful ally?"

Dmitri shook his head. "Not exactly. He wants to make a deal with it or, lacking that, kill it, but he has greater ambitions."

Those plans sounded plenty ambitious to Martin. "What?"

"The mages who came here wanted just to live, save your people our fate, make our home here. He wants to siphon the magic from your world to rebuild ours."

And here Martin thought the master might help. No. Just another predator. "Where does priesthood and worshipping the Father come in?"

A chuckle wafted from under Dmitri's hood. "Though I'm no seer of minds, I can well imagine the images in your head right now. The form of worship you are familiar with has evolved, as has nearly everything else in existence." Dmitri bowed his head and spoke words in a language Martin didn't know. "Worship of the Father and his feminine aspect, the Mother, had existed since your distant ancestors spoke their first words. The enemy of my enemy is my friend. Once the Lady came, the Father's followers believed our story, welcomed us, joined our cause. The original priests all died out as time went by, leaving only mage-born."

Quickstepping to keep up, Martin pushed away thoughts of Peter to recall what Dmitri had said. "You said the Father exists if I believe in him."

Dmitri's hood dipped in a nod. "In people's minds, he is real, and praying to him increases the harvest, allows childless couples children. The people believe in him; therefore, he exists. It's another form of magic."

"The Lady's worshippers? What happened to separate the Father from the Mother?"

Dmitri stayed silent for so long Martin thought he wouldn't answer. "Greed, envy, sloth. Some wanted more of the pleasure; others thought they could only serve by doing without. The more pleasure one group received, the more the others became envious and bitter.

"The creature came here, took advantage of the people's beliefs, and set itself up as the Lady."

"Some believe she... it, doesn't truly live in the temple." Though Martin felt its malevolent presence night after night.

"It does, in a fashion. Right now, it is mostly dormant, feasting on magic. But I believe it senses us, will make a move soon to stop our efforts."

"And—"

"I've said too much already. Repeat none of what you heard from me this night. I only tell you because... because soon I believe you'll have a reason to know. Now, I must study." Dmitri stopped at the door to the Father's temple. Martin hadn't even realized they'd traveled this far. "I bid you good eve."

Martin stood in the street, a million questions on his tongue. He'd not get any answers tonight. Laughter and bright lights called to him from the Lady's temple. Music, wine, warm bodies. Serve the poor? He couldn't imagine those inside serving anyone but themselves. No wonder the common people hated them.

Dmitri had said the current ways weren't like this in the old days. Why did no texts exist of that time?

Churning thoughts put Martin's feet into motion to check on Peter. He rushed past the night workers, ignoring their taunts and offers, breathing a sigh of relief when the tavern came into view.

Light spilled from the open doorway, as well as the last of the eve's patrons. The barmaid wrapped a shawl around her shoulders. Two men escorted her when she'd only ever left alone before.

Good. Peter took precautions.

Or the barmaid took liberties. Somehow, Martin couldn't imagine the headstrong Addie bowing to social conventions.

For a moment, a brief second, Martin caught sight of Peter before the door closed. Peter. Someone easy to talk to, who didn't espouse either faith and try to sway Martin to one side or the other. Merely shared ale and conversation.

And their bodies. Oh, how Martin tried to stay away, not pull Peter into the darkness.

Like a moth drawn to a flame, Martin couldn't stay away.

What was he doing? He should just go. He watched for long moments, how Addie and her escorts closed the shutters while Peter shut the door.

Afraid. Peter was afraid. He should be afraid.

Should Martin go to him? Comfort him? But no. If the demons wanted Martin, he'd only put Peter in danger. And he must protect Peter at all costs. Though he raised his hands and tried his best to focus, no wards came.

He watched until no more light sifted through the shutters' cracks, turned, and shuffled back to his rooms.

Only when he settled into bed did he realize what he'd seen. Of course, he couldn't conjure wards on the Stone's Throw.

The tavern was already warded.

Chapter Thirty-two

A touch of magic helped the scratches heal by morn. Freshly bathed and shaved, Martin stood before his mirror, contemplating his best clothing laid out upon the bed.

This should be a happy moment, for most likely, his friend Cere would be selected for service today, yet no amount of finery could brighten Martin's mood.

Now that he knew the truth. Should he warn Cere? Sneak him out of the temple?

Cere had looked forward to this day. Dread pooled in Martin's stomach. If Cere was Chosen, what would he do? Spend the rest of his life inside the temple walls as a priest, teacher, or oracle?

Serving a false goddess who cared nothing for him.

Never again would he and Martin share a bench in the garden.

A knock sounded on his door. Cere entered without waiting for an answer. "I found this outside your door." He placed a dusty trunk on the floor and crossed to the washbasin to rid his hands of any filth.

Cere, here? How had he even discovered where
Martin lived? Oh. Probably from another guard. They'd
never been accused of being tight-lipped, and Cere's
powers of persuasion were vast.

He looked resplendent in white satin, multi-colored
pearls embellishing his tunic and trousers. Soft
calfhide boots, dyed sky blue, graced his feet. He'd
arranged his hair in elaborate braids, crossed over his
head, trailing down his back.

"You look stunning," Martin admitted. "That outfit
likely cost more than a common man will make in a
lifetime."

Cere turned, arms out to the sides to show off the
workmanship of his clothes. "Nothing less for the
Choosing." His smile melted. "You've been keeping
company with that priest too long if you think the
temple worries about costs."

Was Cere aware of *why* Martin kept company with
Dmitri? "Why did you come here? Won't you be
missed?"

Cere shrugged. "If I'm Chosen, then I'll be
sequestered." He gave a tremulous smile. "And I won't
be able to see you." For the first time since their
meeting, a hint of shyness crept into Cere's demeanor:
a hint of blush on his fashionably pale cheeks, gaze
lowered to the floor.

He would miss Martin? Hadn't Cere just been
practicing his wiles? Martin found Cere amusing,
friendly, but no other feelings stirred in him. *Because
your heart belongs to another.*

The boy, no, the man, swept a tentative gaze over
Martin's body, pausing at a particular area.

Martin looked down. By all the gods anyone ever
prayed to! He grabbed a night robe to fling over his

near-nakedness, clad as he was in only small clothes. Heat crept up his face. Time for a change of subject. "What do you think I should wear?"

Distracted by his second favorite topic of clothing—his first being gossip, or possibly sex—Cere nodded toward the trunk. "You might want to check in there."

"You looked?"

"Of course, I looked. It's... it's hideous. An affront to the Lady, but it's you."

It must be horrible indeed. Martin fought a smile while opening the lid. Despite the layer of dust on the surface, no dirt or mustiness lingered inside. He lifted a deceptively soft garment. Leather? Fine leather, too. He brought the tunic to his nose and sniffed. Definitely leather. A note, penned in an elegant hand, read *You've earned this.*

Black, black, black. Dark as midnight, each item.

"You're not thinking of wearing that in daylight where people can see, are you?" Cere curled his lip in distaste.

The garments were fitted, not flowing, designed to show not a hint of flesh but for hands and head—and not restrict movement during fights. "The least I could do is try them on since Father Dmitri went through so much trouble."

"Father Dmitri, hmmm?" Cere perched on Martin's bed, threw an arm against his forehead, and huffed out a dramatic, "If you must."

A dull blade of regret serrated Martin's heart. He'd miss the young scamp if Cere suddenly disappeared into further service to the evil creature lurking under the temple.

What if he turned into the one thing Martin dreaded the most? Someone who hunted down and killed mages. Would they ever find themselves on opposite sides of a chasm?

"Go on. We don't have much time." Cere bounced on the bed. "Oh! Soft! I'll bet you've gotten into all kinds of mischief in here." He lifted a sheet and sniffed.

"Cere!"

The vision of an angel with the mind of an imp sighed. "Just you. No fun at all."

Yes, Martin would miss Cere. He set his mind to dressing. Each piece fit perfectly. At last, he stood fully clothed in a tunic, trousers, arm wraps, high collared vest likely designed to protect the neck in fights. Rather than plain, on closer inspection, he noticed the intricately tooled patterns. Runes?

"Oh, it makes your ass delectable!" Cere smacked his hand across the seat of Martin's trousers. Martin barely felt the blow, and ignored the suggestive waggling of Cere's eyebrows. He turned right and left, admiring the outfit in the mirror. Some senior officers wore similar attire, minus the runes, but he'd never dreamed of spending so much coin, though the leather added protection.

"You're not seriously considering wearing that, are you?" Cere wrinkled his nose.

"Why not? It's a gift from the Father's priest, so a gift from the Father himself." Or so most of the followers in the lower city might believe.

"Look, my friend, we novices run naked down halls at night and throw mass orgies during breakfast. But you arriving in that," Cere waved a hand to indicate the priest-gifted outfit—"not showing the first bit of skin?" He shivered. "Scandalous, I tell you!"

Martin ran his hand over the dark, supple leather. "So, I'll forever be remembered as defying the social mores of a society with no social mores?"

Cere nodded. "Exactly."

If only Martin didn't squeak when he walked.

Cere stood suddenly, throwing his arms around Martin and taking him by surprise with a punishing kiss. He stepped back, a sad smile on his face, turned, and left Martin's rooms without another word.

Martin ran his fingers over his bruised lips long after Cere departed.

While Martin knew the gardens and the offices of the temple quite well, he'd never before entered the great sanctuary, only seen it through windows. Gleaming marble steps led to an entrance wide enough to admit four abreast. For a moment he recalled the beautiful countess, how she aged, and finally, how she died. She'd traveled this route.

Martin shook off the thoughts. She was beyond help now. The Chosen were no better than the demons, were they?

Once more, he longed to save Cere, but Dmitri swore Cere had his own path to walk. Someone jostling Martin from behind urged him forward into the main chamber.

He gritted his teeth but didn't burst into flames or meet a contingent of bloodthirsty priests upon entry.

White and pink marble everywhere in the octagonally shaped room, with an arch in each wall and eight alabaster columns. A quick perusal showed the downward-leading stairs at the arch opposite the entrance.

There were no chairs, forcing the two hundred or so guests to stand. White floors, pink walls, white ceiling, pink columns. A circular, raised dais sat in the center of the room, bearing an alabaster statue meant to represent the Lady herself.

Martin did, indeed, stand out. Would the creature awake and fell him with a lightning bolt for not presenting himself in traditional worship clothes?

Well, this was him. What he worked for. A hunter. A guardian. Smirks and murmurs met him when he shouldered his way farther into the hall. Even the youngest initiates wore finery, strings of pearls adorning their hair as they flittered about the room, checking to see which notables attended the event.

One glare sent them in other directions.

Boughs of flowers festooned the marble archways of the sanctuary, adding touches of pink, green, blue, yellow, and red—and the occasional fallen petal—to the otherwise too-pristine room. Dozens of perfumes competed for dominance—the winner likely burning out Martin's sense of smell forever.

Men and women posed around the walls, showing off flowing gowns and jewels to the greatest advantage. Several wore the same worn-out pallor of the countess before her death. Worshippers being slowly drained, most likely.

The priests couldn't kill a highborn mage-born outright, now could they? No one with political power cared about the lower classes, but the nobility might take exception to one of their own publicly accused of magery—plus the stigma of having a mage-born family member, based on the carriage driver's outrage at the mere suggestion.

Martin worked his way toward a few guards dressed similarly to himself at the back of the room so as not to stick out too badly, though they wore brown leather instead of black, of much lesser quality. A few he knew from his time in their ranks before his promotion to captain, some as subordinates. They murmured welcome as he took his place among them.

"You've come voluntarily, Captain?" one asked, a look of surprise on his face. "I drew the short straw."

Another groused, "I drew second shortest."

"Don't you want to be here?" Wasn't attending a Choosing considered a great honor? Lots less work than patrolling or any other duties at the barracks.

The first guard let out a disgusted snort, upper lip curling in distaste. "I'd rather watch my nephews and nieces for a sevenday—all thirteen of them—than this lot."

The second guard grumbled in agreement.

Well then.

A trumpet sounded, quieting all conversations.

Heavily adorned novices entered from a side archway. Martin craned his neck, spotting Cere in the middle of the group.

Cere stepped past the masses, which parted to let the procession through, making his way to the central circle. Fourteen positions around the Lady's image, draped in ribbons, lace, and the finest fabrics in every shade imaginable.

Should Martin pray to whatever deity that Cere remain a novice? No good came from promotion in this place.

In the background, a soft, *thrum, thrum, thrum* of a harp announced the beginning of the ceremony. Four priests and the high priestess climbed the stairs, heads appearing first, then the rest of them. Unlike Dmitri's ilk, high-ranking priests and priestesses of the temple were usually only seen on holy days.

Or while hunting mages.

All wore white trousers, heavily embroidered with seed pearls, golden clasps securing their long capes to their shoulders.

The current Chosen were shirtless, both male and female, smooth chests gleaming with a shimmer of oil and sprinkled with gold dust. Whoever pleasured them later would be picking off the dust for days. The priests wore no shoes, their filmy trousers clearly displaying the muscular legs underneath.

So different from Father Dimitri's sect. For a moment, Martin nearly laughed, imagining the man whose face he had never seen so blatantly flaunting his body.

Acolytes came behind, dressed similarly to the priests but in light blue, bearing a litter. A hush fell over the crowd.

The woman on the litter glittered with gold dust from her high-piled golden hair to her toenails. Naked, the embodiment of the Lady herself.

The oracle.

Ageless. Beautiful. Revered.

The voice of the Lady. Long silent.

To a slow drum beat, the acolytes lowered the litter and helped the oracle to her feet, careful to touch only the palms of her hands. To do so elsewhere would smear her gold. Holding still, she appeared a statue. Totally naked, with no hair on her body. Her breasts rose and fell with her breathing, ruining the illusion of an inanimate object.

The high priestess stood beside her, voice filling the room. "Today is a momentous occasion. Today our Lady will pick from her children for a greater purpose. This is a time-honored tradition, as old as history itself."

Really? That wasn't what Dmitri said.

The priestess continued, "For seasons they have grown and learned, worshipped the Lady as she saw fit." She droned on and on about what an honor would be bestowed this day, the Lady's greatness, and so on, until Martin's eyes crossed. When the guards around him started grumbling, the priestess finally said, "Now, the time has come to select the worthy for further service. The Lady has many tasks for her faithful. Step forward for her selection."

Shortly after the last Choosing, Martin knew from Cere, two acolytes died of fever, leaving two open places to fill. A Chosen had been drained of power for killing the countess. The oracle needed apprentices. The ever-swelling ranks required more teachers. Surely all fourteen in the circle would become Chosen this day.

"Our Lady will now make her selection."

Priests stepped up from behind, one for each candidate, to comfort them if they failed or guide them in the Lady's will upon her award. Cere had told Martin the process often enough.

The golden oracle stopped before a young woman, who'd seen perhaps nineteen birth seasons, and closed her eyes. A thrill ran through the crowd, an invisible wave of power.

Magic!

The oracle opened her eyes, lifting the woman's head with two fingers under her chin. Voice soft and melodic, her words carried nevertheless. "I sense in you great faithfulness, a mind for education, and a heart of goodwill. With your patience, you will guide the novices, suiting them for my service."

The young woman gave a tremulous smile, wiping an eye with the back of her hand. "Thank you, My Lady," she murmured, gazing down again.

The oracle moved on. The priest standing behind the girl rested a crown of purple flowers on her head.

"That one's going to be a teacher," the guard next to Martin said.

"How many of these things have you been to?"

The guard rolled his eyes. "Too many. Sometimes I think there's a bit of trickery that I always draw the short straw. At least they feed us afterward."

The oracle approached the next novice. "Although I sense in you much promise, you are not yet ready for the task set for you." She strolled on by, barely stopping. The young man hung his head, receiving a green garland from a priest.

"Well, I'd hate to be him," the overly experienced guard said.

"Why?"

"He's been to five of these things. I've never seen anyone come back for a sixth."

"What happens to them?"

The guard shrugged as best he could under the weight of so much leather and a broadsword strapped to his back. "I don't know. They just disappear."

Cere said they returned home. What if they didn't? The tingly sense of dread took up a place in Martin's stomach.

Sheer force of will likely kept the rejected candidate from crying. Maybe he knew his fate.

One by one, the oracle made her selections: teachers, mentors, acolytes, a future priest. At last, she stopped before Cere, a smile curving her gold-painted lips. "You have faithfully worshipped me with your body and mind, freely increasing the love in your heart. The day will come when you shall open your mouth and deliver my words."

All emotion left Cere's face. His mouth dropped open. What? What had she said? Despite the solemn occasion, the crowd broke into a frenzy. "Oracle! He's to be an oracle!"

Oracle. The voice of the Lady. How Martin wanted to grab his friend and never stop running. But no, the oracle now approached, golden image blocking out Cere's blinding smile. She regarded Martin for several long moments. Was that cold hostility in her eyes?

Her body went completely rigid, and her eyes rolled back. Martin glanced around. This wasn't normal, was it? Was she ill?

When she spoke, her voice was low and raspy, so unlike her former musical tones. "Demon-slayer, you think you know me, but you know me not. But you will, little warrior. I see you."

Fire seared Martin's skin. He bit his lip to keep from howling. The pain abated as quickly as it came. When he opened his eyes, the acolytes were already helping the oracle back onto the litter.

What had she meant? Had no one else noticed Martin's discomfort?

"Did you see that?" he asked the guard who'd drawn the short straw.

"See what?"

"Did you hear the oracle speak to me?"

The guard let out a chuckle. "I've been told the Lady reserves visions for her priests." He elbowed Martin. "I would say to apply for entrance, but you're a bit too old to be a novice."

A flash of gold caught Martin's attention, and he turned to see Cere, a crown of yellow roses on his head, the flower petals highlighting his burnished hair. "Did you see? I'm to be an oracle." His bright smile faded. "The priests said I could come and tell my family goodbye. They're not here, so..."

The priests huddled together in a circle, their low conversation a slight buzz among the larger hum in the room. Spectators crowded forward to congratulate the newly promoted novices.

"I know it doesn't matter now, but I wanted to tell you, I... I love you. You're the only one who's ever seen *me*, Cere, not the merchant's son, not the novice, but *me*." Cere turned and dashed into the crowd, quickly swept along with the tide of revelers.

Martin stood still. Love? What should he do now?

Silence fell. All eyes turned toward the doorway. The crowd parted, allowing a man clad in brown to approach. They drew back as though the very touch of his robes might taint them.

Father Dmitri said for Martin's ears only, "She has seen you. The battle begins."

Martin closed his eyes. That voice. That eerie voice. Chills raced down his spine.

The spectators swarmed through double doors, the scent of roasting meat beckoning. Most of the guards in attendance followed the crowd, but the two next to Martin stayed, one focusing his gaze on Dmitri and lifting a brow before turning away. "Are you coming with us, Captain? The feasts are worth the wait."

Martin clapped the guard on the back. "No, you go ahead. I have other business to attend." He found an opening and made his way outside with Dmitri.

Cere. An oracle. Never again to sit on a bench on a warm day and chatter about nothing. Martin's heart ached. Though he could never return Cere's deeper affection, he did care as a friend.

Martin followed Dmitri into the temple across the street, into the comforting gloom of the familiar training area. The brightness of the temple had hurt his eyes. At the back of the chamber, they stopped. Dmitri stepped forward, tapped his fingertip against the stone surface, and continued tapping out what appeared to be a random pattern. The wall glowed, and the spots took on a meaning: Dmitri opened a...door? Portal?

The stones shimmered, dissolving into nothingness. Martin eyed the doorway with wary eyes. What magic was this? Pulling in a deep inhale, he braced himself and followed the priest through the opening.

Dmitri threw his arm out to the side. "Well, Martin, welcome to the real temple."

The real temple?

Priests shuffled from several directions, forming a loose circle around him, men and women he'd hunted with, talked to, learned from—but whose faces he'd never seen.

Dmitri swiveled his hood from one side to the other, pausing for a moment on each of his number. Fourteen in all, like the Chosen.

All nodded. As one, they swept back their hoods.

Martin's breath caught. What was this? He jerked back, heart pounding, and spun. Around and around. Nothing made sense.

Every priest in attendance had skin like porcelain, gleaming white, even under low light. Their eyes were much larger than his; their ears rose to pointed tips. Their hair fell around them in waves of nearly transparent white silk.

"You're... you're not—!"

Dmitri stepped closer, but didn't crowd. "I told you before. We're not from your realm."

"But... But..."

In his usual calm, Dmitri stood stock still, no emotion showing on his face. Another of their number stepped forward. Dmitri shook his head. "It's all right, Gaveth."

Dmitri had spoken of other realms, said he wasn't from here.

That Martin's mother had been from Dmitri's world.

For all Martin's wondering what Dmitri looked like, nothing could have prepared him for the reality. He would have guessed Dmitri to have been old, yet his appearance said otherwise. Then again, what did Martin know of other races?

For a moment, he stared. His mother. His mother was of these people? His breathing came in harsh gasps. No, she'd been an ordinary woman. Hadn't she?

Dmitri's eyes were two shades darker than his skin. Martin might call them pretty if he wasn't staring at something that shouldn't exist. One thing to be told they were from another realm, another entirely to have all doubt removed.

Dmitri sighed. "While I understand this comes as a shock, we have much to teach you and not a moment to waste."

Martin grasped the priest's—or whatever he was—hand. Hey! No claws. Just long, slender fingers, though the nails formed a point. He searched Dmitri's face. Mum had looked nothing like this man. How could she have been one of his kind?

The others hadn't moved. Hints of leather peeked out of their robes. Tooled leather, similar to Martin's.

Their skin and eyes varied in hue, though their skin glittered like pearl. After the shock wore off, he realized how stunning they were.

"What... What are you?"

"We are what you've known all along. We are guardians."

"But you look so different from me." The robes and gloves suddenly made more sense. Not only could the guardians not show how different they were and be taken to the Lady's temple, the sun likely wasn't kind to their pale complexions. "You said my mother was one of you. She didn't look like you do."

"You have so much to learn." Dmitri shook his head. "Yestereve, I visited the docks. I saw a man easily two heads taller than you, with dark skin and tattoos covering most of his body. He wore three golden hoops in each ear. He doesn't look like you, but can you deny he is from your world? In the mountains of Adulas, all manner of creatures live who don't look like you. Increased magical ability shapes the appearance of my kind. Your mother was less powerful and appeared more like those of your realm. She also used her powers to further disguise herself and ensure any offspring would not stand out."

Thinking back, Martin remembered flickers of images, for a moment seeing his mother differently when she let her guard down. "Was my father one of you too?"

"No. He is from this world, as was your grandmother. Your mother was from ours, which makes you very valuable. Born of both worlds, those with enough skill can use you to open a portal between our realms without requiring multiple practitioners to perform the feat, as we have spent much time and effort erecting guards. Which is why you must learn to control your skills.

"This is the beginner's class," Dmitri said. "More explanations come later. The important thing is that we are here to train you."

Martin narrowed his eyes. "Why?"

"Because in recognizing you, the Lady's oracle has shown us that you are the chosen champion."

Martin shifted his gaze from the priests and priestesses to the walls. They glowed soft blue under the lantern light. He opened his fist. A golden flame licked at his palm. "Wha... how am I doing this so easily?" Always before, he'd had to concentrate, except during a moment of desperation in an alley.

"Because, Martin, you are standing in the middle of magic. Welcome home."

***

"Are you sure about this?" Commander Enys sat in his usual chair, feet on the desk as he'd never do around those he wasn't comfortable with.

A familiar pose when Martin appeared.

"I am sure. I appreciate you finding me, giving me a home and purpose in the guards." How could Martin explain without giving too much away?

"But you have found another path."

"Yes, I have."

Enys let out a long, slow breath, running the fingers of one hand through his shaggy hair. "I always knew this day would come. You never struck me as a man to settle into routine without risking his sanity. I'm sad to lose you. You're an outstanding captain. I consider you a friend as well."

Martin cracked a smile. "Though you've tried to consider me a brother-by-bonding, cousin-by-bonding four times removed..."

Enys laughed, a rich sound reverberating from his barrel chest. "You have no idea how flattered you should be that I wanted to make you a kinsman." His smile fell. "It wasn't to be. But know that your place with the guards is here, should you ever want to return."

Martin studied the room, the dust eddies swirling in the sunlight from the window, the stack of parchment on Enys's desk. An empty plate on a side table said Esmerla once more proved her devotion by sending one of their many children with midday meal.

So many things Martin would miss. He gave Enys a hug before leaving the office for the final time. No looking back. He couldn't, or he might want to change his mind, return to a simple life.

He had a realm to save.

Chapter Thirty-three

P eter's eyes must have deceived him. He'd heard of sailors going mad after too long at sea, seeing and hearing things not of this world. Had he drunk bad ale? Was the lamb he'd eaten tainted? The *Seabird*'s cook always said the crew should stick to seafood.

Once, they'd had to lash a pirate to the mast during a storm to keep him from jumping ship when he'd started seeing things the others couldn't.

Or maybe Peter's mind merely played tricks. Maybe he'd longed to see Martin so badly he'd conjured a reason and the man himself. Peter gave a shudder. Those... creatures appeared all too real, as had the man who'd rescued him. Was it really Martin? Was he well?

Peter had no way to find out without knowing where Martin lived, except that he worked as a city guard.

What could Peter say? "Excuse me, but an ugly dog chased me, and a man saved me. Do you know who he is?"

Ugly dog. Yeah. That must have been it. But no, that being had slitted centers in its eyes and scaly skin, like one of those creatures he'd seen in the southern islands, with lots of teeth and insatiable appetites.

He shuddered. Then, the man he'd met in the streets, in priest's robes. Peter had seen him around a few times or someone like him but always headed the other way, not being one of the faithful. Some of those mystic types might take one look at Peter and see the secrets hidden in his soul. Why had he asked one for a blessing? Could he ask for information?

Not worth the risk to approach a possible threat.

Despite his best efforts, he still watched the door. No Martin. For days.

He glanced up at a vision straight from his memories. Brown hood, brown robes, brown gloves. Not a bit of skin showing. All eyes turned toward the door. The priest ignored the patrons and marched straight to the bar.

Addie hugged herself. "I've not been exactly the devoutest of worshippers," she whispered, "but I never thought they'd come get me like me mum used to say."

She'd done nothing so wrong as to earn a visit from a priest. The Father's priests hadn't taken up killing mages for sport, had they? For all Peter knew, priests *didn't* visit. At least not taverns. Peter placed a hand on Addie's shoulder, urging her behind him. "You go to the kitchen. I'll handle this."

Addie ducked into the back.

"Can I help you, Father?" Peter's heart pounded a hard beat in his chest. Bile burned his throat. What business had he with a religious man? One by one, his customers darted out the door. For a lot with little respect for the Father's teachings, they showed fear at one of his servants.

Cowards. It wasn't them being approached.

"You call yourself Peter, do you not?"

Peter expected the priest to lift his hood, revealing a grizzled head of hair and a craggy face. The priest did no such thing.

"Yes, Father."

The hood swiveled one way, then the other. No one remained. "A few nights ago, you... saw something. Something you've never seen before."

"How... how...? Do you mean it was real? Not only in my mind?"

"Yes, it was real." The priest kept his voice even, betraying no emotion. "I wish I could say otherwise."

"What was that thing?"

"Something you shouldn't speak of."

"I wouldn't. I mean, who'd believe me? But, shouldn't people know?" Given its speed, the thing could take out dozens of lives in a night.

"Ordinary folk cannot see them. There are reasons you do. We cannot let the beings become common knowledge."

"But... Why don't you tell people?"

"Can you imagine the panic, people running from what they cannot see? When one shows up in the city, it's hunted."

"By what?"

"By those trained to hunt them."

Knife in boot. Always on guard. Martin showed up at the right time and saved Peter from the abomination. "Who?" The twisting in his gut said Peter already knew.

"I believe you've met a hunter. Or rather, one other." The hood dipped. "I myself am a hunter, as are most of the Father's priests in the city, and a few priestesses."

"Why are you telling me this?"

"First, because I'd like your silence to avoid a panic. Secondly, because the hunter who rescued you is concerned for your safety."

All the cards lay on the table, apparently. "Why didn't he come in person?"

"He is at war with himself, between what he needs to do and what he wants to do. In time, he'll reach a decision."

"What he wants to do?" Did that mean he wanted to visit but didn't out of some misguided sense of loyalty? Peter narrowed his eyes. "Are you holding him somewhere until he does what you say?"

The priest waved a dismissive hand. "We believe in free will. However, we must help him fulfill his destiny. Tell me truly. If he left the city and never came back..."

What? No!

A chuckle emerged from under the hood. "No words are needed. Your face betrays you. So, he has found a place in your mind, if not your heart."

How could this priest speak so casually of a man loving another man? Didn't the Father consider such affections to be abomination? "I... I don't know."

"Well, though he will not tell me, you've certainly found a place within his." The humor fled the priest's voice. He placed a gloved hand on the bar. "A war is brewing. I cannot clearly see your exact role, yet you will play a part. A big part."

"Again, why do you tell me this?"

"Because Martin will need you. And because there will be danger. You must never tell him I came here, for doing so can affect his choices, his actions. So much depends on him."

Peter scratched the back of his neck, then clutched his amulet as he often did when troubled.

The priest reached across the bar and snatched the charm. "Where did you get this?"

"My mum. It was hers."

"What was her name?"

"Rosemary."

The priest drew back, murmuring, "Rosemary, Rosemary. Then, finally, he said, "Rossmari." His hood lowered and raised. "You look like her, or rather, the illusion she conjured. But her hair was lighter."

Peter scrubbed a hand through his artificially dark locks.

"Ah," the priest said. "I see. Tell me. What happened to her?"

"The villagers killed her, called her a mage."

For several long moments, the priest remained silent. Finally, he murmured, "For that, I am deeply sorry."

"You knew her?"

The priest wafted out a sigh. "Yes. I am sad to hear of her passing. When she chose to flee E'Skaara, I'd hoped she'd have a peaceful life. Though she possessed some skill, she wasn't powerful enough to join our battle."

"Both Martin's parents were killed by mage hunters. Did he tell you?"

"He didn't need to. I have long waited for him. You, however, are most unexpected. Tell me, was your father a mage?"

"A what?"

"Did he have special powers or abilities?"

"I know what a mage is," Peter snapped. "What does that have to do with my father?"

"I sense power in you."

Da had predicted the weather and knew where to find a safe haven for the *Seabird* when needed. There was nothing magical in those skills, was there?

"Now, please forgive me." Faster than the eye could follow, the priest grasped Peter's hand, laying his forearm bare.

Peter screamed when the priest sliced open his skin.

Peter stared at the now-healed wound on his inner wrist. A mark, which glowed if he stared too long. He'd been taught by his mother never to question a priest.

"Why?" he croaked, in a voice hoarse from screaming. That no tenants rushed down the stairs to investigate remained a mystery.

"You need protection, but you might have refused. My apologies, but in this, I couldn't take a chance." The priest followed Peter's line of sight upward. "No one heard us. I put up silencing wards."

How strange that the man never removed his hood or let so much as an inch of skin show. But... "Silencing wards?"

"I've no time to explain. These runes are for protection—your protection. One of my kind warded your tavern long ago, and it appears Martin has marked you as his own. None can harm you here unless the wards fall." The priest rose from his seat at the bar. "Remember, Martin needs you. I see in your heart your need for him."

"But—"

The priest held up a hand, giving his head a shake. "Listen to your heart."

Without another word, the priest vanished. Vanished!

Peter ran to the window, peering out. Nothing. No one.

He stared at the mark on his wrist, recalling the priest's words: *Listen to your heart.*

Chapter Thirty-four

M artin lay on the bed in his new room, mind too full for sleep. Here, beneath the city in the Father's temple, magic lived. Ethereal creatures laughed and joked over dinner.

Had given him a set of enchanted leather armor like they wore. Had treated him like their own.

And yet, he saw the runes. Long lines of glowing text the others said nonmagicals weren't meant to see. When he studied the markings, really focused, whispers reached his ears, murmurings and not-quite-words. What were they trying to tell him?

Fourteen priests and priestesses to teach the fifteen elements of life, by the Father's teachings:

Fire
Water
Earth
Air
Heart
Soul
Mind
Body

Peace
Love
Future
Past
Present
Joy
Sorrow

He hadn't bothered asking why fifteen skills and fourteen priests and priestesses. He probably wouldn't have understood the answer. Or, in Dmitri's words, "Not *now*, but *you will.*"

So much, too much, too fast. Where was Cere? What was he doing tonight? And...

Where was Peter? Was he okay? Dmitri forbade Martin to leave the sanctuary until he grew stronger but swore to Peter's safety. Unfortunately, the master of demons had upped the game, sending fiercer followers. Why? Martin was nothing. A farm boy from a poor community tucked into the mountains.

But mage-born.

Would he, in time, look like the other guardians?

A dear image flashed through his mind. Peter. If Martin's skin faded to milk-white, his eyes appeared nearly colorless... In his conjured image, the desire in Peter's eyes turned to horror, the arms that once held tight pushed away.

Peter screamed. Martin gave chase.

But no. If Peter's very existence hinged on the guardians, Martin lost the option of turning back the moment he'd left his family's home.

Martin bolted upright in his bed. If demons gathered here in the city, what about the outlying villages? Without quite knowing his destination, he ran out the door in search of... anyone.

Gaveth approached from the common training area. "Stop! What's wrong?" Was that concern on his face? Martin hadn't been around the unmasked priest long enough to work out facial expressions but understood Gaveth to be young by Dmitri's standards.

"Where is Father Dmitri?"

"He's out. What's wrong? Tell me." No mistaking the sincerity in Gaveth's eyes this time.

"The village where I grew up. What happened to it?" To the children he'd spared when their parents betrayed him.

Gaveth let out a harsh breath. "I am to instruct you on the ways of the past. Tonight, you're tired, but this much we can do if you let me help you."

"Please." Anything to ease his mind.

"Come with me." Gaveth extended his hand. Martin hesitated too long, staring at the abnormally long fingers with short pointed nails. Gaveth dropped his arm back to his side. "Come." He led the way down a dark corridor, murmuring soft syllables under his breath. A faint glow came from the walls. "With our night vision, we don't need much light, but Dmitri reminded us of your requirements. For now."

For now?

The corridor opened onto a cavern. The dim light shimmered on a rippling surface. A fountain? A fountain without running water, so now a pool. "We're under the city, aren't we?"

Gaveth nodded. "Yes. The oldest known people of your world lived here in these caverns. So close to the source of magic, mages were born. It's no accident that both the Father's and the Lady's temples are here."

He shuffled over to the pool, gesturing for Martin. "It will take you a while to master this skill, but working together we should be able to at least give you a glimpse of what you seek."

The water rippled, something unseen swirling beneath the surface. Martin shuddered, recalling the creatures in the lake near his home known to grasp a leg and pull a fisher out of a boat—or so legend said.

"Focus," Gaveth said, stepping closer, though not close enough to cause alarm. Would Martin ever get used to his new teachers' appearance? "First, I'll show you the past as I've seen it. It will take time, but gradually you'll be the focus.

"Now, clear your mind, and stare into the water. Deeper, deeper, seek out the bottom."

Wait! Was there something on the bottom? An image? Martin stared until his eyes watered. Nothing.

"You're trying too hard. Open your mind. Let the vision come to you."

Time and again, Martin tried. Nothing. "It's of no use..." At the moment he gave up, images came.

That made him wish he'd never asked.

The sun rose and set forty-seven times before Martin left the sanctuary. He knew the others hunted, for they returned shaking their heads and murmuring in hushed tones, cleaning ichor off their clothing.

Tonight, they'd finally deemed him ready to return to the streets, capable of hiding himself from view of the demons and the creature under the temple. The stronger he grew, the greater the threat.

But he must protect Peter.

And defeat his foe before it overtook Cere as an oracle.

The night appeared different to Martin's enhanced vision, crisper, sharper, the ocean scent stronger in his nose. Here and there, glowing runes marked the way, like road signs only the guardians could see.

Autumn had given way to winter during his confinement. The snow would be deep back in the mountains. He no longer worried about the remaining villagers surviving the cold.

Demons laid waste to his village. Looking for him. He couldn't afford any more guilt, unable to change the past. All he could do was move forward, do the best he could with his newfound knowledge.

Tonight, he'd draw new runes that some of his comrades couldn't, not being from two realms. Be they guardian or demon, no eyes would see the spell he cast, but any with harmful intent would find themselves repelled from the site. Whoever had cast the current runes had been adequate, but the demons grew stronger. Sooner or later, the existing barriers would crumble.

He might not be able to see Peter again, hold him, but he could protect him. Keeping to the shadows, Martin rebuilt faded runes in the air at one rear corner of the tavern. The scent of corrupt magic hung on the breeze. Demon. The night they'd gone after Peter?

The knowledge sped Martin's footsteps to the next corner.

He'd completed the final front corner when he glanced up and met dark eyes through the window. Peter paused midmotion of wiping down the bar. One moment turned to two, two to three.

Why couldn't Martin move?

The door opened, and Addie called out, "Well, come on in, then."

He shouldn't have come, or waited until later. But no, he'd been seen. No hope for escaping now. Going to his doom, Martin gave a hard swallow and entered the tavern, empty save for Peter and Addie.

Potential mages, untrained. Their magic now shone in his sight, a faint golden glow.

His nerves jangled. Funny, he'd served as a guard, finely honed his fighting skills, killed demons without flinching, yet the possibility of rejection terrified him.

Smile strained, Peter approached. "To what do I owe the courtesy of your visit?"

Martin whispered, "How long since you last traded a secret for a secret??"

Peter scowled at Martin, arms folded across his chest. Dyed hair topped a face that, while not particularly handsome by local standards, carried an open friendliness, inviting men and women alike to chat. To Martin, no greater beauty existed in the universe. Peter's nearly-black eyes drilled into Martin's. Peter canted his head, whispering into Martin's ear, "You've been gone a long time; I've no secrets to tell." The rich timbre of his tones caressed Martin's spine like a velvet glove.

Addie, the bar, hunting, all faded away, Martin totally enraptured by his lover. "My apologies, Peter. My duties have kept me away of late."

Peter brushed his lips against Martin's. "I've longed to see you. Are you really here, or do I share company with a wraith?"

Martin made a confession of his own. "I've missed you."

Grasping Martin by the hand, Peter shouted, "Addie, you close tonight."

Not waiting for a reply, Peter pulled Martin toward the storeroom and shoved him up the ladder to the room above. A wall-mounted lantern glowed a welcome.

The moment he joined Martin, Peter grabbed him by the back of the head and kissed him soundly, desperate, seeking. He drew back, resting his forehead against Martin's. "That's what you get for leaving me to my own devices."

Somewhat breathlessly, Martin replied, "Then I guess I'll have to leave you to your own devices more often."

"Don't you dare!" Peter slammed his mouth down with no hesitancy in his all-consuming kiss.

Should Martin be thrilled to have been missed, or sorry he'd have to give this up again? Deep in his heart, uncertainty grew. He should leave here, stay away. His presence put Peter at risk, brought the wrong kind of attention.

This is war!

But Martin had never felt so helpless as in Peter's arms. Too weak to fight, too powerless to do the right thing. He wanted only Peter. Why? What was it about this man that drew Martin in, touched his heart in a way he couldn't resist—didn't want to resist?

In Peter's strong arms, Martin found comfort, purpose, a reason to fight an unseen enemy.

He remembered his mother's tales of two heroes. *There are always two.*

Mouth to mouth, hands roaming, tugging at clothing, moans and grunts, and the patter of rain on the roof. Naked, they fell onto the bed, Peter a reassuring weight on Martin's body. Warmth, comfort. Together.

The mat of hair on Peter's chest told the truth of his coloring, ranging from dark blond to medium brown. Martin brushed his lips over the puckered scar on Peter's shoulder.

Martin's own body hair was thicker if lighter, his muscles bulkier than Peter's.

After their second time together, Peter had prepared, a small vial of oil sitting on the crate serving as a bedside table. "I don't know—"

Martin cut him off with a kiss and pulled away to murmur, "I do."

Taking the oil from Peter's hands, Martin shifted, giving wordless instruction. Peter lifted up, allowing Martin to apply oil to his own entrance.

Many times Martin had done the same, had grown skilled in fast preparation. Even so, now his heart pounded, and his hands shook slightly. Why? He was no nervous, untried virgin.

This was his first time, however. His first time with Peter, with someone he... loved. Depositing the oil on the crate, he wound one arm around his lover's back, applying oil to Peter's cock with the other and, at last, at long last, guided him to where he needed to be. Martin pushed back, impaling himself on the head of Peter's cock.

They both gasped. "Am I hurting you?" Peter asked. "I've been told it can hurt if I'm not careful."

Though Peter's length and breadth weren't often found, the brief stab of pain—pain Martin wouldn't burden Peter with—subsided after a moment of careful relaxation. For a long moment, they stared at each other.

Peter grinned. "This is even better than I dreamed." Taking Martin's mouth in a near-bruising kiss, he gave a tentative thrust.

Martin met each thrust, communicating what he wanted, letting Peter know he caused no discomfort. Oh, yes. Amazing. The feel of taut muscles flexing against Martin's skin, the slick slide of Peter rocking into and out of him, setting a slow but sure rhythm.

Wrapping his legs around Peter's hips, Martin angled upward. Oh, yes, oh by the fates, yes! Clinging to firm shoulders, he fell into the moment, the kiss, the connection. Never before had he experienced such closeness, like they were indeed two parts of one whole, moving in perfect harmony. His muscles trembled.

The rightness of the moment. Martin groaned when Peter lightly nipped his earlobe, gently scraped teeth over his shoulder, and sucked at his neck.

Chills raced over Martin's skin.

Peter's movements grew more frantic, and he wrapped his arms around Martin's shoulders, pinning their bodies so closely together. Friction between their bellies stroked Martin's needy cock, sweat making him slide.

So good. Yes. Right there. He wasn't going to last. Putting all his focus into Peter's enjoyment bought precious seconds.

"I'm going to... I'm gonna..." Peter's pace faltered.

Martin leveraged arms and legs to keep the tempo going.

"Ahhhh..." Peter froze, muscles seizing beneath Martin's hands.

Peter shuddered and groaned for what seemed a lifetime, finally collapsing onto Martin, only to raise himself on shaky arms. "Am I too heavy?"

Speech eluding him, Martin shook his head, reached between their bodies, and frantically stroked his cock. He had to come. Now. Why couldn't he...

Peter shimmied down the bed, taking Martin into his mouth. Oh, damnation! Yes! Martin's body defied his attempts to hold still, shoving into blissfully wet heat.

Digging his fingers into Peter's hair, Martin thrust, again and again, pressure building to the tipping point. No, he didn't want to let go, wanted to experience this moment forever, the sultry look in dark eyes, the sex-tousled hair, the perfection that was Peter.

But no, Martin couldn't hold back. He threw his head back on a husky moan, giving a final thrust. Body tight as a bowstring, he stilled, hovering on the edge, caught in the fleeting moment between torture and ecstasy. Groans escaped him, low, throaty, needy.

Martin fell, pulsing down Peter's throat.

Floating. Blissful. Martin vaguely registered Peter moving him, spooning against his side, raining kisses on his face and neck.

In a trance, Martin watched Peter extinguish the lantern, pull him close, and murmur, "Good night. Rest well."

In that moment, Martin visualized the eternally wonderful place the Father once promised his faithful, yet could also clearly see the land of everlasting torment.

For Martin could never enjoy an eternity of wonder in Peter's arms.

Fate wouldn't let him.

Sometime later, Peter quietly said, "The other night, you saved me from those... those... things?"

"Things I will protect you from." Though Martin had no idea how much the protection might cost him.

"Addie too?"

"Any within this tavern."

"What are they? Those... things. They said they wanted to take my soul, use me for bait."

"An evil most cannot see." Martin kissed the top of Peter's head, resting against his cheek. "You should know that I have quit the city guard. If you ever have need of me, find a priest of the Father." Bait. Yes, they'd planned to use Peter against Martin. All the more reason to leave and never come back—if the sacrifice kept Peter safe. "I protect the city from those things, along with the Father's priests."

Peter stayed quiet a few moments, then nodded against Martin's shoulder. "You'll tell me if there's more I need to know?"

"I will." May the Father grant that Martin never have to.

And many thanks to Peter for accepting Martin at his word and trusting him to keep it.

May the trust not be misplaced.

Chapter Thirty-five

N ight after night, Peter watched, waiting until daylight to leave the tavern, even to step out the back door. The shutters stayed firmly in place every night. Occasionally, he caught a glimpse of black or brown clothing from the tavern window, but no one tapped on the door.

Tonight, cool weather brought in a crowd seeking warmth, full bellies, and conversation. Nearly every table was filled to capacity. Only one space remained at the bar. How he'd love for Martin to perch upon the stool, but no matter how many times Peter glanced toward the door, only regulars entered.

Somewhere out there, Martin and others kept the city safe from a horror Peter dared not speak of. He agreed with the priest: telling tales would only lead to panic. As long as the people weren't in danger, the less they knew, the better.

But he had some degree of magic, didn't he? Why should he be safe in here when he could be out there, protecting others and, most of all, keeping Martin safe?

Granted, his powers were hit and miss, striking when he least expected and totally worthless when he needed them, but he could learn, couldn't he?

A young traveler sat on a stool in the corner of the room near the hearth, playing a lively tune on a reed flute. Several patrons gathered around, patting the tables with their hands, stomping their feet to the music.

One older man, deep into his cups, with the leathery skin and weather-beaten air of a sailor, kept the patrons at the other end of the room entertained. "And then we came upon this village. No smoke rose from the chimneys, and the harvest sat ungathered in the fields, covered in fine snow." He waved his hands, pitching his voice high and low, acting out the scenes for his audience.

Scenes that didn't require him to lower his tankard.

"Just the four of us, mind you, and not a swordsman in the group. I said to meself, 'Something be wrong here,' but would me brother listen? No, he wouldn't.

"We found a scraggly mule, mostly skin and bones. Wolves came and went as bold as you please from the houses. We stopped and looked to see if we could find the villagers."

To scavenge, more likely, given the character of the storyteller. The scent of fish stew, woodsmoke, and strong ale competed with the aroma of perfume or soap here, an unwashed body there. Nothing unusual about the night.

Not even the flute or storyteller, though sometimes the musician played a violin or harp, but the stories were mostly the same, designed to scare the faint of heart.

"That's when we saw it," the sailor announced with excessive flair, punctuating his words with a rap of this tankard against the table. This also told his audience they needed to buy another round if they expected his tale to continue.

A man in the well-cut garments of a prosperous merchant motioned to Addie to supply more ale. With a roll of her eyes, Addie complied. She'd worked here long enough to have heard every variation of any story and knew when a man performed for his drink.

Peter would never hear the end of her complaining if she wasn't equally well reimbursed for her time.

A hush fell over the crowd, those nearby leaning in to hear the speaker's every word. "Saw what?" a young man asked.

The storyteller lifted a finger in a "one moment' gesture and took a healthy draft of his ale. "Bones. Skin. Bodies all around, frozen in the snow and ice. Young, old, men, women, and children alike." He lowered his voice to barely above a whisper. "They just lay there. The wolves wouldn't even touch 'em."

Peter caught a flash of purple out of the window. What was that? Green flashed, then blue.

His mind caught up to his eyes when the screaming started.

The door slammed open. A man staggered in, opening and closing his mouth. No sound emerged. He pointed toward the street and collapsed.

Peter glanced out the window. His heart stopped. "Close the door!" No one moved. He charged out the door, heart hammering as he banged the shutters closed. The screaming and scritch of claws on stone drew closer. He darted inside the tavern, slamming the door just in time.

Something pounded on the shutters.

Addie paused but a moment before jumping into action. "Tables! Add the tables."

A few patrons snapped to enough to help, shoving upended tables over the windows, legs sticking out.

"What are those things?" Addie asked. Her hands shook. She'd been levelheaded enough when Peter needed her to be.

He'd never told her of the demons. May he not regret the decision.

"I'm not sure." In a brief moment of silence, Peter heard scratching. "The back door!" He tore across the floor, jumping a fallen chair and winding through huddled bodies.

The back door burst open before he got there. "Run!" he cried, snatching a carving knife from under the bar. He swiped at the first monster. How had the thing gotten past the runes?

The green-scaled thing grinned. "Ahh... the little man wants to play."

Where were Martin and the priests? Hadn't they said only one or two of these things ever entered the city and were soon after killed by the hunters? Four others peered around the first, hissing, reaching around the leader, and grasping for Peter.

"He smells good!" one shouted.

Peter stepped back, gripping the knife. He'd barely escaped one of these things. Five? Never. Chairs scraped across the floor behind him, the screams lessening as, hopefully, the patrons fled the building.

Footsteps grew close. Peter spared a glance over his shoulder. No! "Addie, run!"

She shook her head, a fillet knife in each hand. "Da taught me never to run from anything. By the Father, I don't know what these things are, but you're not facing them alone."

Peter's heart pounded a frantic beat. "You see them?"

"Aye, but by the Father himself, I wish I couldn't." Addie had magic, so could see them. Though, based on his customers' screaming, at least a few of them now could too.

"Kill the female if you want, but not the male," the leader ordered. "The master wants him alive. For now." The thing grinned, possibly the most unpleasant sight ever to exist.

Including sea battles.

But kill Addie over Peter's dead body. The things held no weapons—they needed none. Teeth and claws appeared dagger-sharp. They'd not lure him out into the alley, where his sight would fail, and possibly theirs would not. He took two steps back. If they followed him, Addie still might get away.

He'd never forgive himself if she died in this battle.

His time as a cabin boy on a pirate ship taught him a little about knife fights, enough to avoid them at all costs. Sooner or later, though, the gentlest of men were put to the test.

Peter rocked on the balls of his feet, knees loose, remembering lessons taught by pirates. One of the things grabbed at him. He swiped the knife down. Greenish blood spurted. The creature shrieked. Two more took its place. So, their leader intended to let others do his fighting for him, and their skin wasn't nearly as hard as the last one he'd encountered.

Or the leader merely waited for the others to tire Peter to step in and claim its prize.

Whoever or whatever their thrice-cursed master was, Peter wished him dead. Screaming persisted in the streets. Peter couldn't spare thoughts for those poor souls now. He had his own battle to fight, and if by some miracle he and Addie prevailed, five fewer horrors would stalk the streets this eve.

Where were the priests?

Peter grabbed a bottle so vile he dared not serve the gin and threw it at the leader. The bottle plinked against its head and smashed on the flagstones.

Addie hurled a lantern. The oil and gin burst into flames. The thing screeched, dancing in the blaze, then grinned. "Fire can't hurt me."

Without knowing why, Peter thrust out his hand. A ball of yellow flame shot toward the monster. For one brief moment, the thing stood immobile, engulfed in yellow light. The being exploded, green gore splashing the walls, the floor, Peter, and Addie. The other four demons shared a glance.

The second took the first's place. "You are untrained, mage. Your wild magic will do you more harm than good."

Peter tried again to hurl flame. Nothing happened. "Addie, run!" he screamed, grabbing the fire poker and brandishing the iron like a sword.

Something flew by his head.

"Ah-ha!" Addie shouted in triumph. A dagger protruded from the second demon's eye. It blinked its undamaged eye at them, face slack, then fell backward, knocking down another monster.

Two. They'd taken out two. Three more to go.

Peter peered around the trio.

Four more pairs of eyes gleamed in the darkness.

"Martin, I love you," he said, not caring who—or what—heard. "Addie, as your employer and your friend, I order you to go." Without waiting for an answer, he said a prayer to the Father. "Father, please keep the innocent safe, and accept my soul if my time has come."

He'd go down fighting.

Chapter Thirty-six

Martin stalked the sector, sword at the ready, controlling his breathing to focus on hearing the night. His skin prickled more the closer his quarry drew. Something seemed different tonight, twisting his insides into knots.

"You feel it too?" Dmitri asked.

"What is it?" Martin rubbed his hand over his sword arm. The hairs on the back of his neck stood.

"I'm not sure. But it's wrong."

The night they'd faced two warrior demons flashed through Martin's mind. Were another two stalking them? Had the hunters become the hunted?

A hunter's whistle sounded to the west. Martin stopped, turning toward the blast. Another came from the east. Two different sightings at separate sides of the lower city?

Together, he and Dmitri bounded eastward toward the closest alarm. They cut down an alley and stopped. Two sets of purple eyes stared out of the darkness. Scales slithered over stone, punctuated by a low, rumbling chuckle. "Well, well, well, what have we here?" The thing came closer into the glow of Martin's ball of mage fire.

A hideous thing, with sharp claws and teeth, glowing eyes, and ears like a bat's wings. They flapped slowly, then settled against the demon's head. The thing stood taller than Dmitri even, taller than any demon of Martin's experience.

Its smaller companion slipped out of the shadows. "Ah, I smell a hunter. Tell me, betrayer, how does it feel to hunt those you abandoned? Does your friend here know what you look like under those robes or who you really are?"

"He knows as much as he needs to." Dmitri's voice came out controlled.

The beast snickered, turning to face Martin. "He never told you why he gave up his realm to live among lesser beings. How he was banished after he betrayed—"

"Enough!" Dmitri's booming voice made the alleyway tremble. Really? Dmitri raising his voice? What sorcery was this? He raised his sword. "I'll send you back from whence you came."

"And why would you waste your time? The runes have fallen, didn't you know? Tonight, my brethren overrun the streets, hunting down the precious weak beings you'd try to save."

Martin's breath caught in his throat. Peter! He glanced in the direction of the tavern. Dmitri's hand on his arm stopped a mad dash. "Let us finish here first. Others patrol that quadrant."

"Not for long." The first demon let out a laugh. "You've lost. You know, you should have told the denizens of this realm about us ages ago. Maybe then they'd know to run when we approached." He smacked his lips. "They're so much better when they run."

A scream split the night. Martin bunched, ready for flight. Dmitri held him in place. "Do you think you'd get three paces before these two cut you down?"

Right.

Twin grins flash at him. "If you dare." The taller one charged.

Martin whirled, putting himself back-to-back with Dmitri. The muscles of the priest's back and thighs flexed, betraying his intent. The cassock hid those unspoken tells from their adversaries.

The first demon flicked out a forked tongue, tasting the air, and grinned wider at Martin. "Oh, the sweet scent of magic. It fills you, not like the paltry bits I feed on from others of your kind. You'd make a fine meal if my master allows. Maybe once he's finished with you, he'll reward me with what's left over."

The shrieks from the city grew louder now. Martin shut down the mental images the screams produced. Fear beat against his senses, a palpable thing.

No. Nothing but his opponent could hold his attention now.

He took the first step in the dance. Right foot, sword back. Left foot, swing. *Parry. Thrust. Spin.* Demons might look different, but their muscles moved more or less like a man's. Bunching in the right thigh meant weight on that foot, and vulnerability.

Martin slashed, backing up occasionally to bump against Dmitri's reassuring presence. If only Martin could call the consuming fire down at will like he'd done once before—the night he'd saved Peter.

The demon slashed out with razor claws. Martin jumped back. Claws raked the leather over his chest.

He swung his blade with all his might. *Slash!* Dark liquid spurted from the thing's arm. It howled, a hideous, bloodcurdling sound.

No more wasting time! Martin needed to check on Peter! *Slash. Whirl. Thrust. Spin.* Purple fire burned in the demon's eyes. Step by step, it kept pace. Another scream. Was that Peter? Oh, goddess. What if Peter needed him?

Martin snatched the knife from his boot. Throwing away the dance steps he'd learned to use for fighting, he charged, like he would have a wounded deer back home when he hadn't owned a sword. Steel bit flesh. The thing howled again. Blood spurted. The knife grew slippery, but still, Martin fought. Blindly. On pure instinct. Visualizing where the knife should go, then trusting the blade to its duty.

"Martin. Martin!" Something grabbed his shoulders from behind. He brought the blade up. Dmitri grabbed Martin's wrist in a near-painful grasp. "Martin. It's dead."

Martin stared down at the bloodied heap at his feet. Another lay a few feet away, missing its head. He conjured, flinging blue fire onto the mangled body while Dmitri chanted. The remains went up in a sizzle. Martin swore he heard one final shriek before the body vanished.

Dmitri whispered, "The war has definitely begun."

<hr />

Without pausing long enough to clean his blades, Martin darted out of the alley and onto the main street. Too many people for this hour, when the area should be nigh deserted. A woman sprinted toward him, stopped with wide eyes, running her gaze up his body. She screamed louder and darted past.

He glanced down. Green blood dripped from his gloves, blade hilts, and clothes. Likely his face too. Nonmages might not be able to see the demons, but apparently, they saw the gore.

Dmitri caught up. "Come. We are needed."

Screams and whistle blasts split the night. Hundreds of people stampeded past, many carrying crying children. Likely headed for the high city for refuge in the temples. When others ran away from danger, Martin vowed the opposite.

Especially when the Stone's Throw lay in this direction.

Dmitri by his side, Martin pounded over dirty streets. Blood and fear assailed his nostrils, cloying his senses, leaving him unable to sniff out demons. At last, he found himself in front of the Stone's Throw.

Flames licked through broken windows.

No! "Peter!" Nothing else mattered. Martin charged the door.

Strong arms kept him back. "No," Dmitri hissed into his ear. "I'll go."

Without allowing Martin a moment to react, Dmitri shrugged off his robes, dropping his clothing as he darted toward the door. The straps on his boots burst into flames. Dmitri ignored any discomfort, plunging into the inferno.

Breath caught between his throat and chest, Martin froze, fighting the instinct to dart into the flames. Peter was in there. Martin's mind said no one could be there and still alive. His heart told his rational mind to shut up.

There he stood, fire heating his face, the smoke searing his nostrils. He raised his hands to the heavens. Rain! Snow! Ice! Anything! *Any deities listening, please help!*

Maybe Peter wasn't there. Maybe he'd left with Addie or had been taking one of his walks on the docks...

Which would've put him in the path of demons. Martin reached out with his senses, trying to feel life within the flames. Why couldn't he sense Peter?

Martin's heart began an icy slide into the pit of his stomach. What if Peter died? Was already gone? Crying out his last alone. Had he thought of Martin? Martin had promised to keep him safe.

He'd failed. Hot tears tracked down Martin's cheeks. Had he sent Dmitri to his death in a futile attempt to save a dead man?

All around, people screamed; fire crackled. Flames shot into the sky from the docks, ships blazing. Turning, he witnessed a nightmare world of fallen bodies, burning buildings, screams, and demons running loose in the land.

Tonight, it appeared the demons didn't hide their presence.

Martin cut his eyes back toward the remains of the tavern. Please, let Dmitri find Peter and bring him back alive.

Movement caught Martin's eye. A man, all in black, strode down the street, oblivious to the chaos around him. His long cape swept out behind him, borne by hidden winds. Only his face showed, obscured mostly in the shadow of his hood.

Fear sent chills up Martin's spine. This was no man. His mind couldn't identify what he saw, but the deepest parts of him urged him to run.

Fully a head taller than even Dmitri, this being crossed the street with measured strides. Confident, unconcerned.

The figure lifted one gloved hand, drawing circles with his palm in the air. Sigils ignited, a brief spark before dying. Invisible bands lashed Martin's arms to his sides.

What? No! Martin's heart pounded in his chest, every ounce of rational thought screaming at him to flee.

The man...thing... approached with all the grace of a cat, bootheels making no noise. Though the firelight fell over him, he cast no shadow.

He *was* shadow, stalking forward and placing a cold, gloved hand against Martin's heated cheek. "We meet at last, little hunter. Tell me, did you enjoy putting my friends to the sword?" His words held no malice, just a hint of a growl.

"They murder innocents," Martin snarled.

The man smiled, showing even, white teeth. "What power decides who is innocent and who is not? I once knew of a child, who was, what? Seven summers, maybe? He murdered his entire family in their sleep, painting the walls with their blood. He was most definitely a child. Was he innocent because he lacked age? My friends rid this world of the most heinous among you for all you know."

"They call you master! They kill at your bidding!" Martin tried to flinch away from the man's hand to no avail. Except for the ability to speak, he found himself unable to move.

"But then they're controlled. They do nothing without my wishing it. Are they guilty of following my commands?"

"Then the fault belongs to you," Martin snapped.

The man laughed, a robust sound so out of place in their surroundings. The mirth fell away. He tightened his grip on Martin's jaw to near-painful levels. "You don't know me—yet. But you will, little hunter. Believe me, you will."

A crash from behind him had Martin struggling to turn.

"You wish to see?"

Not knowing how he got there, Martin found himself facing the burning tavern, the roof teetering on the brink of collapse. The man pulled him closer, putting Martin's back flush against his chest. "Flames are lovely, don't you think?"

The heat seared Martin's face, even halfway across the street. His heart pounded harder. No way had Dmitri survived, let alone Peter.

"You can save them, you know," the man who wasn't a man whispered, mouth so close his lips grazed the shell of Martin's ear.

"How?" Martin would do anything, give anything, to save Dmitri and Peter.

"Easy. Give yourself to me."

What? "You want me to... to give up my current existence"—my lover— "to become one of those... things?"

"No, I do not. Look at me." Martin found himself facing the man again. "Do I look like one of my servants?" The shadows peeled back, revealing a handsome man with sea-green eyes and a mane of copper hair. The image flickered around the edges. An illusion. "I most certainly do not. You won't either, though I had no idea the depths of your vanity."

Not vanity. Martin just didn't want Peter to recoil. Another timber snapped. The roof collapsed with a great *whoomph* of flame. Too late! He was too late! He struggled, but his captor's will held fast. Martin focused. Why wouldn't his magic free him?

Again the man laughed, jostling Martin like a rag doll. "You're a mere novice, no matter your strength. I was proclaimed one of the strongest among thousands, survived when they did not, and have practiced magery for thousands of your puny mortal seasons.

"We're running out of time," the man hissed, putting himself eye-to-eye with Martin. Flames reflected in those green eyes. "Soon, they'll be beyond even my saving. So, tell me, little hunter, will you give yourself to me to save their lives?"

Martin stared at the flames. Tears and sweat burned his eyes. "Yes. But I have to see them. I have to know they're okay. Speak to them."

"Done." The man snapped his fingers.

Shadows within the flames took shape, coming closer. Dmitri stepped out of the blazing inferno, Peter draped in his arms—sooty, hair and clothes singed. His chest rose and fell.

Dmitri stopped, staring at the man. "Why are you here?"

Martin didn't have to see the man's face to hear the smile in his voice. "Why, Dmitri. How good to see you again. You haven't changed much, I see."

Dmitri scowled. Peter stirred. Dmitri set Peter's feet on the ground, holding him steady with an arm around his waist. "Martin, get away from him. You don't know who he is."

"Ah, but he will, he will." The man wrapped an arm around Martin's chest, pulling him back.

Martin's skin crawled, being so close to this foul being.

"Martin?" Peter asked, glancing behind him at his ruined tavern. "Martin? What's going on? What are you doing with that man?"

"You cannot take him." Dmitri snugged Peter against his side. "You know he has free will. He must consent."

The chuckle rumbling behind Martin had to be the evilest sound he'd ever heard. "That won't be a problem. You see, he agreed, to save the two of you."

The world blackened around the edges on Peter's horrified face.

Peter screamed, "Martin!"

Chapter Thirty-seven

"M artin!" Peter stumbled in the direction Martin had stood and would have fallen if not for the priest holding him up.

"Come. He's gone, and it's not safe for you here."

Peter barely heard the wails or saw the burning skyline. Martin. That man. That... that... thing had taken Martin. "Where did he take Martin? Why?"

Peter gazed up and up at a pale white face, eyes shining like a cat's in the dark. Long white hair spilled over broad shoulders.

The man holding him was totally naked, muscles sleek but well-defined.

Peter barely fared better. For a moment, an image of Martin flashed through his mind, how he'd looked at their first meeting, burned and broken.

"Who are you?" Peter tried to yank free. The unnerving man held tight.

"You may call me Father Dmitri for now." He paused long enough to better grip Peter's stumbling form. "The immediate answer is that he traded his life for ours. He doesn't know what awaits him, nor that the runes you wear and my power would have saved us. The arrogant prick took advantage of Martin's decency."

This was a priest? This was what hid under layers of brown wool?

"Wait! Martin sacrificed himself for nothing?" The rough tones of Father Dmitri's voice offered no reassurances. "Where did that... thing take him?"

"To another realm."

Another realm? Was that a city? Another land? "We can't leave him there."

Father Dmitri skirted the body of a woman lying on the ground. A man lay slumped against a milliner's shop. Both looked beyond any healing skills Peter might have. "We won't. Now, no more talking until I get you to safety. The lower city definitely is not safe."

They turned the corner. Glowing eyes emerged from the darkness. Father Dmitri backed up, shoving Peter behind him. "No matter what you see or hear, you must never say."

Who would Peter tell? Who would believe him? All other witnesses appeared dead or well on their way.

Father Dmitri held up a hand.

Two of the hideous creatures stepped forward, one's teeth dripping blood. "Oh, see who we have here. You can give him to us. He's served his purpose."

"You cannot have him." Father Dmitri kept his body between the creatures and Peter.

"But he's just a pitiful man. No more than a meal."

By the Father. Peter froze, horror holding him in place.

"You did not hunt to feed this night. This... This"— Father Dmitri swept an arm out to indicate the city— "is an abomination. Killing for the sake of killing."

One of the vile creatures snickered. "Today, tomorrow. What's the difference? Once Thomoth fully wakes, we all die. Unless our master defeats it."

Father Dmitri attempted to reason with these foul creatures. If Peter only had a sword...

The priest made a shoving motion with his hand. A ball of white light shot from his fingertips. The things shrieked, sinking back.

Grabbing Peter's arm, Father Dmitri bolted. He must've been younger than Peter realized to keep up such a staggering pace.

They left the main street, loping steadily uphill to the high city. No flames here, no terrified screams. Lights spilled from the elegant Lady's temple. Sounds of revelry cascaded from the doors and windows, so at odds with the carnage not so far away.

"This way." Father Dmitri led Peter to the other side of the street, so dark it seemed to repel even the soft glow of street lights.

"What about them?" Peter pointed across the street.

"No matter how bold they've grown, the creatures will not tempt fate by coming closer to the Lady's temple." Father Dmitri gestured toward a door, not bothering to hide his nakedness.

Peter didn't say more. He'd lost his tavern, his home... his lover. Was Addie okay? Please let her have been reasonable for once and run.

Father Dmitri guided him through the pitch-black interior without a single waver or without bumping into anything. At last, they came to a door. Letters in an unfamiliar language glowed around the doorframe. Father Dmitri placed his hand dead center of the door. He spoke a few words Peter didn't recognize, even though he'd learned many languages during his lifetime.

The door opened.

Candles chased back the darkness. Who had lit them? No light had peeked out from under the door. Peter saw no evidence of anyone else.

"This is Martin's chamber. Stay here." Father Dmitri beckoned toward a room hewn out of rock, containing a bed nearly as small as Peter's own, a washstand, a desk, and a chair.

Peter's heart rose to his throat. "Where are you going?"

"I must go help the others."

The door shut behind him.

And locked.

* * *

Dmitri let out a sigh of relief. Maintaining a glamour of clothing and the acceptable appearance for this realm for the sake of those they met sapped his strength—strength he'd need for the battle ahead.

The tavernkeeper saw through the glamour.

Dmitri retreated to his chamber to don new clothes. To get Martin back, he'd need to hurry. Xariel taking him meant Martin had become integral to some sinister plan.

Much as Dmitri had been seasons ago.

Xariel.

No time to dwell on the past. Just because Martin agreed to go with the monster to spare Dmitri's and Peter's lives didn't mean he'd agree to everything.

Time mattered.

Dmitri shuddered, flashing back to earlier. Flames, engulfed in flames. Peter lying still on the floor, fire already licking at his body. Martin's lover had been used as bait. He wouldn't have died in the fire, but Martin didn't know that.

Like the demons said, though, Peter's purpose had ended. With his considerable magic, he'd have made a fine meal for a demon.

While the demons' purpose for him ended, Peter still had a role to play. He carried more power than Dmitri ever imagined, hidden by a skillfully made amulet. Only someone from Dmitri's own realm would have such knowledge.

Two mage-born, each with parents from the two different realms, coming together. Peter's mother came from Dmitri's world, as did Martin's. Could their combined magic build a bridge, or seal the rift once and for all?

Though Dmitri had no desire to see his homeland destroyed beyond redemption, he'd not destroy another's to save his own.

He'd had an unpleasant ending lurking in his path for centuries. He'd spare Peter and Martin if he could. Enough people had already paid with their lives for his mistake.

Flames one minute, the next outside, with a living, breathing Peter. But for how long? To reach his destination, Dmitri would have to undo the seals that had held the horrors at bay.

No, tonight, the seals failed if the king of demons himself entered the dominion of men. The flawless skin, lithe body. Even through a moment's glance, Dmitri saw his biggest regret hadn't changed. Still alluring. Still tempting, though wearing glamour.

Could Martin defy him? Had the bond with Peter grown so strong?

So much rode on a little thing like love. The ache in Dmitri's chest reminded him of when the mere promise of the thing tripped him up and sent him into a fate worse than death.

He stared at his hands as he donned a pair of hide gloves. A lot of good love had done him.

But to love the right person provided an anchor, protection.

He must guard Peter at all costs. "Father, please help me," he prayed.

To a deity long silent.

Chapter Thirty-eight

M artin stood on a seashore, watching the waves crashing over boulders. Unrecognizable birds wheeled overhead, crying out to each other.

A dream?

The sky held a hazy gray hue. All colors were muted, shadows flitting on the edges of his vision. He didn't recognize this place, know how he got here, or where the man in black had disappeared to.

But Peter. His wonderful, dear Peter, survived the flames, along with Dmitri. Or maybe Martin's worried mind merely conjured a vision.

Waves rolled onto the shore, lapping at his bare toes. He'd long ago removed his boots and stripped down as much as he dared for comfort's sake. Whatever the place, it put E'Skaara's worst summers to shame for heat.

A day spent exploring showed no way back and gave no indication of Martin's location. If he ventured far enough, would he find a village?

The outcropping looked familiar. He turned. A tiny inlet, perfect for mooring ships. His heart dropped to his stomach. No! It couldn't be.

He ran toward the harbor, stopping at the water's edge. There should be ships here, buildings, an entire city. Nothing but weeds and scraggly trees. Their withered branches mirrored his mood. He climbed a hill he'd last seen under cobblestones, stared at the place where a temple should be, and twisted around, trying to imagine the Father's temple across the road.

Nothing but an empty, blackened crater in the ground.

There should be carriages, gas lamps. And...

He charged down the hill, back toward the water. E'Skaara's main dock should be here, which meant a side street should lead from the wharf to the city proper. Nothing but dry grass crunching underfoot.

One step at a time, he made his way to where the lower city should be. Where the Stone's Throw should be.

Where Peter should be.

Peter.

Pain lashed through Martin's heart. Had Peter and Dmitri really emerged unscathed from the fire? Where was Martin, why was he here, and how could he get back to where he belonged?

Nothingness, as far as the eye could see, except for shadows. Everywhere, shadows. They moved to and fro. With reason? Did patterns exist in their flitting silhouettes?

If Martin stared hard enough, they almost took shape. People? Staring harder brought in the faint hint of walls, gone with a blink. Was he still in the city, but unseen? Could he find the ancient relics he'd visited with Dmitri?

Dmitri.

Martin ran back to the hill he estimated should house the temple. The gardens should be... over there. The sanctuary? Behind him. And farther back, the area reserved for the oracle and the oracle only.

Well, no oracle. He knelt in what he thought might be the center of the room if it existed.

Footsteps crunched dry grass behind him. Martin whirled.

The man in black leaned against a withered tree trunk, sweeping out a hand. "Look around. The creature you call the Lady did this. It used us, leaving the land I love the ruin you see here." He strode forward but stopped before coming too close. "It will do the same to your world."

"What is this place?"

"It's a shadow of the world you live in. We were you, once upon a time. We lived, we loved, we had children, grew old. And died." The man trained his gaze on Martin. Even the sparkling of his eyes appeared muted and gray in this place. "When *the Lady* came here, my ancestors loved her, worshipped her, built temples in her honor. How did she repay us? Abandoned us without a backward glance. Leaving us to die." He turned away. "And die we did. If you look closely, you'll see the ghosts of the lost.

"Everything you've ever been told of her religion is a lie. The Lady so many pray to bears no resemblance to your native form. She'll... it will kill you in the end."

"What about you? You still live."

"I was her oracle. The one who loved her most and felt her betrayal the deepest. In return, she cursed me to outlive everyone I know, watch my beloved homeland crumble."

"Who are you?"

The man sketched a bow. "Xariel, Oracle of *the Lady*, at your service." He spat the name and gave a bitter laugh. "Though it hasn't spoken its loathsome platitudes through me in ages."

"What do you want with me?"

"Much."

Martin backed away. "You're a monster. You killed all those people."

Xariel held up his hands. "Did you see me throttle anyone? Cut any throats? In fact, I think I saved two on your behalf, or have you forgotten already?"

"The demons. You control them."

Fire flashed from Xariel's eyes. "How dare you call them demons! Those people were very much like yours once except for appearance and favoring the night. They were left with nothing. Do you blame them for turning into animals, feeding on what little magic they can find that won't alert that vile creature to their presence?"

"But those were innocent people they killed."

"It's no worse than will happen when your *Lady* bores of them and leaves again." Xariel charged forward, grasped Martin's collar, and slammed his back against a tree. Eye to eye, he sneered, "There is no Lady. It came to your realm where you embraced a lie. It usurped your deity and fed on your adoration. But mostly fed on your magic, eliminating any who might stand in its way."

"Thomoth." Martin's hard swallow didn't clear his dust-dry throat. "We will beat it."

The man barked out a laugh full of bitterness. "Who? You and the few remaining guardians? If six thousand of our best and brightest failed, what chance have you?"

Six thousand?

"Let me ask you—what has Dmitri shown you? Parlor tricks?" Xariel stepped back. Green flames danced over his gloved fingers. "Runes, signs, divination? They are nothing when it comes to the creature's power. Where do you think that power comes from? Fire rages and destroys, but it relies on what it burns for its existence." Xariel swept his arms out to the sides. "This! This is what happens. Thomoth sucked the very life from our realm, as it will yours. I've spent eons trying to overcome the runes keeping me here. And now I have. The foul creature won't do to your world what it did to mine."

"But then why kill the people?"

"To feed the hungry. It's not flesh and blood I long to save, but my home."

"This one isn't that bad."

Xariel scoffed, full lips twisted into a bitter scowl. Blackened timbers littered the ground, the trees standing dead around him. The whole area appeared devoid of life. Even the ocean waves ceased their rolling. "Now, do you understand?"

"But... those things! You control them. Make them stop."

"I don't control them, can't you see? They're the bitterness left behind after ruin. Pity them more than you fear them."

"You're not like them." No scales, no purple eyes. A powerful glamour. Except for his beauty, most wouldn't notice if this... man strolled through the city.

Was it wrong to think of this man as beautiful, this evil being who'd released destruction on Martin's city? Possibly his village. The man lied about not controlling the demons—he had to be lying. After all, he walked right past them, and they paid him no mind. They called him master.

Yet, he'd saved Dmitri and Peter. Why?

In the mountains surrounding Martin's old home grew a beautiful blue flower, so lovely any who saw one wanted to pick it and take it home, were obsessed with the notion until they did. Prolonged contact caused death.

Yes, beauty and danger often traveled hand in hand. But, once the plant withered and died, Da had brewed tea from its shriveled leaves and cured many an ailment among his people.

Beautiful, dangerous, but in the end—useful.

"No, I'm not like them." Xariel let out a sigh. "The one many of your kind dedicate their lives to isn't anything from your world. I don't believe it thinks of itself as male or female. It's old. Older even than me."

Older than him? Xariel appeared of an age with Martin himself, but hadn't he admitted to being much older? "How old are you?"

The man gave a bitter smile. "Older than I have the right to be."

Not an answer. "What do you intend to do?"

After a long moment of staring out to sea, Xariel murmured, "I intend to destroy the entity, freeing your world, this one, and many more."

"How?"

"By destroying its anchor." He fixed his gaze squarely on Martin, the sorrow on his face replaced by determination. "The ones you call the Chosen."

Cere!

Chapter Thirty-nine

X ariel. Beautiful, sinister Xariel.
   Dmitri closed his eyes to the pain. Soft light reflecting off skin, panted breaths. Smiles. Laughter. The heart he'd forgotten he possessed ached.

His thoughts turned sour. "The Lady" so many worshipped would doom them in the end. He'd tried before to convince the people it wasn't what it seemed and had been cursed for his efforts.

None of those people existed anymore. None escaped the creature's callous disregard.

Except for Xariel, more cursed than Dmitri for betraying the one who'd possessed his body.

Power corrupted. With each destroyed realm, the creature gained more. If they didn't fight, it would destroy this realm too.

But Dmitri and his ilk didn't risk telling the truth. Once people made up their minds, there'd be no dissuading them, particularly about religion.

No, the people loved the Lady, who gave them their secret heart's desires. They wouldn't take the blinders off to see who—or what—she really was.

Dmitri fought on the frontlines to save the people who'd so easily turn against him. While Xariel would risk any and all other realms to restore their own, putting them on opposite sides of this fight.

Yes, Xariel had powerful magic. He'd been among the strongest of them seasons ago when Dmitri left and broke their mage bond to prevent Xariel from feeding on Dmitri's magic.

Dmitri's former love had seasons to grow stronger since, gathering energy his servants brought back from this world.

Was something of the man Dmitri remembered lurking beneath the surface?

And Xariel brought those other beings, using them as pawns. Before revenge consumed his every waking thought, he'd once been a good, caring man.

Dmitri's caring man, who'd seen the worlds the creature destroyed; the lives laid to waste. World upon world, lives upon lives, sacrificed to a being who gave nothing in return.

There was no chance Xariel could defeat the Lady on his own, for the guardians had failed when they'd numbered in the thousands. And a smaller chance still for those who yet lived.

What if they combined forces?

With purpose, Dmitri strode to the bridge he'd once shown Martin. The lower city smoldered around him. Bodies lay where they fell, rich and poor alike. A well-dressed man died next to the woman he'd probably left the safety of his home to procure.

Death had no regard for rank or social standing and would not stop. These lost souls were beyond help. For the living, Dmitri must strike a bargain.

Stepping over the rough stones of the ancient bridge, he removed his glove and placed his bare hand on the runes. They glowed. Nothing happened. After so long a time, had the portal closed on this end? The demons came through quickly enough.

Xariel couldn't have gotten through if the wards hadn't fallen completely. Had someone sealed the entrance to keep Dmitri out?

One by one, he plodded through carnage to reach other runestones. The other guardians were out seeking demons, but he'd not heard their whistled signals.

Finally, on a crumbling piece of wall he remembered as having been freshly built, he pressed his palm to the runes. A rumbling reply from deep underground answered. The air above the fallen stones shimmered. Drawing in a deep breath, Dmitri stepped through.

He came out at a near replica of his old home, on a ridge overlooking the city. Or what once had been a city, now overgrown. Drifting by on a breeze, phantoms whose faces he dared not gaze upon.

Family, friends; he'd lost so many during the purge when his world ran out of magic. This had been such a beautiful place once. From this vantage point, he spied the cove in the distance where he'd once...

No! He'd lost his love. Lost his mage bond. Twisting discomfort squeezed at his heart. A coward, he hadn't even told Martin the truth about the man he'd loved.

And lost. There were always two.

Seizing a gnarled stick from the ground, Dmitri waved a hand to remove any small branches. Apparently, he'd brought enough magic with him to strip the twigs and use the remainder as a walking stick.

The ground here sloped steeper than in E'Skaara, the city having worn away at the surrounding crags. No directions were needed. Finding the path took no effort at all.

He strode down what had once been streets, now covered over by grass, and paused, gazing at the spot where the Stone's Throw stood in the other realm. In his own world, a robust woman served potions here, once upon a time, potions Dmitri's mother purchased when Dmitri or his siblings fell ill.

His brothers. Eight brothers, all gone. Four sisters, gone. Mother gone. Father gone. No more chatter from nephews or nieces. Nothing remained to mark the grand estate where Dmitri had grown up except a twisted metal gate, long since rusted.

Only he remained of a once-powerful family line.

Well, he and one other.

He trudged on, entering the circle where the temple grounds once stood. His mind took him back to his younger self, heart pounding, as he stood with a smiling young man to declare their bond in front of their family and friends. The gardens had been so beautiful that day, the breeze fragrant with the scent of the many now-extinct species of flowers and shrubs.

Family and friends now long gone. His mate claimed by the creature as an oracle. Best not to dwell on the past, lest he forget that all his endeavors now were for the possibility of a future for his and other races.

Tossing back his hood, he declared, "I know you're here. Show yourself."

Striding over the rough stones of the ancient ornamental bridge, he removed his glove and placed his hand over his heart.

Xariel appeared, bearing the taint of evil like a whiff of sour perfume. The glamour he'd worn in Martin's realm didn't do him justice.

He'd been so beautiful the first time Dmitri met him. His beauty hadn't faded with time.

"You've come for your little pet," Xariel spat, a cruel twist to his lips.

"He's not my pet. He is my student, nothing more."

"Yes, I know. But you can only break our bond completely by forming another. Don't think I haven't felt your attempts to rid yourself of me."

An old argument, one they had no time for. "I've not tried to bond with anyone else."

"You're here to win back the man you call Martin?"

"While I wish him to remain unharmed and need his skill for the upcoming conflict, it's you I'm here to see."

"Me?" Xariel's scowl softened momentarily, then his face returned to its rigid, unyielding mask. "You've had no use for me in many seasons. Why would you need me now?"

"Because neither of us can win this war fighting on two fronts."

Xariel stayed silent for so long that Dmitri braced for an attack. While he was the strongest among the guardians, Xariel could defeat Dmitri with little problem—providing he'd been able to glean enough magic from his servants to replenish his energy.

Xariel cocked his head to the side, long silver hair sweeping over his narrow shoulders. "What do you suggest?"

Dmitri lifted his chin and let out a deep breath. So far, so good. "Combine forces. Let us put aside our differences. Work together to defeat this enemy."

"My stance doesn't change. If we defeat the damnable creature, I still intend to restore this world as close to its former glory as possible."

"At the cost of another realm."

"If we don't win this fight, it won't be an issue. Neither will survive."

"True." Somehow, being here, standing in Xariel's presence, old feelings came back, the desire to see him smile once more, feel his arms. "You know who you've taken, don't you?"

One side of Xariel's mouth lifted into a smile, causing Dmitri's heart to ache with its familiarity. "A mage-born, with one parent from this realm, one from the other."

"He's more, and you know it."

For a moment, true pain crossed Xariel's face. "I know. How could I not? So, she's dead."

Dmitri hung his head, an ache blooming in his heart that he'd not allowed himself to acknowledge. "Yes."

"How?" Xariel's voice came out soft, a mere whisper.

"You haven't asked him."

Xariel's silence provided answer enough.

"She left the realms as so many others have—drained of her magic and destroyed by Thomoth."

"Don't speak its name!" Xariel roared. He closed his eyes, hands balled into fists. Gradually the rage bled from him. "You're trying to make me care. I'm long past caring."

Brief hope flared in Dmitri's heart. "Keep telling yourself that. I stopped listening long ago."

"If this happens, if we win, where will you go?"

"I have vowed to care for those Tho... the creature harmed. Wherever that takes me." What did Xariel expect Dmitri to say? That he'd come back to this place, live in comfort at the expense of so many others?

Xariel released a snort of disgust. "Your bleeding heart will be the end of you."

"So you've told me... on many occasions." Please, let Xariel consider the reach of his decisions.

"I must think on this."

Dmitri fought a sigh of relief. He'd not lost the argument yet. "Your servants have slipped their leashes. They kill without remorse, for more than survival. But you know that, don't you?"

Instead of his usual posturing, Xariel stared at the ground, voice pitched soft. "That is regrettable."

"You control them. Make it stop."

Xariel stared off at the horizon. "I no longer have a say. The portals are open. They travel where they will."

"You could stop them if you wanted to."

Xariel pinned Dmitri in place with a searing glare. "And why would I want to? They've already lost everything. Their world collapses as we speak, leaving them dying and desperate. And me? The only thing I have, what keeps me going, is the desire for revenge and to restore Eallarial."

"What about Martin?"

"*She* named him Arkenn."

"What of Arkenn?"

"Yes, I still have him, though he doesn't even know." Xariel paused for a long moment. "No matter what I decide, he'll stay here, where he'll be safe."

"He won't agree."

"It's not his choice."

"Is it not? He's a man, Xariel. He's formed a mage bond. You know what separation from a bond mate can do. Would you put him through that pain?"

"He must survive!"

"But will he want to? You know there are always two. So many believed it was us." Such bitter reminders. People misplaced their faith in Dmitri.

"We certainly proved them wrong." Xariel's laugh held no humor.

"We have a new chance. The two of us, with Ma... Arkenn and Petran, also a man of two realms. Whoever we can find to assist. We've sent many mage-born away from the city to keep them from the creature. Some have matured and can possibly return to help. It will be our last stand." Begging? Yes. For this, Dmitri would beg.

"What makes you think we'll be victorious when we failed with a force of thousands?"

Dmitri winced at the reminder of their earlier defeat. "Because we can't afford to lose."

When he spoke again, Xariel sounded like the man Dmitri once knew and loved. "Did you tell him who his mother was?"

"Only that I knew her, that she was from my world, Eallarial." Dmitri's heart stung. So many times he saw traces of the mother in the son, yet dared not tell Martin of his true heritage.

Xariel gave a sharp nod. "Tell him no more."

"You will help?"

"I will consider."

"Don't consider too long. Time is running out." Heart hammering, Dmitri spun on his heel and returned to the portal. He stood on a rise, letting the pain take him as he gazed on what used to be. No matter how hard he tried, Xariel would never restore Eallarial, never restore their families.

Never bring back the daughter who'd sided against him.

Chapter Forty

Martin blinked open his eyes, staring out a window at a sky like gray soup—gray soup with chunks of fat. His pleasant dream escaped like smoke through a closed fist.

Peter. He missed Peter.

Fire crackled in the hearth, the scent of roasting meat making his mouth water. He sat up from the pallet he lay upon. "I don't remember falling asleep."

The man who called himself Xariel shrugged off his spot against the wall. He'd dropped his glamour, appearing to be one of Dmitri's kind. A guardian, with pale skin, eyes, and hair. "I had business to attend. I couldn't risk you running off. You don't know this world. It's not... safe."

"I didn't know you we so concerned about me," Martin snapped. Damnation, his head hurt. Squeezing his temples with his hands didn't reduce the agony.

Xariel waved a hand. The headache went away.

Should Martin thank his captor? No. Instead, he perused the room, seeking weapons.

"Do not try to attack me. I'm far more powerful than you could ever know."

Had Martin been so transparent?

"Your father was a healer, I believe, and your grandmother a nature mage."

"Don't talk about my family." Apparently, Martin's foul temper didn't leave with the physical pain.

"What would you rather talk about?" Xariel added a hint of amusement to his tone.

The cottage prison smelled musty, unused, the bed new and clean. There were no personal effects. This was a prison cell, not a home. "How about why you brought me here, are Peter and Dmitri well? What do you plan to do with me, and when can I return?"

Xariel chuckled. "Wow, that's quite a mouthful. All without taking a breath. You definitely inherited your mother's talking talents."

"Do not speak of my mother!"

The smile on Xariel's face fell. He gave Martin his back, turning toward the fire. The room had been sweltering even without a fire.

Pale coloring, head-to-toe coverings. Maybe they weren't all for hiding. This world's sun didn't seem so bright, the sky gloomy, and the air too warm for Martin's comfort.

Just because Xariel was cold didn't mean the same for Martin.

When his captor once more faced Martin, he offered a laden plate and fork. How Martin would love to throw the offering back, but his stomach rumbled. Making himself weak would help no one.

"Then I won't speak of your mother. I'll speak of a promising, headstrong, young mage who once ran along the shoreline, screaming at birds. Who regularly set her family's house on fire until she learned to control her magic."

Damnation. "You knew her."

Xariel nodded. "I knew her."

"So did Dmitri. You both knew her, and now she's dead. Neither of you protected her."

Xariel hung his head, long, pale locks obscuring his face. He looked so different without glamour. Pale, though not as pale as Dmitri. "No, we didn't protect her. I was sorry to hear of her loss."

"Why am I here?"

Lifting his chin a fraction, Xariel shook off his moment of sorrow. "Because, as her son, and the son of a mage from your realm, you are a key. You can travel from one realm to the other without a portal." He fixed his eerie gaze on Martin's. "And no one can stop you."

"You came to my realm."

"But at great cost."

"Those demons cross freely."

"Don't call them demons!" Xariel balled his hands into fists. "I know what that word means in your realm. The Dreckons are just people. Desperate people. Because they don't look or act like you doesn't make them lesser. Would you kill to feed your loved ones? To give them hope for a future?"

Martin said nothing. What could he say? He'd gladly kill this being for one more glimpse of Peter. "What do you want of me?"

"I do not know."

Martin let out a disgusted snort. Figured. "Doesn't sound like you have much of a plan."

"The plan was to take you and use you to travel between realms."

"Now?"

"Now that I see how powerful you are... Dmitri did tell you of your power, did he not?"

"He did. But I don't see how he can say—"

"He's taught you?"

"Some."

"I can teach you more."

"Why would you?" Martin gave in to the gnawing in his gut and sampled a bit of what looked and smelled like chicken. Tasty. The thing resembling a potato tasted vastly different but still filled his belly.

Xariel released a heavy breath. "Because I can't kill Thomoth on my own."

A memory surfaced of Mum telling Martin stories, how he'd admired the two heroes battling the evil Thomoth. He repeated his mother's words. "There are always two."

"There always have been. The last time two went against Thomoth, they failed. They failed their people, their realm, their families. But most of all, each other."

"My mother told me of Thomoth. And the heroes. She said the creature followed them to my realm." Martin remembered hanging in space, silently observing a thousand or more realms.

"It did. It used up ours. The strength of hundreds of mages created a portal to your world, at great cost to themselves. Our survivors fled."

"You stayed."

"I wouldn't desert my homeland."

"Even if you lost all else?"

Xariel let out a noisy breath. "Even if I lost all else. But come now, we waste time. You have lessons to learn beyond Dmitri's understanding."

Nothing came for free. "What will this training cost me?"

Xariel squatted, connecting his unnervingly pale gaze to Martin's. "Possibly, your life."

Martin sat in the middle of a circle of stones, wearing only a light, thin robe. A breeze ruffled his hair, but even the air seemed lackluster in this place. The enemy who could be a mentor sat across from him, similarly attired.

"Aren't we wasting time? The city was under attack when I left." Martin shouldn't be sitting still. He needed to go back and fight. What of Peter? Or Enys's endless family. Dmitri.

Cere.

"Time doesn't move the same in the realms. Or rather, the portals don't. We can arrive a few days after you left with the right concentration. But to do that, you must learn. You're a powerful fighter with your body. Can you fight with your mind?"

Fight with his mind? "I don't understand."

Xariel pointed to a gnarled tree several paces away. "Join me there."

Martin started to rise.

Xariel lifted a staying hand. "Just your mind."

How ridiculous! No one's mind could move without the body.

Suddenly, Martin felt weightless, standing in front of Xariel—by the tree. He turned his head but felt no familiar brush of hair over his shoulders. Instead, his seated and erect body sat exactly where he'd left it.

The chest rose and fell, breathing, but his eyes were closed. "How?"

"Magic."

A second later, Martin found himself back in his body. He shook himself and opened his eyes. Had that really happened? His head hurt.

With a wave of his hand, Xariel dispelled the pain.

"How did you know?"

"A good healer reads the signs." Xariel nearly cracked a smile. "And I received a pounding headache the first time I tried projection."

"Now what?"

"Now, after you've rested, we'll try again. Farther this time. We need to hurry, before the magic you brought with you fades."

"How is this going to help?"

"It's going to help you retain control when you need to."

An image popped into Martin's head of a waterfall, which withered to nothing, the stream beneath more mud than water.

"Do you see?" Xariel asked.

"Yes. What is it?"

"Where we'll travel to by sunset tomorrow."

By sunset? Really? "I have a question."

"Yes?"

"If Thomoth has always been a threat, why did Dmitri wait until recently to work with me? Wouldn't it have been better to start my training as a child?"

Xariel stared off at nothing visible to Martin's eyes. "Remember the child I told you of? Who'd killed his entire family?"

"Yes."

"According to tradition, when a child is born with immense potential for magic, we must wait, let power grow, determine if the wielder would use the abilities for good or evil. You have found good in those others might not, like pirates and prostitutes."

"How does that—"

"Of your own volition, you have used what little power you controlled to save others, even in your position with the city guards. Don't think that Dmitri wasn't watching you every step of the way. He has but one chance. If he approached you too early, he'd lose the chance."

"So the child?"

"His parents were arrogant. Instead of merely teaching him to control and use his magic, they thought they'd teach him advanced application early, create the most powerful mage ever to live."

"What happened?"

"The child went mad. Killed them all."

Martin winced; the images of a knife-wielding child all too vivid. "What would have happened to me if I hadn't made the right choices?"

Xariel once more fixed his eerie gaze on Martin's. "Then Dmitri would have ensured you were out of reach of Thomoth and waited for a new champion."

"He'd have..."

"Yes, he'd have killed you. This war is far more important than a single life."

How easily this man... being... spoke of killing. Martin would rather die than become so heartless. "Are you helping me, or do you intend to use me against Dmitri?"

"I don't intend to use you at all. If Dmitri and I succeed in our efforts, you'll do the right thing of your own accord."

"And if I don't?"

Xariel shrugged. "Then it won't matter, for we'll all be dead."

Time didn't pass the same in the strange realm Martin found himself in. Days seemed so much longer, or maybe being outside his element took a toll. He had very little time to worry about what might be going on in his own world. Xariel kept Martin's mind busy.

He woke one morn to voices, one the hissing susurrus of a demon. He shot out of bed in the hovel, barely stopping himself from charging out the door. Weapons! What could be used as a weapon? No sword, no fire poker, not even a bread knife.

He crept to the window, peeking out. Xariel sat on the ground across from a demon. Instead of the normal menacing appearance, this one was... crying?

Evil incarnate itself in the form of Xariel was... comforting the creature?

Martin stepped out of the hut. The creature screeched.

Xariel placed himself between Martin and the blue-scaled demon.

"What is that doing here?" Martin spat, working up a ball of mage fire.

With a simple wave of his hand, Xariel extinguished the ball. "Martin, you are in my home. You are a guest here."

"Could've fooled me. Here I was thinking myself a prisoner."

"Are you wearing shackles? Are you staring through the bars of a cage?"

"You've taken me from my home. I can't get back."

The demon poked its head around Xariel. "He doesn't know, does he?"

"Silence, Garamel." Xariel eased away from the creature and gestured to the ground. "Ark... Martin. Since you've ill enough manners to eavesdrop on others' conversations, you might as well join in."

Xariel wanted Martin to sit down with that... that... *thing*?

"Suit yourself." Xariel shrugged, smoothing down his simple brown robe. "Garamel, may I present Martin of the realm currently housing Thomoth?"

The demon hissed, showing a row of sharp teeth. "That *thing* has killed many of my kind."

"*Your* kind have killed many of *my* people," Martin retorted.

Xariel held up a hand. "Silence. We have two choices here. We can hiss and spit and solve nothing, or we can do what we came here for."

"What is that?" How could anyone hope to accomplish anything by speaking to a demon and an evil mage? A demon who, moments ago, had been crying, and an evil mage who'd been offering comforting words.

"We are here to discuss an alliance, to defeat a common enemy," a new voice said.

Martin spun around.

A brown-robed priest threw back his hood.

Dmitri.

Chapter Forty-one

Peter stared into a swirling liquid pool.

"Look more deeply," Gaveth said.

Peter strained his eyes in the low light. The shimmering took on form: a man lying on a bed. Martin!

"How does he look?" Gaveth didn't peer into the pool but stood a few feet behind Peter.

"He appears to be asleep, but is he dead?"

"You are the one who sees. What do your eyes tell you?"

The man on the bed stirred, lips moving. Hope rose in Peter's heart. Martin. His Martin. "Am I seeing true? Is this actually happening?"

"It is."

"He's alive! And appears sound."

Peter heard the relief in Gaveth's voice. "Then he is. Xariel took him, didn't kill him, so has plans that involve him being alive." At *least, for now*, remained unspoken.

"Who is Xariel?" Peter asked.

"One of the two heroes my people thought were destined to defeat Thomoth."

Thomoth. The creature Peter once thought of as the Lady. The reason his mother died. He balled his hands into fists. "What happened?"

Gaveth's voice remained calm, only a slight tremor betraying his sorrow. "We were losing the war. Those of us who were guardians on our world fought in the battle, created a portal, and brought the remainder of our people here, thinking Thomoth would be content.

"Xariel refused to leave his home and swore an oath to see Eallarial returned to its former glory by whatever means necessary."

A chill raced up Peter's spine. "Which included sacrificing other realms."

"Indeed. His bond mate disagreed and fled with their daughter to this realm. She bonded with a mage of your realm and hid in the mountains."

Damnation. A sinking feeling in his stomach, Peter asked, "What happened to her?" Didn't he already know?

"Thomoth's disciples captured her and her mate and brought them to E'Skaara to be drained of their magic."

"They had a son?"

"Yes. His parents sacrificed themselves to keep him hidden. The villagers accused him of magery, but with no evidence. I'm told that village is no more."

The tale told around the fire at the tavern. The village that had been laid to waste. Had that been Martin's former home? "The demons destroyed his village looking for him, didn't they?"

"Yes. Their master had need of him."

"And they killed innocent people."

"Not so innocent. Those villagers might as well have killed Martin's parents themselves, and they would have killed him if his magic hadn't intervened."

"Arkenn."

"Yes. That was his name. He now goes by Martin."

"Where is he? Where did that man take him?"

"To Eallarial. Dmitri is negotiating his return."

Peter ran a hand through his tangled hair, tugging the roots. "He should negotiate faster."

"He has. Already the demons have stopped their attacks. The lower city dwellers are burying their dead."

Peter bolted upright. "Addie. I must see if Addie still lives. If she needs anything."

Gaveth put a hand on Peter's arm. "It's not safe for you out there."

"Why not? I—"

"Need to be here, learning your role. You could go out there and help one person, or stay here, preparing to help many. What would she want you to do?"

Yeah. Addie had spent seasons saving all the mage-born she could. If Peter risked himself unnecessarily, he'd be better off facing a pack of demons than one pissed-off barmaid.

And if Addie was safe somewhere, she'd be looking out for the kitchen girl and the tavern regulars. She'd never had young of her own, so she mothered everyone who held still long enough for her to fawn over.

She also knew where Peter had hidden the remainder of the bounty he'd taken from the *Seabird*, and understood he'd want her to use it as needed.

He stared back into the now-still water. "What must I do?"

"If your mage bond works the way most do, you're the focus, while Martin will wield the power."

"And I need to..."

"Meditate."

Peter sat in an underground cavern for two days, cross-legged on a mat. At least, he thought it was two days. He'd slept once and occasionally found food and drink close by. Sometimes he ate, other times, he didn't.

A silver bowl sat over a small brazier, scenting the room with lavender. Only the brazier and a single candle offered light. Outside could be day or night. Occasionally, chanting or the clang of swords pulled his attention away—the priests readying for the battle they told him nothing about.

He let his mind drift, recalling the image from the pool. Martin. The mere thought seemed to hook something behind Peter's heart, pull and pull and pull...

"Peter?"

Peter opened his eyes, expecting his hallucination to have been for only his ears.

Martin stood in the shadows, skin pale and glowing, like the priests'. Peter's heart skipped a beat. Martin? Here? Now? He stood, wiping the seat of his pants of two days' worth of dust. "Martin? Are you really here?"

Martin gave a grim smile. "Yes, but I don't know how I'm here. I'm back there too." He glanced over his shoulder. All Peter saw was the cavern he sat in.

He dove into Martin's arms, touching him, feeling warm skin. He pulled back and stared deeply into Martin's eyes. "Are you okay? Has he hurt you?"

"He hasn't hurt me. He's training me." Martin gazed around the room. "Good. They've brought you to the temple. Have they told you of Thomoth?"

"The Lady? Or what we call 'the Lady.' Yes. They are teaching me to meditate and be what you need me to be during the upcoming battle."

"How's Addie? You don't know him, but I'd like word about Commander Enys and my fellow guards."

"I'm not allowed to leave the temple." Peter didn't bother keeping the bitterness from his voice.

Martin nodded. "It's better that way. I don't know when, but I'll be back soon."

"You're here now."

A slow smile spread across Martin's mouth. "So I am."

They came together in a rush of breath and lips and tongues, hands everywhere at once. Touching, feeling.

Peter found himself on the stone floor, their combined clothes serving as a bed. He lost himself in Martin's touch, the heat in his eyes, the perfection of a warm mouth on his neck and jaw.

This might be a dream, a hallucination. Peter couldn't care less. Martin felt real, muscles rippling under skin, sounded real, whispering "I love you" into Peter's ear.

Peter wouldn't question good fortune.

Outside, a battle could be raging. Here, in the temple's sanctity, he curled his legs around Martin's thighs, shoved his nearly painful cock against Martin's answering hardness, rocking together like the realm depended on their coming together.

Through moans and hissed breaths and shouts of pleasure, they slid, one against the other, Peter's skin tingling from Martin's touch.

Pressure formed within, building, building. Muffling his shout in Martin's mouth, Peter froze, every muscle tensing. He hung on the edge for one long moment...

Then plunged into ecstasy, convulsing as he shot, spurting against Martin's belly. Martin groaned out his own pleasure, melting into the embrace and adding his seed to Peter's, trapped between their bodies.

Martin collapsed to the side, dragging Peter over, where he rested, head on Martin's chest, the steady *thump, thump, thump* of Martin's heart a lulling cadence.

Peter awoke on the cold stone floor in a darkened room, fully clothed, his pants drenched with his seed.

A chuckle reverberated in the stone room. Peter conjured feeble yellow mage fire. "Who's there?"

Nothing. Was it Martin? Had Martin tried to communicate with him?

Peter reached out with his mind, searching for a connection to his lover. Deeper and deeper, his mind sank into a murky mist. *Martin? Are you there?*

There! Something moved! He chased the retreating figure. Where did it go? Blindly he ran after, deeper and deeper into the strange surroundings. *Martin? Martin!*

The mist cleared somewhat, revealing a small child, a girl with golden curls and rounded cheeks. A child? Here? "Who are you? How did you get here?"

The child looked up with eerie purple eyes. Peter jumped back.

"Do not be afraid," the child said. "We will not hurt you. We have been looking for you."

We? "Me?"

"Yes. The elders have been trying to reach out to your race for ages but could not. Then we found you when you slipped between realms. You are not trained to control your thoughts, which would have kept us from making contact. You also belong to two realms, allowing you access to both. You are rare indeed, and exactly what we need. I take this form so you can see and hear me. You and your bond mate coming together created a path for us to travel."

"What do you want from me?" Though the being appeared nonthreatening, power pulsed from deep within, giving off a golden light.

"One of our kind broke our laws. We stripped away all powers and banished the criminal to the abyss between realms. We did not know it would destroy worlds to regain magic, never knowing it could break free of the abyss."

"The Lady?"

The child cocked her head to the side for a thoughtful moment. "Yes, your kind call it the Lady. Others call it Thomoth. It goes by many names. We had no wish to interfere with other realms and have only found them once they were destroyed. We are sorry for those, but I believe all is not lost for your realm. Though you did so unknowingly, you hung in the place between realms with your mate, as you both are of two worlds. You created a beacon for us to follow."

Could this helpless-looking being actually help overthrow the evil currently draining the world of magic? "What must we do?"

"Thomoth has grown strong on stolen magic. Even now, your kind enter a struggle they cannot win. They will be crushed and your world destroyed."

Peter's heart leaped to his throat. Martin! Addie! All the others.

"However futile your attempts, as the battle grows, Thomoth will tire. At that moment, we will strike."

"Can't you strike now?"

The child shook her head. "In its current state, Thomoth is too powerful even for us. It must be weakened if we are to succeed."

Did Peter dare to trust? "And that's all you need?"

"No," the being said calmly. "We'll need one more thing."

"What's that?"

"Your body."

Chapter Forty-two

M artin jerked out of his stupor to find himself cross-legged on the ground. His three unlikely mentors stared at him from their seated positions around a central fire. Despite them not killing him yet, he still kept his guard up. Yet, they could have harmed him just then, couldn't they? "What?"

"How far did you go?" Xariel asked. "You didn't meet us at the appointed destination."

What? Oh... "I..." Heat crept up Martin's face.

"Martin, are you all right?" Dmitri jumped to his feet and raced to Martin's side.

"Quite all right. It's just that I, that I..."

Dmitri narrowed his eyes. "Where did you go?"

"Um... I think I went back to the Father's temple. In the caverns. Pe... Peter was there." The heat in his face grew molten as he recalled sliding his naked body together with Peter's.

A furrow grew between Dmitri's brows.

Xariel barked a laugh. "Remember, he can cross realms as easily as we cross the floor." He rose and smacked Dmitri on the back with one hand.

Dmitri's scowl would have sent a lesser man running. "Where. Did. You. Go."

"I'm not sure I was even there. Was it an illusion?" Martin shifted, feeling the stickiness in his trousers. If he hadn't gone there, he'd had a highly realistic dream.

Xariel nearly doubled over with laughter. "Remember when we studied at the academy? How we—"

Dmitri shot Xariel a murderous glare. "We are not here to discuss our misspent youth."

Really? Xariel and... Dmitri?

Martin didn't want that mental image roaming around in his head, surfacing at the worst possible moments. "Can we focus here?"

Garamel made a gagging noise. "Please don't make me imagine either of you naked. You're what? Thousands of seasons old? And with skin instead of scales. That would be just"—he made a gagging face—"disgusting."

Aaaannnnnd there Martin's mind took a side trip into imagining scaled beings making more scaled beings and having a lot of fun in the process. He barely managed to accept quietly conversing with a dem... Dreckon. "For the love of all that's holy, can we please focus?"

Four different beings from three distinct realms, and Martin visiting Peter by magical means. What if he hadn't visited Peter? What if Peter had summoned Martin?

Xariel stopped twinkling at Dmitri while Dmitri backed off on his glowering a bit, and Garamel tipped his head back, opened his mouth, and dropped in something slimy.

Martin wanted his old life back, without priests, without Dreckons, and definitely with no knowledge of other realms.

Dmitri broke the awkward silence. "Our few remaining priests have been quietly building wards to trap Thomoth in the temple.

Xariel nodded. "What we should have done last time." He turned to the Dreckon. "Garamel, it won't expect us to have sided with you. Thomoth has accumulated an abundance of magic. Your kind consume magic. Bring all your people that you can, and prepare to feast. But you are not to harm any of our kind or Martin's. Is that understood?"

"And if we win?" Garamel asked, pouring a whole lot of hope into the words.

Martin fixed a steely glare on each of them in turn. Here was the impasse. If he was the key to defeating Thomoth, he had a right to a few demands. "I want to keep the magic for my world. Xariel wants it for his, as do you, Garamel. If we win, then we share the magic."

"What if there's only enough for one realm?" Xariel looked down his long nose, arms folded over his chest.

Dmitri strolled a few paces away, rubbing his chin. He appeared so different from Martin in his natural form, yet his mannerisms were surprisingly familiar. Though if he'd been in Martin's realm as long as he claimed, maybe he'd adopted their habits.

How, indeed. "Then we find a way to share a realm," Martin conceded. "We have to win the battle first before we squabble over any spoils. You say many have tried and failed to stop Thomoth. What right do we have to think we can?"

"The young pup has a point," Garamel said.

Martin rolled his eyes. "I'm not a pup."

"What's wrong with being a pup?" Garamel snapped. "We call our young pups."

"I'm too old to be a pup."

"My infant daughter is older than you," the demon pointed out.

And Martin thought demons were bad when they'd been attacking people in the streets. No, not demons. Dreckons. He'd have to open his mind if he didn't want to be thought of as a pup. "I have a friend in the Lad... Thomoth's temple, training to be an oracle. Is there any way we can move him out of harm's way before the fighting begins?"

"If there is any way to spare lives, it must be only us and Thomoth." Dmitri snuck a quick glance at Xariel, darting his gaze away when Xariel caught him.

Martin might give his mentor a hard time if the situation wasn't so dire. "I'm friends with the commander of the city guards. He can rally his people to get the townsfolk away from the temple."

"Do we have any idea how to kill it?" Dmitri asked.

"My mother told me two heroes would come. Would save us." How Martin enjoyed the stories as a child. Now, looking back, he should have been horrified.

Garamel raised a scaled hand. "I was one of the two in my realm. We failed."

Dmitri and Xariel both raised a hand. "And the two of us for ours," Dmitri said. "You're powerful and have a mage bond, but Xariel and I trained together for most of our adult lives."

Then they didn't stand a chance. "What makes you think this time will be different? And why did you deliberately keep Peter and me apart?"

"Because we wanted to watch you—"

"Have you heard yourselves? Entire realms running out of magic. You've used magic your entire lives. Peter and I have not. Wouldn't the same hold true for mages if there is only a finite amount of magic in a realm?"

Xariel and Dmitri both opened and closed their mouths a few times. Finally, Dmitri spoke. "We draw from the magic of the realm."

"Again, finite. A serpent from a particular area in my realm can sicken a man with one bite and kill a child. The adult serpents. The hatchlings have venom so potent, a mere scratch from one fang kills a full-grown man in seconds." Martin had seen such a death once when he'd been summoned to the city gates to aid a wounded traveler. He'd seen death before, but never so painful or horrifying.

Xariel brought himself up to his full height. "Are you suggesting we're serpents?"

"Hey, don't sound so condescending," Garamel snapped. "Some of my best friends are serpents."

"What I'm saying is that mine and Peter's magic is relatively unused. And there's always two. Xariel, you and Dmitri were the two from your realm. Peter and I are possibly the two from mine. Maybe it's two per realm. Garamel, is your partner still alive?"

Garamel nodded.

"The boy does have a point." Dmitri stroked his chin. "There are always two, but what might we accomplish with two from each of three realms?

Martin let the "boy" comment go while he seemed to be winning his case. "How can we collaborate with the Dreckons if my race can't see them."

"They are only hidden when they want to be," Xariel answered. "If they drop their glamour, they can be seen by all."

Which might be a huge shock to the good people of E'Skaara.

"What now?" Garamel asked.

Since no one else answered, Martin took it upon himself. "Now, we plan how to defeat Thomoth."

Guardians, Dreckons, and locals gathered outside of E'Skaara, mages with staffs to channel magic, Martin's kind with blades and knives.

Commander Enys sent a regiment. They'd shaped up quite nicely once they got past the desire to scream, run, faint, or get themselves to the physician for fear of having consumed tainted ale.

The Dreckons needed only teeth, claws, and insatiable appetites for magic.

The priests hid most of the lower townspeople in caverns, all who'd come. The upper city still lived in ignorance of the evil in their midst and wouldn't fight merely on a priest's say-so.

"The wards are at their peak. We cannot delay further." Dmitri sat at the head of the council table, wearing his brown cassock once again.

Martin, dressed in his black leathers, peered out over the assembled leaders. "Has there been any sign of Cere?"

"I'm afraid not." Enys was dressed in simple brown leathers, with no markings to distinguish him as commander. His stance and authority were all he needed. "My spies made it as far as the temple gardens. A strange mist seems to have permeated the structure itself. None may pass."

"It knows we are coming." Xariel sat next to Dmitri at the table in their tent war room.

"There's one more thing," Enys said.

"What's that?"

"We cannot find the tavernkeeper you sent us to find."

"What?" Martin's heart attempted to escape his chest. He reached out with his mind. Nothing. No traces of Peter. Martin rounded on Dmitri and Xariel. "I can't feel him. Where is he?"

They exchanged baffled looks. Xariel acted as spokesman. Telling. "We've been so busy with preparations that we haven't noted his whereabouts."

Damnation.

The needed two were now one.

Campfires burned across the field, an odd mix of different peoples huddled around. Nothing united warring races like a common enemy.

Martin sat outside his tent alone, sharpening his blades, having turned down offers of company. As much as he cared for Enys, opening up about his deepest fears might strain the friendship. Why alienate one of his few friends if they might all die tomorrow?

Any serious conversation would have to include Martin's magery. How would Enys take the news, having been told his whole life that mages were vile and deserved killing?

Besides, Martin had possibly already lost his reason for living. Where was Peter? Was he okay? What could Thomoth want with him?

The same thing Xariel had: as bait or for Martin's magic. Why? Martin's meager powers wouldn't make much difference in the upcoming conflict.

Dmitri shuffled up beside Martin. "I do not sense Peter in danger. I had the priests scry for him."

"I can't reach him." And Martin had tried most of the day.

"If he's in the temple, the magical barrier keeps you out." Dmitri dropped a hand to Martin's shoulder. "You must keep a clear head. I can help you sleep if you'd like."

"No. I'll stay awake a while longer." Martin continued sharpening his blades, the whetstone creating a gentle, scraping rhythm.

The familiar bob of Dmitri's hood signaled a nod. "As you will."

"He still cares for you, you know," Martin said.

"Who?"

"Xariel."

Dmitri sighed. "I know."

"He's my grandfather, isn't he?"

Dmitri sank gracefully to the grass beside Martin. "As am I."

Wait! What? "But... how?"

Dmitri remained quiet for several long moments before replying, "Our realm is not the same as yours. Children are created with a touch of magic. Xariel and I invited a third into our relationship, a young woman named Magda. She helped us conceive your mother, then left to assist another couple."

"So, was my mother your or Xariel's child?" Fatigue must be lessening the shock Martin felt the explanation warranted.

"She was both."

"And Magda's?" How was that possible?

Dmitri chuckled. "There you go, applying your realm's truths to mine. No. Magda carried our child, nursed her, but your mother was a mix of Xariel and me." His tone took on a sorrowful air. "I miss her. If I'd known she wouldn't be safe in the mountains, I'd have kept her with me or insisted she return to her father."

"Why didn't you tell me before?" All this time, Martin thought himself alone, then reluctantly accepted Dmitri as a teacher. Having a grandfather might have been an enormous comfort.

Dmitri swept out a hand, indicating the camp. "Would you willingly bring your only grandchild into this?"

"Probably not."

"You look a lot like your mother, you know."

"But didn't she look like you and Xariel?"

"There you go again. I believe I mentioned before that she altered her appearance. That was no mere illusion. She changed how she looked magically. Her child resembled the form she took."

Some things Martin's brain was too muzzy to contemplate. Maybe later. If he survived. "Too complicated."

"Quite. If we win tomorrow, I'll explain until you understand. For tonight? Sleep."

Martin didn't remember entering his one-person tent, climbing under the covers of his pallet, or falling asleep.

He awoke to trumpet blasts.

Chapter Forty-three

Once again, Martin dressed in the black leather of the guardians, hair pulled back in a tail at the nape of his neck. Commander Enys approached, leading Martin's favorite mare.

Martin stroked the mare's velvet nose. She snuffled warm breath over his fingers. He'd love to have... an apple appeared in his palm, promptly claimed by the mare.

Enys either didn't see or had his mind on other things.

Martin continued petting the mare while she enjoyed her snack. "I appreciate the gesture, Enys, but I'm no longer a member of the city guard."

"In this, you are the brightest and best of us. The other guards agreed last night. We'd be honored to have you join us again on this day, if none other." Enys handed over the reins and pinned a captain's badge to Martin's tunic. "You, better than any, know what we face. These others, with their strange appearance, I know nothing of. It's you I trust completely. You, the guards follow."

"Don't let that prejudice you against the others. I trust Fa... Dmitri with my life. He, Xariel, and Garamel have a truce. I may not trust the other two, but I trust Dmitri. Today, we succeed or fail together."

"I am not too certain of Garamel, though I find no quarrel with Xariel, even if he does look like he needs a few good meals and time in the sun. Do you think he likes redheads?"

Now was not the time to tell Enys, "That's my grandfather you're talking about." "Don't let Garamel's appearance fool you. I've worked hard to understand that their realm is different from ours. What's normal there may not be normal here." Thousands of realms, thousands of beings that could be friend or foe. The more Martin knew of them, the better. "They've agreed to work with us. We can't afford to turn away any allies."

Enys waved a hand. "No, his appearance doesn't bother me... much. The wily bastard cheats at cards." Turning on his heel, he added, "When this is over, Esmerla expects you at the house for dinner."

Martin exaggerated a put-upon sigh. "Who is she this time?" Would the man ever give up his persistent matchmaking?

Commander Enys glanced back over his shoulder. "No niece this time. I'm told you are to bring your own mate. You should have said something. I'd have stopped throwing female relatives at you." Enys flashed a quick grin and waggled his brows. "I've got a nephew if you're ever interested." He strolled off without another word.

He knew? Enys knew? Apparently, he thought nothing of Martin's relationship with Peter.

A half-hour later, Martin sat on his mare at the head of the E'Skaara contingent, Garamel and Garamel's bond mate on Martin's left, Xariel and Dmitri on his right. He'd wrap his head around the fact that they were his grandfathers later.

If he survived.

Dmitri pulled his horse alongside Martin's. "The first groups have left the lower city, each headed by a mage. Even now, the second wave should be entering the caverns."

"What of the dem—" Martin must learn not to refer to allies as demons but as Dreckons.

"They creep in the shadows, undetected. Thomoth underestimated all the individual realms it plundered. While each failed on their own, we might stand a chance with our combined forces."

Where was Peter? Was he safe? Martin couldn't sense him but somehow knew he wasn't dead or in mortal danger.

How could there be two from his world if Peter wasn't here?

"Go. Confer with the city guards. We shall meet you after." Dmitri dropped back, letting Martin ride on alone. The soldiers knew him. Many had served under him. Hopefully, they would again.

Martin left his horse at the garrison, pausing to slip a priest's hassock over his leathers. He met Dmitri, Xariel, and several other brown-clad guardians at the edge of the upper city.

Thomoth would be watching and on guard. Had it fully awakened yet? Would the runes hold, entrapping their enemy?

They entered the Father's temple, moving down and down to the caverns.

Dmitri took the lead. "I had Gaveth ensure the passage remained open. I'm counting on Thomoth's magical barrier's inability to seep underground. If not, we proceed directly to phase two."

Though the guardians' eyes let them see in darkness, they conjured multicolored mage lights for the nonmagicals in the ranks.

Xariel strode behind. The significance wasn't lost on Martin. One grandfather to the front, the other to the rear. Xariel had only just met him recently, so of course, he'd treat Martin like a toddler. Then again, given the guardians' long lives, that was probably what he appeared.

How long would magery extend Martin's own seasons, providing he didn't die today?

Screams came from behind them.

Martin whirled. "What's happening?"

A bloodied young mage broke through, running for Dmitri. "It's a slaughter!"

They turned and ran back the way they'd come, through the caverns and temple. The dazzling sunlight nearly blinded Martin as they emerged from the darkness.

Still dressed in finery and temple clothing, men and women hacked at any perceived enemy within range with knives, swords, and even broken bottles. They stared with blank, unseeing eyes.

"What the fates is wrong with them?" Martin shouted, sword drawn and dagger in hand.

Xariel sucked in a breath. "They're possessed. Thomoth is sacrificing its own followers."

A woman in gossamer fell into a fountain. Her red blood spread out through the water.

The guards approached, led by the commander. Still, the novices fought. None wore armor. Many traipsed across the bloody ground on bare feet.

The guards looked to the commander for guidance. The first novice to reach the line didn't hesitate, taking full advantage of the guard's indecision. A golden candlestick struck the guard's temple, delivering a death blow.

The next guard struck the boy down—a boy who couldn't have seen sixteen summers.

The guards stormed the grounds, the magical barrier keeping them in the gardens but letting the novices out of the temple.

Was Cere among them? Martin searched faces. In the melee, who could tell?

More and more novices poured forth. Two grabbed Martin, tugging him toward the misty veil. He struck. Both fell. Without pausing to check for injuries, he surged forward, mages at his side.

"It's animating too many bodies to sustain for long," Dmitri shouted, back against the garden wall, Xariel a dark shadow beside him. All the guardians wore their robes, with weightier matters to use their magic on to maintain a proper glamour.

"Watch for me." Martin separated his mind from his body. The barrier didn't stop him. Up stairs, down corridors, he searched. Where was Cere?

With a yank, he returned to himself.

"That's not safe," Xariel snapped.

Bodies littered the once-beautiful gardens. Blood stained the water in the fountains. The faces of the dead were unfamiliar to Martin. He closed his eyes, reaching out for Peter. There! Finally! Peter appeared as a murky dream shape on the edge of Martin's senses.

Martin could easily pull strength from his lover, but no, he wouldn't.

Take it, he heard in his head. *If this doesn't work, I won't need it anyway. You must tire Thomoth if we're to have a chance.*

Dmitri dropped a hand to Martin's shoulder. "Take it. That's his part in this war. Providing you with strength."

Martin drew, only intending to take a bit. Once he opened the connection with Peter, power slammed into him, nearly knocking him off his feet. In the blink of an eye, he went from exhausted to invigorated, having removed the magic dampening amulet..

Guardian, gatekeeper, champion, solace. Card images flashed through Martin's mind, similar to cards he'd read with Peter what seemed a lifetime ago. He pushed past the gray mist with renewed determination, bringing the guardians with him.

Step by step, Dmitri climbed to the main chapel, Martin close on his heels. The once-beautiful building now appeared sinister, a heavy weight of vileness permeating the air.

Priests and Chosen stood in their path, eyes eerily blank. Unlike those outside, these attackers carried swords.

"We've got this!" Gaveth cried. He and the Father's other priests broke off, engaging with the Lady's faithful.

Dmitri, Xariel, and Martin pushed forward. The moment they breeched the sanctuary, all outside sounds faded.

"Thomoth! We've no wish for any more loss of life," Dmitri shouted into the eerie silence. Nothing. Then...

The barely audible click of heels on marble, the rustle of clothing. *Tap, tap, tap,* someone approached. They emerged from their hiding place.

Cere. Dressed in the same clothing he'd worn to the Choosing, only stained and dirty, golden skin showing through tears in the fabric. Cere would be beside himself if he knew how he looked. He opened his mouth, but another's voice emerged. "I see, hunter, that you know who I am."

Martin stepped out of the shadows. "Let him go. He's merely a novice. What good could he possibly be to you?"

"He is my vessel. Allowing me to speak to you. You know you cannot defeat me. Yours isn't the first world I've fed upon."

"No, you go where you will, leaving death and destruction in your wake," Dmitri snarled. Even through the heavy cassock, Martin sensed muscles bunched for launch.

Xariel stopped Dmitri with a hand to the shoulder. "That's what it wants, to pick us off one by one. We need you to stay with us."

"Your followers know who you are now, Thomoth. What you are." Martin stepped away, drawing Cere's attention, giving Dmitri time to compose himself. "They no longer worship you."

"Like I care what the weaker races think. However, you've destroyed my conduits, how I channel the magic from this world into myself."

Good! The runes worked.

Thomoth continued, "This body will have to do, though I'm afraid there will be nothing but ashes when I'm done."

Martin bit back the pain of those words. Cere didn't deserve this. None of the temple dwellers did. "Then what?"

"Then I consume what's left of the magic of this place and leave."

"The people here are innocent. Why destroy them?"

Thomoth laughed, a grotesque sound coming from a sweet young man of easy smiles and trilling laughter. "When I dictated the killing of mages and drew their power for myself, your people were all too happy to comply. They loved that I gave them a reason to destroy who they'd long envied. So they are complicit in the ruining of their own world. As has been the case on any world to which I traveled. I found no need to conquer, just divide the people and let them do the work."

"You killed the mages. My parents. Many others."

"Have you not seen your own kind kill each other when food is in short supply or over some petty bickering? Do you not look out for yourselves?" The mocking tones didn't match Cere's peaceful expression.

Martin struggled to accept that this being only looked like Cere. Did Cere still exist? "You kill entire worlds."

"Do you not sit down and dine on animal flesh? Wear their skins as clothing?" The thing wearing Cere's body sneered. "Why should I care about your kind?"

Now! Peter shouted in Martin's mind.

Martin kept Thomoth's attention, channeling magic through his connection with his lover. He met Thomoth's gaze and looked his enemy in the eyes. Raw hatred and fury, things he'd never expected to see in Cere, and something he hoped to never see again.

It took effort to strike the image of a friend. Every attack would tear at Martin's soul. He launched a ball of mage fire and ducked behind a statue. The stone shattered with return fire.

Lying flat on the marble floor, Martin watched in horror as Cere hurled a fireball toward Dmitri. Xariel lunged, knocking Dmitri to the floor. The flames roared over their heads.

"Ah, little mortals. You can't expect to defeat me." Not-Cere's voice held a touch of strain. Could this magic-eating monster tire?

In his mind, Martin focused on Peter. Nothing. No! He should be safe, wherever he hid. Pain sliced up Martin's arm. He rolled behind an urn. Water! He overshot and deluged himself with water. The fire went out. The pain remained.

No time for a healing spell now.

Thomoth lobbed raw power. A column cracked, sending marble crashing to the floor. Dmitri barely missed a cornice aimed at his head. For one moment, he lost his balance. Thomoth took advantage, slamming Dmitri against the wall with another blast of power.

Xariel and Martin attacked at once, from two directions. Thomoth easily blocked them both, a sneer on Cere's lips. Dmitri recovered, joining them, throwing everything they had at the creature.

Was Thomoth's power unending? All Martin's concentration centered on the enemy. No time to search for Peter or consider what happened outside.

This being destroyed world after world, defeated thousands of mages. Who was Martin to think he stood a chance?

Martin heard a child's voice. "I *want to fight* To-moff!"

A voice from long ago answered, "*I believe you would. There are always two.*"

On the edges of Martin's perception, Peter sent strength. Martin stood before Thomoth and screamed out his rage, his pain, releasing a barrage of energy with the sound. Thomoth fell backwards, the fireball in his hands bouncing off the ceiling in a shower of sparks.

Martin ducked behind a shattered column, peering out from behind his shelter. A blast of yellow fire engulfed Xariel. His scream rent the quiet as he writhed in agony.

Dmitri lunged at Xariel, shoving power toward Thomoth.

And joined Xariel in flames.

What to do? What to do? An image popped into Martin's head of a villager dousing a fire with snow. He channeled energy, focusing on cold, snow, a fire going out, and threw out his hands. The shot encased both of Martin's grandfathers in ice. For one moment, time stopped. Xariel and Dmitri faced each other, light and dark, good and evil, frozen.

But weren't those relative terms?

The ice melted in a *whoosh* of water cascading across polished marble. Xariel and Dmitri dropped to the floor.

Xariel lay motionless, Dmitri panting beside him. Still, Thomoth came.

Garamel stomped into the sanctuary, along with his bond mate. Thomoth hurled a fireball. The two Dreckons glowed, the glow gradually fading as they absorbed the magic. Garamel grinned. "Thank you. What a lovely meal." He approached, nothing but teeth and claws for weapons. Did he plan to kill Cere's body?

Thomoth grinned. "Your race never learned, did they?" This time, instead of shooting a fireball, Thomoth made a "come here" motion with his hand. Garamel screeched. Golden light poured from him. His mate grabbed hold, only to join in the screaming. What was Thomoth doing to them?

In the midst of their agony, Martin swore he saw the pair smile.

"Stop!" Martin stepped out from behind his column. "Let them go!" The golden light stopped. Garamel and the other Dreckon fell to the floor, eyes closed. Were they dead? No time left to check now.

Martin raised a hand. Nothing. Panic caught him in an iron grasp, crushing the air from his lungs. "I'm sorry, Peter," he whispered. No, he was sorry, *Petran*. How foolish they'd been to think they could match Thomoth, who'd already defeated so many others before.

Thomoth's laugh raised goosebumps on Martin's skin as Thomoth raised his hand. Nothing happened. The laughter stopped. Thomoth tried again. Had Garamel somehow tainted the creature's magic?

Through billowing smoke, a figure emerged. No!

Peter strode into the temple. Not the humble man Martin knew, but head held high and steps sure.

"You! You are not wanted here!" Thomoth shrieked.

Peter opened his mouth, but another's voice emerged. "You were warned."

What! Had the monster taken hold of Peter? Another monster? Were there two? "*There are always two,*" he heard in his mother's voice, as clearly as though she stood beside him. Two monsters as well as two heroes?

"It is time for you to return. With me." Peter extended a hand.

Thomoth threw his hand forward. Flames shot toward Peter.

"No!" Martin charged, throwing himself in front of his lover. A primitive part of his brain cried, *Pain!*

Nothing but a pair of strong arms. Martin glanced up into a well-loved face.

One side of Peter's mouth quirked up. "Ah, mortal. How brave and foolish. Thomoth cannot hurt me. Nor I, them." One hand firmly on each shoulder, the being who looked like Peter effortlessly placed Martin to the side.

Hey! No pain. Martin spared a brief moment to rub his upper arm. No burns! And he felt energized.

But wait! Peter approached Thomoth. "No, Peter, stop!"

"Time to come home," Peter said.

Thomoth backed away. "No! You cannot take me back. I have the magic of a dozen realms."

"Had," Peter said, smile bittersweet. "While your level of power would kill a mortal, divided between the mage-born..."

Thomoth extended his hands again. Nothing. "No! I've worked so hard..."

"While you fought, every mage-born in this city has worked together to weaken you. But the Dreckons have sacrificed themselves to atone for their actions against other races. There is no power stronger than a selfless act." The being wearing Peter's body spoke in calm tones, so out of context, no matter how elegant the battlefield. "You have killed, destroyed, and made a mockery of what we are. You have turned lover against lover. Realm against realm. We are creators by nature. We give life. We do not take."

"But they are beneath us. Animals!" Thomoth snarled through Cere.

How bizarre, watching an argument between two people Martin knew who weren't really themselves.

"No," not-Peter said. "They are children. If left alone, they will grow and learn. You cannot have what is theirs. Now, it is time for you to return." Peter placed the palm of his right hand against Cere's forehead.

Thomoth's screams pierced Martin's ears, fading, dying, becoming the voice of a scared young man. "Help him," the being in Peter's body barked.

Martin rushed forward, catching Cere before he fell, easing him onto the marble.

"That... Tha... th... thing!" Cere trembled in Martin's arms.

Peter knelt beside the two Dreckons, now lying still in a final embrace. Martin saw one of their kind look fully at peace for the first time. "I was a moment too late to save them. For this, I am sorry, but I see into their hearts. They came fully prepared to die for others, an alien concept for their race."

He rose and approached Dmitri and Xariel. "You have lost much. You have fought for your people and your world, each in your own way. I cannot restore everything my other took from you; however, what you have inside will start restoring your world.

You must dispel the power quickly. Your bodies are not made to contain so much magic." He drew a shimmering circle in the air. "My kind apologizes for Thomoth's crimes against your realm. They will be dealt with. Now, go. Rebuild your worlds."

Dmitri led Xariel forward. He turned and mouthed "Thank you" to Martin over his shoulder before stepping through the portal.

Finally, Peter approached Martin. "The entity has returned to our realm. Thomoth's machinations cost you both much. For this, we are sorry." He extended a hand. "Come with me."

"What about him?" Martin nodded at Cere.

Peter touched Cere's eyelids with his fingertips. "He will sleep until you return. Come."

Martin took Peter's hand, shrugging off the strange sensation that this wasn't actually Peter.

"Where is the man whose body you wear?" An odd pressure built inside Martin, swelling, surging.

Burning.

"He is here. Unlike our friend on the floor, your lover shared his body willingly, for which I am grateful."

The odd sensations continued, the pressure within Martin growing unpleasant. "What is your name?"

"You may call me Sige, if name me you must. Once I am back with my own kind, we are not individuals, but one. The one you call Thomoth was not content and broke free. Now it is returned."

Sige led the way to the gardens and the low bench Martin often shared with Cere. "Sit."

Martin sat, by now, the pressure threatening to rip him in two. "What's happening?"

Sige sank down beside him, directing their still-joined hands to the ground. "Focus. Drain the power into this world. Think of the mountains, the seas, all the faraway lands." The bench beneath them shook. Screams came from the streets. In the distance, falling debris rumbled.

Peter stared into Martin's eyes. "Quickly. Even now, the magic becomes too much for your control."

Martin did his best to imagine the mountains where he'd spent childhood, the sea he'd sailed with a young man named Petran. All the distant lands Petran spoke of.

Nothing else existed but the hand in his and the flow of magic into the ground.

Tired, so tired. Martin slumped against the being beside him. "I can't continue."

"Shh... rest now. You did well." Soft lips brushed his forehead.

Martin slept.

Martin awoke in a soft bed. Where was he? What happened? The past few hours slammed into him in a rush. The battle. Thomoth. Cere.

Peter.

Martin shot upright on the bed, clutching his head. That hurt. He collapsed against a mound of pillows.

"You should be resting." A young man of delicate beauty sat in an upholstered chair beside the bed, dressed in a novice's flowing, elegant silk.

"Who are you? Where is Peter?" Martin lay in a bed larger and softer than he'd ever seen, draped in silks. Elegant tapestries draped the walls. He clutched the covers to his naked chest, Dmitri's pendant hanging once more from the chain around his neck.

"If you seek Sige, I've sent another to fetch them. They wanted to know the moment you woke." The young man lifted Martin with an arm much stronger than it looked, holding a cup to his lips.

Martin drank sweet water. "Where am I?"

"You are in a priest's quarters."

"A priest?"

The boy cast his gaze down. "A priest of the Lady. They're gone now. The oracle, the priests. Only a few novices remain."

"Leave us," came a voice from the doorway.

The young man bobbed his head and left the room, his silk slippers scuffing against the floor.

Sige sat in the chair the boy vacated and took Martin's hand. The voice coming from Peter's body still wasn't his own. "You are doing well?"

Martin nodded, fighting back a growl. "Are you going to let Peter have his body back?"

The thing sounded surprised. "Of course, after we've accomplished what we must."

"How do I know you won't keep him like Thomoth did Cere?" Dare Martin trust this being? True, it had defeated Thomoth, but what if it decided to take over instead? "How long will that take?"

"A few of your sevendays. Once I find each realm, I must seek out those who can shape the magic and rebuild. Teach them, if necessary. I do not yet know what I will find. Your and Dmitri's worlds were still intact, as were the last two Thomoth raided, and a rift exists between the two. Portals, I believe you call them."

"Will those be sealed now?" Martin shuddered, thinking of Dreckons slipping through.

The thing wearing Peter's body shook its head. "The beings you called demons are no more. To our great sorrow, they were killed when Thomoth fell. Not only did the one named Garamel and his mate sacrifice themselves, as they knew they were doomed, the Dreckons' last act was to use themselves to save others."

Garamel, who'd cried on Xariel's shoulder, and all his kind. Pups. He'd had a young daughter. Gone forever. Even for a former demon hunter, the loss hurt.

Knowing the child was now lost, with the rest of Garamel's people, to save Martin's world.

He could harbor no ill will, for it accomplished nothing.

Sige continued, "If the remaining worlds so desire, I will seal the link. However, I believe a battle won together is a strong bond on which to build an alliance. The Lady's novices who do not wish to enter the Father's service are free to make their own lives wherever they wish."

The being placed a hand on Martin's shoulder. "Rest now. And recover. You will be attended to in my absence."

How could Martin rest when this thing still had Peter? Nevertheless, his eyes slid shut.

Chapter Forty-four

W hen next Martin opened his eyes, Gaveth sat by his bedside. "Enough lying about. Time to step out into a new world."

Martin washed from a pitcher and bowl and donned the clothing sitting on the foot of the bed. Not his black leathers, merely cotton shirt and woolen trousers, the kind Peter or another shopkeeper might wear.

Though shaky, Martin allowed Gaveth to lead him out of the temple and into the streets. Good. All the excess made him decidedly uncomfortable. He attempted to divert his gaze from the new reality of the Lady's temple. The formerly majestic gardens now looked like the battlefield they'd become.

Portions of the surrounding wall lay in ruins, a tumbledown of mortar and stone.

"Novices have begun identifying the dead," Gaveth said. He wore his usual brown robes but with no gloves and hood thrown back, exposing his natural looks. "Sadly, few of Thomoth's followers survived."

Though no bodies lay on the grounds, Martin couldn't look at the place without recalling the dead and dying, hearing their screams. Seeing Cere's friendly face, twisted by Thomoth's greed and hate.

Witnessing something else behind Peter's eyes and in his voice.

The fountains had been turned off, though the water in some remained pink. Martin tried to reverse time in his mind, recall roses and richly dressed novices, Cere's smiling face, but an uglier vision chased the images away.

Martin once stood before the gates, hatred in his own heart, vowing revenge. How naïve he'd been to believe revenge wouldn't come with so high a cost. The expensive mansions surrounding the temple appeared relatively unscathed, save for tree limbs and other debris shaken loose by the quakes. No elegant carriages trundled over the cobblestones, no richly dressed worshippers strode into the temple.

Thomoth was a threat no more, and its departure forever changed the city's way of life.

Martin trudged downhill, passing through the business district and into residential areas without a word.

Black banners announcing death hung from far too many doors.

A cart trundled by, loaded with bodies. For a moment, Martin flashed back to a long-ago time, seeing a three-fingered hand and believing his dear Petran hanged for a pirate. "How many dead?"

Gaveth sighed. "Many. Too many. Buildings fell when the magic returned. Most people haven't felt the change, but those with mage blood do. They've flocked to the temple, seeking guidance. The guardians are teaching those most adept, small spells to help in the recovery. To return this world to rights will take all magic users available."

In a daze, Martin strolled barely recognizable streets. He stopped before the building where his rented rooms still stood, an angry crack in the stucco façade.

Gaveth paused beside him. "We took the liberty of taking your things to the temple." He gave an apologetic shrug. "Looting has begun."

Sometimes, adversity brought people together; other times, it brought out the worst.

They marched with purpose to the lower city, passing ruined houses, families crying over their dead, and some stumbling aimlessly, expressions vacant. Smoke rose from the docks. The farther from the temples they traveled, the worse the damage. Of course, houses in the lower city weren't nearly as well constructed as in the upper.

A blackened ruin remained of the Stone's Throw. A woman sifted through the rubble. Martin's blood boiled. How dare... Oh. "Addie?"

The woman turned, tears streaking her sooty face. Addie!

Addie rushed over, grasping Martin by both arms. "Have you seen Peter? I cannot find him. I'm worried..." She glanced over her shoulder at the burned-out shell that once housed a bustling tavern.

"He's safe. You'll see him shortly." If the being named Sige proved truthful. Addie's survival eased some of the darkness in Martin's soul. One fewer person for Peter to mourn. How many friends and customers had he lost, in addition to his business?

Addie let out a breath and stepped back, leaving sooty handprints on Martin's shirt.

Gaveth waved a hand, and the soot disappeared from the shirt and Addie. She jumped back, eyes wide. "Mage!" That she didn't comment on Gaveth's appearance said she already knew of his kind.

"Get used to it, Addie. It's the way things will be."

She gave a tremulous smile, openly studying the guardian. "So, I can tell women what their children will be without the threat of punishment?"

Addie? Magic? Dmitri once said a mage-born watched over Peter, and she'd worn an amulet.

Martin turned to Gaveth, who shrugged.

"Where are you staying? Was your home destroyed?" Martin owed Peter to see to his friends.

"Nothing left." Addie stared at the ground.

"Come to the Father's temple," Gaveth said before Martin could. "You'll be welcome there, as will any others in need."

Addie smiled, though a haunted look remained in her eyes. "Aye. I will." She turned and resumed sifting through the remains of the tavern, pulling out a broken cup here, a frying pan there.

Martin continued on. The bridge where he'd seen his first runes lay in a mound of dust and broken pieces, the runes no longer holding power.

Gaveth stood quietly by, being there but saying nothing to interrupt Martin's thoughts. Martin nodded at his silent companion and turned, trudging back the way they'd come.

Gery Enys's house still stood, though Commander Enys wasn't home, likely out securing the city. From what Martin knew of Esmerla Enys, she would probably be helping where she could. What about

Enys's huge, extended family? Martin would have to find him later and ask.

He found an empty garrison, all surviving guards deployed to keep what peace they could in the city. Should Martin rejoin their ranks? Suddenly, he felt lost. He'd spent so much time dreaming of the Lady's—no Thomoth's—overthrow that he hadn't spared any thoughts for what came after.

"We would be honored if you stayed with us," Gaveth said, as though reading Martin's thoughts. "At least in the short-term. We have much to teach you and much work to do."

One thing Martin did know about his future: his reason to keep living. "What about Peter?"

He heard the smile in the priest's words. "He will be asked the moment he returns."

Martin worked late into each eve, burying the dead, shoring up any salvageable buildings. Half the time, he wanted to surrender E'Skaara to the destruction and rebuild somewhere else.

Those with mage blood came out of hiding, lending their skills.

The inside of the Lady's temple remained mostly unscathed, with rooms enough to house the injured. There Addie spent her days. At night she made her way to Martin's room in the Father's temple, lying beside him in his bed.

The first night he worried but let her be. She cried in her sleep, often waking from nightmares. Martin held her until she calmed as he was sure Peter would want him to.

She'd once boasted of her large family, how most of the lower city were her kin. Martin and Peter were all the woman had left. She could share the bed.

The surviving magistrates agreed that there would be no upper and lower city anymore. No elite novices supported by the sweat and labor of the commoners.

The bed dipped behind him, and a body pressed against his back. Cere. He, too, had been left with no one, though once or twice Martin awoke to find the young man in Addie's arms. Perhaps Cere found a mother and Addie, a son. She'd taken him on as apprentice healer, though he'd no magic of his own. He'd not spoken since leaving the Lady's temple.

Blood ties mattered not when so few survived. Ships returned to the ports, bringing much-needed supplies and news of the outside world. Other lands had fared better, though magic reached their shores too. The lands protected by magical beings such as fairies and elves fared much better.

Daily, Martin visited the now obsolete portals, hoping for word. But, day after day, he left disappointed.

One day he sat in the courtyard of a badly damaged house, taking a break from house repairs, and looked up to find a familiar figure approaching. Though most of his body remained hidden by a robe, Dmitri had pushed back the hood to reveal pale skin, hair, and eyes. The days being overcast likely offered some protection from the sun.

Though he'd dared not dwell on his grandfathers too much, relief filled Martin. "Dmitri!" He paused. "Are you Father Dmitri still?" Martin wasn't ready to call this man his grandsire out loud. Might never be ready.

Dmitri clasped Martin's shoulder and gave a tired smile. "Dmitri is fine." He perused the area. "I see the survivors have rallied."

"Yes. Many lost everything, all their family."

Dmitri nodded. How odd to see his face and not merely a hood. Though a few of Martin's fellow laborers glanced their way, they quickly returned to minding their business. "Is there somewhere we can talk?"

Martin led the way to the Lady's gardens. No, not the Lady's. The E'Skaara gardens, for now, belonged to all. They occupied Martin's favorite bench. Funny how he'd never realized he had a favorite until finding himself here many times, recalling wanting to bring Peter, and last glimpsing his lover's dear face while seated on this bench.

Dmitri sat with a sigh. "I take it he's not returned."

Martin's hopes sank, and he shook his head. So Dmitri hadn't brought word.

"Patience, Martin. He'll be back." Dmitri placed a hand, no longer hidden by a glove, on Martin's shoulder.

"How goes things in your realm?" *How are things between you and Xariel?*

"Slow. You've seen our world. Not much remained. Xariel and I gathered the mage-born, but it's not enough. I'm hoping some of the guardians will soon return and help us, and I'd like to act as an emissary between your world and mine."

"You have more knowledge and wisdom than I ever will. I'm grateful for your help. What of Xariel?" *Too many lost their lives due to him.*

Dmitri dropped his hand from Martin's shoulder to the bench. "He pays for his sins. He did what he thought he had to, as you, I, and so many others have done. Few remain on my world. We're accepting refugees from some of the other ruined worlds that stand little hope of rebuilding."

"And how about the two of you?"

There are always two.

Dmitri let out a another sigh. "I do not know. We went from lovers, to enemies, to comrades in arms. Only time will tell what awaits in the future. Sometimes I believe the old adage of 'there will always be two' is an admission that we're not meant to be alone." He paused for several moments, staring out at nothing before continuing in a lighter tone. "You'll be shocked to know that I've also gone from Father to father."

What?

Dmitri chuckled. "No one was more shocked than I. But, you see, so many orphans left from the assorted worlds will need guidance. Moreso than priests and teachers, they need parents."

True enough. "I think Peter's barmaid adopted Cere. I know he's a full-grown man, but he's unsure and childlike some days. They both lost their families. It works for them."

Dmitri cocked his head to the side. "What will you do?"

Actually, Martin hadn't thought much beyond staying alive one more day—and finding Peter. "Stay here, I suppose. That will depend on Peter. Why?"

"Thomoth has brought together a dozen worlds, now accessible through portals. Some are habitable, others questionable. I no longer belong here. Nor do I belong on my homeworld. I think, perhaps, you find yourself in the same predicament."

Dmitri voiced Martin's sentiments. A sinking feeling invaded Martin's chest. "Yes."

"I've been discussing with other like-minded souls. Once our two worlds are sustainable, perhaps the guardians should exist again, traveling between worlds, helping them recover. You're a powerful magic practitioner and would be of much use to us."

"And Peter?"

Dmitri bobbed his head in a curt nod. "Of course. He's not even begun to tap into his abilities. I look forward to seeing him live up to his potential." He smiled. "And there are always two."

"There are always two," Martin agreed.

But what if there weren't, now with Thomoth defeated?

Chapter Forty-five

W aste and ruin. Peter stood on a precipice overlooking a valley. Images from Sige showed a lush, green landscape, trees off in the distance. Only dry, cracked ruins remained of a once-beautiful land. In his mind's eye, beings who looked nothing like him toiled and loved, living their lives.

The first world destroyed by Thomoth. No people. No animals.

Thomoth has much to pay for, Sige communicated within Peter's own mind.

A dead realm. So long deprived that magic could never take hold again, its inhabitants long gone. This could have been Peter's realm, Martin and Addie reduced to memories...

"Shh... They are fine, young one," Sige said. A sensation not unlike a warm hug momentarily chased back the pain.

With a sigh, they left the world for another. And another.

On the fourth, they found survivors, though the poor creatures barely clung to life. Sige/Peter placed both hands on the ground, willing a portion of stolen magic back into the land.

Will they ever recover? Peter asked.

They stand a better chance now, with some of their magic returned. Time will tell. If we could have found a way to stop Thomoth earlier, we could have prevented some of the destruction. If not for you and your mate, more realms might have died.

One by one, they explored realms. Some they saved, some they couldn't. Occasionally, they found Father Dmitri's kind, assisting however they could.

Finally, they returned to Peter's home realm and E'Skaara.

A feeling of sorrow came over Sige. *We must leave you now. We thank you for allowing us to use your body, and we apologize for the damages we were too late to prevent.*

Sige withdrew. There one moment, gone the next. Peter staggered, recovering his balance by clinging to a cart. How odd, being alone in his head after sevendays—seasons?—sharing with another. Nighttime. His stomach rumbled. He hadn't eaten since before he'd left this place, Sige providing for Peter's body. With Sige gone, exhaustion took its toll. Oh, to be in a nice soft bed. But...

Before him, the Stone's Throw lay in ruins, nothing but toppled brick and charred timbers. Was Martin okay? Addie?

Martin.

Stumbling, putting one foot in front of the other, Peter wended his way through the destroyed lower city, deserted at this hour and with many buildings too severely damaged to save. However, the air smelled of newly cut lumber, fresh paint, and reconstruction. Step by weary step, he followed his instincts.

He met no one. No night workers, no sailors in search of a drink. Not even a stray dog or cat. Without conscious thought, he trudged down a barely recognizable street.

The Father's temple? What was he doing here?

No one stopped him from entering.

A room door stood ajar. Sige's influence had awakened part of Peter's mind where magecraft lived. The scent of Martin's magic lingered in the room, his very essence.

Tired. So tired. Peter sank down onto a mattress large enough for several people and breathed in. Addie? Addie was here? His heart soared to know she'd survived. Another's scent lingered too, a man's, but Peter felt no jealousy. Whoever slept in this bed with Martin wasn't a lover.

Martin. He wanted Martin.

He'd find him.

In a minute. Peter would close his eyes until then.

As days passed, the magic became a part of Martin, there at his beck and call. He kept his actions hidden, but raising a building worked much better with the wave of a hand, though such exertion left him worn out and in need of rest.

Days spent toiling, nights sharing a bed with Addie and Cere. Someone had even noticed Martin's predicament and procured a bed big enough for three, and a larger room.

No one asked questions. They were far from the only ones seeking comfort in these hard times. The comfort Martin needed would only come when Peter returned.

He slept across the street from the temple he used to stand before each night, vowing revenge. Now, no matter how tired the day left him, Martin trudged to each gateway, hoping. Always hoping.

The days had grown short and now slowly lengthened again. Less light and smoke from the city gave him a better view of the heavens. He stood, breath fogging before his face. Did Peter see the same stars when he studied the sky at night? Did he think of Martin? Or was he still too possessed by Sige to recall the man waiting for him?

Would Sige return him as promised?

Martin strolled to the docks and stared out at sea. Dmitri wanted him to leave this place, explore other realms, and help repair Thomoth's destruction.

The remaining people elected interim leaders and ordained new priests to take over once the existing ones returned home.

None mentioned the Lady, and the king hid in his castle, leaving the commoners to their own struggles.

What place had Martin here? A pile of ashes remained of the Stone's Throw. The city's outlying areas would remain in ruins for seasons until the existing population expanded and needed the space.

He trudged through the streets to the temples. How different now. No gaslights. No people about. The dock areas were the hardest hit. Many a night worker had lost their lives.

"Yo! Martin!"

Gery Enys stood in the doorway of the Father's temple. Martin's heart gave a joyous leap, and he swept his old mentor into a tight embrace. They clung to each other for several moments. No, Martin hadn't lost everything. Finally, he stepped back, discreetly wiping his eyes with the back of one gritty hand. "Good eve to you, Commander Enys."

"Good eve, Martin. Esmerla asks about you." Enys paused. "And a few of my nieces. At least one nephew. You must have dinner with us some night." His craggy face lit with a grin—a weary, forced grin, a shadow of its former self, hiding the horrors in old, familiar conversations.

How many nephews and nieces survived? Martin dared not ask. The pain would be too new, too raw. Dinner with Enys sounded too normal to fit into Martin's bizarre, abstract world. "I'll do that," he said, wondering if he lied. "And thank Esmerla for the invitation."

They chatted, comparing details of the past few days. When the conversation wound down, Martin started to walk away.

"Wait!" Enys shuffled over in his battle-worn leathers. "I hear you saved us. That none of us would have a home if not for you."

"I didn't act alone." Martin didn't want to admit how thoroughly outmatched he'd been. If he traveled with Dmitri, maybe he'd learn enough magic to hold his own next time or prevent the next time from ever happening.

"Still, we owe you a debt." No mention was made about being mage-born. Though mages used their talents openly now, for the good of all, like the embarrassing uncle at the family dinner, no one broached the topic.

"I'm forever in your debt for finding me my first day in the city and bringing me to the guards, where I learned to fight."

"I knew a born guard when I saw one." Enys winked. "I also recognized a young man with nowhere to go. You got a home. I gained a soldier."

"Wait! That first day. You said you waited for your nephew. There was no nephew, was there?"

Enys smiled, warm, guileless, eyes crinkling at the corners. "I wondered if you'd ever catch on." He clapped Martin on the back. "Esmerla will be highly upset if you don't come to dinner soon."

Martin turned away but called over his shoulder, "I will."

He'd barely entered the Father's temple when Addie skidded to a stop in front of him, tendrils of gray-streaked hair falling from under her cap. "There you are! Hurry, you must come!" She yanked Martin's arm until he followed her toward the back.

Straight to his quarters. And the pale form covered in blankets on his bed.

"Peter!" Martin rushed forward.

Addie held him back. "Not yet. He needs rest."

Damnation! Was this Sige or Peter? Martin collapsed onto the edge of the bed and clutched one pale hand in his. So cold. So still. He looked up to find himself alone in the room with a man who might or might not be his lover. The lines that Martin hadn't noticed before surrounded Peter's eyes. Martin longed for those long lashes to lift, revealing the soul-deep intensity of dark eyes. To see that wry twist of lips when Peter tried not to laugh.

Peter had returned. Like he said he would.
But who was *he*?

Chapter Forty-six

B linking a few times didn't remove the sting from Peter's eyes.

"Martin!" he heard a woman's voice call. He knew that voice, didn't he?

Tired. So tired. Peter lifted his hand a fraction. It fell back to whatever he lay on. His hand rose again, this time without any effort on his part. Warm fingers wrapped around his. "Peter! Peter, is that you?"

Martin? Martin! Here! Alive! Lacking the energy to reply, Peter simply squeezed. The connection between them, tenuous of late, bloomed to full life.

There are always two.

Soft lips brushed his knuckles, driving back the cold desolation of the past however many seasons. "I've worried so much about you. Are you okay?"

The concern in the voice made Peter push out the words: "Fine. Tired. Hungry."

"Addie. Can you get him something to eat?"

"Addie? Addie's here?" Peter's voice came out raspy, as though long unused. Maybe it had been.

"Right you are," came a blessedly familiar voice, not nearly as fiercely as Addie normally spoke. Lips touched Peter's cheek, ale-scented breath wafting over his skin. "Rest now. I'll find you a bowl of stew. And Peter? Welcome back."

It took several moments to form words, used as Peter was to someone else in his body doing the talking. "Ho... how long was I gone?"

"We're now heading into spring."

Surely he'd not wandered the realms with Sige so long. "What?" Peter tried to sit, but his strength failed him.

"Shhh," Martin said.

Dear, wonderful Martin, who Peter despaired of ever seeing again. Moreso than hearing him, Peter *felt* him, a reassuring presence in his mind. A mind now free of Sige. Peter's heart would have sung, if possible.

Those resonating tones continued, "You're weak, and you've lost weight. I don't know where you've been or what you've done, but you're here now. We'll fix you up as right as rain."

"Rain. I've been to a world where it never rains, another where it rains for seasons on end, and another where the rain stains everything purple."

"You can tell me all about it once you rest."

"Rest?" If Peter closed his eyes again, would he ever wake? He gripped Martin's hand tight. "Don't go," he whispered, his last reserves failing.

"Yes. Rest."

"Stay with me?"

The bed—it must have been a bed—dipped. A comforting body nestled into Peter's side. The scent of leather, sweat, and Martin. "Better?"

"Better." Peter lay still, letting darkness claim him.

He awoke to snores from three different people.

After four days of rest and food, Peter finally left Martin's room. He still felt wobbly, which gave Martin an excuse to stay close and offer an arm. Never before had Peter been to the high city without Sige present in his mind. Sige, who saw the world in vague shapes of many colors. Those possessed by Thomoth had appeared with an aura of sickly yellow-green; what Peter used to call demons were the color of shadow. Despite their brown robes, the priests appeared with mottled green, the shades constantly shifting.

Martin's aura shone with the rich gold of the sun.

Peter gazed upon the Lady's temple with his own eyes for the first time. Swirls and curlicues enhanced the pillars; marble covered the floors. Everywhere he looked, the finest craftsmanship and immense beauty.

He'd love to tear it down. Sige had seen an ugly gaping maw, devouring lives and magic with no remorse.

While people in the lower city went hungry, here the Chosen had lived in luxury. While the Lady fed on them or used them.

Carts passed on the road, hauling lumber and stone, and Peter had grown used to the rasping of saws and pounding of hammers.

Much of the city still lay in ruins and probably would remain so. The people rebuilt only what they needed. Life went on. He and Martin didn't walk to the remains of the Stone's Throw. Peter didn't have the strength and didn't want to see. How trivial his tavern seemed after witnessing worlds ripped apart, entire peoples vanished.

Martin led the way into a garden by the Lady's temple and settled Peter on a bench. "I've always wanted to bring you here. See what you thought."

Roses in a dozen colors bloomed, though a fountain remained still, with no sound of splashing water. "It's beautiful." Less beautiful when Peter weighed the cost others paid to provide such privilege to an elite few.

An elite few drained of their magic.

The plants probably looked better before the battle, some trampled and broken but still blooming, much like the remaining citizens of this realm.

"Without the constant flow of magic, soon the gardens will bloom and die with the seasons, like everything else." No denying the sadness in Martin's voice, the sorrow in his eyes. He'd seen the worst of the battle, the aftermath.

"How is Cere?" Peter saw the young man from time to time, wide-eyed and afraid, and couldn't blame him. Being inhabited by a benevolent being couldn't compare to having one's body taken over forcefully by pure evil.

Peter understood that Cere had shared Martin's bed in Peter's absence, along with Addie, for comfort, nothing more. Upon Peter's return, Addie and Cere found another room, large enough to house them and the orphaned foundlings they'd taken in.

"Fine. I think he'll be staying with Addie for a while once she's ready to leave the temple. So far, we haven't been able to find any surviving family, of hers or his." Martin paused, looking out over the gardens with troubled eyes. "She's found a house, not too badly damaged. Plenty of room for her and her foundlings."

Peter managed a smile, recalling how quickly Addie decided to take him in that day so long ago, at great risk to herself. She'd made a good second mother. "How many has she claimed?"

"Twelve, thus far." Martin patted Peter's hand where it lay on the bench between them. "Though we managed to find an aunt of two, so she's down to ten."

"Good." Cere wasn't the only one in need of mothering. He shouldn't be alone, and neither should Addie. "What happens now?" What Peter had seen of other worlds, the dead and the dying, would haunt him forever.

"I don't know. I feel I don't belong here anymore," Martin said softly.

"I know what you mean. Sometimes I feel I don't belong anywhere." Peter gave his lover a tight smile. "But with you."

Martin returned the smile, slipping an arm around Peter's shoulders. The sun was warm here. The day peaceful. "I talked to Fa...Dmitri."

Father Dmitri? Ah, Martin's mentor. The priest—being—who'd braved fire to save Peter. "How is he?"

"Fine, and helping the worlds he can to rebuild."

"Sounds like he'll be busy." Though he'd recovered much, Peter still tired quickly. Oh, to drowse here in the sun.

Martin sighed. "He's keeping Xariel busy."

Peter summoned the energy to chuckle. "I can't believe they're your grandfathers. You know I wanted to kill him for taking you."

Martin joined in with a quiet laugh. "That was... unexpected. I'd wanted to kill him too. I'm glad we let him live." He sobered. "I'm sorry, but we couldn't find any of your family. We'd hoped maybe some of your distant kin might have survived. Though many are still unaccounted for."

Peter shrugged, a tight lump forming in his throat. "I'd already thought I was the last of my line. But I have all the family I need right here." He rested his hand on Martin's thigh. "You and Addie."

"I'm sure in time, you'll add Commander Enys." Martin's eyes twinkled. "I think he's still getting over the fact that I don't want to meet his nieces or nephews."

After taking a deep breath, Peter asked the one question he'd been putting off. "What happens now? You and me, I mean." Never would he have imagined society accepting the two of them. With so many more pressing problems, who they loved mattered only to them.

"Dmitri wants to reform the guardians from mages of different realms, who protect all of them. We need to ensure another Thomoth never happens again and that one realm doesn't rise against another."

Peter remained quiet. He'd learned the pathways from Sige, could easily slip from one realm to the next. If he could, others likely could too.

Martin prodded, "Is this something that would interest you?"

What? "Me? Why would anyone want me?"

"You're powerful, Peter. You just need training. Dmitri would like us both."

Had Peter heard right? "Both?"

"Yes." Martin tightened his hold on Peter's shoulders.

Peter thought of the worlds he'd seen, some stunning, some horrifying, and so much he would've loved to have shown Martin. But, there was work to be done. Work magic would make easier.

He focused on a withered bloom, watching in fascination as the petals rose, took on pink and red hues, and joined the other blossoms on the rose bush.

Beauty from ugliness. Rebuilding from ashes.

"My father promised my mum that I'd be more than a pirate." Too bad Peter's mum and da couldn't have lived to see this day. To be free to live without fear.

"I spoke to your father."

Peter whipped his head around to stare at Martin. "When?"

"Before we left the *Seabird*, while you were injured. He told me you and I would be together again someday."

"He knew?"

"Yes, he knew. And I think you're already more than a pirate."

More than a pirate. With Martin. Peter lifted his chin and settled deeper into Martin's embrace. Yes, he'd be much more than a pirate.

He'd be a guardian.

With the man he loved.

For there were always two.

About Eden Winters

You will know Eden Winters by her distinctive white plumage and exuberant cry of "Hey, y'all!" in a Southern US drawl so thick it renders even the simplest of words unrecognizable. Watch out, she hugs!

Driven by insatiable curiosity, she possibly holds the world's record for curriculum changes to the point that she's never quite earned a degree but is a force to be reckoned with at Trivial Pursuit. She's trudged down hallways with police detectives, learned to disarm knife-wielding bad guys, and witnessed the correct way to blow doors off buildings. Her email contains various snippets of forensic wisdom, such as "What would a dead body left in a Mexican drug tunnel look like after six months?"

In the process of her adventures, she has written twenty-five gay romance novels, has won her share of Rainbow Awards, was a Lambda Awards Finalist, and lives in terror of authorities showing up at her door to question her Internet searches.

When not putting characters in dangerous situations she's cosplaying for charity, hanging out at the family farm, writing, spoiling her adorable pet goat, Squeaker, and creating HEAs for the characters who live in her head. Her natural habitats are airports, coffee shops, and the backs of motorcycles.

For more information about Eden, please visit her at https://www.edenwinters.com/

Want to hear about Eden's news and special offers? Join the Rocky Ridge Books newsletter for Eden's doings wherever her muse takes her.

Join Eden's Facebook group: https://www.facebook.com/groups/edensdiversions

Also By Eden Winters

Coming Soon

Something Faire
Petty Crimes

Printed in Great Britain
by Amazon